NEW YEAR NEW YOU

A SPECULATIVE ANTHOLOGY OF REINVENTION

New Year, New You: A Speculative Anthology of Reinvention
Publishers: Alec J. Marsh, Allison Pottern, Brigitte Winter
Editor: Chris Campbell
Acquisitions Editor: Avani Vaghela
Co-Editors: Trae Hawkins, C.R. Kellogg, Victor Pope, Sophia Tao, Brigitte Winter
Copyeditors: Julie Danvers, A.E. Kirchoff, Victor Pope
Cover design: Melinda Smith
Book design: Hermit Prints

This is a work of collected fiction. All events portrayed in this book are fictious and any resemblance to real people or events is purely coincidental.

All rights reserved. This book or any portion thereof may not be reproduced or used in any form without the express written permission of the individual authors, except for the use of brief quotations in a book review.

New Year, New You: A Speculative Anthology of Reinvention © 2024
Collection and introduction © 2024, Chris Campbell.

Stories:
"Better Me Is Fun at Parties" © 2024, F.E. Choe
"The Holy Daughters of Eng Mac" © 2024, C.R. Kellogg
"A Façade of Faith" © 2024, Shannon Spieler
"A Thousand Gomorrahs" by Daryl Gregory. First published in *Tales Of The Lost, Vol. Two- A charity anthology for Covid- 19 Relief* © 2020. Reprinted with permission by Daryl Gregory.
"Father Time Dares You to Dream" © 2024, Trae Hawkins
"The Manifold Aspects of Horace" © 2024, Taylor Lykiardopoulos
"Ugly" © 2024, Julie Danvers
"Aurora Deserti" © 2024, Rowan Copley
"Katabasis" © 2024, Alec J. Marsh
"The Ravishing Moon Princess" © 2024, Charlotte Ahlin
"The Catadromous Nature of Eel" © 2024, Sophia Tao
"The (Re)Creation of New Terraform" © 2024, Adianu Etinose
"Redo" © 2024, Brigitte Winter
"All The Time in the World and None at All" © 2024, Allison Pottern
"12 Hours to Anoesis" © 2024, Avani Vaghela
"Fracture" © 2024, Melinda A. Smith
"Wave Walkers" © 2024, Victor Pope
"Mars Monkeys" © 2024, Neil Flinchbaugh
"No Moon and Flat Calm" First published in *Slate.com*, © 2019. Reprinted with permission by Elizabeth Bear.
"Spaced" © 2024, Catherine Castellani
"Athena's Voyage" © 2024, Nick DePasquale
"My Lover's Music Box" © 2024, A.E. Kirchoff
"Chat_transcript_elsie_user260916_2189-12-13T21-18-32.661Z" © 2024, Ash Howell
"Ada the Last Daughter: On Blackhole Cosmology and Computation" © 2024, Chris Campbell

ISBN: 979-8-9907755-0-3 (Paperback)
ISBN: 979-8-9907755-1-0 (EBook)
ISBN: 979-8-9907755-2-7 (PDF)

Printed in the United States. First printing, 2024.

NEW YEAR, NEW YOU

A SPECULATIVE ANTHOLOGY OF REINVENTION

Edited by Chris Campbell

STORIES BY

Charlotte Ahlin ◆ Elizabeth Bear ◆ Chris Campbell
Catherine Castellani ◆ F.E. Choe ◆ Rowan Copley
Julie Danvers ◆ Nick DePasquale ◆ Adianu Etinose
Neil Flinchbaugh ◆ Avani Vaghela ◆ Daryl Gregory
Trae Hawkins ◆ Ash Howell ◆ C.R. Kellogg
A.E. Kirchoff ◆ Taylor Lykiardopoulos ◆ Alec J. Marsh
Victor Pope ◆ Allison Pottern ◆ Melinda A. Smith
Shannon Spieler ◆ Sophia Tao ◆ Brigitte Winter

To all those brave enough to see the world that is and imagine another.

Table of Contents

Foreword	ix
Better Me Is Fun at Parties by F.E. Choe	1
The Holy Daughters of Eng Mac by C.R. Kellogg	11
A Façade of Faith by Shannon Spieler	25
A Thousand Gomorrahs by Daryl Gregory	37
Father Time Dares You to Dream by Trae Hawkins	43
The Manifold Aspects of Horace by Taylor Lykiardopoulos	53
Ugly by Julie Danvers	65
Aurora Deserti by Rowan Copley	77
Katabasis by Alec J. Marsh	91
The Ravishing Moon Princess by Charlotte Ahlin	95
The Catadromous Nature of Eel by Sophia Tao	109
The (Re)Creation of New Terraform by Adianu Etinose	115
Redo by Brigitte Winter	129
All The Time in the World and None at All by Allison Pottern	145
12 Hours to Anoesis by Avani Vaghela	159
Fracture by Melinda A. Smith	175
Wave Walkers by Victor Pope	191
Mars Monkeys by Neil Flinchbaugh	203
No Moon and Flat Calm by Elizabeth Bear	215
Spaced by Catherine Castellani	231
Athena's Voyage by Nick DePasquale	241
My Lover's Music Box by A.E. Kirchoff	257
chat_transcript_elsie_user260916_2189-12-13T21-18-32.661Z by Ash Howell	265
Ada the Last Daughter: On Blackhole Cosmology and Computation by Chris Campbell	283
Contributors	291
Acknowledgements	299

Foreword

EACH NEW YEAR, millions of us partake in a collective ritual at the stroke of midnight. We strive to become wealthier, healthier, and more connected with friends, family, and the world around us. While we may not achieve our goals every year, most of us, without fail, will try again the next.

The word we use for this ritual—resolution—reveals much about the act and our role in it. It is not a wish upon a star or a prayer to a higher power. It is an agreement, a contract between who we are and who we aspire to be. It is a story we tell ourselves, illustrating how our personal agency can shape reality and shift destiny. This concept is inherently revolutionary—each of us holds the power to write the script of our own lives.

The twenty-four stories in this anthology explore various facets of this revolutionary idea of reinvention: haunting tales that gnaw at us with their hunger, Protean myths that echo from ancient depths, near-future narratives that challenge our understanding of humanity, and portals to distant worlds that envision how these ideas will evolve under new suns.

I hope you enjoy the journey our writers have crafted and find inspiration for your next transformation within these pages.

Chris Campbell
June 1, 2024

BETTER ME IS FUN AT PARTIES

F.E. Choe

Better Me grows like a mushroom. She fruits scalp first. Thick coils of knotted hair pin through the soil like fingers digging their way out, bending up toward the light and warmth of living things.

She is perfect. A dream. The landmarks of our bodies are mirror-twins: my birthmark reflected across the base of her spine, the same mole above my right eyebrow which sits above her left. Our faces are imitations, the one eye (my right, her left) slightly smaller than the other.

And this? I say and point to the raised line at her abdomen. Why keep this at all?

Inches below my own navel, an old appendectomy scar slants to the right while her stitching runs parallel to the left.

She makes a sawing motion against the muscle, the side of her hand a blade.

A convenient wound, she says. Where I cut myself away from the stem.

She shakes her hands through her hair and stretches. Her skin smells of soil, of factory dirt, and an artificial, floral sweetness like bonemeal folded into play dough.

I show her how to bathe, how to test the water with the back of her hand, how she should tip her head back and close her eyes when I rinse her hair.

When she dresses, she is careful to pick a shirt of matching color and style, to pull on a similar pair of black leggings. I watch her adjust and pose, how she folds herself into the same posture as my own. She favors her right leg and laces her fingers together, tilts her chin to focus on the space below my throat when I speak.

We watch the ball drop on the screen of my small television. We count down from ten. We hold our breaths and lean forward for the moment when the couples kiss and the streets fill with glittering furrows of confetti.

THE NEIGHBORS TAKE us for sisters.

How nice, they say, to be with family for the holidays. How strange, you never mentioned.

They pretend not to notice the moss-green stain of her nail beds. The scent of wet clay that lingers on her skin. It seeps into my clothing, the walls, and bedding despite our persistent scrubbing, despite the fastidiousness with which she airs and launders, scrubs and steams and presses.

Yes, how strange, she says. How strange how nice it all is.

When she speaks, she is perhaps a little more docile, a little softer than I expect myself to be.

IN LATE JANUARY we are carrying in the shopping, when a neighbor's cat skims past us in the hall and deposits a dead bird at the threshold of our apartment.

The cat pauses, steps slowly and blinks before rushing forward again. Better Me drops her bags, reaches out to try and touch—to catch, or just, if only to feel for a second what the animal's fur might be like—but the cat slips past, a streak of gray and rust-brown, to the other end of the corridor.

While I unlock the door and try to salvage the cans and frozen fruit, the soft loaf of sliced bread, the bananas that have tumbled out into the hall, Better Me cradles the dead bird in her hands and brings it inside. She sets it on the windowsill between the Pothos and the spider plant, inspects it closely, the tip of her nose almost brushing against its wing.

Hurry will you? Wash your hands and help me with this, I say. The center of the bread is ruined, punched down and compressed underfoot.

It's still warm, she says. Her upturned hand hovers over it, her knuckles steady above its breast.

The next morning Better Me pours coffee, fetches the milk and sugar, cracks an egg into a hollowed-out piece of toast. I notice, relieved, that the dead bird is gone, the windowsill wiped clean, the soft bite of disinfectant in the air.

Your lunch is in the fridge, she says. Don't forget it. You know how you always forget.

IT IS NO wonder that others like her have popped up all over the city.

On Saturday mornings, the cafes and restaurants are overrun with identical couplings. They bounce fussy infants between them at parks. They stand together in line at concerts and museums. They spill across the banks to jog along the river at dusk. Their fluorescent vests catch the lamplight, flare under headlights like sheets of tin. Abandoned halves wait patiently for their mates in the lobbies of movie theaters, at gas station pumps, in the aisles of the supermarket. They exist and disappear together, crowding into the backseats of taxis, turning up side streets, slipping into buildings.

Each evening, I come home from work to a spotless apartment, clean clothes folded at the foot of the bed. Better Me thinks of everything: the shopping, the cleaning, the birthday, anniversary, and thank you cards I never manage to send in time on my own. The grout in the shower is always scrubbed clean, the mirror bare, the toilet bowl smelling faintly yet not unpleasantly of bleach.

At night, we crawl into bed together and pull the cover over our matched selves. She neatens the fold of the sheet under my elbow, tucks her head into the space between my chin and collarbone. I lie still and listen to the soft pull of her breath as she sinks deeper into the steady cadence of sleep, and already I feel so much less alone than I had once thought possible.

In March, our first party. Yet another baby shower for a college acquaintance, a roommate, a friend of a friend I haven't seen since their wedding. I scroll through old profiles and show Better Me photos of girls on pristine, verdant quads. I point to young women I have trouble naming, listing instead their degrees and occupations, the various locations of their bachelorette getaways, their hometowns. She helps me choose just the right gift from the registry, shows me the best way to wrap it, how to curl the ribbon for a bow.

We stand side by side and assemble tea sandwiches. She quarters them into perfect triangles, and I arrange them on a cut glass tray she has coaxed from a neighbor for the weekend.

Better Me watches as I bite into one to taste, and distracted, she nicks herself with the serrated blade. I notice only when I look down to move more sandwiches onto the tray.

Are they ruined? She draws her finger toward her mouth.

Let me see.

A thin, broken line bisects the pad of her left index finger. The wound weeps beads of sap, a clear and candy red.

I hold her hand under a stream of water, feel her fingers stretch open under mine.

Does it hurt much?

Hurt? She repeats the word as if amused by its taste.

At the shower, the women wear pale sundresses and sheer white linen blouses. They coo over each other's infants and tell us both how jealous they are, how great we look these days. They write down predictions of the baby's birth weight on identical slips of cream-colored paper and place them in a small wooden box in the hall. They ask us what we have been up to lately, where we live now, are we taking ourselves anywhere nice for the summer?

Their children adore Better Me. They grab balloons and bat them at her with their fists. They toddle over and cling to her legs, bury their sticky faces in the fabric of her skirt, are content to be lifted up, gently pinched, rocked. She cradles one, bounces another on her lap. She brings her nose to an infant's neck, buries her face in the fold of flesh between its chin and shoulder. She closes her eyes, tilts her head sweetly.

The sedate child in her lap. The other women bending their smooth, flawless necks toward her. To be so wholly captivating and unaware. How easy it all seems.

I wander through the kitchen on my own, the sitting room, the garden. It becomes clear I'm the only one who has brought a Better with her.

You're being so good, says the mother-to-be. She motions to Better Me who has apportioned herself only a small sliver of the cake, just enough not to seem disinterested or impolite.

Better Me pinches some of the crumb between her fingers, lifts it to her mouth, lets it rest on her tongue. She moves her jaw as if sifting through it with her teeth.

Someone taps their fork against their glass. Ready for gifts?

Better Me brings a napkin to her lips, spits.

IN THE MORNING, she wakes me with gentle scratches against my back, traces small circles into the side of my neck, my arm, my ankle. She sets the coffee on the burner while I brush my teeth. She lays out my clothing on the bed and dresses herself in coordinating colors. She helps me with my coat and tells me to have a good day, not to worry, that she will take care of everything.

Should I order in from the Thai place for dinner tonight? she says.

Yes, that sounds good.

Good. I'm pleased. Be careful on the subway. Would you like for me to walk you and wait for the train?

We link hands, press close to one another as we descend the stairs amid a crowd of unruly, unpredictable bodies. It makes her nervous— the thick yellow line of the platform's edge, to find herself so deep underground again, so exposed to the scrutiny of strangers, the howl of the train as it barrels through the tunnel. She brings her free hand to her mouth, presses her knuckles against her upper lip. Her grip tightens on my hand.

Are you sure you're alright? Can you make it back on your own?

Yes, I'm fine. Go, won't you? We're ordering in? Good. Alright.

I'll be here when you get back. We should walk together to the restaurant to pick it up. It's still so dark outside by the time you get in.

AT THE END of spring, my parents are not at all surprised when I bring her home.

Your Aunt Eunice has one too, my mother says as we peel potatoes over the sink.

My father is hunched over the bar with his hands in his pockets. How about something to drink, sweetheart? he says.

They've all gotten a bit lazier for it to be honest, my mother says. You know your aunt. She's always been a little odd. It was hard enough before to get her to go anywhere.

Better Me helps my father find his reading glasses. She spends an hour clicking through my mother's phone and helping her readjust the settings. She sets the table and serves us all first and claps her hands together in delight when we have finished.

She's made a cake. Your favorite, I say. Was up all night baking.

This is true. That morning when I woke, the kitchen smelled of powdered sugar and vanilla. Before packing the cake in its box, we ran our index fingers along the rim of the plate, brought them to our lips, tasted sweetness.

Before we leave, my father pinches her chin affectionately. He has said goodbye this way since I was a child.

See you next time sweetheart, he says. He caresses her cheek with the back of his fingers, as if she is too delicate to touch, to spoil with the inside of his hands.

My mother hugs us both awkwardly. Her gaze passes back and forth between us as we tie our shoes, back and forth as we check our pockets, back to Better Me as she picks up the extra crate of pears mother has bought for us.

I hope you weren't upset, Better Me says in the car. She rests her face in her hand then scratches at a place in the window.

Why would I be upset? I say, focused on the road, my hands steady on the wheel. I knew they would love you right away.

You're perfect. How could they not love you as I do?

ON THE FIRST day of summer, I bring Better Me to an after-work happy hour. She puts on the pale yellow dress that has hung unworn in my closet for months. I have been too afraid to wear it out in public before.

The other Betters are attentive dates. They run back and forth to the bar for rounds, helpfully filling in when we fail to remember specific details of a story or the punchlines of jokes.

So this is your secret, how you manage to get everything done—to juggle everything, we say to each other.

In return we offer inoffensive platitudes. We deflect, try to disarm one another, avoid giving too much of ourselves away.

I needed a wife.

I can be difficult, particular.

I just can't live with anyone else is the truth.

Better Me is charming, a good listener, a pleasure to talk to. She is clever and witty and approachable. She is quick to smooth over lulls in conversation, and we find ourselves grateful to her.

She puts her hand on my elbow and shows me how to insert myself gracefully into conversations. She plays nice and makes me look good. She is endearing, self-deprecating. Alongside her, I appear to be more competent and interesting than I actually am.

She tactfully ignores it each time my boss rests his hand in the small of her back.

None of us can keep our eyes off her. The yellow dress and its delicately tied bows that keep slipping off her shoulders, the mole above her left eyebrow, the way she holds our gazes steady until eventually we cede and look away.

Each time we are apart, when I lift my head to look for her, she is there watching and waiting to meet my gaze. Each time, she looks at me as if I am the only thing worth noticing.

For my birthday, we go to the beach and watch our skin go golden under the August sun. We tangle our limbs in the surf, wade further into the sea. We screech when our toes graze slippery, unseen surfaces that turn underfoot and skitter away like living things. In the afternoon, she shows me how to crack open small, hard crabs and keep the flesh intact. We eat with our fingers. We bring bottles of beer to our lips, the glass tasting more and more of salt, of butter, of brine and roe.

We change out of our wet swimsuits in the dressing room of a surf shop. She watches me in the mirror, and I am suddenly aware of how close the space is, how I contort myself around her nakedness. I shield my breasts with my hands, try to turn away from her gaze, press my arm stiffly against my stomach as I hunch over and struggle to tug free of the damp fabric.

Goosebumps ripple across the skin of her arms and the slope of her shoulders. Her nipples are small, dark knots against the soft swell of her breasts.

She slips an oversized shirt over her head. Will you buy me this?

Yes, whatever you want.

She lifts the hem, reaches for my hand and brings it to her leg, uses my finger to trace the line that divides the dark bronze of her thigh from the pale strip of flesh at the join of her hip.

She laughs, and then I am laughing too. I feel a gentle unknotting at the top of my breastbone, and in that moment I want to give her anything else she might ask for.

We wander back along the shore in the dark. She slips her hand into the pocket of my shorts for the keys and tells me she will take us home. I doze off in the passenger seat on the ride back.

I wake in the parking lot of our apartment. The car unloaded, beads of condensation cluster against the glass. She stands bare legged in the stairwell of the building and grins at the moths whispering in the overhead glow even as they singe against the light.

She peers at me through the windshield, stretches her hand out and beckons.

Ready to come in?

In autumn her cheeks go rosy in the cold air. She blooms, grows plump in the season of dead and dormant things. The beds of her fingernails turn pale pink, the scent of her skin softened to talc. A thin, sheer down of hair claims her body in patches: her temples, her forearms, her lower back, the tender space where her thighs meet.

I wake one night, my throat dry, to find her side of the bed empty, the bedroom door a flat outline of muted light.

I come upon her in the kitchen, her back toward me. She is hunched over the counter, her dark hair a curtain. There is a rustle like dead leaves, the snapping of dry twigs, a lush, herbal iron note in the air.

What are you doing up so early?

She turns and smiles. Folds her hands one over the other before her. In this light her gums look wine-stained, her teeth brittle, her skin paper-thin over the angles of her skull.

On the counter behind her is a soft pile of gray fur.

I say, I'd like a glass of water, please.

Why don't you go back to bed? I'll bring one to you.

She turns back and stretches, balances on her toes to reach in the cabinet for a glass. Before turning the faucet on, she rests a hand on the heaped pelt before her and digs her fingers lovingly into it.

I think of her hands opening toward the cat as it rushed down the hall, softening beneath mine under warm water, raking my salt-soaked hair back from my face.

I need—

You should go back to bed.

I think of the pale, silk threads velveting the most intimate parts of her body, the warm seam of her mouth parted in sleep, the weight of her head resting against my shoulder.

Try to catch a few more hours of sleep before work, she says. Early start and all.

We play each other for Halloween. I run to the bar to collect our drinks as she dances under red lights. She watches me flirt with ghouls and werewolves, a parade of vampires with identical sets of fangs, the bartender whose head is adorned with tiny red devil horns.

A tall, faceless figure in a cheap skeleton bodysuit presses her against a wall. The faceless thing bends and turns its head so that its jaw is against her ear. I watch her hand slide against its abdomen. She shows me each of its painted ribs.

The bartender pinches his nose when he's nervous. Did you realize? He's done it four times already. I counted.

And me? What's my tell?

She licks the end of her finger and dabs at something under my eye.

We walk home with our arms linked. The October wind numbs our hands and faces. She leans into me on the escalator and buries her face in my neck as we descend into the subway tunnel.

On the platform, she taps her toe against the yellow line while we wait, laces her fingers into mine.

When we kiss, we thaw the frozen places where we meet: the tips of our noses, our lips, our cheeks, her chin against my forehead.

We undress in the dark. I feel the weight of her body sinking down next to mine, pressing me underneath her own. And then there is only the hot pull of her breath against my skin, the pressure of her hands. I push deeper into her, and nothing exists but my own need, an ache solid enough to wrap myself around as she pulls it taught and tugs it free.

ON THE FIRST snow, she shows me how to sterilize a needle, a blade. How important the placement of an incision. What little meat and blood she needs each day to survive.

Just think, she says. Soon it will be the holidays. And then, a new year. I'll get you all to myself for a while. Won't that be nice?

How strange it is to be so desired.

She puts her mouth to mine, holds my hand steady as I open myself. It is a tiny wound, almost nothing. A new, unfinished seam no more than an inch. A small price to pay to be not so alone.

THE HOLY DAUGHTERS OF ENG MAC

C.R. Kellogg

Before Jica realized that she wasn't dead, before a clammy dewdrop wound down her armpit, before she heard her own scream claw its way from her throat, there was pain.

Fog had twined with the smoking incense pot on the porch that morning. The man who was supposed to be her father tried once again to teach her morning prayers, but Jica's mind wandered. She wondered, as she did most mornings, what she had done to make her mother leave her in Eng Mac. Why she had force marched her from the Mazie war camp, up the high mountains, into a town of pale-faced mystics and deposited her with this white-haired holy man.

The pounding drum of her heart pulled Jica from black unconsciousness. Her heart said: death has not yet folded its hard arms around you. You are not in the prairie grass of the great beyond.

Her mother had said fallen warriors ran across the plains forever under a sun that did not set. But Jica wasn't a warrior. She wasn't anything but a discard. A stranger with no place and no family.

She opened her eyes, and gray moonlight poured through the crusted slits. Her head throbbed at the brightness.

"In three days," her father said, clearing ash from the overnight fire, "our youth will come of age. Your sister will be one." He pointed to where Vive slept on her bedroll. *She was three years older and, since Jica had been*

dumped here, only looked at her with venom. Discovering new siblings, Jica learned, was not common in Eng Mac.

Her father, the holy man Jam Baruk, had a big belly and a long white braid filled with beads and cymbals. It stretched down his back to tell a history of his life. Mid-back, a faded red knot of Mazie cloth denoted his peace-keeping mission in the plains.

"We will need blue waters from a sacred spring atop the mountain." He slid a disk of flat dough off a wood paddle into the coals. When the dough puffed high, Jica flipped it with the tips of her fingers. This, at least, she had learned how to do.

After four ovals of bread lay on a scarf next to them, Jam Baruk said, "Holy daughters fetch the water." He pointed with the paddle to her and the lump of Vive's sleeping body.

THE IMPULSE TO scratch an itch rocked Jica awake. Her injuries screamed. She stretched the pointer finger on her right hand and her wrist pulsed. Her other hand scraped along something rough until a shock of pain walloped her as vomit rose into her mouth. Pain like lightning burned up her leg into her back.

Jica licked blood from her lips. She opened her eyes and studied her surroundings. The moonlight painted the trees and rocks in white. Embankments rose high above her. She lifted her head and froze.

Jica dangled in a tree.

VIVE BLENDED IN with the forests of Eng Mac. As sisters, they were nothing alike. Vive's light brown hair was woven tightly with white cloth, and Jica's black hair was wrapped in a war bun. The soft pine needles sunk under Jica's feet but pressed Vive up the mountain with a bounce. After she came of age, Vive would become their father's apprentice and connect the tribe to the spirit realm. Jica would keep making flatbread and waiting to go home.

They followed a steep path that climbed out of Eng Mac, past the confluence of three tight ravines. Vive powered up the slope, barely noticing the bundle of food and water tied to her back. Her own satchel dug into Jica's neck painfully.

After only a few minutes, Vive had disappeared in the damp, understory darkness. In Mazie, Jica ran and sparred. In Eng Mac, they climbed mountains through heavy, thick air that tasted of sap and smoke. The air wasn't right in Eng Mac. It felt like whispers in her mouth.

"Vive!" Jica gasped after an age of climbing. "I don't know the way." Jica couldn't keep the whine out of her voice. If Vive had been sent to Mazie, Jica would have welcomed another sister. She would have taught her to fight and where to rest at midday.

Through the gloom, Vive stepped from behind a tree and glared. Jica wiped at her eyes and tried to close the distance, but slipped on the slick pine needles. Her belly hit the forest floor, and she slid a few feet down the mountainside.

"You're as useless as a new fawn," Vive said, appearing silently above her. Vive grimaced, held fast to a low branch, and grasped Jica by the forearm. Even with a water skein and her bundle of supplies, Vive lifted her easily, pausing for only a second before bounding up the mountain.

JICA'S PANIC CLENCHED heavily in her chest. The ravine floor loomed an impossible distance below her. Sobs shuddered out, threatening to break her precarious balance on the bare branch.

She was alone. So alone. She was dying in a tree, forgotten and abandoned. First, by her mother, who lied that she was too young for the war camp. But none of her younger sisters had been returned to their fathers during muster. Only Jica. Sent to the village of her father like a boy.

You are different. That was all the explanation her mother gave. But still, she wrapped Jica's hair in a war bun before their march to Eng Mac.

Jica reached up, ignoring a throbbing wrist, and touched her head. The bun survived her fall. She had re-tied her war bun each day since she arrived in these mountains. The rough flax scratching her fingertips quieted her sobs.

Somehow, she had survived the fall, too.

VIVE WALKED SLOWER *after that. From time to time, she pointed out bad footholds or roots about to snap. And one time she took Jica's hand and pulled her roughly off the switchback into the ferns. Vive pointed to a branch hanging askew.*

"A cursed spirit hangs there. It must take a life to be set free."

Jica studied the branch warily, its awkward movement in the wind now obvious. There were so many ways to die in the Eng Mac mountains and too few involved a sword or spear.

After several hours of climbing, they rested. Vive tore a berry leather apart and handed Jica the bigger half. Jica hid a smile as the leather softened in her mouth. Flashes of sun broke through the mists, making shapes of shadow and light roll through the fog.

"It's a bear." Jica pointed to one a shadow shapes moving through the fog. It was a game she played with her Mazie sisters at midday break, finding the shapes in the clouds. No one could ever compete with Jica's uncanny scenes.

Vive cocked her head and studied Jica. She bit her lip and narrowed her eyes. Eventually she said, "Bears hibernate this time of year."

JICA PUSHED HERSELF upright.

The movement tugged at her leg, splayed at an awkward right angle.

Jica leaned forward and vomited, and the wracking pulls revealed new hot spots of pain.

Her shoulder popped forward unnaturally. A goose egg pulsed loudly above her ear.

She gripped the branch frantically. Her vomit smelled of berry leather and flatbread and Jica wept furious tears until her stomach carried nothing more to purge.

Her twisted leg was wedged in a fork below her. Jica cried out and bit down on her lip. With a scream, she wrenched her broken leg from the branch.

Jica held to the branch like her mother during a night terror. She shook and fought for consciousness because though her mind begged for blackness her heart knew there was no comfort. She was alone.

When the spots in her vision cleared and feeling returned to her leg, she scooted, an inch at a time, toward the tree trunk.

W̲HEN SLIVERS OF̲ sky appeared through tree gaps and the air tasted worse than ever, Vive's pace quickened. Piles of rock replaced thick forest understory and eventually they crested a ridge. With no notice, Vive turned and hopped off the trail, into a bank of hot fog. Her braid flashed, before disappearing into the mist.

Jica followed, tentative. Walking alone through mists, she ached for the trees' company. Soon, a trickle of water joined the sound of her own scuffing footsteps. The sound led her to a pool of water that released hot fog into the air. It was a brighter blue than she'd seen anywhere outside of a Mazie sky.

The water moved in a constant motion like a pot of water over the fire. The moving mass sent shapes of steam and mist into the surrounding air. A strange vertigo pulled Jica toward the water with a tug from her belly.

She wanted to go to the water. To submerge herself in it and let its smoking arms pull her down.

"Jica." A hand pushed at her chest roughly. "Give me your skein and wait over there." Vive was in front of her now, and stern.

Unsteadily, Jica stumbled back. It had been difficult to pull her eyes from the water, but now that she looked into Vive's face, the spell shattered. The water gurgled for her attention, but Jica half ran to the rock's safety. She kept her back to the water, unsure of what magic filled this place, and laid a picnic of their remaining food. She broke the last bread in half and left the larger portion for Vive.

When no more tasks could be found, she glanced over her shoulder. Tendrils of steam licked all around Vive, who knelt at the water's edge, praying. Jica shivered. The mists formed arms embracing Vive, fingers picking through the braid of her hair.

A few minutes later, Vive laid the full skeins down reverently. She whispered a prayer and threw crumbles of bread over her shoulder. She looked unburdened.

"What is the ritual?" Jica pointed at the skeins.

Vive shewed, slowly, and ran a hand down her braid. "Your mother unwinds the braid she has been keeping for you. You drink the blue waters. The ancestors reveal your path and you begin your own braid." She tugged a little roughly at a knot in her hair.

Jica knew Vive's mother was long dead. Who had been weaving her braid? Who would unwind it in the ritual? She chewed the flatbread. She'd hated it at first, but it barely tasted sour anymore.

"Are you frightened?" Jica asked. She refused to look at the water, jostling behind her shoulder.

Vive snorted. "Of what?"

"The water. The fog," she shivered. "It's creepy."

Vive's nostrils flared and gestured at the mists surrounding them. "They're our ancestors. Our dead."

Jica rolled her eyes. She'd heard this lecture during morning prayers for months. "I doubt the dead care to hang around here." In Mazie, the dead were released to the plains. They didn't linger, meddling in the silly affairs of the living.

Without warning, Vive stood.

Jica recoiled at the fury on her sister's face as Vive fastened a skein to her back.

"Let's go."

JICA'S CHEEK THROBBED against the tree. A leather strap pulled uncomfortably at her shoulder, and she fumbled behind her to release it. The skein of holy water. She stroked the rough hairs of its skin and thought of the churning and blue spring. She remembered it pull her toward the water. As if the skein commanded it, her gaze flicked down to the base of the tree and she wobbled.

She couldn't think of the spring. Or how she got in this tree.

Jica squeezed the holy water to her belly. A bundle of warmth to fight the chilly night air. The moon was halfway through the sky.

Long enough for someone to have come found her. But no one would. She was unwanted and alone.

Her injuries made climbing down unlikely. It would be best not to attempt any movement until morning, anyway. But her stomach growled with hunger and her tongue stuck to the roof of her dry mouth. And she glanced down at the water. She drummed her fingers on the leather.

They drank the water for the ceremony, so it would not kill her. She opened the latch and sniffed. It smelled of morning mist. Piney. She dipped a finger in and tasted a drop.

It tasted like…water. Fresh and a little mossy. Jica took a sip. It was warm from her body heat or the spring. Jica took a gulp. After a last long drink, she made herself stopper the skein. Her belly grumbled uneasily.

For a moment, Jica fumbled at the knot until the strap released from the water. She wrapped the strap behind her back and around the trunk before tying it tight. She found a part of her face that didn't hurt, rested it on the tree, and closed her eyes.

"Where are we going?" Jica asked.

The fog lightened as they traveled away from the spring. They'd been following a rocky trail for an hour and had yet to reach the tree line. Jica didn't know much about the mountain's geography, but was sure they weren't going back the way they came.

Vive said stiffly, "We're taking another way down." She hopped over a small boulder and motioned for Jica to follow. Vive had not met her eye since the spring.

Jica was falling. She jerked up in a panic and reached out, only to smack something hard. Disoriented, she struggled backward, but was caught by the rope around her middle. She blinked, remembered her situation and clung instinctively to the tree. She blinked again and realized that she could not see out of her right eye.

Day filled the valley with a bright fog. Mist fully enveloped her tree perch. She could not make out the branch from which she'd pulled her leg. The fog weighed on her shoulders substantially, like a heavy blanket. She swirled her finger in a spiral and the mists clung to her pattern, hanging in the air as solidly as a figure drawn in dirt.

Jica froze. Her leg. Though she could not see her foot in the mist, her knee was straight, not bent. She tested it tentatively. No pain.

Her shoulder, which had been angled out of its socket, now mirrored the other side. Her wrist flexed easily. The goose egg on her head was gone.

Her face didn't feel swollen and the blind eye felt normal in all other respects.

Jica laughed out loud. She rolled her shoulders and checked each part of her body. Daylight revealed gashes, tears and bloodstains in her clothes—but no wounds.

She peered into the dense fog and shivered. The people of Eng Mac said when you died, you became the mists. Had she died? Her heart seized silently that she would not rest with her mother's people on the plains.

Jica sucked in a staggered breath. She tasted ash and flatbread and incense. It tasted like home.

If she was dead, Jica decided, then she had nothing to fear from climbing down this tree. She untied the strap about her waist and wrapped it around her hands. The skein of water sat between her legs, completely cool now in the morning chill.

She contemplated it for a moment, and pushed it off the branch. Jica counted in her head until she heard it hit the ground.

One. Two. Three.

Not as far as she'd guessed. But far enough to shatter her miraculously mended bones. Assuming she wasn't dead.

But not seeing the distance made her brave. She wrapped her arms around the trunk and lowered a foot toward where she remembered a lower branch. After a moment of feeling blind in the air, she bumped into a branch with her toe.

In this way, Jica descended from the tree. After climbing for some time, she found no more footholds. The mists swirled less at this height and, for some reason, Jica guessed that meant the ground was near. She embraced the trunk tightly and prayed she was right.

Then she let go with her legs and slid.

THE CLOUDS LIFTED *and their path sloped sharply. Jica didn't know she could dislike anything more than climbing up a mountain until she tried to walk down one. Her thighs and knees ached. The skein of water jostled its weight with each step. Vive's braid whipped from side to side in the wind.*

After another hour of carefully picking footholds, the last trees disappeared to reveal an enormous scree slide. At the bottom of the slide, a sharp precipice dropped into darkness. She wanted to shut her eyes to the mountain's vastness and the destroyed valley.

There had to be another way down. She turned to ask Vive, who had stopped behind her. The words caught in her mouth. Vive was a step away with a face as sharp as the stones underfoot.

Her sister glowered with open loathing.

"How do we get home?" Jica asked. She tried to keep her voice steady, but she was afraid.

Vive grabbed her by the arms, nails cutting into her biceps.

"You don't belong here." Her breath was hot on Jica's ear as she leaned in and hissed, "And you'll never be my sister."

JICA BEGAN TO pick up speed when her feet sunk into a carpet of moss to stop her slide. She laughed out loud and flopped backwards, rolling on the ground. She jumped up and kissed the tree.

"Nicely done," said a voice.

Jica screamed and whirled. She strained her one seeing eye. Only swirling white mists surrounded her.

"Maybe you don't need a spirit guide after all." The voice emanated around her.

Jica spun in a circle and crouched into a fighting stance. No one appeared.

"Here." The mists eddied and condensed, becoming nearly solid and gray. They formed a tall male figure with a complex braid woven to his waist. Jica couldn't guess his age. Not as old as her father, but older than Vive.

Her breath stopped, but she made herself release it. Don't think about Vive.

The man stepped toward her with palms open. His footsteps dissolved into the mossy floor. Jica backed away.

"Who are you?"

"Hamis was my name when I was alive."

Jica considered for a moment. "So, I am dead."

Hamis laughed, and the sound surrounded her, bouncing through the fog with mirth. "No. Your consciousness is, however, temporarily in the spirit realm."

The finer details of his expression were impossible to make out, but there was a familiarity about the shape of his face.

"How do I get back?" Jica asked.

Hamis pointed in a direction within the veil of mist. Jica stepped that way, then stopped.

"And where will that take me?"

He clapped his hands together happily and sent a brief gust of air her way. "You are as clever as I knew you'd be."

Jica waited. She could walk in any direction, but would it take her off a cliff? To Eng Mac? To Mazie?

"Why would you help me?"

"Because you are a daughter of Eng Mac, and we must bring you home," Hamis said, seriously.

Jica's heart squeezed tightly. "I don't have a home."

"Nonsense. You have a father who prays for you every morning. You have a tribe who makes your clothing and hunts your food. You have a sister who didn't know what she was losing…"

Jica froze. Hamis moved close to her, and a warm hand rested gently on her shoulder. She knew tears must be flowing down her face.

Her words were throaty and garbled. "Why?"

SHE WAS FALLING.

Backwards below her, there was scree. But seconds lingered before her body hit rock. Unbraided baby hairs flew around Vive's face in the wind. Her brow was a tight line and her lips a perfect open circle of disbelief or regret. One arm stretched out, reaching for Jica, as if to pull her back.

Then, pain.

THE FOG DEMON stood a pace away, studying the incomprehensible swirls around him. Every so often, Hamis seemed to respond to movements in the mist he'd seen or heard with a minute nod or tilt of his head. When Jica had collected herself, he gestured for her to walk with him.

"Vive spent her life trying to be the perfect daughter," said Hamis.

"But I'm the opposite of perfect." Jica wiped her nose on her sleeve. "I can barely make flatbread."

"Yes. Perfection is irrelevant."

Jica didn't understand.

When she could speak, Jica pointed to her right eye. "Hamis, my other wounds are healed. But I can't see."

Hamis nodded. "Nothing is healed."

They reached an incline and the mists cleared to reveal a dirt trail. Hamis sighed. "Your eye is the price to walk among the spirits. Through your spirit sight, you've always been able to see us interact with the physical world. Shapes in the smoke. Drawings formed from light and shadow."

She remembered the bear in the mists and the fingers combing through Vive's braid at the spring and swallowed.

Her mother joked with the aunties about Jica's wild imagination, but privately told Jica to keep quiet about the images she saw. Her mother knew about this spirit sight. Hot betrayal filled her mouth as bitter as the moment her mother left Eng Mac.

"You could be the greatest seer Eng Mac has ever produced. But you must forfeit your eye to come back here." He spread his arms, and the spirit fog churned faster and more frantically than before. It condensed in flashes and formed the figure of her father. The plains. A dangling branch. Vive reaching.

She focused on Hamis's words while the mists agitated for her attention. Lose her eye? What good would a one-eyed warrior be to the Mazie, when her mother came back for her? If her mother came back.

The ground underfoot became hard and the trickle of a waterfall on rock rang through the thick mists. The sun grew increasingly bright and Hamis dissolved and reconstituted himself several times before kneeling in front of her.

Blue sky broke through and Hamis turned a lemony yellow. "The sun cuts our time short. I bid you farewell, holy daughter. This is the path to Eng Mac. Left, down the mountain, is Mazie. Right will take you to the village."

His face glowed brightly and a blink later the wisps of fog dissolved.

The path sloping down to the left, toward Mazie, hugged the tall ravine. Puffs of fog lingered in patches, but the sun shone on the mountain's scarred gray face. That way was home. Where the tall grass swished with each footfall. Where her sisters loved her. Where mists did not speak.

To the right was a rockier path that sloped up. The sun had not reached that part of the valley and darkness hung off the sheer path. It would be a long way to fall. But as the throbbing returned to her shoulder and leg, Jica realized she was no longer afraid.

She limped forward. The banks of fog did not follow her. They rolled in the sun like a wave.

Jica stumbled and braced herself on the narrow path. She breathed through the pounding goose egg on her head and, several times, stopped to wipe away tears.

She wondered if she chose the right path and why it hurt so much.

Past the next crag, the green roofs of Eng Mac appeared. Jica appreciated them through her one good eye.

Vive's white braid flicked across her face in the wind. She stood silhouetted against the mountain peak and clear blue sky. For once, the mists cleared.

As Jica fell, she memorized this image of her sister, frozen. More painful than each crack as she fell.

A curious crowd jostled in the village center. As Jica limped down the road, no one turned from the commotion. Her throat was sand, or she would have called out.

Her father's voice, filled with anger and tears, echoed down the street. Through a gap, Jica saw a girl on the ground with a shorn head. Hair, ribbons, and beads lay all around her and she sobbed into her knees. She looked up at where their father stood, and Jica saw Vive. Her eyes were red and swollen.

Their father vibrated with anger, and Jica was afraid. She shuffled past the nearest man in the crowd and kept pushing. Jam Baruk gasped when he saw her and pulled Jica into an embrace. His fat tears dribbled into her hair, but Jica's eyes were on Vive. Vive's lip trembled, and she bowed her head.

Jica gently freed herself.

With her good arm, she bent, grasped Vive's hand in hers, and pulled her to her feet.

A FAÇADE OF FAITH

Shannon Spieler

THE FORMEL OF Soreale had a strong nose, hooded eyes that held secrets, and a jaw that hung back from her mouth as if to emphasize her every word. It was the face you wanted on the religious leader of an entire nation. But where she used to stand like a peak sunflower before the basilica's lectern, now the Formel sagged over it.

Cantorine knew with divine certainty that the woman had less than a season to live. The basilica forbade sacrifices to predict another's death, but after the Formel collapsed the month prior, Cantorine—and presumably every Cardinal with even a hint of ambition—had paid heavy coin to know.

From her front row pew, Cantorine Segal imagined herself in the woman's place leading the week's blessings. She lacked the Formel's magisterial mouth with its prominent vermillion border, but Cantorine was taller. Her nose wasn't as strong, but her skin's warmer tone complemented the Formel's hawk feather cape.

Cantorine had only one true rival for the promotion. At the end of the row, Cardinal Tanoria Reede wore a red robe that matched Cantorine's own. The Cardinals, loosely seated everywhere else, clustered around the woman as if wanting to nestle as close as possible. Everyone loved Tanoria.

Tanoria's face had the whole package: a broad brow from which her nose descended like a grand staircase, that bladed jaw balanced by balcony cheekbones and open-window eyes, with a mouth as quick and twisting as a sand viper. It resembled every statue and painting of their god, Bekna, god of mothers.

Cantorine had half, but Tanoria had the whole.

When the ceremony ended, Cantorine went to her room and stood before the mirror. She imitated Tanoria's smile, but her cheeks didn't rise to show off dimples. Her eyes stayed large instead of crinkling with delight. She squeezed her face and tried again.

"Cardinal Cantorine," Tanoria said at the council meeting later that day. "I know your house has provided oil to the basilica these past years, but the price is…high. I know that the Raptor and her slum pirates have been raiding ships, driving prices up on numerous goods, but as Council Treasurer, I must say that bidding is only fair for the honor of supplying our institution."

A year ago, Tanoria had promised Cantorine a price increase if she declined to investigate Tanoria's cousin smuggling holy relics. The slum pirates were an excuse. Tanoria had always planned to renege.

The negotiated price with her house already included a steep discount. A message from Cantorine's mother was likely speeding its way to her desk. *We relied upon you. After everything your sister has strived for—*

Cantorine saw the genius of this play. She could not prosecute the cousin with year-old evidence. Further, Tanoria looked strong and Cantorine weak when nominations for a new Formel would come soon. Cantorine squeezed her quill hard under the table. She didn't want to just write on Tanoria's face. She wanted to take the quill and jab—

The Formel cleared her throat.

"Of course," Cantorine said. "I only want what's best for the basilica."

Tanoria smiled bashfully, as if they'd played a merry round of cards and she reluctantly took the pot. Cantorine kept her own countenance flat. Better that, though, than to let her lips curl into their true snarl.

The Formel tapped her scroll. "Cardinal Cantorine, let us turn to your inquisitorial business—and the problem of that Doctor."

Her position as Inquisitor was one that no other Cardinal had wanted. If Cantorine fully performed her assigned duties, it was a recipe for unpopularity. If she did nothing, she was incompetent. She primarily investigated and arrested the sick who made illegal sacrifices to Dox, foreign god of healing. The position came with incredible power but required cunning to master. But what had her mother always said? Cantorine was nothing if not underhanded and keen.

Soreale's god, Bekna, who shepherded women through childbirth, was beloved of the other eleven continents' gods—except for Dox. The two gods rivaled each other. Thus, sacrificing to Dox was illegal per basilica law. Moreover, Bekna punished those who took Dox's healing by pocking their bodies with scars. Yet desperation compelled the dying to risk disfigurement. Cantorine tracked down scarred survivors and heavily fined them for the benefit of the basilica's coffers.

"So far," Cantorine said, smoothing her notes, "the Doctor's ship has stayed beyond Soreale's boundary line—far enough away to prevent seizure or arrest but near enough so that everyone in the city knows where to receive service."

"I don't understand why we aren't seeing scarring," the Formel demanded. Her fist pounded her chest, and she winced.

"My best theory is that this Doctor is manipulating the sacrifices so that the scars are hidden out of sight on the body."

"Impossible." The Formel recoiled. "Bekna cannot be so controlled."

Cantorine nodded. "Yet my sources suggest they've been successful. The Doctor charges 50,000 silvers per sacrifice. As we all know, there are few houses in the city who could afford such a price."

At her words, at least three Cardinals flinched or paled.

The ten houses that could afford that sum were ones with daughters seated at this table. Cantorine glanced at Tanoria. If only one of her family members was caught up in the scheme—

But Tanoria sat, arms crossed, a serene smile on her face.

The Formel grunted, then grimaced with pain.

Tanoria left the meeting huddled with her chosen group of Cardinals. She flipped her hair over her shoulder revealing a lace green strap. Typical. Basilica rules dictated modesty from head to toe, yet Tanoria wore orchid-pattern underwear in the shade of lime. The woman got away with everything.

With no one waiting to accompany her, Cantorine entered the hall. She expected to turn left and head straight to her office. She'd see her mother immediately. Best to get that out of the way. Then to the docks—

Tanoria blocked her path forward.

"I apologize about the bidding process. I wish I could honor our understanding." Tanoria smiled at Cantorine as if she expected Cantorine to duck her head, bat her lashes, and agree.

"That's not an apology—it's an excuse."

Tanoria's eyes narrowed. That green strap was a high contrast against her red robe. Cantorine craved a pair of scissors. A single, satisfying snip.

Tanoria caught her looking and smiled even as Cantorine glared.

"You know, Cantorine," Tanoria's voice was low with some grit, "I can't tell if you want me—or you want to be me."

The heat started low and twisted in Cantorine's middle until it reared like a cobra at the back of her throat. Her lips parted, and Cantorine reached out, her hand cupping Tanoria's cheek. That perfect balcony cheekbone.

Cantorine pinched, then twisted hard.

Tanoria shrieked, jerking free. She raised her hand as if to retaliate only to think better of it. Cantorine, as Inquisitor, was trained in the fighting arts. The pink jags on Tanoria's cheek were faint, though the surrounding flesh burned an angry rose.

"I don't want either," Cantorine snarled out, and with that, she stalked down the hall.

What did she want?

She sighed. Cantorine wanted what she always wanted. To be herself.

Though no one else seemed to want that.

THE HOUSE OF SEGAL, as if to advertise their oil business, burned a lantern in every corner, even at midday. Her mother sat at her desk, writing. Her black and silver hair was twisted with a silk band. Her long jacket with its candlewick embroidery spilled over the sides of her chair. The servant announced Cantorine, but her mother kept her back to the younger of her twin daughters.

Anyone else in Soreale would be launching to their feet at a visit from the basilica's Inquisitor. Oh, but not her mother.

Cantorine had taken to counting the ticks of the clock—thirty-four, thirty-five—when her mother deigned to lower her pen. "Of all times. Your sister is to take a consort from—"

"House Telane," Cantorine said through a sigh.

Her mother's nose, the same as her own, flared its nostrils. "The match is essential. It's not just for your sister but for you, too. If you're to have a hope of being Formel and thereby meet your potential, we need you both to rise. If you'd—"

Her mother spoke on, but Cantorine stared past her at the portraits on the wall. Lysena on the right and Cantorine on the left. Her sister's smile was beatific, but when Cantorine smiled for the portraitist, her mother had snapped at her to *please stop*. Thus, her frozen physiognomy was one of mulish seriousness.

Too, there was that day when she'd come home with the news that she'd been elevated to Cardinal. She'd put on a new dress and blown past the servants. She'd charged into her mother's room with a smile, and her mother had met hers with its own.

Before Cantorine could speak, her mother said, "Lysena, you must have heard about this whale oil nonsense in the morning's papers. As if the market could bear it."

She should have announced, "I'm Cantorine—and I didn't," but there was the buoyancy of her promotion. There was her mother's rare smile. It felt like she deserved it.

The warmth lasted until Lysena walked in asking if the news about Cantorine making Cardinal was true. After her mother's mouth stopped working, she'd said, "Such a promotion is the least you can do for the family, of course."

Her mother's words, "Though you have failed us…" brought Cantorine back to the present. Next, her mother was telling Cantorine to invite Tanoria to tea with Lysena. Moreover, her mother wanted her to attend their dinner party on Wednesday—but not bore anyone. She should wear her robes, though. They made the right impression.

In Soreale, a woman's house was everything, yet Cantorine felt like spare furniture in hers. She wondered why she'd come here in person. She could have written a note in reply to her mother's. She supposed she hoped to change her mother's mind.

Her mind replayed the squish of skin as she twisted Tanoria's cheek. Wetness tingled across her own, and for a blink she feared she was crying until she remembered.

Five years old, she watched her father shred leaves and rub their juice into her cheek. The pungent, onion smell stung in her nostrils, but she'd leaned into his touch. Her mother had despised their closeness. Eventually, her mother had returned her consort to his house and forbidden Cantorine from visiting. She'd attended his funeral when she was nine. Cantorine said, "I must go. Basilica business."

Her mother protested. "I'm not done—and why are you smiling?"

Cantorine drew her hand into a fist, watching it shake as if it might explode out of her control. She hurried out.

In a warehouse at the eastern docks, her informants painted a clear picture: the Doctor's ship had arrived at the start of the shipping season. It came into port to unload cargo, before docking outside the treaty line, whereupon the Doctor started seeing patients. Harbor skiffs arrived at the ship randomly, though mostly at night. Some carried shrouded ladies of the houses, but at least one a day came from the slums.

Portraits lay spread out on a desk. For the past two weeks, a street portraitist had drawn every visitor to the boat. The drawings had little shading, yet the finer points of detail conveyed their personalities such that if meeting these people in person, Cantorine would know them at once. The artist was worth her coin. Last week, Cantorine had not recognized any suspects of note, but this week, she had hope.

"Tell me you have something."

"Yes, Cardinal. There's two to mention." She tapped at one drawing. "This is the woman who was on the boat the whole of yesterday. I got close enough to hear her voice. She had a scar right here. A different woman returned ashore with a veil, but I heard her speaking and saw that scar on his wrist. See?"

The artist pulled fresh pages from her folio. The first showed an unremarkable, if highborn, woman. But the second, those cheekbones. The cut of those eyes. The lips looked different, yet Cantorine knew she was looking at Tanoria's baby sister: Ulana Reede.

Cantorine's eyes fluttered. She almost laughed as she said, "You deserve more coin, my friend."

The noble houses were making expensive sacrifices to Criyo to put illusions on their faces.

There'd been a time in Cantorine's younger years when she'd given all her coin and talent for such illusions—to not look like her sister. Holding the miracle required regular prayers and concentration. One couldn't slip and think of the real image. People spoke of it like it was difficult. Cantorine found it so easy. Of course, after surgery, holding such an illusion would have been impossible with the pain. Thus, the face covering.

She still had questions, but they required fresh action. "It's time to see this Doctor." Cantorine curled the portrait to slide into her scroll box.

"Oh," the artist's hands flew up, "there's one more." She tapped a page. "Do you recognize her?"

The woman had long, thin eyes and a scar down her swarthy left cheek. Her hair was chopped in a jagged cut. She was not of the houses and yet…

Wringing her hands, the artist said, "It's Yekaran. They call her—"

"The Raptor." The infamous leader of the slums. The same that had raided her own mother's ships, driving up the price of lamp oil. Yekaran's crimes weren't under Cantorine's jurisdiction, but the Raptor enjoyed running circles around the City Watch. Now, though, the Raptor was involved in a crime against Bekna.

A strike against Tanoria at the same time Cantorine managed to nab the city's impossible-to-catch crime lord. The click was felt in her whole body. All the pieces fell into place.

This was her path to Formel.

They came at the boat from all sides. The Doctor's ship, however, made no move to pull anchor and bolt. After the basilica guards secured the ship, Cantorine stepped onto the top deck. "Where is this Doctor?"

"The Doctor's barred the door to captain's quarters but claimed that the door was open to you, specifically," the Commander said.

Indeed, when Cantorine announced herself at the door, it opened right away. The vinegar and herb scent of dwale gave the room a surgery smell. Two beds sat side by side. On one lay an unconscious Yekaran, the Raptor of the slums. On the other, a young woman, covered head to toe in pock marks. A plague survivor.

Working between them was the Doctor. Cantorine had expected a man, but the Doctor's body had a woman's round shoulders and wide skirt, though the thinning hair and a dot of a mustache suggested masculinity. The other continents weren't as narrow in their definitions of men and women. From head to toe, the Doctor was covered in tattoos honoring Dox.

"Cardinal Cantorine, at last. I am Chun Asai." The Doctor looked up with a smile.

Cantorine blinked. The black slash across Chun's brow was the mark of an exile. Someone who had profaned Dox. Exile meant banishment to the continent called the Eleventh. Chun should be dead.

Yet here Chun was. In Soreale. Doing surgery.

Cantorine had a question on her lips until Chun lifted the plague survivor's nose off her face. The Doctor placed it on a silver tray, and then moved to Yekaran. Her nose came right off as well.

"I am somewhat concerned," Chun went on, "as to how Yekaran will react to your visit." The Doctor put the new nose of Yekaran's face before giving hers to the plague survivor.

"She'll be arrested." Cantorine wanted to be horrified, but the way the new nose fit on Yekaran's face was perfect. The slight hump at the top gave an air of dignity.

Chun pulled out the sacrificial scrolls. "Excuse me. This part is delicate." Back to Cantorine, the Doctor put hands on both patients and whispered the prayers too low for her to hear. The first sacrifice fizzed green in a way no known sacrifice should. The second was the white fluorescence of Dox. The scars should have come then. Black roots should have risen with Bekna's wrath. But there was no such retribution. Better yet, the noses fit perfectly, with no sign of the cut. Like they'd always been there.

Cantorine's heart pounded. "That first sacrifice. It's from—"

"The unnamed god of the Eleventh. I will say that it's a…" Chun's lips pursed. "…A layering of sorts. A buffer between Dox and Bekna. I discovered its application to surgery by chance, but now here I am. You realize you can't arrest me though. I am not in Sorealan waters."

"Regardless, the basilica requests your departure," Cantorine said faintly.

Chun shrugged. "I think you're interested in my work for yourself."

Cantorine froze. The call for a guard was on her lips.

Chun continued. "My patients come for one of two reasons. A select few are like the Raptor—they need a disguise, but most are those who have learned to hate what they see in the mirror. They are the ugly sisters. The weak-jawed sons. The ones who don't fit."

"Why are you telling me this?" Cantorine demanded.

"Because I saw how you admired Yekaran's new nose. Because I know you are an identical twin but not the favored one."

Like the clanking release of a drawbridge, Cantorine felt the fury ready to slam open in her chest. Murder was forbidden by the gods. If she struck Chun down, Bekna would send her creatures in vengeance, but there were so many other ways to hurt a person.

As if reading her expression, Chun said, "The reason I was exiled was for using Dox's magic to break every bone in my father's face."

That stopped Cantorine short.

They looked at each other, and in Chun's gaze, despite the tattoos and mustache fuzz, she saw a reflection she had never seen even in her own twin. Their stare lasted so long it grew comfortable. At last, she swallowed. "I will give you two days to manage your affairs and leave."

"My door is open to you," Chun said.

Cantorine balked. "I am a Cardinal of the basilica."

Chun smiled. "You should be as you wish."

CANTORINE PUT THE Raptor in the basilica cells. With her new nose, no one recognized the notorious criminal. Cantorine should have gone to the City Watch and informed them of her prize, but first, she needed to write Tanoria about her sister's latest surgery. It would be impossible to disprove.

Bekna's blood, if the drawing was true, Tanoria's sister wore a different woman's mouth.

Cantorine would only decline to charge her if Tanoria agreed first, to forswear ever being Formel, and second, to accept her family's bid for the oil contract at last year's price.

Cantorine sent off the message only for a panting courier to rush in.

"It's the Formel," the courier announced. "She's collapsed."

TANORIA'S REPLY REQUESTED that Cantorine meet her in the Mother's Garden.

Cantorine put herself in Tanoria's place. What would she do in the woman's situation? Tanoria loved her sister. She also would do anything to be Formel. She believed she deserved both.

What a nice feeling.

THE CHILD MOON nestled against mother moon in the sky. The dahlias in the garden were plate-sized, and with the perfume of tree-high jasmine bushes, there was no place more enchanting in all Soreale. Cantorine settled on a bench and waited.

Tanoria's stomps were audible as she approached. Larger shapes rustled in the surrounding bushes. Cantorine had assumed right.

"Are you here to accept?" Cantorine asked.

Tanoria's face screwed up in contempt. "No. How could you ever think you had a hope of being Formel? No one likes you. Why would I or anyone else accept your sneer looking down at us?"

A snap and sting down her cheekbones, like her jaw might unhinge and fall loose. Cantorine remembered those long-ago days of trying to make friends with her fellow Sparrows. Truly, she'd have been happy with a single one, but there had been no one.

Tanoria's men stepped out of the bushes. Two hulking bruisers. Handsome to boot.

"Only two?" Cantorine drawled.

Tanoria's expression darkened as behind her, the men swore.

A dozen figures flooded the garden. They were pocked and dirty and night-silent.

Tanoria opened her mouth to scream, but the Raptor herself slammed Tanoria down. Within five minutes, the three figures were bound and gagged and loaded in a wagon.

"We're square then?" the Raptor asked Cantorine.

"I can't promise for the City Watch, but for the basilica."

Both women shook.

EACH THUMP OF the waves broke inside her body, but Cantorine forced herself to breathe. As if to comfort both of them, she raised the blanket and stroked Tanoria's cloth-wrapped face.

"I'm sorry. You've always been whole, and I've been a poor half," she said. "Though I know that's just an excuse, not an apology. Tomorrow you'll be on the way to the Eleventh with the other exiles. Although, I suspect, even there, even with lesser cheekbones, you'll make so many friends."

WHAT DID SHE feel when the Doctor lifted her face?

A numb nothing.

But when the new flesh settled over hers: a long-sought embrace.

Tanoria Reed bowed her head as they laid the hawk cape across her shoulders. The basilica was packed wall to wall. The perfume of roses was so thick.

"Scion of Bekna, mother of mothers, Formel of Soreale, you are so anointed." The Cardinal stepped aside, presenting the new Formel.

Tanoria bowed before them, and the chorus broke out. From the balconies overhead, children tossed down the flower petals. On her left, she passed Lysena Segal and her stiff-faced mother. Tanoria had vetoed the renewal of that oil contract. Some called the decision harsh given Cardinal Segal's disappearance, but needs must.

Outside the basilica's doors, Soreale's new Formel smiled.

She looked like the Formel they'd always wanted. All of Soreale smiled back.

A THOUSAND GOMORRAHS
Daryl Gregory

"We lost Jerusalem," Louis says.

The regulars take this news in silence. Eventually I remember the drinks on my tray and set them out: an extra sugar, dark roast Chemex pour-over for Warren; an Australian-style long black for Edgar; and a nonfat latte for Louis. Louis, scanning the screen of his laptop, says an automatic, "Thanks, Mina," and doesn't notice the design I've poured onto his cappuccino. A rose blooms in white and brown, but he has no time to stop and smell the foam. He has eyes only for data.

There was a time just a few months ago, when the cities began to go silent—first Oslo, then Copenhagen, and then a wave of blackouts across Europe—that Edgar and Warren would have said, Are you sure? Are these just internet rumors? But Louis, though he's younger than the other men by thirty years, doesn't speak unless he's sure. He spends his nights watching his laptop and listening to shortwave radio. He says he no longer has time to date. Which is crazy—if not now, when?

I hover by the patio door, unwilling to go inside. There's no one else in the place anyway.

After a while Edgar pushes back his fisherman's cap, signaling that he is about to make a Pronouncement. Then he sets about lighting his cigar, puffing and playing the flame over the tip, nursing it to life. When he exhales we watch the smoke curl into the lights. Even now, smoking is only allowed out here on the patio, and the other regulars put up with the October chill for Edgar's sake.

"So," Edgar says at last. "We're it."

"I really thought it would be Jerusalem," Warren says wistfully. He stirs another sugar packet into his latte.

"Not Megiddo?" Edgar asks. "If you're going for mythological resonance, the jellyfish should have taken Megiddo last."

"Megiddo's not a city, it's a kibbutz," Louis says.

"Really?" Warren asks.

"There's, like, five hundred people there," Louis says. "The invaders haven't hit anything with a population less than two hundred K." The invaders, who more resemble (in my opinion) gigantic manta rays than jelly fish, first appeared near the arctic, then drifted south and east. They swarm our cities, feed until the streets are empty, and move on, multiplying as they go. Louis has maps of the migration in his bedroom.

"I'd even take Mecca," Warren says. Warren's a formerly devout Christian whose faith has been severely tested these days. Nevertheless he keeps his eye out for clues that the apocalypse is following a Revelations-style game plan. So far, not much luck. The invaders refuse to follow any storyline. We're not even sure what they are: space aliens, creatures from another dimension, manifestations of our collective guilt. All we know is that nothing can stop them.

"But here?" Warren asks. "It just seems so…arbitrary."

Edgar lifts his cup. "To Calgary," he says. "The last city in the world."

I WOULD HAVE thought people would be panicking by now, looting and pillaging. Instead, neighbors help each other pack up, then hug goodbye, and make their way out to the prairies and into the foothills. The city empties like a bathtub; at first imperceptibly, then all at once.

But the regulars keep showing up to the café. "What, should we live out in the wilderness like primitives?" Edgar says. "This is all I want. To sit with friends, talk about the world, and drink a little coffee. If the future cannot provide that minimum requirement of civilization, then I don't want to be a part of it."

I haven't told them that we're down to the final half-gallon of milk. The owners of the café tried to persuade me to flee with them—they were heading north, to a small village they hoped was beneath the notice of the invaders—and couldn't understand why I was staying. My little joke—"If I go, who's going to serve the regulars?"—didn't convince them. Finally they kissed me on both cheeks, handed me the keys, and said, "It's all yours now. Good luck."

And I have been lucky. Four days after Jerusalem fell, the invaders still have not arrived. The café hasn't been broken into, the power is still on, and the water is potable. My espresso machine, a huge Gaggia Milano I call the Red Beast, hisses and roars with gusto.

Louis says that the internet is still working, too, at least in part. "We lost some Tier Twos," he says, and Edgar nods as if he knows what those are. "But messages are still getting through." The invaders have not yet begun to feed on the smaller towns. They're hovering over the biggest cities—Cairo, Chicago, Peking, Mumbai—massing like storm clouds.

"Maybe they've stopped," Edgar says. "Maybe Calgary's not important enough for them, and now that they've taken all the other cities, they'll leave the rest of us alone."

"Why would they stop?" Louis asks.

Edgar considers his cigar. "Perhaps they're done punishing us."

"That would explain the pattern," Warren says. He's a big man, almost a hundred and fifty kilos, and as he nods his jowls bounce. "Cities are the greatest concentration of evil. All those scheming, sinful souls."

"I don't agree," I say. Edgar and Warren turn to look at me. When Louis looks up from his laptop, I flush with embarrassment. I don't usually speak.

"Go on, Mina," Edgar says.

"It could be love," I say. "All these people, falling in love, living together, taking care of each other. They can't stand it."

Edgar looks at me, then glances sideways at Louis. His eyes narrow in contemplation, and I feel the heat rise in my face a second time. I grab the nearest empty cup and carry it inside.

Louis is the first to arrive the next morning. His eyes are puffy from lack of sleep, but he's full of manic energy. I don't need him to speak to know what's the matter.

"How soon?" I ask.

He shakes his head. "They're moving. Tomorrow. Maybe tonight."

"Did you tell Edgar or Warren?" I ask.

"The cell network's down. I wanted to tell you in—tell you all at once." Suddenly he can't look me in the eye.

"They'll be here soon," I say. "At least Edgar. He's usually here as soon as I open."

But Edgar and Warren don't appear by nine or even ten. Louis sits in his usual chair, glancing up at the gray sky. He doesn't want to order until the others get here. Finally I bring him his usual. "On the house," I say. "Besides, it's the last of the milk."

"It's pretty," he says.

"What?"

He's looking at the foam of the cappuccino, where I've poured a four-leaf clover. "Hate to wreck it by drinking it."

"You have to," I say. "It's good luck."

"Do you want to sit down?" he asks.

There's no one else here, and no one likely to come. "Why not?"

Our street is empty of traffic. Across from us, the three arched doorways of the RBC building regard us like solemn monks. Dark, fat-bellied clouds churn over the rooftops. Every shadow makes me catch my breath.

Louis says, "It was nice, that dinner we had in Chinatown."

"We should go back sometime," I say. Louis looks at me, then we burst into laughter.

A horn sounds. A white panel truck rolls toward us, headlights flashing. The vehicle stops in front of the café, and Warren leans out the driver's side window. "We stole a truck!" he says proudly.

Edgar hops down from the passenger side and says, "That's not all." The back of the truck is loaded with supplies. Boxes of canned food, plastic bladders full of water, cans of gas…and building materials:

drywall mix, plywood, two-by-fours. "Those were already in there," he says. "Still, who knows what we might need to build?"

"We?" Louis asks.

"I thought you'd rather not live in a future without coffee," I say.

Edgar shrugs. "I talk a lot."

I think this over for a moment. "I'll go with you," I say. "On one condition."

THERE'S REALLY NOT room for four people in the front of the truck, especially when one of them is Warren, so I sit by the window on Louis' lap. His arm is around my stomach.

We head north on Highway 2, the afternoon sun sinking into the mountains. There are many cars headed in the same direction, and none going the other way. In the bed of the truck behind us is the Red Beast, as big as a Ford engine block. Louis and I took nearly an hour to disconnect the machine from the plumbing, and then all four of us were needed to carry it out of the store. We loaded the truck with enough beans to keep Edgar in long blacks for a year.

"Oh no," Warren says. I look in the side view mirror. The sky above Calgary has gone dark with thousands of rag-winged shapes. A sob escapes me, and I realize I'm crying. Louis presses his cheek against my bare forearm.

No one speaks for a while.

Edgar tips back his cap. "Not to worry," he says at last. "We are carrying civilization with us."

FATHER TIME DARES YOU TO DREAM

Trae Hawkins

WELCOME, FRIEND, AND listen closely! Listen with an open heart, for this is the tale of a town, of a boy, of history remade and reimagined. Dream with me, will you? Watch, and allow hope to enfold you.

Here stands the town of New Cairo in all its glory: the descendants of a people forgotten, rebirthed and rebuilt through perseverance. Sitting snugly at the confluence of two great rivers, it is a beacon amongst the wintry land that was Southern Illinois, radiating unique warmth with blazing wooden pillars sprinkled within its fortified walls! Its houses, too, stand strong, their dozens of inhabitants forever intertwined, be it by blood or societal kinship.

Observe—as I have, with roots reaching far into the ground, branches brushing the chilly air—New Cairo as the answer to a humanity-spanning question: *can we exist in peace?* To such a question, the residents of New Cairo might scoff, or perhaps laugh in incredulity, for what form of existence can there be besides peace? Indeed, to consider another way of living...well, doing so would be a great task for the average New Cairene. Understand, friend, that New Cairo has not experienced chaos. A bold claim, one might profess, but a true one, nonetheless.

Perhaps context might shed additional light on New Cairo, beginning with its past, and ending with what may be a luminous, iridescent future.

There stood Cairo, a ghost of a town. Poor and ignored, its population under two thousand and declining every year. Its people were mostly dark of skin—a thing that mattered, before, and determined its inherent value. Enter world wars and nuclear violence, emergency bunkers issued to those deemed worthy of surviving the end of the world. Yes, it was a horrible time, and the people of Cairo—desperate, defeated—dug into the earth and holed up in a makeshift bunker.

And as the world around that tiny town burned and froze, flooded and devoured itself, Cairo endured. (Do not despair; the world may have devoured itself, but New Cairo is not the only surviving settlement. There are others, though their stories are their own, and this is New Cairo's.) When its residents emerged from the ground, freshly formed and full of hope, reborn into a world where dark skin and empty pockets no longer made them *less than*, its leaders made an executive decision: to leave the world as they knew it behind.

So, they did, and when the oldest of its people died, so too did any knowledge of the twisted world before.

Now, New Cairo is hundreds of years old, boasting a population of fifty thousand. Watch with me, please. Do not be shy; my trees have eyes aplenty, their every leaf spectating in anticipatory pleasure. Watch how the New Cairenes prepare for winter, spreading across the snowy ground like little brown beetles, reinforcing their walls, gathering and storing meats, and quadruple-checking their vegetables for edibility. Do you see, there, how the sallow-skinned man bends and huffs near the town's center, sweat pouring down his dark face? And do you see how readily others relieve him of his duties, usher him into the warmth of his log cabin home? *This* is New Cairo, where one cares for the next in communal greatness.

Survival, however, is not why New Cairenes live. Look closer, now, at the swaths of paint—made by town alchemists—decorating the surface of every building. Bright and vibrant, the murals plastered onto the homes and hospitals and schools are ever-changing; each began as a small thing, gradually growing as each New Cairene added to the illustration of whoever painted before them. And look! Oh, how they dance and chant and beam so widely, honey-roasting pecans gathered in the summer.

New Cairo was once a bud, and I swell with pride at having witnessed it watered with communion. Swell with me, will you? Swell as they congregate, smile lines etched onto dark cheeks.

Today is a special day, you see. Once the festivities have died down, they march toward the bank of the Ohio River. (That's right, *all* fifty thousand have gathered; remember, New Cairenes care for one another. Those who cannot walk, or have lost the will to, have been assisted. No one would willingly miss this day, after all.)

At the Ohio River, they send off their voyagers, who will travel across the remains of a ravaged country in search of information. Magazine pages, tourist pamphlets, photography albums—such things have impressed upon New Cairo only the most beautiful of the world before, from technological advances to what was modern medicine. And so the voyagers set across the frozen river on muscled horses, hoping to find in the ruins of before the secret to rebuilding the world.

Honesty propels me to say this: New Cairo *is* the rebuilding of the world. What they seek is a misguided portrayal of what *was*, and under no circumstances should they—

Oh.

You see them, don't you? Heads bowed, mouths set in determination. You see them, yet you cannot *feel* them, as I do. They are praying, unified in yearning for knowledge of the world before. Within them burns the hope of a life protected from precarity—of winters survived, sicknesses endured, and lives lived for bountiful decades. Inexplicably, such hope has taken root within myself. I, too, wish for their safety. And although I am only an observer, albeit one with more power than you, perhaps, I—

I am compelled to comply.

Understand this is not an easy thing, nor something my kind might advise. Come, as my leaves shake—not from the cold, I assure you—and my grass blades dance, and every animal wearily watching the New Cairenes scurries in unsettled surprise, for I am bending myself against better judgment.

There. He is young, only sixteen years old, though inside him dwells something unplaceable. Something gleaming, ambitious, and, more importantly, virtuous.

At four, he trundled into a burgeoning snowstorm to rescue a neighbor's cat. At nine, he held onto his sister's hand for seven days and nights, until the grief of their parents' deaths loosened its grip on her. Every week, he teaches children how to merge mind and body, to paint and craft and build. Yesterday, he fell into a dirt ditch, and—contusions blooming purple and oblong on his deep, brown skin—spent the evening filling the trench, so others might avoid the harm he endured. Do you understand, friend? He *is* New Cairo. He is humanity.

And who am I to deny him the knowledge he seeks? The knowledge sought by the tens of thousands crowding the lake's bank? Follow along, please, as I compile myself—empirically—and press my knowledge into a single flake of snow, so tender and soft and insubstantial, and as the young teen pleads with the sky to protect the voyagers, the flake that is me (and you. *Us*, perhaps.) touches upon his dark brow.

We shall call him Josiah. As he inherits the knowledge of a world long gone, he falls writhing to the snow, his mind expanding to accommodate the influx of knowledge. The fastest of New Cairo carry him to town, where he quickly recovers and asks to rest for the remainder of the day. And as everything lulls back into a sense of normalcy—the people outside resume their dancing and sharing of food, and kids build snowpeople and singers sing proudly, their voices ululating through brisk air—Josiah curls into his bed.

I have given him what he wanted, but…well. It's a bit much. He alone now holds immeasurable knowledge: precise medical formulas, cures for diseases, blueprints for inventions he must first conceptualize as possible. There is happiness in his consumption of the past. Colorful cultures, diverse in a myriad of ways from clothing to music to food to speech bring him comfort. So, too, does he feel warmth spread through his core as he beholds the beauty of fashion in all its facets, of horizons with rising suns, of a drink called 'coffee.' The joys of one hundred and eighteen billion people—indeed, our knowledge extends that far, and even farther, should Josiah wish to probe there—reside within his thin body. And it is euphoric.

But.

I know. I, too, wish there was no *however* to this exchange of knowledge. One might think Josiah lucky, for he is alone in his ability to behold such vast amounts of beauty. But, but, but. I am no perfect being, and you can certainly sympathize with this lack of sublimity. To share is to share *everything*, lest we risk disinforming those we seek to preserve. Naturally, then, Josiah has inherited the goods of the world before, along with—

Poor, poor Josiah. Things were so ugly before New Cairo, weren't they?

Although the word 'war' did not exist to him, it makes sense as he chews on its jagged edges. New Cairo is not immune to disagreements, and he has seen arguments turn violent. War, to him, is not an inherently evil concept. It is the events that happen during war—lines crossed from reactionary violence to sadistic, psychological, and physical brutality—that open his mind to the concept of *evil*.

Imagine, if you will, Josiah's world held tautly together by threads of logic. Now, watch as our knowledge affects him so. Watch as the horror of human trafficking—the exploitation of bodies for the sick pleasures of heartless beings—unravels those threads of logic. Overwhelming accounts of evil, from the conception of human life to the death of the world as we knew it, break him down, bit by bit. It happens chronologically, though he withstands it all, pushing back against despair, his heart fleeting about, his breaths ragged and piercing. Chattel slavery nearly unmakes him, yet still he holds tight.

It is when he has consumed the knowledge of a small town called Cairo, Illinois—the city that became New Cairo, once bustling with potential, then broken down by lynching militias and prejudiced police—that he truly disappears into himself, made unwhole by it, his world having lost all sense of coherence.

In an attempt to remedy the nausea twisting his stomach, he considers the possibility of hallucination: perhaps he is simply daydreaming about events that never happened! Yet he feels, and therefore knows, that what he has ingested is *history*.

Between bouts of poignant disillusion, however, Josiah determines with relief that none of the evils that governed the past currently affect his home. I have told you, before, that New Cairo has never experienced chaos. This much is true; violence directed toward others for arbitrary traits, mistreatment of animals, lands being stolen and forced from under the feet of those who nourished it into vibrancy…such concepts do not exist here. Evil does not exist, in New Cairo.

Josiah understands this. But the potential for evil? Surely, it is here, waiting to sink its teeth into every corruptible human. As this thought settles into him, Josiah becomes fearful. Fearful that the evils of the past might soil his mind—if they have not begun doing so, already.

(Worry not. This is not *that* kind of story.)

Let us leave Josiah, for a moment, to wrestle his world back into coherence. Come, and observe New Cairo once more. I fear I may have presented you with a false picture of the bright, bright land. But you see them, don't you? With winter falling over the town, the New Cairenes' work is twofold. See their strained expressions of working toward a goal that not everyone may realize. New Cairenes are a hopeful people—indeed, they understand hope as undergirding all else—but even hope cannot combat the objective truth that no winter passes without death.

Watch them swing axes at trees for firewood. (Please, do not fret! Trees may be my eyes—as are leaves and wind and hail and air itself—but I willingly and painlessly give myself to those in need.) Watch the town alchemists stuff jar after jar with medicinal herbs, knowing their supplies won't make it to spring. Watch butchers gather to discuss meat stocks, farmers frowning at rotten vegetables. New Cairo exists in perpetual danger. Such danger has pooled their hope into the voyagers, who travel eastward. (I regret to inform you that they will return empty-handed; what was the East Coast is now underwater.)

Yet the New Cairenes hope. See, how thousands of them gather in that tall, tall building? They are praying to the Earth, for they worship

Her. She is not me, of course, though She allows me to make use of Her limbs. My leaves rattle in appreciation.

And—there! Josiah has risen from bed, and is now standing outside the building, listening to the humming and thrumming of voices in soft prayer. And he becomes aware of what he can do. It would be simple, to share his knowledge—our knowledge—with his fellow New Cairenes. Not verbally; the information is too vast for simple speech to convey with any sort of sufficiency. But share he can, just by willing his thoughts into the minds of others. That is what I have given him: the power to share.

Silently, though, he trudges from the building and into the forest, where he plants his hands on a tree and attempts to empty himself of what he has learned. You see, he has determined that history is doomed to repeat should he share the past. Every injustice that made the past the chaotic, evil thing it was…Josiah thinks New Cairo is better off without any of that. After all, how might one repeat something they don't know exists?

Unfortunately, the plan fails. Josiah has infused the tree with our knowledge, but it did not transfer out of him, as he'd hoped. (It appears he does not comprehend the specifics of monodimensional fields of space-time omniscience. Curious.) He stumbles away, slouching into a nearby bush. Observe as he scratches at his scalp, at odds with himself. His seeds of knowledge may save New Cairo from the suffering of sicknesses without adequate medicine. Yet monstrous weeds may emerge from such seeds, destroying his home with violence and injustices that have not yet affected his community.

A rustle of leaves wakes Josiah from his despair. A girl—a friend's aunt's babysitter's sister, though family, through and through—emerges from the underbrush, chasing a butterfly. Do you see the horror dawning on Josiah's face? The butterfly has landed on the tree he infused with our knowledge, sucking sap from its sticky, dark bark. Josiah considers redirecting the girl. Should she touch the tree, she, too, will be inflicted with the past.

She will become a monster, meticulously crafted by knowledge of the evils of before. How long will it take for her to begin believing in inherent differences between people? How long before she views her values as absolute? She will—

The girl stops before the tree, holding out a hand. The butterfly detaches from the bark and lands on her palm. She coos softly, bending to place it inside a dry log, where it might survive the cold. (It *will* survive—laying dozens of eggs in that log, all of which will eventually become as beautiful as their mother.)

And despite himself, Josiah laughs.

Yes, he thinks himself ridiculous! He knows New Cairo. It *is* within him. It is him. Oh, how silly he has been. Watch, now, as he approaches the girl, who is startled by his laughter. Watch him guide her to the tree and explain its dangers. He does not hold back; he tells her the great things he has become aware of—holiday celebrations, organizations created to connect those with similar interests, cat cafés! And he tells her the bad—eugenics, land disputes, police brutality.

Yet she is not fazed. See how she places her palm against the tree's rough surface. Listen, as the girl yelps out, elated at the beauty of before, then falls to her knees at the horrors. But look closer! I assure you, you have never seen such a small child wear such fierce determination.

It is with this determination that she and Josiah spend the next several hours weighing their choices, their primary concern to protect the community they have cultivated. They laugh and envision New Cairo's future, so large and glowing and full of joy. And the future Josiah feared—corrupted by evil—seems so small, so unlikely.

When Josiah and the girl return to New Cairo, it is with smiles across their faces. And as they lead all fifty-thousand people into the forest, toward the tree that will be their salvation, they rely not on fear of what may be, but hope of what is to come.

As long as the people of New Cairo—born from the ashes of a crumbling, evil world—understand where they come from and what they stand for, they will fight against devolving into the world of before. They know—as you do, now—that all they need is faith in their ability to reject the cultures that undermined their humanity in the past. Luckily for them, that faith has existed since New Cairo's birth.

Oh, how kind and welcoming their footsteps feel as they march through underbrush and approach the tree! How sweet the chorus sounds as they laugh with nervous optimism!

Hold your breath, will you? Just for a moment, while Josiah guides yet another hand onto the tree, tears falling down his cheeks. Hold your breath, as he does, and do not panic. New Cairo has been untouched by chaos, and I suspect that will not change.

There. You may exhale now, with hope tickling your core. Good.

We have hoped, and so it shall be.

THE MANIFOLD ASPECTS OF HORACE

Taylor Lykiardopoulos

ANIMATOR SANNUEL OF the second nib-rank sits at his drafting table, half-finished frames jumbled before him. Around the workroom, the other monks bend before their work, laying down the fluid lines of Horace's will. The only sounds are the scratch of pencils and the whoosh of capsules through pneumatic tubes—the monks' vow of silence is strictly observed. Yet though Sannuel's pencil is fresh from the space station's recycler and sharply pointed, he cannot draw.

The lines simply will not come. He has excuses: His hand cramps. The tube system distracts him. His mind is exhausted by the frames he drew the work period before and the one before that, so exhausted that holding a pencil fills him with disgust. He cannot draw because today's nourishment block was so foul he could not eat even his second-nib-rank-animator portion, though he was dreadfully hungry. He cannot draw because there are too many frames to complete, and he knows he will not do them justice; not with the joy and vigor that Horace deserves.

He must draw, and yet his hand reaches for the velvet pouch cinched into the waist of his animator's robes. The pouch holds his most prized possession: a figurine of Horace. The one exception to an animator's vow of poverty, Sannuel's figurine is no mere toy. He takes it out, dazzled as always by the lapis of His Brilliant Coat, the bioceramic polymers of His Four-Fingered Hands, the synthetic diamonds shining in His Beneficent Eyes. Years of handling have left it patinated and the right foot was chipped from wrangling a goat during agricultural work period. It no longer precisely matches His Copyright Image, but that is immaterial. An adept animator needs no figurine to remember the face of his god. Instead, with the figurine, Sannuel reaches for a younger version of himself. The one who first beheld His Light and felt His Joy.

His contemplation is interrupted yet again by the tube system. But this time, the capsule drops onto his desk. He cracks its seal with unsteady hands, revealing the bright green slip of script paper within. Scripter Walton wants Sannuel in his office. Urgently.

IT IS UNUSUAL for a scripter to see a low-ranked animator alone. Furthermore, Scripter Walton must know their picture, *Gopher Trouble*, is already several work periods behind schedule, and Sannuel is sworn to deliver hundreds of frames before work period's end. Still, Sannuel hurries to the meeting as fast as his robes allow. The scripters are a wily bunch, and it does not behoove one to keep them waiting.

"May Horace's Light shine on you, Sannuel," Scripter Walton greets him. Walton sits with his hands crossed over a small notebook, the kind where scripters keep their most private prayers. Walton is a large man, a scar over his temple that Sannuel can tell wasn't caused by a goat. His robes are decorated by a dense constellation of celluloid ribbons that indicate completed shorts and even, over his heart, two feature film tassels. Sannuel is awed, yet a cautious inner voice wonders why such a decorated scripter had been sent to a backwater monastery like this one

"Until The End," Sannuel completes the blessing.

Walton's office is snug, insulated from the workroom by thick panels. Even the station's ventilation system is hushed. Sannuel looks to the story wall, where green beat cards should map out *Gopher Trouble*'s grand design, but finds it blank. This surprises Sannuel, for it is not the order of things to take down the story wall before a picture is done. But Walton is of another monastery, and they may have different rites.

"Does life in this monastery suit you, Animator Sannuel?" Walton asks in a gravelly voice.

"Oh yes," Sannuel replies, swallowing some nervous saliva. "It is an honor to be cloistered in one of His nunneries or monasteries."

"But do you like it?"

Sannuel hesitates. It is an odd question. He flips back the sleeve of his robe and scratches the spot where rough polyester meets the back of his neck; a red patch has developed that is beginning to concern him. "It is no easy thing to devote oneself to craft. There are those who have given up much more than I to serve His Wily Way." Walton's sad, interested eyes and careful nods embolden Sannuel to speak further. "But I do not know if I can live my life to His standard, Scripter Walton." Now Sannuel is tearing up, the words hard to push through a throat unaccustomed to speaking. "Some days in the monastery I cannot feel His Joy at all. Though I try, Scripter Walton. I try very hard."

Walton nods gravely. "Horace sees your effort, Animator Sannuel. His Beneficent Eyes fall kindly on you indeed. He has seen fit to send me a vision."

A bright joy rises in Sannuel's chest. Visions from Horace are rare, and come mostly to the leaders of His Licensed Subsidiaries.

Walton makes a frame with his fingers and peers through it into the great mysteries beyond. "I saw you and I secreted away on one of His ships, spreading His Light to the outer rim." His hands drop, and his eyes return to Sannuel. "Even now, a ship sits in spacedock capable of making such a voyage."

Unbidden, an image in Sannuel's mind: Horace's Joy spilling over an emaciated rimchild's face. Sannuel had grown up comfortably in a citystation of the central band, and knows little of worlds where Horace has yet to penetrate. His heart inflates: Horace has chosen him for a special mission. Yet a sterner voice tempers. The vision has not come through proper channels.

"But the Councils of Burbank and Orlando have decreed no such a mission?"

At the mention of The Councils, Walton's lip curls. He leans over his desk, speaking softly and with great gravitas as if he spares even His All-Hearing Ears the words. "The Councils of Burbank and Orlando are corrupt, Sannuel. They care only for tithes and power. If they could ever feel His Joy, they no longer do."

Sannuel crumples. The words are heretical, dangerous, and, as he looks within to judge for himself, true. Budgets have become so threadbare that pictures rush out long before they're ready. Care of the needy and those cloistered in His nunneries and monasteries has been cut to its very bones.

Still, Sannuel does not trust Walton any more than he trusts The Councils. The scripters' powers of invention go beyond any other acolyte's—some say that in their training, they worship even at the silver screens of other gods. Sannuel must resist these honeyed words.

"Perhaps if you mentioned your vision to the abbot he may lobby for a Council writ to pursue it?" Sannuel already knows he will not report their conversation. Walton has shown him kindness, and he could not bear seeing him whipped for heresy. Still, the ease with which Walton committed them unnerves Sannuel. Walton's recycler-fresh robes are unruffled, even as he stands.

"Your loyalty to Horace becomes you, animator. Truly you bask in His Light." Walton opens the door, dismissing Sannuel. "Few around here do."

Back at his desk, Sannuel struggles to work amid the buzzing of Scripter Walton's blasphemy. To animate requires a steady hand and a tranquil mind, qualities he channeled easily before he began to wonder why the nourishment block was so foul or the sleeping pads so thin. He reminds himself that to animate is to give Horace's form fluid life—to stoke His Light. As long as the faithful continue to make and show His films, Horace will fill the universe with His Joy. Sannuel touches his velvet pouch and prays for the strength to continue His work. And to his surprise, Horace answers.

A cell-shaded image streaks unbidden across his mind. It is a clip he studied in training. Horace toils in the garden of his consort, Petunia. Many large rocks must be cleared from her flower bed. But Horace's strength fails him. His Spaghetti Arms cannot budge the rock-laden wheelbarrow.

Petunia, seeing his distress, comes to him. In an intriguing gesture that Sannuel has often returned to after lights-out, she plants, on Horace's cheek, a kiss.

Sack-like muscles rip from Horace's arms. His spine shoots straight as an antenna. He balances the wheelbarrow atop his head and throws rock after rock up after it, toting the whole precarious tower from the garden in a single trip.

And it is this aspect of Horace that Sannuel wills himself into now. Horace The Mighty. Horace of The Mittened Fist. Horace Whose Arms Will Grow Large Enough To Comfort The Entire Universe.

Pulse quickening, Sannuel licks his pencil and begins.

BY THE END of the work period, Sannuel has completed nearly an entire scene of *Gopher Trouble*. It is the scene where Horace bursts into his space station's storeroom to find the troublesome gophers gone spherical from eating His raw nutrient paste. But just as he draws the lines of His Steaming Anger above Horace's saintly head, the quiet shatters with a trumpet call.

Hunched heads arch from the drafting tables to the workroom entrance, where a liveried herald plays the fanfare of the High Council of Burbank. And beneath that herald's arm, Sannuel can see the rolled scroll of an official Council writ. Six members of Horace's Legion trundle in behind, stiff plates of body armor reducing their walk to a bumbling waddle. But Sannuel knows there is nothing humorous about the blaster pistols clutched in their fists. Even now, the troops reek of blaster dust. And behind them all, Sannuel catches the shimmer of an executive's studio blue suit.

The troops halt. The herald snaps the writ unfurled, its sinuous calligraphy glorious to behold. Walton emerges from his office. Sannuel wants to call out in exuberant celebration, but Walton's scowl stops him. Walton is as grim as the closing credits of a tragedy.

"Hear Ye!" the executive calls, his reedy voice filling the workroom's hungry silence. "The High Council decrees all work on the present picture, *Gopher Trouble*, halt immediately. All frames are to be destroyed, and any prints obliterated."

Sannuel startles. At the word *obliterated*, the guards lurch forward, snatching frames from the drafting tables and cracking pneumatic tubes into recycling bags. One animator, who has gone deaf with age, continues to work, and his pencil leaves a jagged streak as a guard tears it from his desk. When the monk grasps for it, the guard backhands him across the temple.

"The High Councils commend your work. Though market forces are not always kind to His Licensed Subsidiaries, the only true way is His Wily Way. His Light will bless the Cosmos until The End."

A guard in a snub-nosed helmet reaches Sannuel's desk, bag bulging. A rubbery hand grabs his stack of completed frames and, before Sannuel's horrified eyes, lets them cascade into the bag. Sannuel watches as they fall, flickering into abortive motion. The raucous gophers. The ruined station. His Steaming Anger.

THERE IS COMFORT in the routines of the monastery, and Sannuel tries to find it now, as he sits on the floor with the other second nib-rank animators for the evening screening. Usually it is blissful to be bathed in His Light. But the glow of the screening only illuminates the visions of destroyed work that roil Sannuel's mind.

Gopher Trouble was not perfect. Sannuel would have been the first to point out its disjointed second act. In fact, the whole concept of a mammal tunneling into an orbital habitat had been implausible at best. But *Gopher Trouble* had been his work. Its destruction haunted him throughout second work period, even as he had trudged through goat waste, clouds of atmosphere forming and reforming in the pasture module's muddy sky.

Scripter Walton had arrived late, made a beeline for the trough Sannuel was filling and slung a bag of goat feed between them.

"Make no reaction to the words I am about to utter," Walton said. His eyes darted to each goat around them as if appraising their digression. "I've just come from a meeting with our blue-suited friend. There's a script he wants punch-ups on. You might like to know what it's about."

Sannuel, channeling His Beneficent Face, sliced the bag and let feed cascade into the trough.

"It's called Buggy Goes Supernova."

Sannuel's grip wavered. Pellets spilled. Ornery goats jostled against his legs to pick at the loss.

"It's a Buggy picture. Horace doesn't even make an appearance."

Not since the dark days before humanity left its desiccated homeworld has a Buggy solo picture been made. Buggy sits low in the pantheon of Horace's companions. His crude antics cause no end of trouble for His Serene Beneficence, and are barely compensated for by Buggy's aw-shucks charm. Yet even some inside the monastery have advocated for Buggy to receive a larger role. The faithful must treat Buggy warily so as not to eclipse His Light.

At the screening, Sannuel makes a show of stretching to sneak a glance behind, where the executive sits by the abbot in pride of place. In what must be an attempt to curry favor, the program tonight features Buggy extensively.

Sannuel is sick of seeing Buggy's pig face. His fingers reach into his sleeve, finding the hidden slip of script paper Walton had slipped him as they crumpled up the spent feedbag.

"My offer stands," Walton had whispered, "I'd like company on the voyage, but time is limited. I leave tonight."

Sannuel reads the script paper by the light of the silver screen. *Closet B34 at the stroke of 27*, it says, and the words thrill him so. But leaving the monastery without permission bears the most awful punishment. He shoves the slip deep into his sleeve so he does not scream. Why is it so hard to follow His Wiley Way?

He forces himself to watch the screening, hoping against hope that Buggy's antics will soothe his troubles. But to his surprise, he finds that an obscure picture is starting, incongruous with the rest of the program. It is from an era, no longer fashionable, when His Studios were taken by the surreal and the macabre. Sannuel hears confused shuffles as the sound of synthesized tremolo fills the hall. Perhaps the brother projectionist has once again mixed up his reels. A title card fills the screen, its letters violently jagged. *Haunted Horace*.

It opens to Horace, guttering torch held aloft, creeping down the long hall of a terrestrial ruin. Ghostly figures slink in the shadows. Tremors shake His Knobby Knees. A skeleton peeks from a suit of armor, visor snapping shut just as Horace looks back, the movements scored to the mechanical tick of a grandfather clock. Despite His fear, Horace soldiers to the end of the hallway, where a great door looms.

The era is not his favorite and yet tonight Sannuel finds himself captivated by the picture's creeping build. His racing heart finds its twin in His Anxious Sweat, his trepidation an aspect of His Bated Breath.

Horace lays His Four-Fingered Hand upon the great door's crepuscular knob, triggering an explosion of light and sound. In synchrony, Sannuel and Horace gasp as a great skull escapes the door—its visage a mask of agony and fear. Horace yelps, turns tail, and flees as fast as His Grounded Feet can carry him. The film dims out and a title card marks *The End*.

Sannuel pants. The other monks shift in their seats. The executive is visibly unnerved by the odd picture. Surely the projectionist will be disciplined for this lapse. But to Sannuel, the message is so clear he wonders if Horace ordered its creation and screening just to deliver it to him:

The way will not be easy. But Sannuel must flee.

At the 27th hour, Sannuel steals down the darkened corridors of the monastery on His Tippiest Tiptoes. Ever the showman, Scripter Walton greets him with a conspiratorial nod before jamming his pen into a vent's control wafer. Sparks shoot across the room, which fills with the smell of burnt hair. The vent swings open, and they wrap their hoods around their mouths before crawling in.

The way is narrow, linty, and treacherous. Their robes stifle the worst of the noise, but with every step Sannuel waits for the stray bump that will give them away. Through the vents, the familiar station is made sinister by the odd angle. Each cell is a tidy room with an exhausted tenant, some clutching their Horace figurines even as they sleep. Sannuel feels a pang of recognition as they pass the room where trainee animators lay shivering in their bunks, sixteen to a room. He remembers the years of mustering his will each day to grip his pencil and draw to his superiors' satisfaction. He wishes he could tell the trainees that it will all be worthwhile once they've reached the second nib-rank, and feels a deep sadness that it is not so.

At another vent, Walton's eyes twinkle with His Curious Glance. When he looks back to Sannuel, though, his face is wary.

As Sannuel approaches the vent, he can smell air gone stale as a crush of bodies overwhelm the ventilation system. First Sannuel spies wisps of robes tossed around the room's periphery. Then, in the center, sheets and sheets of nude flesh. Two masked forms, portly enough that they must belong to the abbot and executive, engage in unspeakable acts with the other monks which are not technically intercourse but nonetheless break everyone involved's vow of celibacy. Worse, as they engage in these vile contortions, the abbot and executive wear masks of Horace and Buggy.

Sannuel lets out a shocked yip. Walton looks back again and if Sannuel were to draw him, daggers would stab from his eyes. Sannuel looks to see if the sound has been noticed, and is disgusted to find the orgy uninterrupted.

"Did you know of this?" Sannuel whispers to Walton once they've reached the trachea where the vents of the station converge, a huge fan funneling away all their wasted breaths.

"I've known…the like," Walton admits.

"Did you know it *intimately*?"

Walton shushes him. "It's the custom, Sannuel. I'm surprised you haven't participated yourself."

"Do oaths mean nothing to you? And what of the vision you told me of? Was that a fabrication, just like your virtue?"

Walton wipes his brow, smearing sweaty streaks of lint. When he speaks, his voice's flatness belies its depth, like a shadow drawn of the darkest ink. "Perhaps I misread you, Sannuel. I took you to be one who seeks an out from these ascetic confines, who would appreciate the fleeting chance I offer." He rushes on, an orbital mass gone off its tether. "Make no mistake: in our texts, we scripters hold the truth.

Horace is a children's entertainment gone out of hand. He is powerful, but he is no god."

Sannuel grabs for the words to fight back, to show the clear lunacy of Walton's atheism. But he is exhausted, mind smudged by endless heresies. When he draws breath he finds his mouth empty.

Walton softens. He regrets saying so much so soon. A scripter is nothing without an audience. "We deserve better, Sannuel, than to live off the empty fantasies of so long ago."

Sannuel reaches for an aspect of Horace to steel himself, but his search is for naught. Horace never gives up, never loses faith, and so he has no guidance to offer Sannuel now that he grasps for faith and finds it wanting.

SANNUEL AND WALTON crouch behind a crate of goat jerky, a burst open vent behind them. The cargo ship lies at the spacedock's other end, but there is an obstacle in their way. A sleek shuttle, tinted studio blue.

"They can't be back from the, uh, event," Walton whispers.

Nausea flushes over Sannuel as he remembers. Copulating in His Copyright Image! But if Horace is all-powerful, why did He not stop it with His Mittened Fist?

"The shuttle windows are dark and I cannot see," says Sannuel. "We must walk on His Tippiest Tiptoes."

"Best not chance it," says Walton. "Stay low and Sannuel," Walton flips his notebook to a spread packed with carefully drawn star signatures, "if anything should happen to me, show this to the ship's computer. It will chart a proper course."

Sannuel frowns at the crude linework, touched by Walton's generosity. Walton is a snake. But he is a serpent that offers escape from a lion's den. Sannuel offers a wan smile in thanks, daunted by the gravity of the task before them. "May Horace's light shine upon you, Scripter Walton."

"Until The End, Sannuel."

They scramble on hands and knees from crate to crate: goat skins, goat cheese, and the occasional crate of films intended for His

Distribution Channels. At each jerky crate, Sannuel sneaks a sniff of its aroma. The monks eat jerky on only the most sanctified of occasions.

With sore knees and bated breath they cross the spacedock's middle, leaving the darkened shuttle behind. But as they approach the cargo ship, a new problem arises. The crates around it have already been loaded, leaving a flat expanse of scuffed metal. With no alternatives, they creep forward on their stomach, making the most of their cover. They inch along with their backs spasming until the asteroid-pitted mass of the cargo ship looms large.

They are close when, behind them, a door whooshes open. Laughing voices ring. Sannuel and Walton press themselves against the floor but the door is not far. It is easy to see the executive, surrounded by guards, Buggy mask under his arm, pleased expression replaced by sudden doubt.

"Identify yourself, fiends!"

Sannuel flinches, ready to stand and accept punishment. But Walton's limbs are tense. Sannuel realizes they will not be surrendering today.

Walton scrambles to his feet and makes a throat-rending cry for freedom.

A choking cloud of blaster dust issues from a guard's pistol. The shot hits a crate of jerky, filling the spacedock with sulfurous barbecued goat. Even in awful danger, Sannuel's stomach growls.

"Run, man," Walton yells.

The distance is not far and yet every centimeter is thick with death. Sannuel's robes toss around his limbs while blaster bolts sizzle and spark against the hull. It is only through years of habit that Sannuel's mind turns to Horace. Even as he runs, he grabs his velvet pouch and prays for deliverance from His own soldiers.

Blasters dull. Sannuel's eyes fill with His Light. Crafty Horace bolts across Sannuel's mind, pursued by a cruel hunter. But the hunter's bullets are no match for His Wily Way. Horace slips between the rounds like a hailstone through mist.

Reality crashes in. Above Sannuel, fresh scorchmarks pepper the cargo ship's hull. But all have missed, forming around him a fiery silhouette. And in that form, the animator can make out the shape of His All-Hearing Ears, His Four-Fingered hands, even the outlines of His Grounded Feet. It does not take years of study in the aspects of Horace to see that a miracle has occurred.

Blood gurgles in Walton's throat. He has not been so lucky. A blaster bolt fizzles in his chest.

Walton raises his notebook in an outstretched hand.

"Go without me, blessed one."

Walton's eyes are those of a child, filled for the first time with His Light.

It is not difficult to show Walton's instructions to the ship's computer and slip away before the blaster dust clears. Easy, too, for the ship's recycler to produce the tools of an animator's craft: pencils, paper, and celluloid.

Sannuel munches on yet another strip of goat jerky as he considers how to spend the long years of his journey to the Outer Rim. One part hopes to finish *Gopher Trouble*, as he now has time to complete Scripter Walton's final work to the standard it always should have been. Yet Sannuel finds himself called to a new project, one far more ambitious than any he's attempted before.

It will be a feature. About a servant of Horace whose faith is tested, only to find the Light of His Wily Way.

UGLY

Julie Danvers

THE PRINCE IS giving a ball!

Relax, you aren't going. For one thing, you're not invited. There are ways around such obstacles, but they're not open to you. Not with those thighs. Sorry not sorry.

Wait. Come back. I see we aren't ready for candid truths. I'm passionate about my work, and I often forget: intimacy takes time to develop. We'll get there.

The name's Gus. *Greedy* Gus, according to some, but let me tell you: everyone's selfish when they've got a family to provide for. My wife gave birth to a litter of twelve last night, and she's pregnant again this morning. Hungry mouths give you a new perspective on the moral high ground.

Point is, we're in a position to do one another a favor.

I need to get fat for the winter, and you need to get thin for the ball. No, not just the ball. For the life you want. The life your stepsister had.

You name it, Ella had it. Attention. Pretty dresses. Love. Until she disappeared. Ran so fast she left a shoe on the palace steps.

What did she leave you, Stasia? Aside from her share of the housework. None of her fine clothes, and certainly no note of explanation sent to the little stepsister who'd been her worshipful shadow. She overlooked you, the same way everyone else does.

But I've been watching you from the wainscotting for a long time. And unlike everyone else, I believe you've got something. Let's call it...*potential*.

I can help you. I can transform you from pathetic, unwanted grub to desirable, dare I say *sexy* butterfly. But not out of the goodness of my heart. No. Talk about a fairy tale. This is a case of mutually aligned interests. You want to taste the life of a princess. I want to taste buttery crumbs falling from a royal table.

But before I can do anything, you need to get down low. Crouch into a ball where my hole in the wall meets the floor. Imagine how much closer we could be, if your stomach weren't in the way.

There. Now you're on the floor, at the lowest point you've ever been in your life. Now we're ready. Now we can start.

You learned a lot by watching Ella. Everyone pretended to be extra-nice to you when your mother married her father, but no one ever had to pretend to be nice to Ella. Smiles in her direction came automatically, as did cries of "that hair!" and "blue eyes!" and "ooh, those dimples!"

Sure, all your relatives *said* you were pretty, but no one was making exclamations over your plain brown locks.

You gleaned that hair should be flaxen, and bodies tiny, albeit with enough padding to manage full breasts and a dimple or two. But also, there should be absolutely no fat on your body, ever. There are great rewards for girls who can perform this miracle, and that's where our little talks together will make all the difference.

We'll focus on making there be less of you. No matter what, that is your go-to solution for every problem. I guarantee it will work. And it gives you control. No matter what happens, you can always make yourself smaller.

It worked for Ella. Do you have any idea how hard it is to fit into clothing made from scraps collected by woodland creatures? She did not have a lot of material to work with. A strand of pearls, a few curls of satin ribbon fashioned into strategically placed bows. But when the important night arrived, she made damned sure she fit into that dress.

I was proud of her. But I never told her, and you'll never hear me say it to you. Pride makes you big, and if this is going to work, you need to stay small in every way possible.

You also need to get better at keeping secrets from your mother. She's never been able to find me in the walls, but she knows I'm here, offering my services to her daughters. She means well when she tries to turn your attention away from our work and onto your studies of herbalism and midwifery. She doesn't understand your potential the way I do. You won't need to work at anything once you're smaller.

Beauty changes the rules. You already know this. After Ella's father died, your mother declared it high time for *everyone* to start helping out around the house. You'd been mending clothes and sweeping floors your entire life, but no one tut-tutted about mistreatment until your mother expected the same of the poor, beautiful orphan. Remember how Ella's crotchety old godmother winked and looked the other way when Ella snuck out, even though she was supposed to finish the washing-up? Told her to have a little fun, for once?

Ella caught you spying on her, once, after one of her frequent fights with your mother. You must have suspected lunacy or deviltry when you saw her talking to me with her ear pressed against the wall.

"Go away, Stasia," she said, not unkindly. She must have seen the worry on your face, because she added, "Don't you mind about your mother. There's more than one way to contribute, and mine doesn't involve mops and buckets. I've got my own plan for making this family's fortune. She'll be thanking me on bended knee by the time I'm through."

Maybe Ella's need to escape your mother's house was more desperate than any of us realized. Or maybe she found a richer, handsomer prince to run off with. Should you be visited by such good fortune, I'd appreciate a letter at the very least. I do worry about my charges.

You knew she was sneaking out, and you half-suspected what she was up to. You'd heard the story circulating about town: an unknown lady of surpassing beauty had caught the eye and the heart of our good, gentle Prince. But on the night of the last ball, the mystery woman fled his royal embrace.

Wherever she ran to, it wasn't home, because you haven't seen Ella since that night.

Her disappearance is sad, yes. All her hard work with me down the drain. The chance to move into the castle snatched from my paws. I do hope Ella's all right. Thoughts and prayers, etc.

But this glass slipper is half-full: with Ella out of the picture, it's your time to shine. I can't believe how much everyone's overlooked your potential. I really think it's your mother's fault for pushing you in the wrong direction all these years. She calls you strong, but that's just another way of saying she doesn't believe you're beautiful.

Let's look at what we have to work with. The Queen is rumored to have a magic mirror that only tells the absolute truth, but you don't need magic to be honest with yourself about what you see. Long brown hair wrapped in a sensible bun. An unremarkable chin, a serviceable nose. Cheekbones that insist on adding roundness to your face. Where are your collarbones, though? I'd like to see them protruding beneath your skin.

There's an epithet you've given yourself: *ugly*. You know it's harsh, but admit it: you need harshness, if you want to sparkle the way Ella did.

Face facts: there needs to be less of you.

SHIT. OK, CHANGE in plans. The Prince has canceled the ball. He's decided on a different method of finding his mystery woman. The official story put out by the Palace now is that the glass slipper didn't fall off by accident. Instead, the woman left it behind deliberately, as a clue, because women love to be pursued. It's a test of the Prince's commitment to her.

He's vowed to try Ella's slipper on every single woman in the kingdom. If the shoe fits, he'll marry her. Apparently, he's not the kind of man who looks at faces.

It's a dumb move if he's searching for Ella. But it's a smart move if he's searching for a princess. Hinging the kingdom's future on footwear lets the Prince stay in control. If there's something about a woman he doesn't like, all he and his witnesses have to say is that the shoe didn't fit correctly.

We'll make sure he sees something he likes in you.

This is good for us. I'm going to be honest, you wouldn't have stood out at a ball. You'll never be as pretty as Ella. But you could be smaller, and no matter what anyone else says, that's what counts.

IT'S THESE MOMENTS I live for: when the student surpasses the teacher.

Your broad feet are too chunky for the slipper. You hate yourself for not being born with tiny, perfect feet. But hate can only get you so far without commitment and action.

You know how you can fix this, right? Of course you do. You're my prize student.

You do it in the pantry.

The meat cleaver's in there, as well as all of your mother's medicinal herbs. There's not much time. The footmen are on the muddy lawn making lewd jokes. They have the slipper, but your foot remembers where it pinched. Your big toe, that was the trouble.

There's nothing for you to bite down on. So you set your teeth against every insult you've ever hurled at yourself, every time someone's eyes slid over you and settled on Ella, and you swing the meat cleaver down as hard and fast as you can.

It takes two more chops, and a bit of sawing. By the end, your mother's arm is around your shoulders, and she's holding you while you sob. I don't think you were aware of her coming in. You definitely weren't aware of having screamed.

She's not angry. She's telling you she understands. She sighs and says now that you've done it, you might as well see it through. You don't have much time. You'll have to run out there and tell them you need to try on that slipper again.

I almost get emotional myself when she says, "Your little toes," and turns her face away, but when she looks back at you, she's composed. She stops the bleeding with one of her powders, some mix of herbs and magic. You haven't always paid attention when she tries to teach you the medicinal qualities of her blends, but you're grateful for her knowledge now.

There's still the question of what to do with your discarded toe. You're looking at it with unexpected compassion, though you know that extra appendages are just your large body taking up more space than it deserves. I'm sure it served you well in life as you walked, balanced, danced. You won't be able to do any of those things nearly as well now. But there will be less of you, which is what matters.

Your mother puts the toe in a little bag, to wear around your neck. You've just been through some trauma, so maybe you're not thinking straight. The second she leaves, I scurry up your shoulder and whisper reason into your ear.

"You can't wear it, hon. Throw it on the ash heap."

"No."

We both reel a little from the steel in your voice. You've so rarely said no to me.

"Stasia, it's a *toe*. In a *bag*. It's not an accessory that screams 'dainty princess.' After all the work we've done"—

"I know exactly what we've done," you say, and the anger in your voice—*toward me!*—makes me fall silent.

You're still shaking as you stuff the bag with the toe into one pocket of your cloak. You scoop me into the other, and limp out to meet your Prince.

THE PRINCE IS about to leave, when he and his footmen see you limping over.

You ask him if you can try on the slipper again.

He takes in the bloody bandage around your foot and looks at you, really looks, as though seeing something new, this time.

"Very well," he says, with an overblown reluctance in his voice that tells you his hesitation is an act; a show for the footmen, who will no doubt gossip in town. For the first time in your life, you feel powerful. You see he knows exactly what you've done, how far you're willing to go for him. And he knows you know he knows. Your relationship has barely begun, and yet a dynamic has already changed between the two of you.

You know it before the slipper is even halfway on your foot: you are about to marry a prince.

When we get to the castle, he tells you, in conspiratorial tones, that he knows you're not Her. "You just gamed the system. It's fine. I need an excuse to get out of a marriage my mother's trying to arrange, especially after things got complicated with my ex. It's better for the kingdom if they think this is true love."

Ok, so you won't have love. You should have known when you cut off your toe that this wasn't about love, and if you didn't know it then, you should definitely have known when your trick *worked* that you were not walking into a Happily Ever After situation. But don't worry about that. Keep your eyes on the prize: you will be a princess. Who needs the love of one man, when you have the love of a country? Who needs love at all, when you can have anything else your heart desires? At least you're not stuck in the country scrubbing floors anymore.

Most of the time, your husband acts like you don't exist. Even when you have sex, it doesn't feel as though it's necessary for you, specifically, to be there.

Still, that's no reason for you to look at me the way you've been looking at me. This isn't *my* fault, ok? I helped you get everything you wanted, and if you're unhappy, then I suggest you address it the same way we always do: get smaller. It got you this far, didn't it?

You need to stay away from the other small mammals and birds who live in this castle. They aren't like the mice and chipmunks from the country. They're filling your head with all kinds of ideas, and I don't recommend befriending any of them.

You accuse me of wanting you to be miserable. This breaks my heart, it really does. I've only ever wanted for your success.

And let's be honest, when you feel at your most hopeless, your most lost, that's when you thrive. Look at you. The love of a kingdom. Nice castle. Comfy bed. Rich, powerful husband. No one can touch you. And even if they could, what can anyone ever do to you that's worse than what you've already done to yourself?

Your mother-in-law is a piece of work. She does indeed have the rumored magic mirror. A mirror that can tell her the truth about anything in the world, and what does she ask it? All day, every day: "Who's the fairest of them all." Beauty is the only thing she and the prince care about. You start to wonder if this is why the kingdom, as a whole, has developed an unhealthy obsession with appearance.

The castle food is as rich as I'd hoped, but that means your collarbones disappear again. The Prince notices and tells you if you ever can't fit into that glass slipper, he'll replace you with someone who does.

His threat fills you with fear. You don't doubt he can do it. Women are interchangeable to him. And you've played right into his hands from the start, by stepping into Ella's shoes.

So we redouble our efforts. You give me all your food. After a few weeks of hard work, there's more of me and less of you than ever. But you are losing your prince.

There are stories of a princess in the woods, fast asleep in a glass coffin. You don't know what it is with your prince and glass, unless it's just that he's attracted to fragile things. He comes home to you smelling of wildflowers, his lips smeared red as blood.

Against my advice, you confront him.

"So what if there's someone else?" he says.

"That's not the point," you say. "She's *asleep*."

"No, the point is that I need an heir, and you haven't given me one. Your priorities need to be with the kingdom. As a princess, it's your responsibility to care more for your people than for yourself. I'm surprised you don't see that."

You don't know what to say. You do care about the kingdom. You aren't trying to be selfish.

So when it happens *again*, to a princess slumbering in a castle surrounded by thorns, you follow my advice and keep quiet. You try to make there be less of your body and your voice, amid this epidemic of sleeping princesses. You bite your tongue and say nothing, until your prince brings home a pair of twins for you to raise. Their mother is…incapacitated, he explains.

It's too much. You forget everything I've taught you. You are loud and red-faced and you take up a lot of space when you are yelling at him.

He does not take well to this. He locks you in the tallest tower in the castle, and says you can come out when you're ready to stop being such a shrew.

What were you expecting? He's a prince, for God's sake. Women don't yell at him.

He pushes you to the floor, the straw feels hard and full of sharp angles. I scurry out of your pocket as he locks the door. When you clear away some of the straw beneath us, we both freeze as we recognize scraps of a dress. A strand of pearls, a few curls of satin ribbon fashioned into bows.

Those are bones, poking through the straw. You pull yourself away from them and start to dry-heave. I feel a little queasy myself.

We finally know what happened to Ella.

"STOP CRYING," I say. "Stop it now. It makes your face all blotchy." It's not that I'm insensitive to tragedy. But if the Prince catches you ugly crying, we'll be stuck in here forever.

When you can finally get words out, you say, "This can't be it. This can't be all there is."

"What else were you expecting?"

"Not this. Not Ella, dead. He's a prince."

"And you're a princess. Like you always dreamed."

"Then it's a nightmare. How could I work so hard, and end up this unhappy?"

"You can work even harder. We can fix this, I know it."

"There's no fixing this. I was wrong."

Before I can ask what you were so wrong about, we both inhale for good, healthy screams, because Ella's bones are moving beneath the straw. A second later, we realize it's not the bones, but the castle mice.

One of them puts a paw on your knee and gives an inquisitive chirp.

"They're a bad influence," I say.

You turn away from me. You cup your hands, hold the mouse to your cheek, and tell her all your troubles.

During our imprisonment, the castle mice don't bring you dressmaking materials or hairstyling products. They bring you gold coins, letters, legal documents that were secreted away in the corners of desk drawers. Did you know that when you married, you obtained deeds to farmland, partial interest in ships, the ownership of a castle or two? The mice bring you a little bag to put all of these papers into.

You recognize the bag. You tip it over and shake out something you've grown exhausted with the effort of *not* thinking about: your big toe.

It used to seem so much bigger, this ungainly stump protruding from your foot. But maybe it never deserved your hatred. All it ever wanted was to help you stand.

There's something coating your fingers. Surely not blood, after all this time?

It glitters. You examine it more closely.

Your mother must have put a pinch of her old herbs at the bottom of the bag. It was a special blend of hers. What had she called it? Oh, yes. *Fairy dust.*

You smear dust onto the healed-over nub at the end of your foot. Your face contorts in pain as blood flows again. Nerve endings open. You place the big toe carefully at the end, and watch the skin knit together. You give all five toes a good wiggle.

With your foot healed, you can rappel down this tower with relative ease. You release your long, brown hair from its bun. It's never been beautiful, but it's always been strong. You're thin enough to squeeze between the bars on our window. (You're welcome, beeteedubs. At least I'm good for *something*, if only for getting you out of the mess I got you into).

You put a pair of scissors the castle mice brought you into your pocket, tie the end of your hair in a tight knot around one of the bars, and then loop your hair around your buttocks to form a seat. Then you rappel down, your feet bracing you against the tower wall. When you get to the bottom, you snip your hair off and walk away.

You go home and show your mother all the properties that are now, by rights, half yours. You hire an attorney who sees the funds are directed to you. The prince doesn't raise a fuss for two reasons. One, he has the twins. He's got his heir, so he no longer needs a wife. Two, the bones of the woman in the tower. He threatens to kill you, of course, but you tell him that if anything happens to you, your attorney will reveal what happened to Ella.

"No one would ever believe you," he says.

"Maybe not. But everyone knows your mother has a magic mirror. All anyone has to do is ask it where she is. Is that a question you want people to start asking?"

"My mother would refuse to allow the courts to use her mirror."

"Then that's as good as an admission of guilt."

He glowers at you. "You aren't pretty anymore. You used to be a lot more fun."

"Really?" you say. "There was a time when you thought I was pretty *and* fun?"

His desire to hurt outweighs his desire to manipulate. "Well." He snorts. "Something like it, anyway."

Our goodbye is hard on both of us. You release me back into the walls of your mother's home.

"Can we still talk?"

"No."

"But you need me."

"No, Gus. I need *me*."

"I can make everyone love you."

You wiggle your toes inside your good cloth shoes. "I'm already loved."

I don't understand. "You could be so pretty."

"I'd rather be me."

And with that you walk away.

I meant it, you know. You could be so pretty. But if you'd rather be yourself, then go on. Don't come crawling back to me when it all goes sideways.

I'll find someone else. I'll get back on top again.

In fact...

Hey.

You there. Yeah, you with the funny hair, and the face with the thing. You know what?

I think you've got a lot of potential.

AURORA DESERTI
Rowan Copley

The heat of the afternoon was just starting to break as Salome pulled her car into their driveway to find the ash pile. There were telltale staples scattered around, and the charred corner of a wooden frame which must have escaped the fire. It now lay by the three cow skulls on their expanse of the Chihuahua Desert that they called a yard. William might have set fire to his entire *Aurora Deserti* series that he'd been working on, given that the pile was maybe ten feet across. She'd loved the scenes of untamed desert interwoven with fractured light, and their sudden absence after seeing them every day for months was palpable. She took a moment to say goodbye.

She walked up the steps to let herself into William's studio, keys jangling unnecessarily in her hands because he had not locked the door, to find him sleeping on his red couch. Probably deep in a funk, if he'd burned everything. The blackout curtains were drawn to keep the desert sun out, the only light on was his table lamp illuminating a small blue rock and some sketches. She let her bags fall to the ground and picked the rock up. It reminded her of turquoise, but glittered in her hands as she turned it over.

"Watch the shadow."

William was walking over to her, navigating around an easel.

"What am I looking for?"

"May I?"

He held it under the lamp on the desk in front of him. Its shadow made a kind of undulation as he turned the stone, like how the light lands at the bottom of a sloshing swimming pool. Salome caught her breath. It was beautiful and uncanny, not at all the way shadows work.

"Where did you get that?"

He turned to her, his eyes filled with a fiery intensity which punctuated Salome's travel-weariness with a slight worry in the pit of her stomach. Then he shook his head, at a loss for words before finally shrugging. *Things just kind of happened*, she could almost hear him saying. She'd find out soon enough.

He'd been growing out his hair since they had moved here from New York, and it looked like he'd been sleeping very odd hours the past two weeks she'd been traveling. She put her hand on his chin, his scraggly new growth approaching lumberjack length, and laughed.

"And *who* has been shaving your face?"

He laughed too, his freaky seriousness melting away.

"No one to complain how scratchy it is."

Then she pulled him towards her and he kissed her, and put his hands in her hair, and his scratchy kisses were like the sunshine she'd been living without. It was good to be home.

You never try to hide things from me, but there are depths in you that even you can't always fathom. To you, sanity and the merely possible are social contagions to be avoided. Mind germs that hinder your full creative potential.

But that stone in my hand, the blue shimmering unreality of it, was like a loaded gun you'd picked up by the side of the road.

The morning after William showed her the stone, Salome took her coffee up the rickety wooden stairs of their house back into William's studio. Early-morning sunshine filtered through the windows and onto the numerous easels filling the space, many of which were conspicuously empty after William's bonfire of the *Aurora*. The pieces that were left were a mute testimony to his not being idle while she was away, as well as his penchant for leaving work unfinished. The stone still lay where she'd left it last night.

She picked it up, feeling its heft in her hands. During the night the knot of anxiety seemed to have relaxed somewhat, leaving her with a puzzled curiosity. So this was William's new obsession. The stone was translucent, the color of pale sky, with glints which made her think of glitter, all smooth flowing curves except for one edge which was broken and sharp like glass. It was beautiful and unusual, for sure, though the way that William had looked at it last night was like a holy relic. Maybe if Salome had found it when she was on one of her solo hikes, she would have ascribed to it a special significance as well. She heard the creaks of the staircase, so she put it back on the table where it seemed to belong.

"How's Marlene?"

He stood in the doorway with his own gigantic mug of coffee and a bag slung over one shoulder. He looked less manic than last night.

"She taught me how to shoot her rifle, and we spent most of the evenings at the ranch with her dad's telescope. So, as Marlene as ever." She glanced around the studio to confirm the painting series was all gone. "Do you want to tell me about the ash pile? Is that what happened to *Aurora Deserti*?" She had been waiting for William to tell her that he was ready for her to bring the paintings up to Santa Fe and hopefully get them in a gallery.

He flicked his hand in dismissal. "Obsolete."

She tried not to be exasperated. "Okay." She glanced at the old leather satchel hanging at his waist. "Going somewhere?"

He paused, a curious smile on his lips that she knew well. It reminded her of a time in New York, which had been last year and a lifetime ago, when he'd had another bizarre proposition for her. He'd lured her to a kink party where the dress code seemed to be exclusively black leather. William had worn white breeches and a pith helmet, while Salome had dressed as a fluffy cat. It had probably been their last truly fun night out in the city, before she'd had to take a week off work nursing William back from a breakdown, before the incident with the landlord, before she got fired, before that egocentric and crowded and trash-filled place started feeling like a living hell.

"I want to show you where that rock came from," William said. "Come with me?"

They drove south from Marfa through the flatlands, settling into a comfortable silence. Salome read her Carlos Castañeda book while he brooded on the horizon and rolled the blue stone between his fingers, the feather and bones on the rearview mirror knocking together as the truck hit bumps in the dirt road.

"That book any good?"

Salome made a face. "I prefer my grandmother's. She's less full of herself."

All she remembered about her grandmother was sitting in her lap, looking up at a craggy-faced old woman stroking her hair and calling her a princess. She'd been a fascinating woman, magnetic even. Born to German and Apache parents, she was someone who never felt she belonged to any particular place, according to her out-of-print book that Salome had spent months acquiring. She'd fought pitched legal battles against corporations over water rights and summited mountains, but one day she'd disappeared without a trace. Of all the spiritualist books Salome had picked up recently, she'd yet to find a better one.

Being the flat, hot countryside, in this part of the Chihuahua desert it was not uncommon to see the mirages that looked like phantom water on the road or off in the distance. More rare were the mirages on or above the horizon, bubbling upwards into the Fata Morgana mirages named after the Arthurian witch Morgan le Fay.

Every time Salome glanced up from her book she could see the clouds moving slowly past them, blowing east towards Dallas. They passed another bare expanse of flat yellow before William spotted what he was looking for. There was a slight fluidity in the intersection between earth and sky, like a distant but enormous lava lamp getting warm. He turned the car onto another dirt road, directly towards one that looked as if Dali had painted an anvil.

"You're trying to drive *into* them?"

His expression as he glanced over at her was all she needed to know the answer, his fingers twirling the stone with more nervous energy between them as he held the steering wheel with his palm. But the mirage stayed firmly on the horizon, until it was late afternoon and William conceded it was time to head back into town.

"I believe in your experience of whatever it was, William," she said as they drove back. "But this wouldn't be the first time."

He sighed, shaking his head. "This isn't like those times."

It pained her to say this. But it seemed to help, and the fever which had driven him earlier had broken.

He'd had inexplicable experiences before, some terrifying, some even dangerous. There were probably a dozen from the days when he was regularly taking hallucinogens. Even in his childhood Will had been prone to bouts of intense spiritual ecstasy and had frankly disturbing memories of a "friendly monster" in the woods behind his house growing up.

"Where did the stone come from, then? If I just hallucinated everything?"

"Yeah. I'm wondering that too."

They drove in silence for a while, surrounded only by the giant blue sky and endless expanses of caliche and scrubland.

"What next?" she asked.

"Maybe we should tell Beck about this."

THEY SHOWED UP at Beck's house the next morning and immediately set to work brewing a pot of hair-raising coffee, the only thing he drank before noon. Salome and William had met Beck right as they'd moved here. Beck was just the guy behind the counter of the motel they were checking into, and a rambling conversation about his boss' supposed involvement in the occult had led to them staying up late into the night swapping stories of the weird. Ever since then, Beck had been a regular at their house.

As soon as they got coffee in him and caught him up to speed, Beck started having ideas. He lived for stories about the paranormal and conspiratorial, he collected them like the family matriarch might collect photographs of her grandchildren. He sat on a stack of ufology books in his living room, turning the stone over in his hand.

"What exactly were you doing before you found this?" he asked, looking up from the stone. "You must have done something to unlock these…mirages."

William was looking a little sheepish. "It's a bit of a blur. I was meditating a lot, sleeping outside in my hammock. A thunderstorm had rolled by that morning. Things started to unfold, potentiate."

"Hmm," Beck said, nodding like he understood.

"Did you drop acid?" Salome asked.

"Not even. They just appeared before me, and I walked up to one until I could touch it. Salome, when you're next to it, it's undeniable. The unity of all things." He shook his head. "I sound *crazy*."

"You sound like a witness to some sort of divine apparition."

Beck was pacing as William told his story. "What if it was real, though? Maybe you actualized it, this place. And that rock. Maybe it's like all that psychic energy, crystalized? This is what quantum physics has been telling us for years."

"Quantum physics has nothing to do with psychic energy," Salome said, though her usual skepticism of Beck's confused miasma of science was half-hearted.

"That's one perspective," Beck replied. "But what if this rock *is* solidified spirit crystal?"

"Try licking it," she replied. William laughed.

Beck snapped his fingers. "Of course! Why not?" Then he licked the blue stone like it was frozen yogurt.

"Sure," Salome said. She'd been about to dismiss the whole adventure as a lark, but seeing the hope in William's face stopped her. "Let's do this."

"Here," Beck said, handing the stone to her. "Pure crystallized psychic manna. It's a little salty."

They squeezed into William's pickup and drove. The houses gave way to the great flat expanse of yellow shrubland until that was all they could see in every direction. Salome felt an anxiety she couldn't quite put into words, and she didn't want to spoil the others' giddy excitement.

The sun got higher, and the Chihuahua around them took on the feeling of a baking oven as critters escaped to where shade could be found. They watched as the illusion of a lake slowly formed ahead of them on the road, as Beck shared a story about how one of the tribes in the region might have simply vanished rather than be subjugated by the colonizing Europeans.

Billowing cumulus clouds moved slowly past them, blowing east towards Dallas. She didn't notice exactly when it happened, but soon they were driving across the phantom lake itself, the ground beneath them a shimmering facsimile of a mirror.

"Holy shit," Salome said.

"Holy shit," agreed William. "This changes everything, right?"

Beck rolled down a window to get a look at what they were driving over, speechless. Salome was trying to put words to a nagging feeling, lurking somewhere beneath the amazement.

"Oh," she said. "It's the Veil."

"Explain," William said, leaning over her.

"From her book." She stopped herself long enough to fill Beck in on her grandmother: her book, her activism, her disappearance without a trace. How her relationship with the area had been an irresistible pull when she and William had decamped from New York.

"She only mentions it in passing. She made it sound like this... *storm* that comes around only very rarely. And how it's a thinning of the boundaries."

"Boundaries between what and what, though?" Beck asked.

"I don't know. I thought it was a metaphor." She trailed off without having to add *until this*.

Ahead rose the towers of a full *Fata Morgana*, impossibly large and close. Salome could almost make out their three-dimensional shapes, but then something would shift and she wouldn't be sure.

William got out of the car and walked to one of the columns, which was a monstrous blob rising up hundreds of feet and wider than a car. It seemed to be filled with a translucent dark yellow liquid that swirled around inside, its massive form resting on a mirror ground that was too soft. Salome took it in from the hood of the truck, holding her knees to her chest, until she could finally bring herself to step on the mirror ground.

William swished his hand through the column, the yellow liquid-air swirling and eddying around it. Then he brought his hand out of the column, still holding a viscous strand of it. His fist closed, the strand retreated back into the column. When he opened it, there was what looked like a translucent yellow stone in his palm.

"It's not blue?" she asked.

"When it cools, it will be."

"You guys, this is crazy," Beck said, emerging from behind the column with his phone in hand. "We have to start telling people about this place."

Salome shook her head. "It's not safe here."

But Beck didn't seem to hear her, as he stared at the melty mirage tower in front of them. "I mean, my shaman is going to have a field day."

William turned to her as Beck got lost again in his own amazement. "Do we even have a right to keep this secret? We don't even know what this is."

She shrugged. "Maybe not."

"You guys?" Beck was pointing them towards the top of the column, from which small tendrils were starting to reach down like melting wax.

Salome took the keys from William's hand as he stared at it, stupefied. "Time to go."

If Beck had kept this to himself like we did, maybe we wouldn't be here. But I don't blame him. The lights were impossible to ignore; something was happening out there. It's a good thing that most people scoffed when they heard about it, but the thrill-seekers, adventurers, hippies, ufologists, and others from the weird fringes of society still came.

This place has always felt like a borderland, but now it did more than ever.

WILLIAM WAS SUNBATHING almost naked on a lawn chair, a beer in one hand and the other hand resting on his laptop. Salome was half-paying attention to the video William had put onscreen, where Beck was being interviewed by a fringe video blogger.

"That stupid rave." William closed the laptop. "They don't know what they're playing with."

She said nothing, just reading her book in silence.

"You think your grandmother is still in there?"

She put down her book. "In *where*?" But she knew what he'd meant.

"You know. *Beyond*."

"I think she's gone. William, why are you asking?"

He shrugged. "I should be the one to figure these things out. I was the one who called to them, first."

She didn't like where this was going. "You're being ridiculous. It's not...fate, or something."

"You don't understand."

"You don't understand! You think you painted some landscapes and summoned the gods to West Texas? And now your fates are inextricably linked? This is just something that's happening, and whatever it is we should stay out of its way until it leaves us alone."

But William was shaking his head, giving her this sad look.

Salome was fuming. "Why? Why are you like this?"

THE MORNING AFTER the rave, they sent out a search party for the missing kids, remember? They found one in the foothills, who claimed he'd been there and back. Found him naked in some bushes talking about how he had gone to the other side to become one with everything, well, no one took him seriously. His friend Dayvan wasn't so lucky to return. All that was left was a pile of his clothes, his hair, and fingernails and toenails.

I've been thinking about the conversation you had with Beck afterwards, trying to tie it into your ideas about abductions, or quantum consciousness, or maybe panpsychic Buddhas. You had that look, that kind of hunger.

Where did you think the rest of him went? Who do you think he left behind?

"I can't drive down the goddamn road at night anymore without seeing them," Marlene said, notching another arrow. "It's creepy. 'Specially if they're, like, alive?"

They were in her backyard on the edge of town, where Salome had been staying for the past few days since her argument with William. Salome sat in the shade of an umbrella to keep out the early evening sun's light, which even now was making the air hot.

"I just want it to be over already."

Marlene glanced at her. "You really think that old woo-woo book by your grandma is right about all this? No offense."

Salome shrugged. "Best we've got, I guess? Better than whatever quantum stuff Beck is using to explain it."

Marlene notched another arrow. "*That* asshole should've maybe kept this to himself."

Salome's pocket vibrated and she took out her phone to see that William was calling her. She briefly considered not answering it, before feeling a pang of longing for him.

"What?"

"Salome." William sounded especially solemn. The silence lingered before he spoke again. "I just called to say that I…I care about you."

"Okay." She couldn't bring herself to meet him halfway, even though he was trying.

"I might be gone for a while. We both knew it might come to this."

"William…don't do this."

"Goodbye, Salome." She heard the click. She immediately redialed, but couldn't get him to pick up.

Salome leaned back, mouth agape. The *finality* in his voice…

"That William?" Marlene hovered over her. "What's up with that boy now?"

Salome stood up. "I have to go."

"Something wrong? Where are you—"

But Salome was already halfway to her car.

The mirage stone didn't break apart like a regular stone. It was softer, like a half-dried translucent clay. Still, with a hammer she found in the toolshed, Salome was able to get her small stone broken into blue bits that sparkled in the glaring light from the ceiling.

She couldn't stop her hand from shaking slightly as she brought the first bit to her mouth. But she managed to get it down with a gulp of water. She swallowed two more, and pocketed the rest.

She drove west, flooring it. She didn't even have to think about which direction to go, because there were so many light balls on the horizon in that direction. It was more than she'd ever seen before and almost as if they were congregating. The way they floated made them look discombobulated and lost. But they weren't. There was a nexus that they clustered around, and Salome drove straight towards it for as long as the highway allowed.

She slowed as the effects of the stone took hold. Her vision started to take on the qualities of the mirage, as if she had altered the world around her instead of herself. By now the vortex was close enough to see, and there was a second source of light beneath the floating light orbs. What looked like electricity sparked and crackled across a slowly moving whirlpool made of a dark purplish material.

She turned off the road entirely to make her final approach, slowing to a crawl to drive over the occasional bush on the flat desert plain. Eventually she was close enough to leave her car and walk to the edge of the whirlpool. It towered above her, translucent and illuminated at points that shone like lanterns into the interior. Within the column, there was a calm center without purple. An eye. Inside was William. He was floating in slow circles, eyes closed, hands crossed against his chest like a corpse.

"William!" She called out to him again, yelling as loudly as she could, but he couldn't seem to hear her inside of the silent purple hurricane. "Will! Please!" her voice sounded hoarse to her ears. She tried running into the whirlpool with a head start, but as soon as she touched the eddying purplish stuff she felt it trying to grasp onto her as well, a gentle pulling like if a feather became a hand.

She tried to brush them aside and shoulder her way in towards William, who was just out of reach. But he seemed further away, and everything was becoming fuzzy, unwoven, and purple—

As she came to, she started to feel her body again. It was a minor miracle that she wasn't too far from her car, since she was completely naked. *What happened?* She sat against the truck, still not able to completely stand up. A light breeze was far too cold on her head, and she found that she was completely bald. She checked her hands, and every finger was missing its nail, as if it had simply fallen out. She'd made it through the storm.

She found the pile of her clothes where they'd fallen, and pulled them on. She thought she had seen William, only he had been a baby. Maybe he'd been flying? And there was a huge shaking of everything, and she'd been tossed and turned and…and in her mind she saw a gigantic bird creature, craggy-faced and stroking her hair as she lay in its lap.

She *had* seen William, she'd reached out…somehow and…and his eyes looked at her, and he looked *sad*, but…

When Marlene opened her front door, Salome couldn't find anything to say. But Marlene didn't ask her questions either, just held her for a while. Finally Salome found the words to speak.

"He's staying in there. I think he wants to."

"Oh, honey."

The next few days were just recovering. Marlene offered a place to stay so she went there, and then a few nights stretched into weeks. She couldn't quite say why, but when she thought of William, she knew that he was safe and where he wanted to be. She felt like she should be angry, or hurt, and sometimes she was.

She decided that she liked how she looked almost bald, so she took to shaving it so it was short enough to be velvety.

Over the next few days, the lightstorms let up, and eventually the tourists left. Eventually, she started going back to the old studio, and picking up a paintbrush.

She finished her letter and sat back on the chair, putting the pen on the table. Then she collected a few things into a small box: the letter, paintbrushes, sketches. And a striking blue stone, the color or turquoise but translucent.

One painting sat in the corner, unobtrusively. The massive expanse of desert, shattered into a hundred pieces by a shock of purple electricity. And in the center, a huge, irregularly shaped blue rock that glittered in the sun, casting shadows like a sloshing swimming pool. The painting still had the effect on her of being in a small sailboat on the open ocean. That was the feeling she'd tried to capture as she'd painted it, taking a few nights to lay down rough and bold colors before adding the detail work to make the stone, mountains, and sky recognizable. It was her own contribution to William's *Aurora Deserti*.

She took the painting and the box down the rickety wooden steps to the desert floor. Marlene was standing by the pile of wood, frames, and sticks, wearing cowboy boots and her best bolo tie.

Beck was there too. After giving it some thought, Salome had reached out to him, and they'd shared a beer as they navigated anger, confusion, and sadness, and after he'd offered to do whatever he could to support her she'd decided that he deserved to be here.

Salome put the box of things on top of the pile, but left the painting leaning against the stairs. Then she nodded at Marlene, who handed her a matchbook before pouring on some lighter fluid. Salome said some words, lit a match, and threw it on the pile. Flames erupted and began curling the paper into ash.

Finally, Salome put the letter on top.

I'm leaving you a trail of breadcrumbs to follow back out. If I'm right about what this thing is, then maybe you'll find your way home with them. But I know that this is probably goodbye.

We didn't just move here on a lark. It was for you to find your next frontier, and me to return to my childhood cradle that I've spent my whole life alienated from. I wanted to do this with you, my beautiful agent of chaos. But I see now that it was impossible for you to stay who I wanted you to stay, and I can't stay angry at you for that. There will always be a place for you in my heart—and if you'd like, someday, in my life.

I love you, my tornado
— Salome

KATABASIS

Alec J. Marsh

THE FIRST TIME Persephone died was the first time she felt pain.

The first time Persephone found the sunlight again, she crawled out of her own grave.

The first time Hades took Persephone, it was called a rape, in the Hellenic sense. An abduction. A shocking rent of flesh and faith. She was only a girl, and girlhood was all she truly understood.

When the earth ruptured and Hades dragged her down, she fought the way the young fight aging, the way a warrior fights death. Remember the Greeks on the wine dark sea, remember the sea they loved could drown them. Persephone, too, drowned. Her husband's arm was an anchor and her chiton was a heavy weight. Rich black earth filled her lungs, she tasted loam and copper on her tongue.

When she landed in the underworld, she could neither see nor hear. Everything had a sheen of unreality, bleached of color and sound and joy. Pity her, of course. Pity all young girls, forced into an adulthood that had always seemed eons away, suddenly caught in the river of time. Never again would her joy be uncomplicated. Always, there would be darkness on the edges, a promise that life would turn and turn.

She was a queen to the darkness, shrouded in sorrow. Life went on, every day a dull imitation of the world above, but still there were days. When a girl is in the dark, it is safer to be in the warm, tight embrace of a lover's arms. As tenderly as loss wraps a girl in sorrow, Hades wrapped her in his bedsheets. In his arms, she was more powerful than she had ever been before.

She rose from Hades' bed each morning, and he watched her, and he reveled in the way she warmed his room. Her skin had the glow of the rosy-fingered dawn. Her hair was the gold of the afternoon sun. Her eyes were the blue of twilight. She was everything he had lost.

Hades made her a crown of golden metal to substitute for sunlight, with rays like Helios and lilies that dripped with pollen. He wanted a queen, who could hear the pleas of the dead and rule with justice and wisdom. He wanted a wife to share his burdens, and she had too many of her own to take his.

A part of her loved him, because he loved her. Because it is better to love, when love is all there is to warm the darkness. Because, as much as she hated him, she saw the hurt in him, and she couldn't help but love.

An entire kingdom knelt for her blessing. They gave her a new name, a new purpose, and they never knew how beautiful she was when the sunlight sparkled in her eyes. She thought only of the softness of spring soil, and the way her feet froze against granite pathways.

She was loved, and she was held close, and it would never be enough. She was a queen, but once she had kept people alive.

She was supposed to stay forever, queen of the dead. But the winter ground on too long, and she couldn't take one more second of the suffocating dark. She bared her teeth against the grave dirt, tore her nails bloody, and pulled herself back to who she had been.

THE SUMMER BURNED hot and blindingly bright. It sank into her bones and brought her heart into a strong and steady rhythm. Vines sprouted under her feet, birds erupted into song as she passed, and everything smelled of green.

The first day of spring was glorious, a day so beautiful as to be holy. Persephone had forgotten what a gilded eternity of sky spread out above her felt like. She did not know, in the dazzle of new life, that even spring could lose its luster.

She reveled in pleasures of the flesh. She bit into ripe peaches and let their juices dribble down her chin. She breathed deep the yeasty promise of wheat and barley, ready for autumn ales.

Steady as the path of Helios across the sky, her days grew hotter. Everything smelled of cracked earth. People shouted late into the night. Each day, people slept a little less. It was too hot to go to bed beside someone, and besides, she only had a husband when the nights were longer than the days.

What was once the spark of possibility became a furnace from which there was no escape. There was nowhere to hide from the sweat between her shoulder blades or the dust along the road. From sunup to sundown, she toiled for her harvest. Her power came from her ability to work the land. Perhaps she had created new life, perhaps her people were grateful for it, but she was no queen in the fields of wheat.

She had forgotten what it was like to serve in the kingdom of her mother. Her days stretched out in a haze of labor, and every day the horizon beckoned, a distant dream of freedom.

The summer dried her out, brittle and yellowed as old grass. She missed her husband, who saw her as a woman and a queen, who worshiped her smile instead of the work of her hands. She missed the closeness of her grave, the quiet, the peace. After a summer of work, she missed long nights of rest.

Somehow, she had become as little herself in the summer as she was in the winter.

The second time Persephone died, she welcomed it. She let herself drown, and there was peace as the dirt filled her lungs.

She put on her golden crown with hands baked brown after a summer in the sun, and she walked the rest of the way to Elysium, her feet bare against the cool and soothing stone.

Elysium welcomed her and offered up its pleasures. The people of her kingdom knew how to prepare for the long dark, and how to thrive despite it. They gave her alcohol distilled between stones and dripped down to waiting vessels, clear and strong and tasting of lichen. They gave her jams and pickles, and this time she did not see them as a pale imitation of a vine's fresh bounty. She marveled at the gemstones, the labyrinth of the tunnels, the heat of the mineral baths. There were no peaches in her husband's kingdom, but there were pomegranates, dark as gemstones, bright pinpricks of juice.

And Hades, well—

He might be pale as ice and dark as midnight, but he was hot as flowing magma and he loved as strongly.

The pleasures of the flesh were sharper in the dark, concentrated and desperate, brandy instead of wine. She reveled in her body, for as long as Hades kept his mouth on her. In answer, she gave him ripe peach juices, her lips like pomegranates, her sighs like a spring breeze. Two people who had only ever served came together with grateful relief.

Hades loved her, desperately. He worshiped at her feet. He buried his face in her golden curls and breathed deep the promise of a spring that would never come. More than that, he laughed with her. He asked her advice. He ruled with her.

She was older in the dark, and she enjoyed a satisfaction that a girl would never understand. A youth will always fight against the horror of aging. When she faded into a ghost, she remembered that the spring will come. She will turn, and miss the cold as well. Her sadness will be replaced with mania.

The second time she suffocated in the dark, Hades opened his arms and let her go. She burst forth into the spring, aflame with the heady anticipation of fresh leaves and birdsong.

Persephone has never been a goddess of the sunlight. She has always been a goddess of the threshold, the spring and the autumn.

Now, every fall, she surrenders to the drowning, and the earth holds her tight, a caress.

Now every spring, she cracks open the earth and walks free, eager again for the sun on her face.

Now she is a woman, and she understands.

THE RAVISHING MOON PRINCESS

Charlotte Ahlin

It started with the teeth. That was easy enough: the Moon Princess brought her first paycheck to Apo Apsis Dentistry and Piano Repair, where a man in a pinstripe suit appraised her rotten, yellowed mouth.

"Only enough monies for one pretty tooth, doll-baby," he said. He had a thick Venusian accent and a thicker mustache. "Bring more monies, we fill you up with white, shiny teeth."

The Moon Princess lay under a searing lamp and eyed the case of gums. They were alive: big, pink, and throbbing. Hippo and walrus for the more ostentatious clients, plus row upon row of perfect human teeth that could be plucked, fresh and bleeding, for a transplant.

"Which tooth you want? Nice, white front tooth?" Dr. Apo grabbed a pair of pliers.

"I don't know," the Moon Princess said. She'd borrowed a blue dress from Tessie (with a slit up the side), and she freed one leg, just in time to brush against the dentist's pinstriped thigh. "Help me choose?"

An hour later, the Moon Princess walked out with a mouth full of new teeth and a mild wrist cramp.

She kept her old teeth in a little pink sachet. They were beige and crooked—she'd ruined them on cryo-candy back on Ceres, and chewing tar when there was nothing else to eat.

If you eat too much tar, her mother would say, *the huldra will come and take you away.*

She set the sachet on her bureau, in the tiny room above Moon Maidens' Cabaret, so she'd never forget where she came from.

Two weeks later, after a screaming phone call with her mother, she threw the pink sachet out of an airlock.

Next were the kidneys.

She'd been at Moon Maidens for two years, and she was behind on rent.

"It's because Gibbs won't take me out of the chorus," she told Tessie. They shared a bathroom and a very thin wall. "I'm the best—no offense, Tessie, sweetie—but I'm the best he has, and he's *wasting* me."

She squeezed herself into a sequined corset.

"No one wants to come to the moon anymore," said Tessie, through the wall. A curling iron sizzled on wet hair. "Gibbs would rather jack our rent than drop admission prices."

"Mm-hm." The Moon Princess applied lipstick (oxblood and purple) and tried not to scowl. She couldn't afford the wrinkles.

"And you're not the best in the chorus," Tessie added. "You dance like the gravity's turned up too high."

"Because I'm not a chorus girl," the Moon Princess said. "I'm a headliner."

The next Monday, she took a lunar buggy to the Sea of Vapors, to see a man the Moon Maidens affectionately called the Butcher.

He offered two months' rent for her kidneys.

When the Moon Princess snaked one hand up his coat (white, spattered brown with old bloodstains), he removed it, gently but firmly, so she had to cry.

"Please," she spluttered, "I'll be thrown out, and I've nowhere to go." She looked up into the Butcher's squashed, ugly face and let two fat tears roll down her cheek (touch of menthol on the tear ducts, worked every time).

She got four months' rent for both kidneys and her spleen. Half a month went to a stupid little pump to remove waste product from her blood, now that her kidneys were gone, and another half to a strappy violet dress with a plunging neckline, even though she didn't have the right kind of underwear.

"Where the hell are you wearing *that*?" Tessie asked.

"Wherever the hell I want," the Moon Princess said. "Do you think I need to do my nose?"

Tessie was right about lunar tourism, though—Moon Maidens' sat on the main drag of the Bay of Love, on the "shores" of the Sea of Tranquility. A short buggy ride from the Apollo site, yet business was grim and getting grimmer.

The oyster bar closed, and the Luna Moth Glowing Garden. The Grand Zero-G Ballroom was shuttered and replaced with a chintzy bounce house. The hot dog carts stayed open (though the petting zoo was conspicuously empty).

They still got the odd dignitary from off-rock, but the days of splendid outings to the moon, of moon-buggy picnics in fine evening gowns, were over.

The Moon Maidens were already performing *Starlight Lover* and *Come Kiss Me in the Black Abyss* to half empty houses when the Looney Lunar Coaster decapitated a girl on school vacation, so the Moon Princess borrowed a hammer and went to see Mr. Gibbs.

She put her kidney pump on his desk.

"Whoa-ho-ho, baby-cakes, Gibbsy is busy," he said, without looking up from his scotch. He had a stately office with peeling green wallpaper. On the desk (fine mahogany stained with drink rings), a herd of projected racehorses flickered as they galloped in a figure eight.

"C'mon, Velvet Imperial! Get the lead out!"

Mr. Gibbs was short and stubby. His hair had long ago migrated from the top of his head to his ears and nostrils, and while he wasn't the worst lover the Moon Princess had ever known, he was far from the best.

"You said I'd get my own number, Gibbs." He still didn't look at her. "Two years, you said."

"Look, you're a doll, dollface, but we're getting murdered, killed, eviscerated—the roller coaster thing? Girl loses a head? Heads don't grow back. Need sure-fire acts, honey-bun, proven money-makers. Gibbsy can't gamble—come ON, you miserable cow!"

He slammed one hairy fist down on a projected horse, but the grainy little creature phased right through and kept on losing.

"You've got it backwards, baby," the Moon Princess said. "Martian royals are on the rock tomorrow. You need a nice big distraction from the headless broad. Something *new*."

Mr. Gibbs waved her off. "Maybe next year, kid, huh, maybe next year, sugar-pie, baby-love, sweetness, now wouldja let me lose my money in peace, huh? Wouldja?"

The Moon Princess moved her kidney pump to the dead center of his desk, where the little horses fizzed right through it. She raised the hammer and brought it down with a CRACK on the mahogany, inches away from the stupid little pump.

"FUCK—what the—"

She raised the hammer again.

"I'm two days overdue for a pump, Gibbsy. Toxic waste is building up in my veins. But I'm going to smash this thing apart right in front of you. Then I collapse in your office and die." He was looking at her now, with his big dumb eyes—she hated that, the baby-innocence in men's eyes, their eternal bewilderment—and his stubbly jaw hung open.

"One dead girl is an accident. Two is a shuttered operation." She raised the hammer higher, even though little white lights were popping at the corners of her eyes, and she could feel her knees going wobbly. "Make me headliner."

"You're bluffing," Gibbs said. "You're fine."

The Moon Princess unbuttoned her high-neck blouse (cream and gold, secondhand), so he could see how her veins stood out, toxic-blue. "Wanna bet?"

Stella Starbuck took terribly ill that night. *Food poisoning*, some theorized, or a flare up of the old Venusian Itch. Whatever it was, she was in no condition to perform, and a chorus girl who styled herself *The Ravishing Moon Princess* covered last minute.

How lucky! that one of the Martian royals just so happened to be there, after a day spent commemorating such-and-such at the Apollo site.

The perfumed letter that arrived by pneumatic tube, inviting the Second Martian Prince to the Bay for a *very special evening*, was never widely spoken of.

Either way, he was there when the Moon Princess descended on a papier-mâché crescent in her signature violet dress, platinum hair set in hasty finger waves. She'd saved up for lashes so long and arachnid, she could barely see through the haze of lights.

She was nearly nervous, but she'd promised herself never to feel such pedestrian things.

There were coughs and shuffles. A tinkle of martini glasses and some low-level discussion of whether the Méliès Margarita was overpriced, would the roller coaster reopen, did the hot dogs make anyone else feel sick?

But when the Moon Princess warbled out her first note, all of them—the T-shirted tourists and the smoked-stained regulars, Tessie in the wings and the Second Prince of Mars—fell into the awed silence usually reserved for watching clouds of gas and dust collapse under their own gravity in the cosmic dance of creation.

(In other words, a star was born.)

Next was the hair.

She'd dyed it so religiously with toilet bleach and peroxide that her raw scalp was starting to poke through. She went full follicle transplant in white, tinged with lavender. And her new nails would grow in pre-polished; she just had to swallow phosphorus to change the hue.

On her first date with the Second Prince of Mars (the things that happened in her dressing room didn't count), he offered to pay for new irises.

"Lilac really is your color," he said. They stood on the observation deck of the Red Spot Tavern, drinking helium gimlets as the perpetual storms of Jupiter swirled below.

"You think so?" The Moon Princess tore her gaze away from the whirls and eddies of ammonia hydrosulfide (best to feign starry-eyed wonder, even though she'd been hoping for a tour of the Martian palace).

"Only if you like," he said. She loved his voice—that soft, interplanetary lilt. The sound of boarding school and private spacecraft. "Only if *you* want to change them."

Three days later, she had light purple irises that would darken with her moods. She regretted it six months in, during their first fight.

"You *are* upset!" he said. He'd taken her to Neptune. Diamond rain pinged off their glass igloo. "Your eyes are almost black!"

"I'm happy!" she snapped. She wore a dressing-gown (emerald-green) and the tacky astatine hairpin he'd given her at his ski lodge on Io. "Maybe you just bought me faulty eyes."

"Davina," he said, and reached for her.

The Moon Princess tried to melt in his embrace. She was, after all, looking out at a roiling sea spattered with diamonds, with an empty platter of Titanian caviar and a genuine prince who wasn't even ugly—his nose was crooked and his ears stuck out, but she liked those things about him. She liked everything about him.

That was the trouble.

"You won't take me to Mars," she said. "You won't put our picture in the papers." She turned to face him, for dramatic emphasis. "You're ashamed of me, Alshain."

"Davina," he said again, "You don't know how it is."

"I do," she said. "Prince Altair will be emperor, and you won't. Why does it matter who you're seen with?"

He ran his hands through his mop of black hair. "It matters," he said.

"You can't date a performer?" It came out tremulous and hurt.

"I can date a performer," he said.

"You can't date a nightclub performer," she said. "Not from a seedy little club in a dying tourist trap where the air smells like cheese on a stick." Not a girl with a bumpy nose and baby fat and a lingering asteroid belt accent.

He said nothing.

"But you could date," she said, "A system-wide super star?"

He chuckled. "I suppose."

She met him with her steely lilac gaze. "Well then?"

She had her cheek fat out and her vocal chords shaved. Her nose was done twice (the first came out too cutesy) and her ears once, but she held the line at new kidneys.

"I don't want someone *else's* kidneys," she said, though the Martian prince couldn't understand why.

"He's poison," Tessie told her, on their last day as Moon Maidens. Tessie's whole life was crammed into a steamer trunk and an *I went Looney at the Bay of Love!* souvenir tote. "You look crazy, Davy."

"Green isn't your color, Tessie, darling," said the Moon Princess. Her life didn't even fill a trunk (and the astatine hairpin would eat a hole through the side, anyway).

"I'm not jealous," Tessie said, but then she shrugged. "Or maybe I am—you monster, I can't believe you're leaving me."

"Because you're such a miserable little hanger-on," said the Moon Princess.

"Says the has-been waiting to happen."

"Surely. But first I have to have *been*."

"I'll call!" Tessie said, flinging her arms around the Moon Princess, "And bang around all night to keep you up, like old times."

She never did.

The new apartment (three bed two bath, on a gated station orbiting Mars) was quiet, with thick walls.

She gained three pounds on her tour of the Jupiter Trojans, and another four playing the Quicksilver Room on Mercury, so she had her stomach removed.

"Only if *you* want to," said the Second Prince of Mars.

By the time she was opening at the Ishtar Opera House on Venus, her cheekbones could cut fused silica.

They went to Mars and rode canal boats under a scarlet sky. She met Prince Altair and Princess Tarazed in the fire gardens of the Red Palace, though there were no photographs.

Then two things happened: her song, *Moony for You*, hit number three on the inter-planetary radio charts, and she found her first wrinkle.

She sat in her dressing room at the Royal Oceanic, a few miles below Europa's ice sheet. A wide window looked out at the subsurface sea, spotted with bioluminescent shrimp, but the Moon Princess had her nose (recently retouched, at no small price) pressed against the vanity mirror.

"That was unbelievable," said the Second Prince of Mars. He offered her a bouquet, but she shooed him toward the great floral heap in the corner. "Davina—when you dropped from the ceiling? Did you *hear* the gasps?"

"Never mind that," she said. "*Look.*"

The prince looked.

"What? You want to re-do your eyes?"

"No—what's wrong with my eyes *now*?" She swept aside a stack of fan mail to get a closer look.

"Nothing," he said, quickly. "What's the matter?"

"My forehead!" she moaned. "*Look. A wrinkle.*"

"Oh, that," said the prince, giving her a cursory glance.

"You can *see it*?" She pulled at her face miserably. "I'm an ugly, hairy huldra."

"Darling!" He kissed her forehead. "It's nothing. Besides—you can have it fixed for a song, now."

"What do you mean?"

The Second Prince of Mars grinned. She couldn't help but smile at the way it made his ears stick out even more. "The bioengineering regulations," he said.

"Oh, Alshain, you know I don't follow all that."

"Cloning reform," he said, "It's a new dawn, Davina."

It was:

A new spine (heels gave her back pain) and plasma infusions to stay vibrant. New kidneys (finally), since these had been grown in a lab and not cut out of an aspiring chorus girl, and a daily dose of pills to kill and regenerate her every living cell bi-monthly.

The Prince couldn't avoid photos anymore—*Under Ruby Skies* and *Raining Diamonds* topped the charts, and *Cosmic Love* smashed every record. When the Moon Princess performed on Phobos, the crowd was so big it shifted the moon's orbit by three feet.

"Don't worry, darling," said the Moon Princess, holo-signing another palette of tour posters. "You'll always come first."

"Not now, Davina," the prince said. "I'm up to here with these bleeding-heart lawsuits—surely they'd *rather* I clone miners *without* sentience? Ridiculous people."

At the Stratus Spa, swaddled in sulfur clouds high above Venus, the Moon Princess had her epidermis stripped and replaced. It felt like being flayed alive while the esthetician murmured at her to breathe.

When she returned, red and raw, to her estate on the Plains of Elysium, the prince was away at his mining colonies. She called, to take her mind off her agonized nerve endings.

A woman answered, mid-laugh, "Hello?"

"Oh," said the Moon Princess. "Is Alshain there?"

"No," said the woman. "Sorry, no—he just stepped out."

The Moon Princess heard a man's voice, distantly.

"All right," she said. "Tell him Davina called."

She sent the housekeeper and the cook home and sat alone in the big empty parlor.

When she accepted her first Silver Harp at Kepler Hall, reporters asked where he was—"Is the Princess without her prince tonight?" and "Any truth to these rumors? Your split from Prince Alshain?"

"Oh, I've got something planned for Alshain," she said.

At the ribbon cutting for the prince's new Plutonian mine, amid bobbing icebergs of methane, she presented him with a jar wrapped in gilt paper.

"For you, darling," she said.

The prince's brow was furrowed these days, more often than not, but he gave her one of his grand winning smiles and unwrapped the jar. Flashbulbs popped.

Inside was her still-beating heart.

The Moon Princess opened her coat (real faux sable), to show where it had been cut out. The new heart was silver and pearl, with a little glass window in her sternum to watch it pump.

"My heart," she said. "For you."

In later years, when Ursula Majors sent her lungs to an ex-husband, and Sissy Centauri plucked her eyes out onstage, they were understood to be low-rent copycats. No one, anywhere in the system, would ever again make a gesture so grand and romantic and all-around foolish.

The Second Prince of Mars furrowed his brow.

Her face was on lunch pails and porn rags from Venus to Vanth. *Her star*, they said, *will never burn out!* But when Alshain turned up in the tabloids, canoodling with some baby-faced blonde, the Moon Princess walked out her door and kept walking.

She was found collapsed, three days later, on the rocky Martian plains, bare soles ripped to bloody shreds (she opted to have the feet replaced afterwards, since she'd never liked her big toes, anyway).

Heartlessly Hopeless and *Broken Heartless (For You)* didn't even chart. She upped the epidermis peels (twice a month).

She's starting to look strange, fans noted. When most of her face sloughed off at the Xanadu Mirrordome, the radio comics had a field day.

Her get-well cards barely filled one drawer.

The limb extensions that were meant to make her lithe and lovely started to buckle. Her knees bent both ways. Uranian Cruises cancelled a tour after her nose caved in onstage, and bony spikes broke the skin all up and down her spine.

Her nails grew in black, polished, and sharp.

The phone stopped ringing. The stars spun on.

One night, in her big empty house, she called her mother on Ceres.

"Who?" asked the woman on other end.

The Moon Princess explained. "Oh, honey," said the woman. "I think this house has seen a couple generations since then."

"Me too," said the Moon Princess. "I don't have any of my original parts."

The woman said nothing.

The Moon Princess could hear the briny hiss of Cererean vapors, tinny and distant.

"Do you still have cryo-candy?" asked the Moon Princess. "Do you still have huldra with silky white fur? I never thought they were real, but mother always insisted."

The line went dead.

She played a dive on Aphrodite Terra, where university students with dyed-blue skin screamed at her for something to do with cloning.

"Those miners are *people*!" cried a girl with bobbed brown hair.

"Tessie?" said the Moon Princess. "Tessie, it's me, Davy!" Young blue Tessie wouldn't wave back.

The Bay of Love had changed when she returned to the moon for one-night-only. There was trash on the boardwalk. Moon Maidens' Cabaret looked small and shabby to her now, and the Maidens were less adept at singing than at removing their clothes.

"Hi-ho, gorgeous!"

A boy of six sat in the front row at sound-check, twirling his cigar. "There's my starlet!" Blonde hair flopped into his eyes as he drank a scotch on the rocks.

"…Gibbs?" she said. "You look…different."

"I look different! I do! Me! Look at *you*," he said.

Her poreless skin had started to pucker. It sunk over the contours of her skeleton like wet tissue paper. Her lavender-white hair grew faster now, and so did, for some reason, her ever-lengthening toes.

"You're a kid, kiddo" she said.

The six-year-old nodded, emphatically. "Whole new me! I'm a baby, baby-cakes! You got yourself a little baby-clone?"

"No," she said. Most of the *Cosmic Love* money was gone, and the Martian royals had come after the Elysium estate, which she didn't know she was meant to pay taxes on.

"Oh, you *gotta* get yourself a clone-baby, baby-love," said Gibbs. "Waiting for puberty is a bitch, but I never felt so *alive*."

The Moon Princess smiled (her smile was wider now—sometimes it met at the back of her head). "You saying I'm not cute, Gibbsy?"

"Hey! Hey! You kidding me?" The Gibbs child looked up with great solemnity. "Sexiest fucking corpse I've ever seen."

When the Second Prince of Mars came to visit, days (years?) later, he looked so old—salt and pepper hair, eyes that crinkled. He stared at her, then wept (the constant cell regenerations had done interesting, snout-like things to her nose and jaw).

"My god," he kept saying, "my god, Davina, you did all this for me—now look at you, look at you."

"Alshain, don't cry." She reached for him, but he recoiled (her fingers were longer, too).

"I was a fool," he proclaimed. "A fool—none of the others—they never meant—but Davina, please—I'll pay, a full consciousness transplant—a new clone. A whole new life. With me."

She thought perhaps she was dreaming (her dreams had gotten interesting, too—lots of snowdrifts and cryo-volcanoes that spoke with her mother's voice), but he meant it.

Royal Martian guards (clones, non-sentient) escorted her to a facility, just past the asteroid belt.

"I grew up on an asteroid," she told the guards. They stared ahead, blankly.

The doctors in their white coats (no bloodstains) showed her a girl in a great glass tank.

"Who's that?" the Moon Princess asked.

"That's you," one doctor said slowly. "We're putting your mind in there." People talked like she was stupid, now.

"Oh," said the Moon Princess. The girl behind the glass did look like someone she'd known, once, only rubbery and dead.

The Moon Princess tried to think her rubbery and *alive*. She tried to think herself young. Adored. But she'd already *been* young and *been* adored and held her still-beating heart in her hands.

She thought of Alshain, the warmth of his arms, and his wide, wounded eyes. She thought of chill, salty ice, and the way her lovely white hair brushed the elegant bone-spikes of her toes. She thought of home.

The tank girl's heavy, dead head bumped against the glass.

A pretty child, no doubt, pretty like any old chorus girl. But the Moon Princess had already been in the chorus.

What she'd never been, the Moon Princess thought, was covered in soft white fur.

"And if I want something different...it's prepaid?"

The tabloids were thrilled to report that the Moon Princess, after years as a system-wide darling (and decades a talk show punchline), died tragically during a routine consciousness transfer.

Best move for her career, quipped Sissy Centauri, rising star.

Tucked away at the back of one issue was a fluff piece: *Watch Out, Campers! Huldra Sightings on Ceres!*

And somewhere, amid briny rivulets and belching volcanoes of ice, stalked a long, bony creature with lilac eyes. It thrummed and hummed strange melodies, fur spun from moonlight, before it vanished into fine, salty vapors (high humidity, good for the skin).

It was only weeks later that Prince Alshain of Mars suffered a bizarre light-sail crash. He was halfway through a slingshot 'round the moon when a scrap of space debris was sucked into his engine at precisely the wrong moment, causing a one-in-a-billion destabilization.

A freak accident, everyone agreed. *Such carelessness to leave trash in orbit all these years!*

Even odder, some said, that forensic analysis identified the space debris in question to be a little pink sachet...

...filled with rotten human teeth.

THE CATADROMOUS NATURE OF EEL

Sophia Tao

EVEN MY TWIN Lydia does not know I am an eel-person. If I ever told her, she would show up with a knife in the dorm we share and open me up from chin to tail. She would pry apart the squelching whiteness of my belly to have a look inside and see whether I was telling the truth. Of course she would see that I was, but then I would be dead, and whether I was telling the truth would not matter.

So I have to pretend I am not one. I attend my classes like a human would, with my eyes turned forward. I imagine that the cold breath of Nova Scotia's winter is air my gills can breathe. On weekends, when I go home to my flesh-father—that is, Lydia's father—I pretend to care about school, and current events, how the Thunderbirds are doing. I masquerade as the person they expect me to be.

I never go home to my fish-father. He does not let me. He says I cannot go until it is my time.

When it will be my time he does not say.

When I was younger I used to beg and beg for him to let me go home. Just once, I would say to my fish-father, desperately, with a deep and immovable ache, but he never relented, it was always no. And so ever since the time when I was thirteen, the last time, I never tried to go home again. And the Urge went away too.

Except today it is back. I feel the Urge again.

During dinner it begins: I feel a deep and alarming stirring in my gut. Lydia and I are on a double-date at Mr. Gao's. The date was Lydia's idea, because of course it was. Eel do not date, we only let our fertile material loose in the waters. And even if we did I would not have picked a cheap noodle place with light so fluorescent and unblue that it hurts my eyes.

At least it does not serve seafood. Lydia believes I am violently allergic to seafood, so she always vets our dining venues carefully.

"And then we went to Davie's place," says the big man with the lobster-hard muscles, sitting across from Lydia, "and he was like, come on dude, one more shot. I mean, I was already nine shots in and real fucked up"—he affects a burp—"but I said sure, why the hell not."

Lydia laughs vigorously.

She puts a hand on his arm as she does, glittery holiday nails digging into his carapace, snowmen that I helped glue on. I think about how my fish-father once told me that lobsters are actually quite shy, despite how much they like to wave around their big claws. Once you get to know them, he said, they can be quite sensitive, even neighborly.

My own date, thin and moist like kelp, pours me another cup of green tea and tries again to make conversation. "So you're in pre-med," he says. It is the second time he tries to open with that particular topic.

Before I can reply, the Urge comes for me. My lungs seize up. My mouth turns dry.

"I feel a panic attack coming," I interrupt Lydia's conversation. I can barely force my next words out. "Can...can you take me home?"

She looks at me with a face I know. Angry mouth puckered around angry teeth, a human expression that says, *Really? Now?* It makes the terrible pain in my gut worsen, as if her disappointment has clawed its way into my pinkish intestines and is working on extricating them inch by inch.

"Please," I manage to say, and my voice is so hoarse that even the lobster man and the kelp man are staring at me. But Lydia is my twin and she has learned to resent my Urge, so she does not look at me. Her eyes stay on the noodles floating belly-up in her bowl, mouth twisting in a way that fish mouths cannot.

She says, "Anna, can you not ruin things for once?" Then, louder, "Seriously, *for one night*, can you think about something besides yourself?"

She is right. I am embarrassing her. I try to suppress my Urge.

I try very hard, because I hate seeing that bitter look on my sister's face, the look that says her life is better without me. But the Urge is stronger than I am. And as the night goes on, I can no longer ignore the agony of my insides constricting, or the excruciating stone-dryness of my skin. I feel the need to coil. It becomes harder to breathe the land-air, and even though I desperately try to keep breathing anyway, it does not work and I begin gasping.

The lobster man leans forward with concern. "Are you all right?"

Lydia frowns. When she speaks it is calm but hurried. "There's nothing to worry about, Josh. My sister likes to be dramatic sometimes. It's been that way since we were kids. She's always fine after." She gives me another *Can we not do this right now* look, which is as sharp and barbed as a hook and makes me feel awful.

By now my mouth is moving involuntarily, opening and shutting, opening and shutting. I know Lydia hates me now. She always hates it when I get like this. I know I cannot embarrass her any longer in front of the lobster man, so I get up abruptly and go outside, into the winter.

None of them come after me, which is good, because Lydia would not want her friends to see me when the Urge gets strong like this. I crouch in the alley behind the restaurant to gather myself. Usually the Urge goes away after some time. I try to wish it away, the way I could always wish it away when I was an elver, young enough to still be translucent.

But this time it does not go away. Even when the night has become completely dark, when the murky clouds have completely covered the sky-lights, it does not go away and I am still hurting. Perhaps it is because I am older now. The need to return home gets stronger as we age. Eel are catadromous, which means that one day we all must return to the sea.

We all must return to the sea. Even the other lifeforms, eventually; it is natural and it is primal. Even the life borne by the first tidal gasps of earth's womb knew how. The trilobites and the coelacanths, they all knew the way home.

It is only later that creatures learned to fear the sea. Creatures like Lydia, they will keep fighting their way out of the water, fighting and fighting as long as muscle and lung allow them.

My body is stiffening. It is beginning to coil up. I cannot fight the Urge much longer.

I look around and find it empty here, the sidewalks silent except for the indifferent buzz of street lamps. Nobody is looking.

I know that Lydia will likely be able to keep the lobster man and the kelp man busy. I am reassured that it will not be like the time when I was thirteen, when there were sirens and harsh lights and so many voices shouting at me. If I go to the sea now, my flesh-father will not cry and clutch me so tightly I choke. If I go to the sea now, Lydia will not scream, *What's wrong with you?*

Why do you want attention so fucking badly?

How can you do this to me? To Dad?

If I go to the sea now, nobody will notice that I have gone.

The Urge grows stronger. I start walking.

At first I make an effort to walk like a human. But as soon as I see the beach the Urge grows so strong that I cannot help it anymore, I fall onto my stomach, using my muscles to propel me forward, slitheringly, along the rough sand. Blindly I am driven forward, ensorcelled by the lull of the lullaby waves. I do not notice as rocks make deep cuts in my flesh.

I am almost to the sea when I hear my fish-father's voice in my head.

Not yet. It is not your time.

"Please," I rasp. I know my fish-father hates it when I beg, but the Urge is so strong now, and I am so desperate. I desire, feverishly, the sweet release of the sea. Ferociously I thirst for the feel of home, the endless coolth of it to hug me and let me know I belong. But still he forbids me.

Still he says no, so I cannot go into the sea. Instead I just lie on the empty beach. Neither able to go in one direction or the other, neither forward into the darkness of sea or back towards the darkness of land. The beach is liminal. It is the only place an eel-person is allowed to be.

The clouds break and the sky-lights come stuttering out.

The Urge grows stronger.

I feel myself stretching. I am always my true length, but I am not always conscious of it; at this moment, however, I feel very long. I feel the full expanse that is me, my wet head, my soft chin, my dorsal fin spanning from back to tail. I can account for every tiny scale scintillating on my surface, and every last one lusts for home.

Please, I try to tell my fish-father again, but this time it does not come out as sound. *Help*, I beg, but again only silence. I think it is because fish do not naturally speak, they can only gasp.

My muscles are twitching now, seizing. The pain of the Urge is becoming unbearable.

It reminds me that I am made of flesh. That though I cannot speak with my mouth, perhaps I can speak the only way fish can, with my body.

Eel bodies are not very eloquent. We only have the one length of us, no appendages to help mime at glyphs, no limbs to tittle or to crossbar. Even so, there are some things we are capable of saying.

In some human movies they get stranded on islands. I remember Lydia and me watching one together, with me coiled around her on my flesh-father's worn couch, watching the men in the screen arrange pebbles on the beach. I remember being fascinated by how they managed to make meaning out of only ocean-waste. By how they announced their existence with stones, which are the most silent creatures of us all.

The shapes they made are ones I can make too, even as an eel and even stretched as I am. I fight through the clouding pain of the Urge to curl my body into an S. Then I fight the seizing of my muscles to clamp my mouth onto my tail, an O. Then, again, S. When I am done I do it all over again.

I cannot speak so I use my body as a semaphore. I am silent so I must force my physicality into language, contort the flesh of me into meaning. I do it until I can no longer, until the Urge has become so strong that my body is spasming and thrashing, and breathing land-air becomes so difficult I can only lay on my side, with my tail flat on the sand, gills erect, mouth panting. Until I am too weak to move, and there is nothing left for me to do but hope that my body has been loud enough. When fish scream, they scream with silence.

When I wake up next there is old linen beneath me, which tells me I am on the couch at my flesh-father's abode. My wounds, where I have scraped my belly on the beach rock, are already bandaged. The blanket wrapped around me smells like Lydia.

"Yes, she had an episode," I hear her saying from the kitchen. "But we're lucky she didn't go in the water this time." I am surprised that her voice quivers.

"Good thing you noticed she was missing," my flesh-father says. "Good thing you brought her home."

THE (RE)CREATION OF NEW TERRAFORM

Adianu Etinose

"If I'm being honest, Rami is exquisite," I tell Oyeh, "which makes him far more sentient than I imagined he'd be."

Oyeh is braiding my hair in preparation for your arrival. We're squabbling over you like opposed thumbs, Rami. At any rate, I should be prepared and beautified long before you are legally permitted to sweep me up.

House Ivie is our temporary quarters until you carry me away to your palace across the island and Oyeh returns to the stars. Still, Oyeh and I stay in a place of great beauty. The walls are made of hurricane-proof glass, and the hallway is made of the same star-dusted stone my father's palace was comprised of before it collapsed.

Oyeh pauses from braiding my hair. "Then you don't want to kill him."

I shake my head, and the tight strands whip against my skin. "I don't."

Oyeh draws out a long, exasperated sigh. "Grandma won't like that, Abi. She won't like that at all."

"Screw Grandmother, then," I snap.

Here is one truth and one lie. Rami, you are exquisite, and I have no intention of killing you. However, the manner in which I tell the truth is woven through with silver. You see, I'm pretending. I'm lying to you.

I never told you the true reason why I'm rushing our marriage. I'm doing this to protect you. Grandmother asked me to assassinate you because she knows that you love me and that we have fostered a relationship, one that was once founded on outward beauty entirely.

I'm not sure that outward beauty still is, to a large degree, an impetus.

At any rate, she believes you to be impossibly strong, so much so that you are akin to a god. In other words, she perceives a threat in you. She believes that you hold your entire kingdom under your duress, and the moment we kill you, the kingdom will be ours.

You know that our people have been adversaries for millennia. Because of a lover's quarrel, dragons, elves, and octo-kin have held each other in the grip of war for millennia. Funny how history repeats itself when others don't learn from past mistakes.

In any case, I never confided in her my feelings towards you. I made sure my dealings with you were all covert, self-contained via messages, our means of communication over the past five tides.

Grandmother suspected, of course. Before she let me go, she warned me. "Ndi will kill him," Grandmother told me, "if you don't finish the job."

I won't. She'll have to sic Ndi on you, and I'm going to make sure Ndi does not prevail.

I lied to Oyeh, too. I never told her that you and I met long ago, when the two of us were young tidlings. I was nine tides, and you were eight. We met beneath the awning of a castle as beautiful as one could imagine with battlements and soaring walls made with deep cobalt blue stones and a fist full of stars strewn throughout.

It was night, but I could still see the violets of your eyes because your irises glowed.

"Raaaa-me." I mispronounced your name on purpose, but you didn't seem to mind. In fact, you probably found it funny.

When I asked your sister, Ankh, to pronounce your name correctly, she would repeat it over and over again. As much as I asked, she would repeat, and you snickered and snickered. I smiled, suppressing a giggle. I loved to bring you joy.

Later that night, you walked over to me and kissed me. It was my first kiss, and the sweetest. You had an accent that I could hardly understand, an Isles accent, but the little I could understand was brilliant.

"You're a riot!" you told me.

"Excuse me?" I said.

It was the first time I'd heard anyone call me "a riot," and I laughed and repeated the phrase to you, the first of many times I'd steal it. Your brilliance and your masculine beauty drew me to you.

For this reason, as well as your morals and keenness of observation, I love you.

I've always wanted to marry you when I grew older.

My wish will soon become reality because we're about to marry in a few days.

YOU ARE A tide younger than me, eighteen tides to my nineteen. I'm an octo-girl, and you're an elven boy.

You're all bronze skin and almond-shaped, expressive, violet eyes with long lashes and lips that I could peel back like the buds of a rose. The only vulnerable features of your face, your body.

You're all lean, cut muscles and dark, curling, thick hair that you've swooped into a bun. You're tall, which means that you're unlike the other boys who I look down upon.

"Rami," I tell you.

"Abi," you say. You're playful. It's banter.

You turn, gazing at the world around you. Your eyes catch on the star-laced stones that span the ground beneath my bath and the hallway that glints beneath the moonlight like polished onyx. You glance toward the hurricane windows and the school of fish that kiss the algae forming against the glass.

Next, your violet eyes take in the mer-children. They dance beneath the high tide, their red tails pivoting this way and that to the beat of the ocean's song.

If you were to venture out of the palace and into the waves, you'd smell the puma lilies and their sweet fruit. Their taste is a combination of a tangerine and tart cranberries. The puma lilies bloom in this season, and I can tell by your nearly rapt gaze that the ocean is calling you.

You'd enjoy the tidal heat, what surface dwellers call summer. You'd enjoy the oceanic sun beating across your back. You're so much at ease beneath the waves.

Now, you gaze once more upon me, and I'm desperate, hungry for your kiss. I tilt my head in wanting.

You smirk, but otherwise, you don't move.

At last, I return your smile and pick up my paintbrush. You are my first subject for the tidal year. "I've mastered this technique," I tell you, "and I've been dying to paint you, Rami."

This is an earnest statement, one that perhaps you don't understand, but my hearts race at the thought of your expression. I turn and watch your reflection in the panes of hurricane glass.

For the moment, the two of us are alone. I sit up from my seat so that the rest of my torso is out of the water. The glass dome of my room echoes with the sounds of splashing water and the friction of paper against pen. I exchange the brush for the quill, and my fingers touch the cool, textured felt of the easel.

My submerged room is warm in the heat of orange tide, and the current is warm against my scales. Out of the sheer, unyielding glass that is my window, I can see the moon glittering from high above, and I can see the cove sisters dancing beneath the song of the tidal women, their red and gold tails shimmying, the mer-boys playing.

With raised brows, your eyes meet mine, your wild eyes darting back and forth as you take in my expression before you finally grin. "Abidemi?" You offer to take my hand, which I place in yours. "It is my immense honor to be a highly sought-after subject of an artist of your repute. Thank you, kindly."

I blush, and my nearly ebony silhouette glows with a dark amethyst phosphorescence.

You gasp, almost dropping my hand, and then, slowly, you recover yourself and hold my hand with both of yours.

I drop the brushes that were in my hand, but I smile because I'm just as delighted to see you again. "Rami."

You're probably wondering how a girl of nineteen tides with a form as lithe and changing as the ocean can possibly love a boy like you.

I feel the same way because you know what I am and my dealings with your world. We octo-girls want more than your elven arms can hold.

That was why I greeted you with eight arms upon your arrival, and then, when you looked with awe, or perhaps fright, at my curling form, I seduced you with my humanoid body.

I have legs that go on forever, dark curves and ample thighs that suit this skinny girl. But I won't flaunt them. Not now, anyway. For now, I'm just a girl who sits in the water, an interstellar mermaid from oceanic space.

You don't know me very well. I've kept my history a secret from you for so long, but I want you to ask me where I'm from. I want to discuss.

Instead, you raise my stained hand to your lips, so that the warmth of your breath fills me with want. I'm aching for the soft, eager kiss that I've never had nor ever asked for.

I should have, and now is my moment to make it right.

You watch me with heavy lids. You elven boys can read emotions, and perhaps you are one of those who can, to a limited degree, read thoughts because you ask, "May I…have the pleasure…?"

Your question is unnecessary, but I know you want to convey your passion through your tone.

The fever catches me, too. I nod. "Please."

And you kiss me. Your kiss is tender, but it's lacking because you pull away. Let's remain chaste, you seem to say.

"Please…" I murmur once more.

You flaunt a mocking smile. "It wasn't enough. You wanted more."

I nod.

You're silent for a moment, gazing at me through heavy lids. "I'm quite famished, too." You release my hand and cup my chin and crush your lips into mine over and over.

I kiss you back, and I'm breathless because I'm stunned that you would have me when others never worked up the courage.

You pull up your tunic, and my eyes are rapt upon the firm muscles of your abdomen as you climb into the bath, the water splashing everywhere, the taut skin against your rib cage stippled with droplets. Yours is the type of body that could cut a girl to pieces, straight lines and jagged cuts laced with poison.

I want to trace the veins that cord the gamut of your arms, your muscles, your hands. I love how you make me feel. I'm breathless as I say your name, breathless as though I don't have the gills to breathe through water. "Rami."

I WANT TO warn you of Grandmother's plans, but Oyeh is delighted to see you. She's hovering around in our room, complaining that it's her room, too, smiling and flirting with you, licking the inside of her mouth.

I know that you notice, but you seem oblivious as to the reason for her behavior. That's the confounding part about it. I'm sure that you can read minds, so why can't you read hers? Maybe Grandmother is shielding you from the obvious. Perhaps Oyeh's flirting is obnoxious, but she certainly means no harm.

You smirk in my direction, and then for a second, your expression changes. Then, you tidy up your wan expression before I can analyze it fully.

Did you frown?

You probably did, but ice trickles down my back at the thought of you hiding your expression from me.

I know it's my fault. We tell each other everything, but I've let you down in not being forthcoming to you. I love you, but I never say it, not in the company of my friends and certainly not in the company of my sisters.

WE'RE ALONE ONCE more.

It's NIGHT AGAIN, high tide. The octo-girls have returned to their coves. We have nothing to do but catch the rise and fall of our bodies and thrill from the heat of our touch.

I rest with my back against you, and you're eating the apple that I'm sharing with you. It's a green apple, and it's so sour and delicious. I can taste the honey of your kiss in the bite of apple that I'm savoring.

Rami, it's my turn now. You hand the apple to me, which I take from you.

I take a bite and hand the apple back to you.

You take the last bite. The sound of you crunching makes me think of illicit places and the two of us being in the midst of them, us engaging in more forbidden activities than my mother would ever allow.

Outside sunlight fills every shadow and envelopes the sky with light. Though I love the rain, the change in weather is beautiful because it suits the occasion. I'm about to make a profession of love in telling you the truth of my feelings and the truth of my dealings with you.

I have so much to tell you now that I finally have the courage to confess my love for you, my desire to fight alongside you against Grandmother, and my most intimate thoughts concerning my dealings with the goddess Ndi.

I begin. "I love you, Rami…." That's one. "Grandmother sent me on a mission to kill you…" That's two. "Ndi and I were friends, but she's jealous of you," I tell you, "And she's under Grandmother's orders to kill you if I don't follow through."

You say nothing. You're all long lashes and violet, blank stares.

"Rami…"

You pause from crunching our apple, and your warm, muscled body tenses and, perhaps I'm imagining it, chills.

"I wanted to believe that I was hallucinating," you murmur. "That those thoughts weren't true perceptions but the machinations of a delusional, depraved mind."

You put our apple on the table and grip my waist.

"Rami…"

Your huge hands are now fists against my stomach. "But there is one thing that I don't understand. Why? What is your grandmother's motivation?"

"She wants your kingdom," I say, "But not you. She wants our children but not you. She wants a willing, submissive, granddaughter, but not you."

A low growl escapes your lips.

"She thinks you're too powerful and that love will slacken and dull your senses. She wants the goddess Ndi to kill you while you're in love."

"Then she anticipated that you would confess everything to me."

"But she didn't anticipate that you're clairaudient," I chime.

Now, you relax your hands, but you grip me tighter and kiss my ear. "That's true." You say at last. "Now for my final question. When?"

It's clear that you read my thoughts based on your one-word question. I've finally developed a theory of mind for you.

I know exactly what your question means. You want to know when we should expect Ndi's attack. You want to defend yourself.

And I want to help you. "On the night of our wedding, the moment we consummate our marriage."

Now that we're alone, I've a chance to admire the paintings that line the walls.

Depictions of lions and wolves, leopards and hawks, and water birds and hunters line the walls with scenic revelry. The hunters scour the meat from the carcasses of animals and lead tamed beasts in the hunt. Your cartouche sits among the frescos.

I smile at the scenes because some styles never grow old. People here still line their eyes with ochre makeup that kisses at the ends.

You watch me silently. Your eyes are glowing violet, and you're comfortable with me once more. That is what my theory of mind is telling me.

You nod once.

"Rami…" I shake my head. "I don't know that I'll ever understand you all."

"Speak."

"I don't know how you Keshutians are so…courageous."

You watch me with heavy lids. You're in a fit of passion, which is confounding and confusing. "Continue," you say.

I grin and swivel my body while clasping my hands. "If I didn't think you so clever, I would say that you're courageous to the point of being a fool."

You chuckle as though you didn't know that I would say that. "Oyeh is on our side."

I gasp. "How do you know? How is this possible?"

"Your sister," you say, your violet eyes boring into mine, "knows more than she lets on."

I let out a breath. "What do you mean?"

"She's forgiven the two of us."

"Forgiven me…?"

"Yes. We made a poor effort of hiding our affections from her."

"Oh…"

You take a sip of wine from your chalice and hand me a folded papyrus scroll. "She had hoped that I would choose to wed her instead of you."

I'm nodding. Tears sting my eyes as I press my forehead to your chest. "She knows this? And she still…" I sniffle and wipe my nose with a cloth you give me, and now I stand and look over the papers.

The words are written in the delicate penmanship of nobility, in the mother tongue of my ancestors. This must be Grandmother's handwriting. "How did you get this?"

"Oyeh offered me your grandmother's strategic plans as a show of solidarity," you tell me.

I sigh and cover my face with my hands. "Rami? She loves us."

"I WANT TO finish your portrait," I tell you, "That way I'll be able to visit you wherever you go."

We're laying in your bed, and we've just finished.

This wasn't our first encounter with heaven, but none of the other times we'd loved were as sacrosanct as this. Literally.

Our bed was prayed over, and we were bathed and cleansed before we made love.

You're extremely strong is the only conclusion I can come to after experiencing your love.

You snort, possibly from overhearing my thoughts. My spoken words probably add to your reaction. "You're passionate."

"I am!" I say.

You pull back and poke my nose. Now you grin with satisfaction. "You are."

Your violet eyes are like dual suns. I can't stop gazing at them.

Now you frown.

"Rami," I murmur. "What's wrong?"

You return to your tense smiling before you drop the act altogether. "Nothing."

Now I rise from our bed and kiss your ear. "Rami. You can tell me."

You turn away.

I'm breathless as I say your name. "Rami."

"The palace," you murmur. "They'll want the palace."

I gasp.

You rise from the bed, throwing your clothes on, and you storm out.

You tell me that you've arranged for guards to watch the palace while we try to sleep. We've had little sleep since the festivities the night before. You've managed to quell two uprisings, defeat two legions, and come back in time for dinner.

All of that seems impossible, but I let go of my doubts and hold on to the boundless beauty of wonder. "How did you do that?" I say, between forkfuls of fried oyster and sear-fried potatoes.

"You wouldn't believe me if I told you," is all you say.

I've mostly finished painting you in the weeks before the wedding. All I need to do is finish painting your eyes. The lighting is always the same, what most surface dwellers would call gloomy.

The gloom befits the moment, for once.

Your eyes are heavy, from mourning the future loss of your childhood home and from that pervasive sense of desire we have despite the weather, despite the circumstances. We're young; we're still passionate.

Even the way you lounge is suggestive. I shouldn't have doubted how potent my passion is for you.

I face the portrait once more, frozen in the face of doubt. I close my eyes. I hope I can truly honor you by painting you in perfect strokes.

"You will," you tell me.

I smile, and the warmth of your reciprocated grin fills the hollow of my back. I sigh and lift the brush, tearing up. This is the sad but beautiful moment when our lives are sundered apart, isn't it? I have an intuition that is.

"Be sure you use the right shade of violet," you say, adding, "More red than blue."

I nod, sniffling.

"And if you would," you murmur, "Please include yourself in the picture."

I turn and face you. The pain in your eyes is too much. You don't have to tell me. I know my prediction is true. I face the portrait once more.

"If you need a reference to aid you," you continue, "I could provide a mirror. Or I could always telepathically communicate your features."

"A mirror would be nice."

"I shall fetch one for you."

It is now evening, and the sun is setting. We've barely slept.

I've finished your portrait and mine in a few hours. My picture didn't require the same amount of detail as yours.

And you and I made love over and over again, and we've been laying in the bed, watching the horizon.

Dark clouds fill the sky and seem to rise from below.

I hear you sneeze, and now, you cough, too, once and then twice. Now several times more. "The palace," you gasp between coughs, "is on fire."

Flames catch on the curtains, on the bed, on the tables.

"Fire...?" I say. Ah...so this is how the paradise we've made for ourselves is ripped from beneath our appendages.

You rise to your feet and take hold of me. "Yes. Fire." Now you lift me in your arms.

Tears stream down my cheeks.

"Ndi is forcing us out." You press me against your chest, the air finally seeping back into your lungs, and you carry me to the balcony. "She's culling us from safety." You laugh, but your eyes glint. "Fine, then. We'll play that game."

We've reached the balcony. Smoke rises from the cliffs and the rocks below. The village is dusted in a strange, green flame.

"Dragon fire," you murmur as we look on.

I turn to face you, my arms around your neck. "Dragon fire?"

You nod. "This is arson. The work of my kinsmen."

"Rami..."

You frown, now, truly frown. All traces of your smile are gone. You shout out orders to the armed guards, some of them women who coil the rain from the storm towards the palace. The rain cycles and cycles, and the flames crack like lightning.

"Rami."

You jump into the air, holding me to your chest, and your wings burst through your tunic. You grip me as we take flight.

Now I KNOW why Grandmother was wary of you.

You're a dragon. Why didn't you tell me? Were you afraid of how I'd react? I'm not angry, Rami. I'm just saddened you kept this secret from me. I'm just saddened that you didn't think that you could trust me with this knowledge.

With tears streaming down my cheeks, I gaze up at you. I expect to see anger, hatred or some hint of emotion in your eyes. I don't expect to see warmth.

We pause mid-flight and land in a field. Green papyrus reeds fill every direction, and in the distance, we can hear the Wile lapping against the coast.

Rain streams down my cheeks, and you wipe the droplets with your free hand, your other hand cupping my chin. "I'm so sorry," you say at last.

"No, no." I sniffle and shake my head. "It's okay. It's all right." I'm trying to avoid your gaze, but your violet eyes bore through mine.

All is silent save for the lapping of the Wile against the reeds.

"Besides," I tell you as I turn away from you and fold my arms, "I should apologize, too."

Your smile is lazy and beautiful. "I suppose we both have our secrets. And I am in favor of divulging them. Are you?"

Despite my tears, your violet eyes light my vision like dual suns. "Rami? Of course I do."

You wipe my eyes and kiss me over and over.

REDO

Brigitte Winter

3.

In our third timeline, I met you on New Year's Eve.

I had slept off a migraine half of that day, so I wanted nothing more than to spend the evening by the fireplace cuddling with Jamie and our ancient basset hound. But New Year's Day would be my fifth wedding anniversary with Jamie—our "wood" anniversary—and he had gotten tickets to a burlesque show because he thought he was hilarious. Predictably, he insisted that it would be wasteful to skip the show because the tickets were $50 each. Plus, booze was included. Plus, he could watch women dance out of their clothes, which was significantly more interesting than watching me sit around all night in the oversized sweater and leggings I'd been wearing since Christmas.

"Plus, Mary," he said, "maybe you'll surprise yourself and have fun for once."

And so I pulled a black slip dress over my leggings and twisted my unwashed hair into a bun, and Jamie and I squeezed into the dingy black box theater just as the first dancer finished her set. Jamie muttered something about me making him late again before disappearing to the bar. He didn't ask me if I wanted anything, which was fine because I didn't. My temples pounded along with the bass blaring from the too-close speaker. Everyone in the audience was standing, and the guy directly in front of me was well over six feet tall and completely blocking the stage. The back of his jacket was a maroon velvet that looked so soft and dark that I longed to press my face against it until the bass stopped pumping and my brain stopped throbbing.

And then the bass stopped pumping.

I pushed up onto my toes to peer around the velvet jacket as slow piano and the first rich notes of Des'ree's "Kissing You" wrapped around me and pulled me forward until I found myself standing in front of the tall man.

By the time you glided onto the stage, I had somehow edged my way to the front of the crowd. They introduced you as Ale Mary. Your sequined teddy glinted like a disco ball with every slow, luxurious spin, and your arms were clad in long feathery wings, which you used to cover and uncover your body in delicious, teasing motions. You were the most glamorous woman I had ever seen.

And each time you spun toward the audience, you looked directly into my eyes.

By the time the song ended, Jamie had made his way to the front of the house and draped his heavy arm around my neck. I barely felt it.

"I have to pee!" I yelled over the music, untangling myself from him. He nodded, eyes glued to the stage. The next dancer was already down to pasties and a thong, flossing a purple boa between her legs.

I didn't want to fight the crowd to the back of the house, so I slipped through a door to the left of the stage. I realized my mistake as soon as the door clicked shut behind me and an icy wind whipped down the alley outside the theater with enough force to make my eyes water.

"Shit." I grabbed the door handle and yanked. Nothing. "Shit. Shit. *Shit*."

I spun around and growled, eager to kick the nearest dumpster or brick wall or some other big hard alley thing, and nearly collided with you. My eyes pricked with embarrassment, but I was not going to cry in front of you.

You extended a gloved hand. You were holding an old-fashioned cigarette holder, smoke curling off the tip and spiraling into the frosty air in serpentine curls. "Want a drag?"

"Um, I...I don't smoke."

"Me neither." You laughed, and your whole body shook with a raw, chaotic energy that complicated the graceful, glamorous persona you'd presented on-stage. "I needed some air, so I bummed this off one of the gals. I found this prop cigarette holder in the green room; couldn't resist trying it out."

I shuddered as another frigid blast of air cut through the alley, bringing a swirl of snow flurries. You stopped laughing. "Oh shit. I'm so sorry, darling," you said. "I'm blabbing while you're freezing. I think I'm still jittery from my set. I always talk too much when I'm jittery."

As you spoke, you unwrapped the fat infinity scarf from your neck and draped it over my shoulders like a shawl. Your hands brushed down the sides of my arms as you did it, and I smelled your perfume—sweet jasmine and vanilla mingling with something muskier. I shivered again at your touch, a rush of warmth heating my cheeks and tingling over my scalp and down my spine.

"Why j-j-jittery?" I shivered. "You were amazing."

"Thank you." You grinned and dipped into an exaggerated bow. "Getting all jittery is part of the fun of performing. I'd have to drive off a cliff for the same adrenaline high I get from dancing." You winked. "Dancing's safer."

I reflexively looked down, away from the wink, and right at your chest. Without your scarf, your cleavage rose over the scooped collar of your faux fur jacket. Your breasts were covered in goosebumps.

"If you're going to stare at my boobs, it's only polite to tell me your name."

"Oh, sorry, um…" My cheeks went hot again. "I'm Mary."

You gasped. "You're kidding me."

"I'm not." I wanted nothing more than to melt back through the locked door and vanish into the crowd.

"I'm also Mary. Like, legally. Not just for the show. Well, Marian, technically, but it's close enough. That means I'm obligated by law to show you the nearest open door back inside." You grinned again. "Which is a shame because I'd really like to keep talking to you."

You were standing so close that I could feel your warm breath against my shoulder. I could see your smile lines cracking the makeup around your hazel eyes, the way you kept licking the red lipstick off the inside of your lips, the way your tongue—

"I'm married!" I announced, and then instantly wished myself dead.

You laughed again. The snow flurries collecting on your false lashes sparkled in the light from the streetlamp illuminating the alley. "Me, too." You raised an eyebrow. "Buy you a drink?"

And so I followed you back out to the street and around to the theater's front entrance. As we climbed the steps, my head spun with a wave of dizziness so intense and unexpected that I reached for your hand and squeezed it tight. You squeezed back—three short pulses—and the gesture felt somehow familiar, a happy memory I couldn't place. The harder I strained to remember, the dizzier I felt. I didn't want my migraine to come back, so I slipped my hand from yours and opened the door for you.

The theater lobby was empty, and muted bass pumped behind the closed doors to the house. A bored bartender with a glittery mohawk sat behind a bar near the coat check, their chin propped on their fist. The clock over their head read 11:16 p.m., and the short hand's proximity to twelve—to the crowd swarming the lobby to celebrate the new year and Jamie requesting a midnight kiss and a sober ride home—made something twist in the bottom of my stomach.

The bartender stood as we approached. "What can I make you?" they asked.

Without thinking, I blurted, "Two Stoli O and gingers, please."

You perched on a stool and looked up at me with pinched brows. "How did you know?"

"How did I know what?"

The bartender plunked the drinks onto the bar, and you passed them a credit card before I could dig into my purse. "You ordered my favorite drink," you said.

"Oh."

You sipped your drink and crossed your legs. "I mean, I'm not mad about it."

"Lucky guess." I had no idea why that drink popped into my head, why I still felt so dizzy, or why I was so helplessly drawn to you.

"Lucky." You covered my hand with yours, and that was that.

We talked while we drank, a desperate ping-pong of frenzied question and response, with topics deepening in intimacy the closer the hour hand climbed toward midnight.

Where did I grow up? Here. I'd never lived more than ten miles from where I was born. I'd always wanted to live near the ocean, but I was worried it was too late to start over somewhere new, and Jamie burned easily and hated the beach.

What were you like when you weren't performing? Boring. Happy. A technical writer with a cozy government job and three Siamese cats.

Had I ever been with a woman? Yes, but not since Jamie and I became official in college.

Was your husband here tonight? Wife, and you were separated.

What would Jamie think if he saw you stroking the outside of my thigh? I didn't want to know, but I also didn't want you to stop.

Should we maybe go for a walk, find someplace more private?

You slid off the stool and pulled me toward the other side of the lobby and into a pop-up photo booth conveniently tucked behind a heavy black drape. The booth was full of photo props—a bedazzled bowler hat, a rainbow-colored boa, several different cardboard mustaches on sticks. There wasn't much distance between the prop table and the camera's touchscreen, and the slender space between our bodies buzzed with energy. We were nearly the same height, and I could feel your breath against my lips when you spoke.

"I'd really like to kiss you," you breathed.

I closed the space between us, pressing my lips to yours, lightly at first, and then with greater urgency. Somewhere in the wild tangle of arms and lips and hands and hair, a flash lit the booth, and then another, and another. You pulled away from me, laughing and pointing at the camera. "Guess we'll have a souvenir to remember tonight," you panted, "like it's possible to forget how you taste."

"How do I taste?" I smirked.

You smiled and closed your eyes, sliding a finger down the front of my throat and between my breasts. "Like Stoli O," you laughed. "But also like something warmer—honey, maybe. Or sunshine. Shit, you've made me a romantic. What's your email address for the photos?" You reached for the touchscreen. "Just kidding. I'll delete them. You should have seen your face. You believed me for a second."

And then we watched the photos fade into a text screen, and my chest squeezed so tight I couldn't breathe.

Thank you for sharing photos to our live album!
Follow @BigTeaseBurlesque to see how you look.

7.

"That's how I found out what you'd done," Jamie says. "At least that's how it worked in our third redo. I got to learn you cheated with her again in a Facebook album, along with the rest of the world." Jamie shuts his eyes and takes a deep breath, in and out. I imagine him counting to three, slowly, the way our couple's therapist taught him. "It took longer in other timelines," he says. "Sometimes years."

A dull pain throbs behind my eyes, blurring my vision. So much of the story he told me seems familiar. It feels distant—like something I overheard years ago at a cocktail party, or the plot of a book I haven't read since high school—but somehow undeniably true. I slide my wedding ring up and down my finger. It's grown tight over the past twenty years, and it digs in sharply each time I force it over my knuckle. The pain grounds me.

And I remember.

I remember details from the story Jamie told me, but also…other things. The tall man with the maroon jacket. Des'ree. Your face. The way your laugh bounced off the alley walls. Your fingers in my hair. Tart orange on your tongue. I remember all of it.

"I don't remember," I tell Jamie, pressing my fingers against my throbbing temples. "I don't remember any of it."

"Of course you don't." His voice is velvet. He sits next to me on our big comfy sofa and strokes my hair. "I shouldn't have pushed you to go to the show that night. I didn't in our fourth timeline. We stayed home, made a fire, watched the snow fall outside. It was perfect. I felt so close to you." He pulls my head against his shoulder. "I love taking care of you."

"What do you mean?" My body stiffens each time he strokes my hair, but I know I shouldn't pull away, not if I want to hear more. And I want to hear everything.

"Your headaches were so much worse after that fourth jump—not an uncommon side effect of the redo process—so we stayed home more often. We made adjustments to keep you healthy."

We made adjustments to keep you healthy. His words shudder down my spine and twist around my stomach, drive me from the couch to the big front window, the one that looks out over the beach. It's February and probably freezing outside, but the day is bright and the water is calm. Jamie moved us here a decade ago, one of the most thoughtful things he ever did for me. Then he made partner faster than anticipated, and my migraines got so terrible and unpredictable that he encouraged me to stay home and pursue my art full time. A big canvas with a half-finished painting of a sunset rests on an easel by the window.

Did he move us here because he thought it would make me happy, or because we'd be six hundred miles away from you?

"How many times?" I ask him. "How many times did you do it?"

"Marry you all over again? Seven. Seven times, and I'd marry you a thousand times if I had to." I hear his slippers shuffle across the hardwood floor. He rests his hands on my shoulders. "That's why I'm telling you everything today, for our anniversary. I want you to know how hard we've both worked to earn this celebration. Because we're worth it."

And with another flash of pain behind my eyes, you are back again.

"Because we're worth it," you said, sprawled naked and flushed across your bed. One of your fat Siamese cats, Ursula, perched above you on a shelf stuffed with worn sci-fi paperbacks and creative writing textbooks you'd carried with you since college.

"Run away with me, darling," you purred dramatically, lingering on the "aaaah" in darling. The quilt was printed with purple tulips, and I imagined you lounging in a garden.

"You look like a painting," I told you. "A portrait of a fancy Renaissance lady reclining by a fountain. I'd love to paint you in a place like that."

"Only straight white cis men are into time travel fantasies." You laughed.

Jamie squeezes my shoulders and your bedroom fades. Your sudden absence wrenches the breath from my lungs. I imagine myself drowning in the ocean beyond the window, my body burning for air while his hands hold me just below the waves.

"How does it work?" I ask him. "The time travel, I mean. The redos."

He spins me so we face each other, and smiles. His dark hair is streaked with gray, but it still spills over one eye when he looks down at me. I loved him so much in the first years of our marriage. My chest used to ache when he looked at me like that, with his cheeks dimpling like an eager little boy, his eyes peeking through his hair and suggesting all the naughty, amazing things he wanted to do to me, whether we were home in our bedroom or pushing a cart through a crowded grocery store. We met when I switched schools in second grade, so I know the story of every tiny imperfection on his beautiful face—the two chicken pox scars on his left temple because he couldn't help scratching them when he was eight, the way his front teeth cross slightly because he was too impatient to wear his retainer after his braces came off in ninth grade, the scar in the center of his chin from trying to impress me by diving into the shallow end of the pool at Mimsi Patrick's sixteenth birthday party. Always impatient, always impulsive.

"You really want to know, don't you?" His smile widens. "Well, I really want to tell you. Today, I want to tell you everything."

He laces his hands with mine, and his familiar wedding ring is warm between my fingers. Our rings are simple gold bands, scratched and dented over the years. They belonged to Jamie's parents, and his grandparents, and very likely multiple generations of great and greater grandparents before them. I felt strange accepting them from his mom and dad, who were very much alive and still together when Jamie and I got married, but they presented the rings with such enthusiastic ceremony that it was impossible to refuse them. Plus, Jamie had just started law school, and it seemed likely that we'd be in debt forever. Free was an excellent price for gold.

Jamie guides me to the mantle over our big stone fireplace. Before he dropped the "I've married you seven times" bomb, our twentieth anniversary morning plan had involved chocolate chip pancakes, pajamas, and a wood fire. The pancake batter is still mixed and waiting on the kitchen counter.

Three framed photographs stare back at us from the mantle, each a wedding portrait: Jamie's grandparents, his parents, and us. Jamie scoops up the photo of his parents with his free hand and smiles down at it.

"Do you see how happy they look?"

His tall, willowy mother is wearing a long-sleeved, perfectly seventies wedding gown that I was blissfully able to refuse because it wouldn't zip over my boobs, and her head is resting on his dad's shoulder. His dad's powder blue tux is somehow overshadowed by his gigantic square glasses, but his grin is contagious.

"They do look happy," I admit. "Your parents were always crazy about each other."

He lets out a staccato laugh, the same one he uses when he's bested me at trivia, even when we are on the same team. "They weren't always crazy about each other," he says. "That took work. And three redos."

A sick feeling sucks at the pit of my stomach.

"For my grandparents, it wasn't that easy," he continues. "My grandfather redid their marriage five times, and then they decided together on a sixth redo to celebrate their twenty-fifth anniversary, right before my parents were married."

In the photo of Jamie's grandparents, his grandfather stands behind his grandmother, wrapping his arms around her waist as if they are posing for a prom picture, the familiar rings adorning their interlaced fingers.

"It's the rings," I say weakly. My mouth is dry, and my tongue feels heavy.

He frowns and grips my hand more tightly. "How did you know that?"

"I—"

"Have you used them?"

"No! Jamie, I—"

"Have you gone back to see *her*?"

"You're hurting my hand."

He lets go. "I'm sorry. Oh, shit. I'm really, really sorry."

I turn away from him and ball my hands into fists so he can't see them shaking.

"Mary? Can we hit rewind on this conversation? This is not how I wanted it to go."

My eyes sting with the tears I keep blinking back.

"Sweetheart? Listen to me. It's just that you're not supposed to remember any of it. That's how the rings work. We can wish for a redo together like my grandparents did for their anniversary, and then we both remember our last timeline. Or one of us can make the wish for both of us, and only that person remembers. Either way, we always go all the way back to the morning of our wedding day and start over again. Each time I've made the wish on my own, the memory of the redo has been my burden to carry. And I've been honored to carry it."

My head throbs again, and I'm dizzy with all of the truths I'm fighting to hold at once: The truth of what Jamie has done, but also the dozens of electric conversations I shared with you on the commuter train where we met in our first timeline together, the impossible softness of your skin, your loud and bawdy humor, your vintage lingerie collection, the way you'd snore into my hair when you fell asleep right after sex. And at the center of all of it, the sudden deep, throbbing ache of the loss of you, of the many lives he stole from us.

"Mary, love—" He grabs my arm—too hard—and I spin free of him, nearly tripping over the LEGO castle Annabelle built last night before bed.

Annabelle.

My God.

I sink into the sofa.

"Jamie, I need to know something."

He nods. "Anything." He sits next to me and slips his hand under mine. His eyes are big and mournful. He wants to make this right.

"In the other timelines, did we have a baby?"

He presses his lips into a straight line, but I know the answer. I know I never wanted a child. Annabelle—our sweet, stubborn, hilarious daughter who hates marzipan, loves seahorses, never brushes her hair, and wants to be the Easter Bunny when she grows up—she exists because he willed her to. And any minute, she's going to bound down the stairs and ask why we haven't called her for pancakes.

"You needed a reason to stay," he says quickly. "And it worked. We made it twenty years this time, seven of them with Annabelle. Before we had her, we never even made it fifteen."

"You're a monster." My voice comes out flat, limp.

"Well that's a bit dramatic, don't you think?" He pouts and squeezes my hand, which rests on his like something dead. "It's not like I killed that woman. I just gave us more chances to get things right."

I stand and pull the wedding ring from my finger. It leaves an indentation on my skin, white and shiny as a scar. I drop the ring into the chest pocket of my flannel pajamas.

"What are you doing?"

I walk toward the front door.

"You have no idea what I've been through, what I've sacrificed for us!" he calls after me. "You think those headaches are bad? That it hurts to forget? Imagine what *I've* experienced. Imagine what it's like to remember *everything*."

I pull my winter coat from its hook and step into my boots.

"Don't do this, Mary!" He's shouting now, loud enough for Annabelle to hear. "I've started my career over seven times. Seven times, I went from senior partner all the way back to first-year associate. Seven times I watched my father die, watched my mother fall apart grieving him. *Seven times* I watched you leave me, again and again—for *that woman*—no matter how hard I worked to take care of you."

I wrap my fingers around the doorknob. It's cold and hard in my palm. He doesn't understand what he's done, what he's taken from me, from you. And I don't need to explain it to him. I don't want the last word. I want my freedom.

3.

You looked from the photo booth touchscreen to my stricken face and back to the screen again. "Well, I guess we're screwed," you said.

My heart pounded and my cheeks burned. I felt like I was going to cry, but a strangled laugh came out instead, and once I was laughing, I couldn't stop. I laughed so hard that my sides ached and I propped my back against the wall to keep from doubling over.

"It's not funny." You crossed your arms and pressed your lips together, but soon you were laughing, too, and then tears were streaming rainbow rivulets of eyeliner down your cheeks. "Is this fate?" you hiccupped. "Am I doomed to mess up every good thing in my life?"

I forced down a few deep breaths until I could speak without laughing or sobbing. "I don't believe in fate," I said. "Fate is just an excuse lazy people use to avoid taking responsibility for their choices."

You sniffled and smiled. "I like you," you said. You linked your fingers with mine. "I like you a lot."

I closed the distance between us and kissed you again. "I like you a lot," I said.

"We were doing better in the alley," you said. "Come outside with me until we get caught? You can bring your coat this time."

7.

Jamie stands and crosses his arms. "You won't do it." His voice is steady. He isn't yelling anymore. "You won't walk out on Annabelle."

I laugh sharply. "Why not? Men walk out on their families all the time."

The words taste bitter in my mouth. I take a deep breath and change course, walking back toward the kitchen.

"What are you doing?"

"Making breakfast for Annabelle."

He follows me. "This is the right thing, Mary."

I click on the gas stove. The burner flames a searing blue.

"You can't go back, you know." He rests his big hands on the counter, fingers splayed, trapping me in the corner by the stove. I can barely move my arm in a wide enough circle to scoop the pancake batter into the pan.

"Those other timelines were erased the second we left them," he says. "Everything you shared with that woman is gone. She won't know you if you find her." He grabs my forearm and squeezes so hard that I drop the spatula. "Will you stop for a moment and listen to me? This is important."

"Let go." I try to pull my arm away, and he tightens his grip.

"I've learned from my mistakes and grown into a better man because of you." He presses his body against mine, bracing himself against the counter with his free hand. The hard marble digs sharply into my lower back. I can't breathe.

"Jamie, back up. Please." I need air, and he's so much bigger than me, and he won't let me go.

He'll never let me go.

"I've given you everything you asked for, everything you needed, even when you didn't know you needed it yet."

And everything he's given me—his lies, my headaches, our beautiful child, this gilded cage we live in—will tether me to him whether I walk out that door or not. And he knows it.

"Mary?" His lips curl into a boyish half-smile.

Unless—

My heart pounds so hard that I can hear the blood rushing in my ears. I reach behind me, feel for the familiar edge of the wooden block. And then I pull the carving knife from its slot and slam it down on the counter. The knife slices through his fingers with a thud and then clicks against the marble.

He shrieks, releasing my arm and crumbling to the floor. He leaves his severed fingers on the counter by the mixing bowl.

I pick up Jamie's ring finger with a shaky hand. It's slick with blood, and the wedding band slides off easily.

"My God, Mary!" Jamie sobs and curls his body around his wrecked hand. "What are you doing?"

I pull my wedding band from my pocket and slip it back on.

I push his ring onto my middle finger and flip him the bird. "Erasing this timeline," I say.

My stomach lurches.

The kitchen falls away and I plummet through harsh white space. I tumble, heavy, accelerating too quickly.

A bright, searing pain behind my eyes.

The sharp scent of burning hair.

A ripping sensation as twenty years of life are shorn from me, layer by layer: Jamie, Annabelle, love, fear, guilt, resentment. Every beauty and every horror equally excruciating as they tear away.

And then—weightlessness. Humming warmth. I shut my eyes and savor the slow, steady beat of my heart.

My feet find the earth. I open my eyes and take back my life.

1.

I FINISH MY story. The sun is starting to set over the tulip garden, and the cool breeze prickles my arms. I imagine the truth I've loosed skimming across the rows of purple flowers and vanishing over the horizon, free. I should feel relieved, but a tight, stuck feeling hardens in my chest. I'm not ready to look at you, but I can hear you breathing beside me, steady and even.

"Bit much for a first date, huh?" I ask with a strangled laugh.

You don't say anything, but you also don't leave.

I extend my hand and peer between my fingers to watch the colors shift over the horizon from soft pink to flaming orange. My two gold rings shimmer in the sunset glow.

And then you catch my hand and lace your fingers through mine, running your thumb across the rings. My pulse quickens at your touch, same as always. My need to hold you, to *have* you is an unbearable ache, but this has to be your choice.

My eyes find yours.

"So, what happens next?"

ALL THE TIME IN THE WORLD AND NONE AT ALL

Allison Pottern

January 1, 2006

12:01 am

The time traveler was late.

3:05 am

Sometimes he finds himself staring at the sky and forgetting what time he's in. Haze, cloud, stars. Sometimes it seems he can feel the earth turning beneath his feet, time unspooling around him. One moment, he's in his hometime, sweating in his winter gear, waiting for his transfer. Now here he is in a New York City that no longer exists, skyscrapers looming up around him, slush in the streets. Then he is 18,000 years ago, when there is no calendar. Only ice, a thousand feet thick.

::

The doctor was in her office, despite the federal holiday, the abysmal hour, and the ludicrousness of being in work heels in the middle of the night. Her husband had long since stopped asking about her strange habit of "taking space" on New Year's Eve and much of the following day, because she rarely asked for it otherwise.

A travel mug of black coffee cooled on her desk. The lamp beside her chair filled the room with a warm glow and the small couch for patients sat empty and expectant. She had already watered all the plants in her little office, rearranged her desk, shuffled her notes. The time traveler only came for an appointment once a year and she was determined to be professional. If not, she might lose her damn mind.

3:30 am

Some partiers still stagger through the winter-dark streets, confetti scuttling in the gutters, the sky coal-gray with cloud. The time traveler walks with his face wrapped tight against the icy wind, hands shoved into his coat pockets. He's survived much colder; had just returned from the Pleistocene, where he'd only lost the tip of an ear to frostbite. He'd come to love the cracked-ice color of the sky back then; the deep, guttural creak and groan of the glaciers; the crystal-clean wind. He'd gotten a commendation for that tour.

The doctor's building is up ahead on the right, all steel and concrete; its windows blank, black mirrors. Two young women in high heels, puffy jackets, and short skirts brush past him, laughing. Their hair smells of perfume and champagne. They seem so very much alive.

He knows better.

::

If the time traveler showed up, this would be their fifth session. The doctor kept careful notes, though she was pretty sure the time traveler himself would disapprove. She wrote them up after each session, then set them aside so she could focus on the rest of her patients, on her marriage, on her real life. Until the dark gutter of the year came around and she couldn't help but pull out those frantic scratchings and pore over them for clues to her own sanity. All the notes were in her handwriting, on the notepaper she preferred, but the words felt alien. A little like the time traveler himself.

3:40 am

When the time traveler was taught temporal theory as a fresh-faced guppy at the Time Center, the instructors used the metaphor of time as an ocean. They could track travelers through the waters of time, they explained, using individuals' unique time signatures. Like tracking whales by their individual songs across the ocean depths. Meaning: someone is always watching.

The more the time traveler learns about time, however, the less the metaphor makes any sense. Not that he'd even known what a whale was back then. Now he knows and the metaphor still doesn't, well, hold water. But it taught him one thing: that no analogy—or system—is perfect.

Like sonar, when too close to an electro-magnetic field, the temporal tracking system is subject to interference. The turnover of the year in these centuries with global time zones is exceptionally prone to noise, especially this close to the turn of the millennium. Which means that, if he travels to the Eastern Seaboard of the United States between midnight and 05:00 EST on New Year's Day, especially in the early 2000s, his already-hard-to-read time signature should be invisible.

But he has never calibrated his own transfer without a pre-assigned target lock, and he overshot his target. Right day, right city, six years and a couple hours late. At least he is still in the interference window. Not bad for a first try.

He walks up to the front door of the doctor's office building and places a trembling hand on the door. Next time he travels here, he'll find a way to convince the doctor to see him. He hopes that can be soon, because he feels as if he's either sinking or dissolving—he's not sure which.

But, for now, the sooner he can return to his hometime and confirm he's left no trace of this transfer, the better.

Very little surprises the time traveler anymore. But he does not expect the door to the office building to be unlocked.

3:50 am

The time traveler arrived, finally, in her doorway. He seemed hesitant, surprised, and much neater than previous years—a white man in a dark coat, his face wind-burned, his rust-colored hair combed back. His gray scarf was draped around his neck and, most shockingly, his full beard was gone. It made him look younger than she would have guessed. He pulled his hands from his pockets and the breath went out of her.

Damaged ear and missing first two knuckles of ring finger, left side, she'd written. She'd just read it, on the very first page of her notes. It was a detail she remembered year to year with great clarity; the story he'd told of how he'd lost the finger to the ice, while drumming his four remaining digits on his knee. She looked to his ear. Still ragged, like an alley cat who'd been in a fight. But his left hand was whole. Which could only mean one thing.

"How long has it been for you since we last met?" she asked automatically, before he could ask, before she dared say anything else.

"Never," he said, stepping cautiously into her office. His accent, always strange and unplaceable, was more pronounced than ever. "Or, I should say, this seems to be my first time meeting you."

January 1, 2007

12:02 am

She could hold both ideas in her mind: existing in a reality where time travel did not exist, was in fact irrelevant; and that, in a tiny, pocket dimension of a single day, once a year, time travel was very real. The mind was capable of all kinds of compartmentalization, could bend to accept even the most abnormal circumstances as a given. She'd encountered patients who lived so deep inside illusions, that only medication and intensive rehabilitation could peel away the protective layers of self-deception.

Was she falling into the same trap? She'd decided it didn't matter, couldn't matter. It was Schrodinger's Box, like the curled question growing in her belly. A person and a non-person; a fullness made of light and possibility; a present and a future, neither entirely knowable. Impossible to look at too closely without everything falling apart.

Of course, the man she counseled on New Year's Day was a time traveler. Of course, there was no such thing as time travel.

Either way, it provided plenty of fodder for sessions with her own psychotherapist.

He staggered in, looking haunted, exhausted, hair in disarray like he'd run here. She couldn't tell the status of his fingers without staring at his clenched fists, pressing down on his knees. His coat was black, for once, not gray. Last year, he had been all nervous energy. This year he was silent, except he claimed it had only been a week for him, since they'd met in 2006. She wondered where—or, sure, *when*—he had been.

::

The time traveler has just come from his parent's funeral.

He had been in the ice age for nearly six months, while in his hometime, mere moments had passed. Sometime, between the yawning maw of frigid days and a handful of heartbeats, his parent, whom he hadn't spoken to in three years hometime, died quietly in their sleep.

Three years of silence might as well be a lifetime. Now his parent has been dead for two weeks and also six months and will be dead forever and yet, here in the doctor's time, is not yet born. Still, somehow, time continues to flow over them both in a never-ending stream. One he is allowed to swim in, but his parent is not.

Others had made his parent's post-mortem arrangements, while he had scavenged time for someone, anyone, to talk to. And now he doesn't know what to say.

The doctor watches him with an open face. No edge of expectation or eagerness, just calm, patient eyes, hands draped gently in her lap. Like she has all the time in the world to wait for him to speak. As if she isn't also, already, dead.

At the Time Center he can't speak like that. Talk of ghosts is something they all think about, but never discuss. It would get him slashed from the deep time project. He would be sent straight into therapeutic neuroplastic treatment—"brain massage" as they call it—and restricted to the Anthropocene. Or, even more likely, benched from travel indefinitely.

So he's comes here, to her. To find his way through the ghosts and back to…what? Or is it when?

He sits silently, beneath the doctor's gentle gaze. And, this time, that is enough.

January 1, 2008

12:00 am

She secretly hoped he wouldn't come.

But here he was, looking as wrung-out as she felt. He was looking far less funereal, but his usual gray coat was wrinkled, and his beard short and unkempt. He drummed five fingers on his knee. Maybe they'd have another silent session and just stare into their own thoughts for the next three hours. She didn't mind that. She'd been living in that space a lot lately.

If he hadn't come, she would have had a quiet, dark morning to sob into her patients' couch. Her husband was getting tired of her sobbing, so the privacy would have been welcome for them both. She knew she needed to fill the prescription her psychotherapist had written for her, but the sad place she was in was also comforting, in a way. Heavy, muffled, so she didn't have to move or hear or speak.

Their fertility specialist said it would all take time. Schrodinger's box had been Pandora's all along.

After three failed embryo transfers in a year and a half, her husband was ready to give up. He wanted to travel—to Thailand, to Tibet. She worked harder, took on more clients to cover mounting medical costs. *Why do you keep putting yourself through this?* he asked, sometimes in accusation, sometimes in pity. She tried to feel something for her husband in those moments, but it was hard. All she had left was grief. And hope.

::

The Center has been sending him on short transfers.

Short transfers should be easy. A day of observation and recording, two at most. Half-drowned London in 2133, to witness the first introduction of extra-terrestrial flora, a not-quite-algae, that would eventually re-oxygenate the dying ocean. 1657 on the North

American continent, observing herds of American Bison prior to their near extinction. Pompeii, in late August of 79 BCE in the days after the volcano, the ash still settling. And half a dozen more. They're testing him, but he's not sure for what. He should feel something, in these moments. Awe, maybe, or at the very least pride. He used to feel that way, didn't he? Instead, he does his job and feels nothing. Or, only slightly better: dread.

He knows it shows on his face when the doctor asks how he's been. What can he say?

"I've been traveling," he answers. "It's been hard."

"Tell me," she says. And he does.

January 1, 2009

1:15 am

"You talk a lot about what you miss from your work in the ice age," the doctor said. They had, in fact, been talking about the Pleistocene for nearly an hour. Again. "But you don't often talk about your hometime."

The time traveler sat spine straight, hands clenched in his lap. She wondered if his posture was a commentary on her new couch. "There is not much to miss. I was recruited from an early age," he said. "My hometime…it is in some ways even less real to me than the other times I visit. There is little waiting for me in my present, except the means to return to the past, to the things that do have meaning."

The things that have meaning: her infant daughter's tiny hand clenched around her finger and the sweet smell of her head. The timelessness of sleep-deprivation. The small hollow of terror and joy that lived behind her sternum, always. The soreness in her breasts knowing she'd need to excuse herself, eventually, to pump milk for her baby.

"There's talk that they might send me into deep time again. Back to the glaciers." He looked up at her, his face eager, desperate. "But I'm not sure I'm ready."

It took everything she had to resist looking at his hand.

Her breasts hurt. Her head hurt. "What do you think it will take to make you feel ready for your next deep dive?" she asked.

"To just be able to feel *something*," he said, his voice cracking. And put his head in his hands.

::

He tries to find a way to ground himself, like the doctor taught. Five things he sees: the spider plant on the doctor's desk; the dark circles under her eyes; the familiar seaside painting on her wall; her brown hands sitting loosely in her lap; his own cuticles, bitten to the quick. Four things he hears: music from somewhere outside her building; the ticking of a clock; her breath; his own. Three things he feels: his heartbeat, like he is being chased; the scratchy fabric of the ugly, new sofa; the hunger in his gut. Two things he smells: the slightly burnt scent of the space heater; his own sweat. The one thing he tastes: bitterness.

January 1, 2010

12:00 am

They are sending him back.

They are sending him back to the Pleistocene, but further: 36,000 years ago for this tour. There is non-stop training, environmental and temporal resistance work in preparation. No one has said anything, but he understands that this trip is a steppingstone. If he can survive 36,000 years, there will be little to stop them sending him deeper: 100,000 years, 200,000. At those depths the temporal pressure changes don't fluctuate significantly until closer to a million years. Even that is in their sights, he can tell. This is what he's wanted, been working towards. But he feels constantly nauseous, and he isn't sure if it's the medical treatments, high-intensity training, or the existential dread.

It's risky, fitting in another appointment so soon after the previous, especially for safe dates drifting further from the year 2000. But his deep transfer is scheduled for two weeks and the doctor hasn't fixed him yet. He doesn't know what else to do.

∷

Part of her had thought he wouldn't come.

Her notes from last year had been longer than usual, more convoluted, full of speculation about their disparate positions in time. She had become more and more convinced that his next appointment would be with a *previous* version of herself, that the journey he was about to embark on was one she had already helped him process, or at least tried to.

But here he was, looking so ill she almost reached out to help him sit. But they'd never touched, not even to shake hands, and she didn't dare test either of them. Instead, she handed him a bottle of water. He gulped it down.

"I'd like us to take a slightly different direction today," she said, before he'd come up for air. "I want to understand what drew you to time travel in the first place, so maybe we can connect that to the choices you're making now."

His pasty forehead glistened with sweat. "I told you, I was recruited," he said.

"Recruitment requires consent. But you were so young. Do you think you understood what being recruited to the Time Center meant?"

He sat still for so long, she wondered if her question had registered. Finally, he said: "I thought I did. The Center said I was made for the work—I have a time signature impression score near zero. That's rare and ideal for travel. It means there's hardly any chance my actions will affect the time currents." He fell silent for a moment, took another sip of his water. "They promised adventure. Being part of the long arc of history. They were not lying. But they did not tell us what we would miss, living outside our own time."

Made for the work, she noted. "It sounds lonely," she said. He flinched, the water bottle crunching in his hand.

"I suppose it is. But I like being alone," he said.

"Lonely and alone are not always the same thing," she said, closing her eyes for a moment, pulling her thoughts together. Her own lonely places sat heavily inside, the grinding away of her self in the face of parenthood; her child climbing all over her, never leaving her alone; the way she and her husband never laughed together anymore. She'd been marooned by all the things she'd wanted—motherhood, her marriage, this life.

Sometimes, when her daughter was screaming or she'd had a particularly difficult session or she found herself wandering the house helpless with insomnia, she thought about the time traveler, alone, struggling against the currents of time to reach her in the past. It gave her strength, in those moments, to comfort her daughter, her patient, herself. She may be just one small pebble in a vast ocean. But she was also a destination. The currents had to move *around* her.

"It sounds like you are resigned to your role at the Time Center," she continued, opening her eyes. She had to push him. "But if you truly feel you don't make an impression on the world around you, then why do you choose to be here?"

12:15 am

Choice, the time traveler thinks, that's the thing. Time travel does not account for an individual's wants or needs. It dilutes them, neutralizes them. All you can do is hold your breath; hope you don't get pulled under.

"I'm here," he says, anger building in him, "because you're like me. Hardly any impression score to speak of. You don't make a difference either." He practically spits the words, and he knows his rage is not at her, but at the currents he can feel beneath the surface of reality, even here, taunting him.

But her expression is smooth-water calm. She's waiting for him to continue, and he hates himself.

"Do you remember what I said?" he says, trying to make her understand. "About whales?"

"Time travelers are like whales in an ocean of time, yes," she says, nodding.

"That's something The Center gets wrong," he says. "Whales can withstand drastic changes in pressure. Human bodies aren't built to dive through deep layers of time. Doing so is difficult and dangerous.

It requires training and careful return procedures. Not everyone can do it."

"Like decompression sickness," she murmurs. "But you can? Survive it?"

The sun glinting off a glacier, as far as the eye can see. "Yes."

"So, you are making an impact at your job. That's making an impression, isn't it?"

"You don't get it," he says, through clenched teeth. "Flailing around in deep time makes no impression on today. Time may not really be an ocean, but it is vast. And someone like me—like us—can't do anything to move it."

::

She had to start thinking like a time traveler.

In their first session, he had said to her *I need help learning how to change*. But that was a future-him, one who'd gone into the ice age a second time and returned one finger short. That version of him knew what he needed because of what they talked about now. She felt the years of their sessions pile up behind her like dominoes ready to fall.

"But we're not in deep time," she pointed out, "We're right here, right now. And even so, the information you bring back, that can affect your tomorrow." She scooted to the edge of her chair. "Choice is not just an either/or. Even if you feel you don't have a choice, you get to decide what to do with the consequences, with the outcome, how you feel about it, how you allow it to help you grow. Growth is change," she said, leaning back. "And you do that every time you come to my office."

The time traveler's face was a mask of grief. It was an expression she recognized from the mirror. The babies that never were, the kind of marriage she used to have, or maybe only dreamed she'd had. The time traveler had lost someone and in that losing, had lost himself.

"Your parent, the one who passed," she began, quietly. "Their death was outside of your control. Can you choose to change that?" The time traveler looked away; his whole body curled around the heart he wanted to protect.

"No," he whispered.

Time comes for us all, eventually.

"We may not be able to change everything about our pasts. Maybe not even our present. But you *can* choose to connect with your present," the doctor said. "And you can choose how to heal for the future."

January 1, 2000

4:30 am

Y2K has not killed her. In fact, while everyone around her had scream-counted down to what could have been Armageddon but wasn't, the associate had kissed a man she'd only just met. He was Pakistani too and had a nice laugh. She thought she might want to kiss him again. She was ready to be over her ex-boyfriend already, out of this vortex of self-loathing. It was a new millennium. She'd kissed a stranger and stayed up the whole night. Anything was possible.

It was stupid early, but there was a vibration to the city, beneath the sharp, winter darkness. Gold and silver confetti clung to her boots. The only places open were the street carts selling super-heated diesel fuel, but that was what she needed. The vendor handed her a cup of hot black coffee, just in time for her to nearly collide with another customer.

"Doctor?" the person said.

"Associate," she responded, reflexively, her stomach tightening. She was still learning how uncomfortable it could become when a client, outside of the office, realized just how much she knew about them and how little they knew about her. Her mind flicked through the rolodex of her and her boss's white, male patients, but couldn't come up with a match.

"Sorry," she said, trying to make light of the moment. "It's always so hard to recognize people when we're all bundled up. Have we met?"

"No, I must have been mistaken," he said. He had a slight accent she couldn't place, but she could hear a smile in his voice. "I've gotten ahead of myself. Could you direct me to Times Square?"

"It's gonna be a mess, even now," she said. "You sure?" A tourist then, grappling for a piece of history.

"I've been through worse," he said, with a shrug. She thought she could detect a beard under all that scarf. "Can you point me in the right direction?"

"Happy to help," she said, with a smile.

758995.023345 Ω

00::17::85

The director stands in front of his childhood home. The tropical heat makes him ache for ice.

Before his sessions with the doctor, he could not have managed a trip to this time and place. Experience for one thing, and Time Center policy. But with a life full of deep time transfers, he's learned to read and ride the currents, even when they're all tangled like this. He also knows that people tend to look the other way, when you're the one running the Time Center, if you need to make a little visit to your own past. As long as there's no insider trading.

He can almost hear his younger self's heartbeat, in his childhood bedroom, stuttering with the fear of his upcoming first, real, transfer. Or maybe it's the rapid fire of his own, old man's heart.

The director puts a splayed hand to the front door. Above, the sky is a thick, mottled haze, ripe with the colors of sunrise. From inside comes thin strands of music; his parent, alive and well, with only a thin door between them. It is a song he remembers. It is a song he is hearing for the first time.

30 Ma

DAWN

He stands on a beach, a temperate one for once, the midnight sun at his back. Give it another 20 million years and this too will be ice. The ice always comes back.

Wind whips around him, the water churning into white caps, as he holds the scope to his eyes. Out in the newly minted Southern Sea, he sees them, a small pod of early mysticeti, their grey bodies surfacing with a burst of spray and tail. He's been tracking them for the duration of his tour here, which is almost complete.

He wades into the water deep enough to release the hydrophones. They will dissolve in a matter of hours, leaving no trace, but in the meantime, he'll be able to listen to and record the calls of these magnificent beasts. Almost done. Then he can go home.

He pushes out into the water and rolls onto his back. Floating relieves some of the ache in his bones. The ocean is so frigid, churned up from the depths, that he can feel it through his chronosuit. Deliciously, glacially cold.

Already, the hydrophones are picking up a song beneath the waves, a call and response. Two beings reaching out across a vastness until, for a moment, their ripples touch.

12 HOURS TO ANOESIS

Avani Vaghela

07:03 EST / 12:03 UTC

```
Dear Operative of the National Service
for Data Retention and Reclamation:
By 00:00 UTC on 01/01/2053, over 90%
of civilians and Operatives will lose
COMPLETE ACCESS to any data stored in
either their brains or their implanted
Augment Drives. This is irreversible
and final. Please direct questions and
feedback to the SDR_Admin channel. We
are online to answer your questions
and help you during this transition.
— Pygmalion, on behalf of the SDRR IT
Staff.
```

VISHAKA'S GUT TOLD her the message was real. For one, it was cryptographically signed, and the key checked out. Forging a message from the Service was possible but would require about five years and 10 million dollars of effort. While the public charter of the Service made them out to be diplomats with very good memories, it was an open secret that the operatives' extra large, high performance augment drives made them ideal spies and data mules. The Service cared about opsec. The skin above her eyes tensed, pulling at her nose. 00:00UTC was 12 hours from now. 12 hours to global anoesis. 12 hours before the world reset.

Vishaka, the accidental adult in the room, carefully docked her console, stepped over to the living room, slipped out of her flats, lay on her kitchen floor, and cried.

8:30 EST / 13:30 UTC

"Aloe, Teak, Minnow, Mercedes, Obake. Pygmalion. Aloe, Teak, Minnow, Mercedes, Obake. Pygmalion."

An answering machine for the Service repeated the list of agent names, followed by the Service's head of IT, on every line she called.

Aloe was Vishaka's codename. She didn't know Teak, Minnow, or Mercedes, and her last contacts for Obake were a defunct chat room and a P.O. Box in Cabo. There were generally about 25 active Agents at the service at any time, scattered around the world, and she didn't immediately see why the 5 of them were singled out. She pulled her console from its cradle and laid it on her grandmother's antique oak table, the centerpiece of her paisley and linoleum war room. She shook two amphetamine pills out of the bottle she'd set aside for emergencies, chugged them down with Sunny D, and logged in to the Service admin channel.

```
>> ALOE:  I would like a global
agent status.
                << ADMIN_BOT: Welcome Aloe. I am
                glad to see you. You, Teak, Argent,
                Minnow, and Obake have logged into
                SDRR systems in the past 72 hours.
                Other agents are presumed non-
                functional at this time.
```

It was pointless to accuse a bot of being cold, so she instead did her best to reflect the bot's self-composure.

```
>> ALOE: Please define
'non-functional'
                << ADMIN_BOT: Agents Willow,
                Magnolia, Heron, Burkin, Gadfly,
                Antimony, Pike, Rowan, and Ash are
                confirmed to have suffered full
                memory corruption. Their bodies
                have been collected, and their
                implants have been repatriated to
                our facility for diagnosis. The
                remainder are presumed corrupted
                but have not yet been recovered.
```

"Recovered", "Repatriated." Artificial synaptic ribbons threaded through the brains of new augment patients within weeks of implantation, the existing connections turning from scaffold to skeleton. The drives were as indelible as the data they were designed to store.

Vishaka's shaking hand knocked over her tea mug. The Service had killed at least 9 agents. Likely would kill more. Likely would kill her when she was blank and couldn't understand what was happening. She could picture Magnolia, sitting on the floor with her big eyes and wild curls, looking up at the men who would have, what? *Oh God. They couldn't retrieve data if they shot her. Neurotoxins were out. Brain cells die really fast no matter what...* Vishaka threw up. These were—had been her friends. And if she didn't want to join them, she had to throw everything she had at the next 10 hours.

```
>> ALOE: Can corruption be avoided?
                << ADMIN_BOT: All users who
                applied yesterday's automatic
                update are vulnerable to the
                corruption introduced by the cls2
                security patch.
>> ALOE: Who has this patch?
```

```
                << ADMIN_BOT: 99.9926% of users are
                known affected.
>> ALOE: Am I affected?
                << ADMIN_BOT: Yes.
```

Vishaka felt foolish for having held any hope that somehow, miraculously, her update hadn't gone through. All augment drive companies relied on the same hacked together open source library, so of course she was affected—everyone was. She took a rag from under the sink and, with a blank expression, cleaned up the vomit from the floor.

She had to assess the situation, calm nerves, and then come up with a plan to save humanity. Vishaka needed to gather her resources. Her next step was to reach out to an expert on neural memory interfaces. She texted Pygmalion.

10:30 EST / 15:30 UTC

Brunch was a welcome respite from thoughts of dead friends and imminent loss of self. Vishaka sat at her table picking at leftover sauerkraut from New Years' with rotis she'd made that morning, before the news broke, and washed it down with a bottle of Jack Daniels she pulled from the stack in her oven. She'd failed to contact any of her colleagues at the Service, including Pyg. She needed another backup plan, in case she couldn't find the error and fix the code in the next 9 hours. What minimum knowledge would she need to have to survive? She started a list, loading data into her augment as she went:

1. "Making roti"
    1.1 "How to make flour"
        1.1.1 "How to grow grain"
            1.1.1.1 "Kreb's Cycle"

Restoring the world was going to be turtles all the way down. She didn't have time for this. She had to try loading it all in anyway. She started with a few classic resources. Scouting manuals. The Long Now disc. Werner's "Where There Is No Doctor". For the rest, she'd have to think of every edge case. She would also need to do a lot of shopping in the next few hours.

12:15 EST / 17:15 UTC

OPTION 1: SHE needed to figure out how that tiny bit of new code corrupted her augment drive's neural interface and, from there, reverse or at least halt the effect.

Option 2: She needed to squirrel away as much knowledge as possible, and come up with a plan to automatically structure and disseminate it, to rebuild modern civilization.

AUGMENT DRIVES WERE essential to operate in the modern world. One of the biggest wins of the Cortez presidency had been full government support for early data augments for all schoolchildren, so that the poor weren't forced to memorize times tables while wealthy children blinked twice to store them indelibly. A tiny drive, even 128GB, was enough to store 4 full copies of Wikipedia as memories, with space left over for 4 copies of the complete Shakespeare to fill in the cracks. People who had grown up with augments tended to not know how to remember anything "by hand", saving neural memory for those episodic interactions that non-consensually sear themselves into the psyche. Augments integrated brilliantly with the brain, but needed a constant update stream to function with external apps.

NONE OF THE employees she'd reached out to at MindMeld or Sykilink, the two companies that made augment apps, responded. Likely they ate their own dog food, and applied their patches earlier, so they were already out of commission. She needed other agents. She poured the dregs of the bottle of Jack in her tea and opened her console:

```
>> Aloe: Vishaka Wilson ,17060 12th
St, King George's County, VA 22485.
+1.540.663.1632
```

Vishaka let out a breath she hadn't realized she'd been holding as she transmitted her contact details to the SDR general chat. Her cover was blown for the next nine and a half hours, but it was the best chance for other agents to find her. She could make all of the plans, but she had priorities. Let them save the others: she was doing the world a favor by finding them. She needed to focus.

On to option 2. Rebuilding the corpus of civilization could also use other agents. Compared to civilians, agents had incredibly large, secure augment drives: at least a terabyte, roughly 200,000 books at 200 pages each. A pair of agents could interface and quickly access each other's repositories. Three, and they'd have a cluster capable of rebooting the anthropocene. *It may also be good to have some backup.*

13:00 EST / 18:00 UTC:

Vishaka had been calling Pygmalion every hour, on the hour. This time, someone picked up Pyg's phone. The voice sounded like hers. It made a series of sounds and cries but no words.

"Hello?, Hello?"

The voice responded, "Haaoh," creaking into sounds worn and unfamiliar.

"Pyg. Pyg!…Marissa. This is Vishaka."

"Mris," the voice tested, trying to recover a memory

"Ma—Ri—Sa. Marissa. That's you." Vishaka started switching to video, but realized that there was no way Pyg would be able to give permission on her end, and thought better of it.

"I'm so sorry, Pyg," Vishaka said as she hung up.

Vishaka's heart burned. Vishaka imagined Pyg in her 10th-floor penthouse, surrounded by appliances with tastefully hidden controls and a few days' worth of organic produce, unable to recognize an elevator or toilet. Unable to remember her medications. Pyg would likely be dead in a week. Vishaka could save her if she flew right now.

She wasn't going to.

She justified her choice with how little time there was left and how much good she could do, and she tried not to think about how she'd feel if she didn't suspect that, at some level, this was all Pyg's fault. She'd met Pygmalion while working on hypnosis in the Service. Vishaka had been unsuccessful in controlling the test subjects, and Pyg had come in to make them forget everything they heard or said in a session. She started meeting Pyg for lunch after that, listening to her stories of engineers and databases and badly misconfigured programs. She'd had a vague notion of what Pyg did day-to-day, but beyond Pyg occasionally asking to update her systems by hand, they didn't talk about details much. Now, she had a guess as to why.

With Pygmalion out of the picture, trying to fix the code and save everyone's memories felt increasingly distant. Vishaka looked at her lists. If she really had to basically restart civilization alone, she would need supplies.

She turned back to her data-list and wrote:
    107. Supplies from the Before Times
        107.1 Water
        107.2 Food
            107.2.1 Camping meals
            107.2.2 Iodized Salt
        107.2.3 Twinkies
            …

Half an hour later, armed with every credit card she could dig up, she hailed a cab to town.

End of the world blues: meet shopping therapy.

15:07 EST / 20:07 UTC :
She parked the rented U-Haul full of camping food, multivitamins, wine, water, and other supplies in her backyard and recruited a neighbor to help carry her haul. A stop at the library had netted her more field medical guides, a Boy Scouts' handbook, several pictographic

"learn to read" primers, and a book about edible plants for wilderness survival. A base town in Virginia was probably not the wilderness the authors had in mind, but it was something.

After cleaning out a grocery store, she'd stopped at a military surplus store and bought most of their inventory, including as many blankets and first aid kits as she could get her hands on. Then, it was time for downtown. She was generous with luxuries: cashmere socks, a Dutch oven that cost more than she made in a week, boxes and boxes of overpriced tea, and the piece de resistance: an Eames lounger, complete with the footstool. Tomorrow, she'd have no credit card bill or late fees, and she intended to enjoy it.

15:30 EST / 20:30 UTC :

A CALL CAME in from a blocked number. A thin, tinny voice identified to the screener as "Minnow to Aloe."

"Are you calling regarding M. Valdemar?" Vishaka called back and asked.

"I'm sorry to inform you he has died".

Having received the expected response from Minnow, Vishaka threw herself into a dining chair and exhaled. "Hi, Minnow, nice to meet you. I've got a plan."

"We don't have much time."

"I know. Do you know what happened?"

"The Service happened. Pygmalion happened." Minnow had a way of ending every word a note higher than he started, which sounded to Vishaka like a 6-year-old child attempting a serious conversation.

"How?"

"They apparently restarted work on the Hypoxaria protocol four months ago."

"How? How was this not all over the Service?"

The line dropped for a moment into garbled static.

"Our job is to keep secrets, and Pygmalion is a *damned* good memory engineer. The Service hired them to modulate people like us. Our memories are deep, perfect, and last forever. Don't you think the Service would have made sure they could change those memories if they needed to? Are all new agents this goddamned naïve?"

Listening to Minnow swear reminded Vishaka of an irate chipmunk. "I just called Pyg, Minnow. They're completely out of commission. They didn't do this on purpose."

Minnow continued: "Let me spell it out for you. Your pal was trying to delete something from all of our brains, they fucked up, and now everyone, even civilians, is about to have their memories wiped."

"What were they trying to delete?"

"Something that doesn't fucking matter, Aloe, unless we fix this in the next two hours."

Vishaka bit her knuckle. Having Minnow was better than not having him. She had to come up with a plan. Fast. Two agents gave her possibilities she should have thought through earlier. Minnow was a resource, and she needed all the resources she could gather.

"Here's the plan. I've put pictographic instructions for loading data from our consoles onto our drives. I'm planning to be staring at it when the clock hits. You need to, too. We can't read our own data, but we can read each other. I'm putting together a database that will give us enough to start with to re-learn language and reading and some basic survival from there. I'll send it to you when I'm done in case you have any requests."

"What language?"

"Just English. Sorry. I was short on time, and it's the most useful. No reason we can't get the rest back eventually, but we'll start here."

Vishaka felt a thrill at her decisiveness. Now, she was responsible for both of them, and Minnow was falling in line.

"One more thing, Minnow. Have you contacted anyone else?"

"I have. Teak is holed up with his kids and wants the whole Service to go fuck itself. I haven't found Mercedes or Obake. You still haven't asked the important question, you know."

"I haven't? What is it?"

"If Pygmalion is brain-wiped already, who made the recording?"

16:20 EST / 21:20 UTC:

There wasn't much more prep to do. She'd uploaded her library haul into the database and supplemented it by downloading all the baby books she could find. Her English would suffer for a bit, but she would be able to talk about farm animals and fire trucks. One of those two may come in handy. Minnow had grudgingly agreed to meet her on base a half hour before erasure to do the data share and, ideally, kick-start Anthropocene 2.0. Her brother had left his dorm and would be home with their parents, safe, in half an hour. The generators she had bought for her parents and herself had been delivered and installed, a testament to the quality of service an open checkbook can buy. She had sent her brother instructions to set it up, and programmed the house displays to screen her Survival 101 on loop when the time came.

Vishaka sat slumped over her makeshift kitchen war room, paper cups emptied of coffee and burrito wrappers surrounding her docked console and scattered handwritten notes. She felt like she should cook herself something while she still remembered how, but all of her spare motivation had drained into getting the database perfect. Minnow had asked for some frivolous additions; engineering diagrams, and advanced construction plans requiring dozens of directable workers to follow through on without reliable power. She badly needed to keep Minnow on board, though. Two agents working together could hold an entire library. They could travel from town to town, serving as preachers from a forgotten age, instructing the people on how to be human. She'd contacted the Service, and the bots were already busy setting up infrastructure. Autonomous cars a chargepoint apart, with destinations set, so no one had to know where to go or how they worked. Broadcasting devices. Food stores for the two of them to miraculously discover to win the peoples' trust. Vishaka was stunned at how quickly the Service had gotten through the logistics of putting this all in place.

MINNOW'S QUESTION LINGERED unbidden in her internal monologue. She didn't have time to solve a mystery. She had lists to make, instructions to record, and hieroglyphs to invent.

"Teak, Aloe, Minnow, Mercedes, and Obake. Pygmalion." Who made the recording? If the admins knew what agents were still active, they would just connect them directly. Pyg? Would she have put her own name at the end as a clue? Was it an apology?

VISHAKA REALIZED SHE needed to stop and focus on what mattered in the next 2 hours. She'd have time to worry about how they had gotten there if it still mattered in the morning. She pinned up her braid in a deft, practiced motion and plugged in her dataport to start a full data backup. Her console said it would take about half an hour. Trapped in her chair, she started ribbing what would now be a cropped sweater.

```
5.5:
Error. Data object <Hermione> could
not be transferred.
```

VISHAKA WAS DEEP in binding off her knitting when she heard the error tone in the back of her head. *I just checked for corrupt files last week.* She restarted the transfer, but the error came back up immediately. "Hermione." Pyg must have added the file to her last update. The only Hermiones she knew were Shakespeare and Harry Potter, and Pyg was definitely not a Potter fan. More mysteries that she didn't have time for. She looked at her watch, added the object to the skip list, and proceeded with the transfer.

17:00 EST / 22:00 UTC:

PHONE CALL FROM Pyg. It was a voice recording, with a standard Service anonymity filter. Timbre evened, tone normalized, accents shifted to NPR standard.

"Hello Aloe. I'm sorry, but it was my only way out."

Out of what? Vishaka wondered, hearing traces of desperation even in the heavily modularized voice.

"I thought we could stabilize the Hypoxaria protocol. It almost worked, but there was a bad update. Jeremy from the cls2 team caught on—it doesn't matter. Even if it wasn't my fault, I should have tested for it, worked around it. I had IT put a data blob in your and four other agents' brains. It's not a vaccine *per se*, but it'll keep any data on the drive part of your brain safe from the wipe. I changed the Service voicemail to the agent list so you can find each other."

This barely makes sense. I understand why she trusts me, but Minnow spoke like he didn't know her at all. And she hates Teak. Also, why wait until T-2 hours to tell us?

"You're too real to be my Galatea, so I called your blob Hermione." Pyg's voice broke on the recording. "I enjoyed those evenings when we'd drink too many daiquiris and argue about Proust. It was nice having another lit nerd to talk to. Um, er, yeah. I'm sorry."

She seemed so achingly human for a moment that Vishaka wanted to believe her. Believe that this whole mess was a tragic case of hubris and bad dependency management. Believe that Pyg had actually been her friend.

"I never wanted to hurt any of you."

Click.

She was going to be fine.

Why was the Service stabilizing Hypoxaria?

She was going to be fine.

Vishaka gulped the remains of her cold coffee to clear the acrid taste rising in the back of her mouth. She was going to be absolutely fine. She'd be able to read, ravel to her parents and remember what was safe to eat. She would keep all of it.

The adrenaline that had fueled her since Pyg's notice this morning still reverberated, barely tethered, in her throat. The last 10 hours had been focused and dedicated, highways in the middle of the night. Now, time had snapped back to the infinite, and every path forward was a buzzing cloud of possibility. She needed a new plan. She had four agents, a few scattered cultists, and kids under 5 to rebuild civilization with. That was a much better scenario than she'd been planning for.

Why was the Service stabilizing Hypoxaria?

17:40 EST/ 22:40 UTC

"Minnow, I have some news."

"Is this about the message from Pygmalion?"

"She called you too?"

"Yea. It sounds like we all got a similar message. The Service wanted to keep an eye on its best agents. We each have a blob in our storage that'll counteract the virus. It's up to us to rebuild. About right?"

"Who else have you heard from?" Vishaka asked.

"Teak."

"Was he in a better mood once he found out he was keeping his memories?"

"No. Turns out saving him and not his family made him even angrier. He told me to go fuck myself. Same to you."

"Ok, I have a plan. We still both load ourselves with my info database. I just sent you the database and the route I mapped for you. You are going to start by teaching Service members to read, giving them the data, and then sending them out. I'm going to start by looking for survivors."

"People will die."

"I know. But more will die if we don't."

There was a pause on the line.

"What if, Pyg—," Minnow started.

"No. There isn't time to argue. We still need to move fast. Let's meet on base at 8 tonight. I'll get you started, then I'll head out."

Vishaka didn't wait for a reply before hanging up.

18:00 EST / 23:00 UTC:

One hour. She rechecked the recorder and set up a call with her parents, two of her father's sisters and their families, and the awake third of her extended polycule. This was her core. She told them what was about to happen. Her cousin Pratik laughed and walked out of frame.

Everyone else listened while she told them to copy down the pictographs she'd put together for accessing the main recordings she'd made. She didn't tell them how long she'd known. She didn't tell them that her memory wouldn't be wiped, out of both doubt and fear. Instead, she said she loved them. They said they loved her. They reminisced, savoring details anew, leaving out the callous words and infidelities now that past transgressions were on death's door.

Her father took over organizing the family, leaving Vishaka to sit back and revel in someone else leading a part of the charge. She slipped off the call without saying goodbye but left it recording so that she could play it back for them tomorrow when they didn't know her.

20:00 EST / 1:00 UTC

Vishaka walked into the Agent Briefing Center on base to find a tall, wide, dark-skinned person, more wall than man, waiting inside the doorway. Behind him were a dozen people working on their consoles, either at desks or in small clusters near the whiteboard.

"Minnow?"

They nodded. "Hi, Vishaka"

Vishaka looked haphazardly at the activity of the center. The people with Minnow weren't agents. She was certain of it, even if somehow they'd masked the telltale drive ports that protruded from the top of her and Minnow's spines.

"But…How?" Vishaka asked, with an unfocused gesture. "This wasn't my plan."

"No, it wasn't," Minnow sat down on the corner of the desk and reached back to pull a console off the dock. "I had the same amount of time to prep that you did. While you were busy playing Lone Ranger, I was tracking down why the Service was going after us in the first place. Look at this."

Vishaka pushed the console aside, "These people. What do they remember?"

Minnow smiled, clearly pleased with himself.

"Everything other than what was in their augment data cache. So, they've lost a few days, some work data, but nothing catastrophic."

"But—"

Anticipating her question, he continued, "I called engineers together from every neural startup and every professor I could find. They managed to build a patch that countered most of the data corruption The original issue was something about cache invalidation. The bug made it impossible to know what data was good or not, and they figured out how to mark the good data."

Vishaka had been standing perfectly still, long enough for her heel to start hurting, but her legs felt frozen.

"And…everyone else?"

"Our patch went out 2 hours ago. Apart from a handful of people who got early data corruption, everyone is okay."

Vishaka wilted into a chair. Minnow walked over and held out the console. "Are you ready to see why?"

"I should have done this," Vishaka said, ignoring him entirely. "I should have saved everyone."

Minnow knelt, "No. We saved ourselves."

Quietly, still kneeling, he held out the folded, rubberized glass book to her and said softly, "Look at the goddamn console, Vishaka."

Vishaka held the console tentatively, opened the panel, and started reading. Her eyes flickered over the text, then slowed to intent scanning, and then stopped moving altogether. The last lingering drops of the day's urgency were replaced by stillness. Vishaka was a statue, her chest moving in sporadic rasps as she remembered to breathe.

Minnow waited, watched, and finally said, "You wanted to save Pyg."

Vishaka stared in aphasic silence.

"Your heart was in the right place. You wanted to save them all."

"This says that Pyg had augment-dementia, Minnow. That means that their temporal brain cells were dead. I copied their entire augment to myself because I didn't trust anyone else to do their job. I had to become them. And me."

"And then you kept doing it."

"And then I kept doing it. "

Vishaka paused to reconstruct and continued, "And then I realized that if I wanted to stay sane while hosting the brains of so many other people in my augment, I needed to be able to partition my brain—to temporarily forget who I was. I'm the one who tried to restart the Hypoxaria project. I'm the one who did all of this. The data block Pyg sent—"

"You mean you, acting as Pygmalion, sent," Minnow interjected.

"Right. Sending the data block to the top agents was the backup plan." Vishaka was increasingly animated, pacing across the narrow conference room as she re-evaluated the situation.

"Do you remember anything about why?"

"I told you. I needed to temporarily forget the rest of the people I'd copied into my augment so that I could run whichever one I needed to."

"No, Aloe. Why did you restart one of the most dangerous experiments in Service history instead of just asking for help?"

"Because I'm the only one who could," Vishaka blurted.

"You couldn't, though, could you? You almost killed us all." Minnow said the words gently but with no comfort. "Thanks to you, though, we've managed to kickstart a whole new data-sharing scheme, complete with safeguards so no one can ever do what you did again. Welcome to the new and improved Service, Aloe."

"Call me Hermione."

FRACTURE
Melinda A. Smith

10.

THE SECOND-TO-LAST TIME I saw Dad, I was ten, wearing the Mickey Mouse shirt he'd bought me when I was six. It was way too small. Maybe even then I knew to cling to what I could.

Dad flung open the shutter-style closet doors and wrapped his large bear arms around all his clothes. He wrestled them out, bending the cheap metal hangers so their hooks straightened into daggers. I looked on, remembering him wrapping those arms around me.

He stuffed his clothes into trash bags. I stood in the bedroom doorway, shoulders hunched. Dad looked at me.

"Put on a shirt that fits. You look like a whore, like your mother."

I didn't know what a whore was, only that it was bad because of the way he spat it out. This was somehow my fault.

I froze when he stomped out, then scampered after him. Kids are like dogs. Even after you hurt them, all they want is your love.

I stood on our welcome mat and watched him drive away.

I wore my Mickey shirt for days. Mom didn't make me bathe.

THE LAST TIME I saw Dad, I was sixteen. By then, I knew what the word *whore* meant. But he'd sent a few birthday cards, so maybe he still wanted to see me.

Mom had just yelled at me about a boy I was dating.

"I don't think he's right for you," she said. "A girl should be with someone who treasures her."

I looked her square in the face and put my hands on my hips.

"How the hell would *you* know?"

Mom's eyebrows had been knit together. They released, and her eyes turned shiny with tears.

"I didn't mean—" I started to say. But it was too late. "Whatever."

I grabbed my purse and walked out.

The last card he sent me had a Staten Island address—a couple hours from Hoboken, if the trains were on time.

When I got there, I double-checked the envelope. The house's wood siding was rotted, chipping paint flecks over crabgrass. A hose sat out in the weak afternoon sun, leaking over the concrete path. My stomach turned. Did Dad really live here?

The car in the driveway had a Mets decal. It was Dad's house, alright. He was obsessed. I made a fist and banged on the door.

Grumbling and footsteps.

Dad opened the door. His graying beard had what looked like hot sauce in it.

"The fuck do you want?" He said, slurring.

I stood up straight and brushed my hair out of my eyes. Pulled the hem of my shirt down.

"Dad, it's me."

He squinted, and then let out a little breath. The corners of his mouth twitched upward. His arms lifted a little. He wanted to grab me into one of the bear hugs he used to do, squeezing me and lifting me to the sky. I know he did.

Instead, his arms fell.

"You look like her."

A stench filled the air. Something like vomit and the yeasty smell of old beer. I covered my mouth and nose.

The spark in his eyes vanished.

"You should go." His body was swaying.

"Dad, I thought we…You wanna get pancakes or something?"

"Pancakes? It's the middle of the fucking night."

I checked my watch. 2:54 pm.

A hot stream of vomit sprayed across my face and chest.

I screamed and stumbled back.

"Already said you should go." He burped and slammed the door.

I grabbed the garden hose and turned the valve, drenching myself in cold water. I heaved sobs and gagged a few times.

No one would sit near me on the train.

The memory sits above my head like a cloud.

I remember every detail:

Mickey Mouse; the bent hangers; the word *whore*; a Mets sticker; vomit-crusted hair; a cold train ride.

The memory is vivid. Pregnant with trauma and disappointment.

Only…I feel nothing.

9.

THE NIGHTMARE GOES like this: She walks toward me, backlit by a strong light. Each limb, each movement, breaks the light into smaller beams that radiate like branches around her silhouette.

Her gait is familiar.

She nears. Falls to her knees.

"Help me. It hurts." Her voice trembles. Echoes in my skull until it becomes my voice.

She looks up. It's me there, on my knees. Her face—my face—is melted by devastation, like a funhouse mirror. I lift my hand to touch her shoulder, and I can't reach her. She's right here and, strangely, just beyond my fingertips.

"I don't know what to do," my voice squeaks. "I don't know how to help you."

"It hurts," she sobs. "It hurts so bad."

Mostly, it comes at night. But here and there, I get a flash of her. In moments where my mind slips just under the surface of consciousness. I'll be staring at the clouds and my brain relaxes, like eyes unfocusing. The therapist in me wants to point to clear nodes of trauma in my life, places where I took a turn, grew needles instead of leaves.

But I've dealt with my trauma and view it with only a practical lens now.

8.

"Shel, I think I'm losing it," I say quietly, sliding into a booth. Even though the morning rush has ended, the café is still crowded.

"Well, can I sit first?" they ask, unraveling their scarf. It's one of those infinity ones, so really, they're just unlooping it.

They sigh and look at me. "The dreams again?"

I nod.

Shel leans forward to brush an orange hair off my sweater.

"I see you brought Bryce along."

"Yeah."

"Glitches are normal," says Shel. "Jeremy's brother was seeing weird things, too, and his doc says that stuff happens all the time."

"Yeah, but—"

"Another fun side effect of our BrainLames."

My eyes dart to the raised line nestled in their hair, which they wear shaved on one side, dyed pink to blend in with the scar.

They catch the attention of a server and ask for two americanos. Rico's is one of the last places in the city to keep actual servers. Luddites like Shel and I come here to feel normal.

I run my finger along the raised scar on my temple. I voted against the BrainFrame initiative when it was on the ballot. After it passed, everything moved so quickly. Suddenly it became mandatory to install them. Implantable computer chips were the way of the future, they said. Now, babies are getting BrainFrames in utero. Easier that way. No scars. No sign at all that humanity's losing.

The neural operating systems came with basic "govie" apps for tracking our health and whereabouts. Then, third-party apps started coming out—map apps that integrated with the brain's spatial awareness centers; or Trax, which lets you hear music right from your auditory cortex; and hundreds more.

Shel snaps their fingers in front of me.

"Yo, Janie. Where'd you go?" They're squinting at me. "You having one now? A nightmare?"

"No." Then, in a low voice. "I just hate all this tech."

They shrug as if to say, *What are you gonna do?*

Our drinks come.

"Shel. I think I messed up."

They lower their coffee, lips still pursed from blowing on it.

"They're not glitches, the dreams. They're—"

Shel cocks their head.

I swallow. "I installed an app."

7.

ONE GLASS OF wine and I find myself reading the description of Fracture on my phone's app store.

> When you recall a memory, your brain pulls it out of long-term storage and rewrites it based on your current thoughts and emotions. Fracture separates the who, what, when, and where of a memory from the feelings tied to it. Then, your brain puts the memory back in long-term storage, rewritten exactly how it was—without the emotions.

That's more scientific than I thought it would be. The app works a lot like CBT or EMDR, where we have patients revisit trauma and help them rewrite a less emotionally charged narrative. These methods take months. Years, in some cases. Maybe Fracture could speed this process up, bringing peace to patients sooner.

And isn't that what technology is for? For doing what we want to do, faster?

Still, something about it feels wrong, like therapists shouldn't be leaning on brain tech. It's almost like cheating.

But my patients are using this. I should go through the process so I at least know what they're doing to themselves. And I think about David. How well he's doing.

I hit the download button.

"Welcome to Fracture," says the dialogue box on my phone. "Pairing with nearby discoverable nOS. Found: *Jane_Ward_548094345*."

I confirm.

Another box pops up.

"Try your first *Fracture*?"

Pinot runs through my veins. I imagine a future where therapists like me won't be needed. We're at a turning point. I need to either play nice with tech or find another job.

I click *YES*.

6.

I CHECK MY office voicemail.

"Dr. Ward? I'm calling from Dr. Alisi's office. I'm just going through his voicemails because he's been unexpectedly—he's out of town. Anyway, I'm just letting you know. He'll call you back if... I'll have him call you when he's back."

I can't remember a Dr. Alisi or why I would've called him. Maybe he—

A brisk shave-and-a-haircut knock interrupts my thoughts.

My nine o'clock is on time for the first time in ages.

"Come in."

David walks in, and plops onto my couch. He chews his nails.

"Hey, how are you, Dr. J?"

"Shouldn't I be the one asking that?"

"I'm fine. Really good, actually." His smile seems genuine.

Still, I worry he's masking, suppressing latent emotion. He's fidgety. Doesn't know where to put his hands. He's not wearing his wedding ring (and hasn't for a while; there's no tan or indent).

"I know what you're thinking," he says, holding up his hands. "Holly was murdered. And I saw it happen." He notices a hangnail and chews it off.

A month ago, he couldn't talk about what happened.

I watch him carefully, nodding for him to continue.

"I mean, I miss her, don't get me wrong. I'm just not sad about it. You know when something just feels off—like it's missing or something? Like that."

As though losing a wife is like jet lag.

"Here, look, I'll Blinq you this website, and you'll see," David says. "What's your number?"

"Oh, I don't use Blinq." Neural texting is just too weird.

He looks at me like I've just said I churn my own butter.

I pull out my phone and he punches in the website the old fashioned way.

"Fracture," I read. "Oh, David, this isn't. . ."

My shoulders fall. I didn't think David would turn to the junkie apps. When BrainFrame came out, big pharma played catch up by developing apps that did things like block pain or help people sleep. Of course it took about thirty seconds for med apps to start getting abused.

David taps on his thighs.

"David, did you—is this something you installed?" My eyes move from David to his phone and back. "Who makes this? Department of Tech?"

"No, it's not a govie. It's made by EverTech."

That name sounds familiar, but I can't place it.

Anyway, the app isn't federally developed, which is bad.

With D.O.T., you know what you're getting. Nowadays, any asshole can write code, and people just download it without thinking. I read a story the other day that some hacker cracked the supposedly impenetrable encryption in some woman's OS and installed a virus without her knowing, like with WiFi on the subway or something.

"EverTech," I repeat. Damn, if that name isn't ringing all kinds of bells. "Are they legitimate? Do they have trial data?"

"I dunno, maybe. But it's not like the feds are any more trustworthy. I mean, where's the data on the govie apps?"

He continues drumming on his thighs. I realize he's got a music app running.

"David, can you turn it down?"

"Oh, sorry, Dr. J. Sometimes I forget it's even on." He closes his eyes to see the app dashboard. "I got into oldies recently. Beastie Boys."

I take a deep breath. "Why don't you tell me about this Fracture app?"

"Yeah, okay," he says, straightening up. "So when someone goes through something shitty, there's the feelings part, and then there's the facts of what happened. Right?"

"Trauma has emotional and declarative memory components, yes."

David smiles. "Yeah, that." He pauses, thinks for a moment, then continues. "Anyway, Fracture erases the emotional part."

I skim the summary on the website.

"You think it's stupid?" he asks.

I shake my head. "My concern is that using tech to meddle in our emotions seems dangerous. I mean, the app has access to your memory centers."

I look up at David. He isn't listening to me anymore. He's closed his eyes and is bobbing his head to a beat only he can hear.

5.

IN FRONT OF Giuseppe's, a firetruck blares by. I cover my ears and stumble back.

"I feel dizzy," I say.

"You know, I think we both had one too many beers," Matt says, smiling. "But hey, blind dates are intimidating."

I admonish myself for not being more careful. I've heard hundreds of stories like this that end terribly.

The beers were strong; I don't even remember most of the date. *Jesus, Jane.*

"I'll get you a RideX," he says. "It's on me."

What a good guy. I hope we go out again.

Matt waits with me for the RideX.

A tear runs down my cheek, and I don't know why.

4.

GIUSEPPE'S IS A nice place. Though it's no Rico's. The seats are metal. Everything here is metal, now that I think about it.

"You want anything stronger?" Matt asks.

"No thanks," I say. "Just a ginger ale."

I need to keep a clear head.

He types our order into the table's touch screen—small salad for me, meat-lover's pizza for him—all the while talking about work.

I smile politely. My skin prickles.

His eyes flash as he goes on about new versus returning users, and customers interacting with the brand.

He's not leaving me much of an opening.

Our food comes. I poke at my salad. Matt shoves a bite of gooey pizza into his mouth, cursing at the hot cheese. After a long swig of beer, he freezes.

"Oh, hang on," he says, closing his eyes. Checking a neuro app, probably.

"Finn—he's our sales and accounting guy—anyway, he just Blinq'd me. Sorry, lemme deal with this."

His eyes flutter; he's Blinq-ing back.

I get a quick-flash image of writing notes on lined paper with my girlfriends in middle school. We'd fold them elaborately, pass them across class—giggling about getting caught. Even texting has its charm, with all the emojis.

Now we have computers in our heads, and software that syncs with our brain's language centers.

It feels like we've died, in a way.

I don't say these things aloud. I know I'm the minority.

"Holy shit," Matt says. "We just hit a billion downloads!"

My stomach clenches. "That's—"

I don't know how to finish this sentence.

Fucking awful? Yeah, that'd do it.

He orders another beer, then closes our tab. The table scans his BrainFrame wallet.

My body is numb.

Almost instantly, his second drink comes, and he takes a sip.

"Matt." Maybe he'll be reasonable.

I take out my tablet and show him the article I read last night.

His eyes scan it.

I drum my fingers on the stupid metal table, waiting for what feels like an hour.

"Okay, so?" He says, shrugging.

"So? Fracture is…basically torturing people. You have to shut it down."

He laughs, raising his eyebrows.

"Shut it down? Over some yahoo pseudoscience?"

"I—"

"I don't care what this guy says," he says, pushing the tablet back to me. "Nobody else will, either. I'm not shutting anything down."

"What about you?" I ask, my voice shaky. "What have *you* erased? He's out there, too, you know."

I stand up, causing the chair to clatter on the tile behind me.

"Matt," I say, my hands flat on the table. "Shut it down. Or I'm gonna call whoever I need t—"

Matt pulls out a tablet.

"What are you doing?"

"Accessing your tagged files," he says. "Hang on."

"My—"

And here's my own proof that emotions belong in this world: My stomach is shifting; my mouth is dry; my heart is racing in my chest. Even though I have no idea what's going on, my body does.

"EverTech information is proprietary. We upload a null device file to anyone who collaborates with us. Anything that you see or hear about EverTech or any of its apps or employees is flagged in our app so it can be deleted at any time. You know, for security."

I let out a breath as though it was knocked out of me.

"But I didn't upload any—"

He looks at me like I'm an idiot. Obviously, I am. He installed it without me knowing.

"You're a fucking monster," I say under my breath.

He shrugs and taps on the tablet.

3.

BLEARY-EYED, I PUSH open the door at Rico's. Bells on the handle jangle and I breathe in the air—thick with the smell of bacon, pancakes, and coffee. The clatter of dishes, the yells of "order up," the simplicity of cooks making food to fill bellies—these things warm me. They root me in the real world and remind me why I love it.

They remind me of why I called this Emergency Breakfast.

Shel isn't here yet. I collapse into our usual booth. There's a rip in the retro vinyl bench. It's always been there, that tear, right next to my left leg. I run my finger over it, glad they've never patched it.

A burst of bells and a rush of cold air. Shel, equally bleary-eyed, floats through the door.

They fall into their side of the booth.

A server whips around the corner. "Coffee?"

"Two gallons, please," Shel says. Then, to me, through a yawn, "Okay, what's the emergency?"

I ignore my pounding head and gather my thoughts.

"So last night, I—" I stop, thinking of a better way to start. "Shel, you ever hear of the Milgram experiment?"

They raise an eyebrow that says *duh, of course, I haven't.*

"It was in the 1960's. An experimenter in a lab coat would sit a subject down in front of a button. They'd tell the subject to press the button, and that it would shock somebody. They even played recordings of people screaming in pain."

Shel winces. "Oh yeah, I remember this. The subjects did it anyway, right? Supposedly explains Nazis or something."

The coffees come and Shel orders our usual—two Breakfast Special Number Twos.

I sip my coffee. "Well, it demonstrates that people—even good people—will do what they're told. They might have reservations about doing it, but they'll ultimately do it."

"I don't buy it," they say, brows raised, eyes serious. "I don't care who is telling you to do what. You have a choice. You *always* have a choice."

They're right. I need to talk to Matt.

2.

I RUB MY eyes. Staring into a laptop screen late at night is the worst habit. But I never got used to those neural pdf apps, the reading in my own head.

Bryce is lying on his back next to me.

An email alert chimes. It's from an MIT address. I open it.

> Dear Dr. Ward,
> My name is Winston Alisi and I'm a theoretical physicist. We've just published a paper in Nature about our recent discovery of The Mirror Particle, which is the final piece of evidence that more or less proves the Many Worlds Interpretation. (Our finding has made quite a splash in the domain of theoretical physics this week but hasn't quite made waves in the normal world yet). The paper is attached.
>
> I'm writing you about something I think you need to see, given your position. I'm working on an op-ed piece; wanted you to see it/weigh in before I send to the Times next week.
>
> If you're interested, please call my office to set up a time we can meet to discuss.
>
> —Winston

I've heard of Many Worlds. But I Google it just to make sure I understand it.

> Like a tree whose branches emerge from the same trunk, so too does one universe split into many. We like to believe we inhabit a single, linearly evolving universe—*the* universe—but this is no more true than a tip of one tree branch is the singular output of that tree.

Okay, so different outcomes can exist in parallel. Got it. And somehow this mirror particle proves it. So, I guess there's a me that never dumped Roger. Yikes.

Still, I'm not sure why Alisi sent this to me.

The op-ed is called "Therapy Hacking in the Brave New Many Worlds".

I open it and skim ahead to find out what he means by "therapy hacking."

> Take the new app, Fracture, for example. It bypasses lengthy—but ultimately beneficial—therapy work. And just like magic, we are left with memory of the trauma with none of the emotional fallout. But at what cost? In a parallel universe, we've created a version of ourselves that not only bears that pain for us, but doesn't even have the memory of said trauma. Using Fracture is tantamount to creating people to torture.

So in one world, the person has only the memory, and in another, they have only the hurt? I imagine the pain of being called a whore without remembering it happening, and a pit opens up in my stomach.

Bryce jumps into an old cardboard box in the corner of the room. His tail disappears inside.

I read on.

> Humans have a long history of feeling very okay with suffering as long as they don't have to see it. We've all heard of Milgram's famous shock experiments. But here's a lesser known part: The farther away Milgram moved the person getting shocked, the more willing the subject was to shock them.
>
> What pain might we inflict, I wonder, if the recipients are separated by an entire universe?

The pit in my stomach widens.

It seems like an unavoidable side effect of humanity, that we hurt each other. And then, once we do, the pain has to go somewhere, so we pass it on to the next generation like hair or eye color, recycling the hurt, unless we do the proper work to process our trauma and stop the cycle. Fracture is a shortcut. And now with this many worlds thing, it's just as bad as inflicting pain on purpose.

If I were to use Fracture, I'd be no better than my father.

It's late, so I only get Dr. Alisi's voicemail when I call.

1.

PsychCon is crowded. After the morning talks, I stroll through the vendor booths.

One at the end of the row catches my eye. EverTech printed in big, blue letters. I've never heard of it.

But their tagline intrigues me.

Tech that supports total body and mind health.

The guy running the booth turns and smiles.

"Jane Ward," I say, shaking his hand.

He looks at my badge. "Ah, PhD in cognitive psych, cool."

The man hands me his card. *Matt Finch, CEO, EverTech.*

"What does EverTech make?" I ask.

"Our company wants to support mental and physical health with all the advantages our BrainFrames have to offer."

I nod, raising my eyebrows.

"We've developed apps to help people manage their eating, keep them on track with sleep—stuff like that."

"Huh." Instantly, I think about David, who sobbed for an hour in my office on Friday.

"What about mental health?"

"Yeah, we've got a great meditation app."

I sigh. "If we have to upload tech into our brains, shouldn't we get something better than that?"

He raises his eyebrows.

"Sorry." I blush, realizing I've just dismissed his whole company.

"No," he says, eyes focused. "Go on. What would you want an app to do?"

"Well, unless you can create some magic app to help people process their traumas, then—"

"You'd be surprised what we can do."

My stomach growls, reminding me it's lunchtime.

"I have to be honest, Matt. I hate all this tech."

He laughs. "Me too, if you can believe it. Look, I get it. But here's the thing—we're in this world, whether we like it or not. Apps are gonna get made and people are gonna upload them. So isn't it better if people like us—who *care*—are the ones steering the tech?"

He has a point.

He looks at his watch. "Let me buy you lunch? I'd love to hear more about this idea of yours to tackle trauma. You know, we hire consultants like you all the time."

I think about David. About how much I wish I could just press a button to help him feel better. An idea for an app starts to form.

"Sure," I say.

Couldn't hurt.

WAVE WALKERS
Victor Pope

Wave Walkers weren't dangerous—as far as we knew.

Our tour guides were quick to reassure us at every apprehension that what we were about to do was a safe, controlled interaction. That the Walkers usually didn't even notice the humans bobbing at the water's surface, eyes skyward, trained on the incandescence of dusk searing the tree line high above. Waiting.

The water wasn't warm. I was in the middle of warming it up a little in my immediate vicinity when I first saw the Wave Walker crest the ridge, a massive, circular shadow that gleamed at its edges, pushing dusk into darkness. I wasn't prepared for its sheer scale. It triggered an uncomfortable tingle in the back of my brain that told me I was not supposed to be here, that nobody and nothing was in control of this creature.

And when I saw the second Walker rise beside the first—another leviathan eclipsing the last dregs of the sun—I missed my next breath, my fear carried on a weightless pulse in all directions by the Fathoms.

"Two Walkers!" shouted one of the guides from the rocky shore, sixty feet away. "You are very lucky!"

A cold current swept through the lake, splashing a swell into my mouth, making me choke.

I coughed and kicked for lift, then cleared my throat before refocusing on the Walkers dominating the ridgeline. They were both way over my head, and only getting higher.

It was my first time in the Fathoms, and I was determined to make this trip a memorable one. I didn't want to spend another vacation chasing white sands and perfect surf or untouched slopes and fresh powder. I was sick of parasailing, didn't care to hang glide anymore. Surface Plane was old news to me now; home had a way of losing its luster after you'd crossed every border and found the grass was only greener in filtered photos. So I'd taken my first step through the Breach thirsting for everything novel. Bracing for my initial encounter with the substance that still defied particle physics, the cool pressure that nestled on your skin and responded to emotions, to thoughts. The Fathoms, it was called, the substance inseparable from the place it permeated. And when I stumbled through the Breach, bile kicking the back of my tongue while my inner ear attempted a backflip, I knew why.

For most people, being in the Fathoms would be enough. You certainly had to jump through enough damn hoops to get here; vaccinations alone took four months. So even as I sat through the introductory cultural demonstration outside of security in Basshwivoh, watching the Fathomers speak with only quick bursts of dialog and subtle, motionless pushes on the Fathoms to weave their meaning into dual waves of sound and feeling, I was thrilled. At first.

Like the other four people in my tour group, I was bristling with small pulses of excitement, hyped from the adrenaline of arriving somewhere so far outside my purview. But for me, those feelings dulled during our bean-heavy breakfast and side of braised insects.

I sipped the juice—local citrus with a subtle tang—and tried to smile my way through small talk while the rest of the group was busy bounding with eagerness, their emotions rising in a tangible feedback loop.

An older woman whose name I'd already forgotten started waving her arms around again, her excitement rippling off of her and across the low wooden table that held our breakfast. "You ever felt anything like this?" She looked to the teenage daughter of the family of three, who all sat on the other side of our alternative protein spread.

"Never," said the daughter, beaming.

I watched the parents perk up with the daughter's constant pulses of elation. They looked at each other.

The mother radiated with delight. "Not even close," she said.

"It's like...happy water," said the father, a warm wave of joy beating in time with his belly laugh.

Then they all looked at me.

"Me, either," I grinned. But that was it. I crunched a spoonful of spiced insects on top of stewed kidney beans in a misguided attempt to fill in for my lack of passion. The Fathoms could not be fooled.

A slight twinge of unease slipped underneath their cheerful pulses, like the bitter aftertaste from strange citrus.

I sipped my juice again. The conversation moved on, but I didn't really move with it.

I knew I was jaded. I wasn't ready to be confronted with exactly how much.

This was why I needed to see a Wave Walker. It was the only creature that defied capture on film, their presence revered across every inch of the Fathoms. A legend you could only look at with your own eyes, sure to inspire awe no matter who you were, where you'd been. What you'd seen before.

I'd read the stories since I was a teenager. About how they walked on nine legs that curled back in on themselves with each step, supporting the Walker's rear ends before being brought down in fluid movements again. How they made no wind but churned up water, twirled throughout the clouds at dawn.

I wouldn't be happy until I'd finally caught sight of one in all its otherworldly glory. But honestly, I wasn't even sure that would do the trick.

THE WAVE WALKERS ascended the mountains surrounding our lake. They were absolutely magnificent—from a distance. They eased their nine legs down and kept their crown level, gelatinous feet picking through trees. The trees themselves didn't wobble or toss their branches, but all the insects ceased their groans, chirps, and titters in a rush to abandon perches on leaves and limbs. The mountain trembled at their exodus, a glistening murmur of iridescent wings fleeing over the lake, out of the way. The guides had told us there would be no other animals. They knew not to rest here this late in the day.

"They're coming," said Cassidy, floating several feet ahead of me. Even though we'd just met this morning, I didn't think she sounded exactly excited. "They're coming." Her voice carried over the quiet. I felt a tart twinge of apprehension across my face from an errant push of Fathoms. Couldn't tell who it was from, maybe one of the family of three further up.

Water rose to meet the Walkers. From where, I didn't know. But we were being pulled towards them in a tide of their own making. The father of the family flopped his arms, tried to swim backwards.

"Don't splash," the guide called. "Relax," he said. Then repeated himself, "Relax."

I laughed. We were being dragged towards two colossal, ethereal creatures making their way across a foreign landscape in an entirely different plane of existence. The best we could hope for was a mild panic.

And I was no optimist.

I'D BEEN HANG gliding before in Surface. Gliding in the Fathoms was nothing like it. For one, you didn't need anything besides yourself. In the same way that you could work emotions into semi-visible waves that other people could feel, you could fashion your will into the physical.

If anything, it was akin to body boarding—without the board. I'd waited for the rest of the group to pass on our way to the bus in Basshwivoh, eyeing the downhill slope to the station. It was perfect: not too narrow, not too steep, not too crowded. Just casual shops soft-selling souvenirs and snacks with inviting, open fronts. I bounced on my toes and pushed down with my forearms, testing my hang time. Then I took two steps and leaped forward, arms slamming down hard on the thin press of Fathoms I had created, core tensed into a laser-straight line, like I was doing a plank.

And I floated.

I couldn't help but giggle. I was floating down the street, gliding past the store owners seated in front of their shops. One raised a hand and offered a smile. Another whistled and yelled, "Nice!" from across the road. And I wasn't embarrassed at all. I was gliding against the wind—sun high overhead, throwing my shadow down five feet from my toes—and laughing like I'd never done taxes, never had to make rent.

But I was picking up speed now, and the group was coming up quick in front of me. I twisted in the air and lost control, landing awkwardly on my left ankle and scraping my right palm on the cobblestones as I tumbled.

I winced, partially at my rolled ankle and partially at the collective "Oooo" from the tour group. A warm pulse of concern braced me from the right.

"You okay?" asked one of the tour guides. He kneeled down next to me, looking at the ankle I was holding.

I glanced around to find everyone staring; my ears burned. "Yeah," I said, then popped back up by pushing off the ground and standing on my right leg. "I'll be alright."

He glanced down at my ankle again before pushing over a slow wave of reassurance. "The bus is right over there. Very close."

"Thanks," I said. Then I dusted myself off and tried to walk normally for the thirty feet to the bus stop. Nobody was convinced.

I had painkillers in my bag, plus a wrap of gauze I kept exactly for times like this. With my hobbies, I was no stranger to minor injuries on trips. I bit down on a bitter grin as I hobble-hopped down the hill. I guessed that was why they called it gliding; you had to come down eventually.

Some, sooner than others.

THE SWELL TOOK us higher. It was not a current so much as a pull, a gravity. The water moving all at once and the five of us being brought before their feet. We were going to greet the Wave Walkers, and it was entirely on their terms.

I was scared. My heart hammered on my ear drums, and I sucked in cool evening air through gaps in my teeth. From this angle the Walkers were less translucent, more silvery and material, and I could see smaller cilia fanning from their crowns, bristling in different directions, almost as if they were feeling their way through the Fathoms.

The water was rising, my heartbeat chasing it, and I felt something was missing. I was...lighter, like I'd forgotten my backpack on the way out the door for work. But my life jacket was secured around my shoulders and waist. And I was leaning back, anyway, taking in the full scale of the Walkers on their saunter down the mountains. They were tremendous; a pair of islands shuffling their way to another ocean. That was when I realized what was wrong. The Fathoms were no longer carrying our emotions outward in even directions. All the fear seeping off of my skin felt like it was being siphoned off. Up. I couldn't see the pulses in the growing dark, but I knew it must have been true. There was nowhere else to go. The Fathoms were being drawn to the Wave Walkers.

And the Walkers were being drawn to us.

"What brings you on this little excursion?"

I looked over to find the older woman leaning into the aisle, staring straight at me. Making conversation was one way to distract from how fucking terrifying buses were in the Fathoms. Like surfboards with rickety recliners under a sunroof of green glass. Oh yeah, and it was *flying*.

"I wanna see one," I said. "And I needed a vacation. My job can't bother me in another dimension." I brought a fist to my mouth to beat back a wave of nausea as we pulled through another sharp turn.

"Oh, come on, lad," she said with a laugh. "Not worth the hassle just for a vacation."

Excitement was sliding off her in sheets. I laughed, too, nervous about the bus but enchanted by how unguarded she was, how fresh her emotions felt on my skin. We took a quick dip and the sinking feeling flashed me back to the endless days trapped in remote meetings. Late calls with 'emergency' assignments and eleventh-hour asks that peeled weeks off my calendar like receipts on cheap takeout. *Vacation* was a loaded term, sure. "How 'bout you?" I asked.

"When you get to my age, you stop being so scared of dyin' and more concerned with livin' a little," she said. "And I want a new hair color," she added, winking. "Even if it only lasts a couple weeks."

We banked again, changed altitude way faster than I'd experienced on any flight in Surface Plane. My ass flew out of my seat and then thumped against the thin cushions as we turned and rose once more, wrenching a sudden pulse of fear from me—which was lost in the laughter and excitement surging across the aisle.

"Now we're talkin'!" she yelled, hand stretched in the air like she was on a roller coaster.

The woman was beaming, and my little wave of alarm couldn't overcome her elation. I was probably thirty years younger than her and jealous of her joy. She wasn't traveling to forget about her work life or outdo past experiences or encounter a single creature. She was fully committed to every minute of the ride, not just the result. I was grateful for a sudden drop in altitude to hijack my jealousy before the Fathoms picked it up, maybe tainted her radiance.

"I wanna feel like a kid again," I blurted, surprising myself.

She grinned at me. "Well, lad," she said, "hopefully the Walkers can help with that, too."

She lowered her rollercoaster hand and extended it to me. "Let me reintroduce myself. I'm Cassidy."

"Daimen," I said.

"If it's any consolation, Daimen," she began, "you still look like a scared lad from where I'm sittin'." Her wink did a lot to ease the sting.

We climbed again.

THE FIRST LEG kissed the water. It didn't seem weight-bearing as much as guiding, sensing. So when the second and third legs from the first Walker landed on either side of the family of three, they did a very admirable job of not openly freaking the fuck out. Because this was where we'd been told there was magic.

If you got close enough to the Walkers, then your outward appearance could be slightly altered. Previous travelers had left the lake's waters with blue hair or burnished skin, others longer eyelashes or fewer wrinkles. The alterations weren't exactly random, but were far from understood, at least by Surface science. Fathomers had strict rules about attempting to capture or study the creatures, but didn't mind sharing their grandeur with those brave enough to take the plunge. What was almost guaranteed, though, was that nobody left the Walkers unchanged. This close, it was easy to see why.

One of the legs paused on the water's surface, shy of the family, but only just so. The mother kicked closer, reached out to touch the Walker, fingers approaching its translucence—then passing right through. But not without a response.

The Walker changed from thin silver to deep green exactly where her fingers were, spreading through the rest of the leg in a slow roll from the point of contact. She jerked her hand back, but the spread continued around the leg, making its way up the trunk, towards the crown a hundred feet above our heads.

"Your hair's green," yelled the daughter. "Mom, your hair's green!"

The daughter reached out next, putting her fingers through the green edge of the same leg. Now it turned orange, and the daughter was delighted. When she pulled her hand away, her skin had gone a shade darker, then another. Like she was instant tanning in starlight.

"I'm not missing out on this," Cassidy yelled. She swam over to another one of the Walker's legs, this one also oddly still on the water. I looked up and found the crown of the first Walker, the wave of green and orange thinning the higher it went, but still visible. When Cassidy dared her hand against the other leg, it rippled dark blue. She laughed, high and pure, and I saw her hair streak with bright red in the places silver had been. Her hand twirled and twirled inside the Walker, as if she were mixing watercolor.

And then something strange happened.

"Relax!" the tour guide screamed from the shore. "They don't want to hurt you. Relax!" I looked over to see him splashing into the lake, full sprint.

When I tracked back to the family, I saw the Walker flicker a bright yellow from another leg. The yellow kept flickering from the same point: the father.

The guide dived in, a line tied from his waist to his partner still on the shore.

The father was focused on the Wave Walker, its crown coming down to meet the surface. He couldn't take it. Even from sixty feet away I could see him thrashing, trying to escape. But the Walker's leg didn't let him. He was surrounded by it, pushing, screaming, throwing his arms at what he couldn't touch. His wife and daughter were yelling at him, trying to reel him back in. But this was the Fathoms. Emotions were more contagious here.

Another yellow flash from the Walker, then another. Except now the other leg that the mother and daughter had touched was also turning yellow. Because they were panicking, too. Even from where I floated, I could feel the sympathetic response bouncing back and forth between the father, mother, and daughter. It was sticky and clammy and claustrophobic. It gave me goosebumps and tightened my throat. A good portion of the panic was being siphoned into the Walker's other legs, turning them a clear yellow, too.

That was when I felt the same panic from a different direction. I looked to my left and Cassidy was wide-eyed, arms straining in the water to get away from the hysteria. But she was even closer than I was, and the Walker still had its pull. The leg nearest her also began flashing yellow.

Behind me, the guide stopped swimming. At first, I thought maybe he didn't dare approach the group in the midst of a panic. Except his head was tilted upwards to observe the Walker. It wasn't only the panic loop he was worried about. He did his best to push pulses of reassurance on the Fathoms across the fifty feet between him and the rest of the group. Most of it was simply being absorbed by the Walker, sifted upwards to the crown, which was still closing in on the family, the yellow wave crawling over its curves.

I swam away as best as I could, an instinctual need prompting me to get the fuck out of there. And I had a chance, since I'd been farthest back in the group. Except when I turned to fully extend my arms into a freestyle, I encountered another problem. I stopped mid-stroke and gawked up at the silver shadow suspended against the sky.

The second Walker.

It towered over me, nine legs coming down around all sides to meet the surface. I must have lost it in the commotion on the lake, too focused on the panic loop to notice this one's calm, continued stroll. How the tips of the legs bent back upwards after a moment, returning to the crown while maintaining their curve, nestling along the inner edges of the fuzzy cilia busy tasting the Fathoms, like resting your chin on your knuckles. Thinking.

More screams behind me.

I craned my neck to look back over at the rest of the group. The first Walker was now fully yellow, casting them in a sallow luminescence. And in that light I thought Cassidy's hair looked more like iron instead of ruby. Saw the daughter point at her mother and say something I couldn't quite catch. But the mother's hair was now wispy and white. The daughter held a hand up in front of her face and screamed. The father was still splashing and thrashing at the Walker, though only in fits and starts now. It seemed like the guide's pulses of reassurance were having at least some effect.

When I turned back to my Walker, I found it much closer than I had left it. I fought back the first shock of fear, since I'd seen what happened when you panicked. Besides, I was already too close to outrun it, had no hope of fighting back, either. The Walker had me firmly in its gravity; the least I could do was meet it with the respect it commanded. And damn, was it beautiful.

This close, the crown was a tender silver, streaked by starlight like I'd never seen in Surface Plane. Around me, the legs were slowly moving closer in, joints on the water forming oblong shapes while the ends intersected with the crown—now directly over my head. I kicked over to one of the legs, then slowly reached out to touch it.

But I didn't. Because I saw the leg move, ever so slightly, back from my outstretched fingers, the silver joint sliding across the dark water.

I let my hand rest back in the lake, spread my arms and legs, and floated. I didn't come here for a new hairdo or to get rid of wrinkles. Hadn't crossed the Breach and braved these damn buses and panic loops for a bucket list checkmark, either.

I was in the presence of legend.

And it had not asked for me to be here, or to piss in its pristine lake, just so I could give it a fucking high five. I breathed out, closed my eyes. Thought about why I had been so dead set on getting myself into exactly this situation, when simple thrills were to be had swimming with great whites or base jumping or even talking to a stranger on the train. The Fathoms were not only a new frontier for Surfs like me, they were a chance to dream. To spread out your arms and glide downhill without being an eleven-year-old on your bike. To feel the laughter from a new acquaintance bubble off your skin like champagne. To encounter ancient creatures that strolled the world at their leisure, frequenting their favorite lake in the first breaths of nighttime.

I opened my eyes and the Walker was close, so close now. I looked through its crown to the sky behind and couldn't believe the spectacle. It was like each spot of starlight was a kaleidoscope of fractal colors that only became more gorgeous the more I stared. This one ice blue at its center but sparked with orange and violet in overlapping circles. That one pale green before exploding into rose spires with teal studs at their tips. I laughed. I'd never dreamed the sky could look so incredible. I could feel the Fathoms pulsing from me, and I couldn't stop laughing.

My Wave Walker responded. The cilia around its crown weaved themselves together into a cape extending down to the surface of the water around me. But I wasn't scared. I was laughing still, staring at the stars with a wonder I thought I'd lost somewhere between folding laundry and scheduling meetings, going to bed early just to wake up earlier for work. Where had this laugh been the whole time? Tears were blurring those breathtaking stars, and the Fathoms were pouring off of me, breezing the Walker's new curtain and sending ripples throughout its crown.

That was when I noticed the screaming had stopped. Not only that, but the other Walker was no longer standing still. It had resumed its graceful stride across the lake, a soft shade of olive overtaking the yellow staining its legs. And it wasn't the only Walker changing colors.

I had to wipe my eyes to make sure, but when I did, I was not disappointed. My Walker was glowing all different pigments in tune with my ripples of Fathoms. The hues were faint at first, but grew more saturated with each passing moment. First sea blue, then pine green and sunset pink, a splash of twinkling silver. The colors bounced all around in radiating waves, overlapping and intersecting and blending into inconceivable spectrums.

I laughed again, sniffled to clear my throat. I was still drifting in the swell under the Walker, except we were above the others, almost even with the crown of the first, the only sound water lapping at my earlobes. When had we lifted so high?

I looked around at the mountains and the sky and the lake and the other Walker, painted with all those coursing colors, and my mouth hung open, airy laughs bubbling into the new night. All of it, down to every last atom, was absolutely wondrous. I could see that now.

We lifted even higher, the cape coming closer, the colors through the crown expanding into new palettes with each passing moment. And I couldn't bear to blink.

From far away, I thought I heard someone calling my name.

But I ignored it.

I never wanted to come down.

MARS MONKEYS
Neil Flinchbaugh

Carol opened the front door just as the delivery drone hovered down the snowy stairs, leaving a package on the porch. It was addressed to Billy Fornof and bore a sticker that practically shouted in red letters: *MARS*.

That son of a bitch. He was two weeks late.

Carol scooped up the box and gave it a good shake. Something lightweight jostled around inside. Almost immediately, her gaze drifted toward the trash cans on the edge of the sidewalk.

Billy had already forgotten the Christmas gift fiasco, and God knows he'd be better off leaving the whole disappointment in the past. She turned the package over. It was bound to be something cheap and thoughtless, perhaps even wildly inappropriate for a seven-year-old boy, like novelty beer glasses that said "Beam Me Down the Hatch, Scotty" or "I Went to Mars and All I Got Was Drunk." She could make both their lives a lot easier by just tossing it right now.

But—no. She couldn't bring herself to throw out a present for Billy. Not even one from Mark.

She closed the door against the cold January air. The living room was dim, even gloomy, with a single glaring light coming from the dating show paused on the hologram. She trudged upstairs with the package. Shook it again.

Whatever it was, it sure wasn't a puppy.

The sounds of Billy's video game got progressively louder with each step. She reached his room, cracked the door open, and peeked her head inside.

"House, mute sound." The room went suddenly quiet. "Billy? You alive in there?"

"Hi, Mom."

A giant 3D hologram filled the room with an electric glow. The game showed two hands holding a laser gun. Billy sat on the floor, eyes glued to his game.

"There's a package for you."

The laser gun fired red bullets at a bug-eyed alien, and it silently screamed, thrashed, and exploded into a burst of green goo.

"It's from your dad."

He gasped in that way that only kids do before they learn how important it is to hide your true feelings. His head whipped around, mouth spreading in a toothy grin.

"Dad?"

His voice was so sweet, so pure. It just broke your heart.

She showed him the package with the gaudy red *MARS* sticker. He jumped to his feet and followed her to the bed, his eyes never leaving the package.

"What is it?" he asked and grabbed hold of the gift.

"You'll have to find out." She didn't let him have it just yet. "You going to come downstairs and eat with me tonight?"

He tugged one more time, probably testing her grip strength. Then he nodded.

"Okay." She let go of the package and flipped on the nightstand lamp. Weak LED light banished the darkness from their corner of the room. Billy tore into the box, scraping at the tape with his teeth.

"Oh, don't bite it…" But it was too late. He ripped it apart and froze, unblinking, mouth hanging open.

"Ohhh…" It was the sound he always made when he was excited. Usually he followed it with, "Moony!" Tonight, though, he just stared.

"What is it, honey?" She scooted closer and looked over his shoulder. The corners of her mouth pulled into a frown.

Really?

"Sea Monkeys?" She reached into the box—Billy was too flabbergasted to move—pulled out the package and turned it around in her hands. "Sea Monkeys." She shouldn't have said that. At least not the *way* she said it—her tone screaming, *I am* not *impressed*.

"No, Mom." He grabbed it from her hands like she was a drunk waving around a Waterford champagne flute. "They're *Mars* Monkeys. See?"

Mars Monkeys, the package said in bright green letters alongside a picture of a shrimplike alien family. The whole thing was a lazy rebrand of Sea Monkeys, an incredibly old toy consisting of a plastic tank and brine shrimp. Aunt Dee had given Carol Sea Monkeys on her tenth birthday. It had been a cheap gift then, and it was a cheap gift now.

"That's what they're going to look like. See, Mom?"

Billy was so happy, though. So in awe of his father. Daddy the astronaut. Daddy the spaceman. She stroked his hair, licked a finger and wiped a little piece of cheese off his cheek. Bless his heart. He wasn't old enough yet to understand the difference between *actual astronaut* and *construction worker who happened to work on Mars*. But someday he would be. Hopefully, someday soon.

"Isn't that something." She wrapped an arm around him and gave a squeeze. He let her hug him for a minute, then shoved her away.

"We have to put them in water." He shot out the door, footsteps pattering down the stairs.

Carol stood to follow him. An alien with a laser gun danced around on the hologram.

He hadn't even bothered to pause his game.

CAROL STOOD AT the sink in their dingy little kitchen, with its built-in table and its laminate countertops, and rubbed her tongue along the raw spot on the roof of her mouth. Pizza bites. Burned her every time, but she still kept coming back for more.

That felt like a life metaphor she didn't want to think too hard about.

She sighed and kept scrubbing. The freaking dishwasher was broken again. She couldn't afford another repair bot right now, so back to hand-washing. But it wasn't so bad. The lukewarm water actually felt kind of nice. She enjoyed pretending it was a little stream of water redirected from a hot tub. Made her feel like she worked in a spa or something.

Strange that her fantasy wasn't *going* to the spa, but *working* there. Maybe that was a sign that her nursing job was too stressful. Or maybe she was just a realistic dreamer.

"Welcome to Earth. We come in peace. Take us to your leader."

Billy was sitting at the table with his nose against the cheap little plastic tank. If any good came from that present, at least Billy was spending more time with her. Ever since she told him the Mars Monkeys had to live downstairs because of gravity.

"Mom, how long will it take the Mars Monkeys to come alive?"

"I don't know, honey. Aren't they swimming around?"

"No."

"Well, finish your broccoli."

He groaned on instinct. Carol could relate. She'd dumped her broccoli in the trash when he went to the bathroom. Billy took a bite and stuck out his tongue. Poor kid. At least it took his attention away from those stupid Sea Monkeys.

Sorry. Mars Monkeys.

Carol was suddenly seized with an urge to tell Mark what an idiot he was. Billy wanted a dog. Asked for it specifically. Then Mark had all but promised Carol he would buy one, so she started dropping hints to get Billy excited. *Dad sent me a picture of a dog the other day. Did you tell dad what kind of dog you want? I hear they have little green dogs on Mars now!*

No. Instead he sent his son a bargain-bin box of crap. Stupid brine shrimp from Mars that had died en route. They could survive without water by going into a state of suspended animation—at least, that's what the box claimed—but interplanetary travel was surely beyond their evolutionary achievements.

She dried her hands and took her phone out of her pocket. "Voice mode off." She didn't want Billy to hear this.

The keyboard appeared and she began a long and winding message that quickly spiraled out of control. Before she realized it, she was bringing up the alimony and the damn cat (RIP Mister Fluffers). She stopped and read back over the train wreck of a text, then put her thumb firmly on the backspace button until it was erased. Better to keep it simple.

He wanted a dog. She stopped, scrolled to the most recent message, and checked the timestamp. Almost three weeks ago. The one before that was eight weeks ago.

"Screw it," she muttered under her breath. She tapped *Send* and slipped the phone back in her pocket.

"Mom. Do you think they're dead?"

She sighed. Rubbed her tongue over the burnt spot in her mouth. And in the sink, the jet from the hot tub felt like regular sink water again. Her imaginary spa job faded back to reality.

You can only fool yourself so long with stuff like that.

CAROL'S FORTY-FIRST birthday came on January 19th, and while she wasn't usually one for resolutions—they seemed to fizzle out faster than Billy's sparklers—she had a feeling this year would be different. Ever since the divorce and the rocky months leading up to it, she had felt like a float tube in the wave pool of life. Even worse, Billy was stuck in the middle of this crap situation. But last night while watching him fiddle with those stupid Mars Monkeys again, she realized something: he was obsessed with Mark's present because he wasn't getting the love he needed. That was something she could change, though. She *would* change it.

And if she showed up Mark in the process and helped Billy realize which of his parents really deserved his adoration, well, that was Mark's own fault.

She trudged up the porch steps, already tired from the big box she carried. She rested it on top of the newel post and gave her arms a good shake. The street was snowy and quiet. Peaceful.

"You doing okay in there?"

The box shuffled around a little. She peered through an air-hole, but her head blocked the light and she couldn't see anything.

"That's okay. I'm used to being ignored. I have a son."

She lifted the box again and opened the front door. As she did, she glanced at the porch. No packages.

Stupid. Of course there wouldn't be. You send your son a present on Christmas. But on your ex-wife's birthday? She can go screw herself.

Inside, she went straight toward Billy's room. Halfway up the stairs, though, she stopped.

Where was the noise?

"Billy? Billy, you here?"

She listened. No video game. No music. Her heart skipped a beat. She shouldn't have left him home alone. Even for only an hour. He was only seven, after all, and—

"In here, Mom."

Carol exhaled and started toward the kitchen. The box jostled in her arms. "Shh. You're a surprise."

In the kitchen, Billy was playing with those stupid Mars Monkeys again. He had the tank open and held one hand over it, crumpling little brownish flakes with his fingers. The flakes landed in the water and turned it cloudy.

"What are you doing, honey?" She carefully set the box on the table. Then she saw the bag on the table next to him. Goldfish food.

"I got them some new food."

"Oh, honey that's not for…Where did you get that? Have you been using Mommy's headset again?"

She scooted her box a little closer. He mumbled a reply, still focused on the tank of Mars Monkeys.

"So," she began, determined not to let this ruin her surprise, "you know it's Mommy's birthday today. But instead of getting myself something—"

"Aren't they supposed to be getting bigger? They don't look like the box *at all*."

She stopped. Took a breath. She just needed to divert his attention and he'd forget about them. He was only seven. Kids were easy to distract.

"Hey. Look. I want to show you something."

She waited patiently until he finished crumbling the flake of food and looked at her.

"That's good. Now give them some time to eat." She slid the tank away, then pushed the box in front of him. "I got us something for my birthday."

"Wait. *You* got *us* something? Aren't you supposed to be the one getting presents on your birthday?"

"Oh, did you buy me a present?" She raised her voice in mock excitement, stared at him in exaggerated anticipation. She could see little gears turning in his head.

"Well…See the thing is…I spent my money on this fish food, because I know you want me to learn asponsability."

Asponsability. She suspected that sometimes Billy mispronounced words on purpose to sound cute and get out of trouble. It usually worked. "It's okay. I won't expect presents till you're ten. But here. Open it."

A ghost of a smile appeared on his face, vanished, and appeared again. "What is it?"

"I don't know. Open it, silly."

He was too short to see down into the box while it was on the table, so he scooted a chair and stood on top of it. Carol didn't like that, so she stood behind the chair and held it steady.

For a minute he just looked.

"Well? You going to open it?"

"What is it?"

"You'll have to open it."

"Why does it have holes?"

He knew. He totally knew.

"I don't knooow. Why do you think?"

He held still, watching the box. The excitement was growing. He stuck one finger carefully inside one of the air-holes and held it there a moment. Probably wiggling it around inside.

"Eww!" He pulled the finger out and showed it to her. "Something licked me!"

"Something licked you?" That smile. Worth its weight in gold. "What could it be?"

"Is it…" He lifted a corner of the box, peered inside, then threw the lid onto the floor. "It's a German Shepherd!"

"That's right!" She hugged him and kissed his cheek. It wasn't a German Shepherd. Mark was the one who put that breed into his head, but Billy wouldn't know the difference. Besides, when you're adopting a free puppy from the shelter, you kind of take what you can get.

It was an adorable puppy, though. Labradoodle mix with tan fur, a patch of white on his chest, floppy ears, and big, glassy eyes. He had a tendency to tilt his head to the side, like he was a little bit confused. Cute as a button.

"Thanks, Mom!" Billy put his hand in the box and let the little guy lick his hand. Oh, to have been recording that moment. "Can I pick him up?"

"Sure you can. Just be careful."

He gently lifted the puppy, holding him at arm's length. "He's so little."

"That's because he's a baby. He'll get bigger."

"I wouldn't be so sure, Mom. I've learned pets don't always grow up the way they're supposed to."

Ha! Take that, Mark.

"Well, we'll have to see. What do you want to name him?"

"Ummm…" He scrunched his face, pushed his lips off to one side. "How about…the Martian Mutt!"

That wouldn't do. She'd have to steer him toward a better name some other time.

"Tell you what. We'll think about it. Now why don't you hold him closer? Like a baby? That's right, put one arm underneath him, like that..."

Billy did like she said, holding the puppy close. He petted the top of its head and even rocked it back and forth. Carol's chest grew warm.

"Good dog." Billy's voice was tender. In that moment, Carol saw him as a fully grown man. Her son was going to make a great dad someday. He would be patient, loving, understanding—Mark's DNA be damned. He leaned in close to nuzzle against the puppy, and it unleashed a flurry of licks on his face. It was super cute, but then Billy let go and dropped the little guy onto the table.

"Careful!" Carol reached out, but she was too late.

The puppy landed on the edge of the box, knocking the cardboard onto its side. Then he rolled onto his feet and began wagging his tail. No harm done.

The dog explored the tabletop. Sniffing around. Looking over the edge. It looked like he considered jumping onto the floor, but thought better of it and turned around. Then he made his way to the tank with the Mars Monkeys and began to drink the water.

Billy let out a horrified gasp.

"*No!*"

He lunged forward and onto the table. The sudden motion scared the dog and he jumped and knocked over the tank of Mars Monkeys.

Water spilled all across the table, covering the laminate surface in a cloudy liquid that was half fish food, half dead brine shrimp. The puppy started licking the water off the table. For half a second Billy stared, and then he screamed.

It was a horrible sound. He sounded like—well, like a kid who just lost his puppy. The dog didn't like that one bit, and ran back inside the box to hide. Carol instinctively grabbed the roll of paper towels from the counter and ripped off a handful of sheets.

"Mom, no!"

He dashed in her way and grabbed her arm to stop her from mopping it up.

"Oh, Billy, for Christ's...crying out loud." She had to take a breath. This was too much.

"You'll kill them!"

She closed her eyes and counted, like her therapist suggested. *One. Two. Th—*

"Mom!"

Not enough time for three, let alone ten. Here she was, less than an hour into her resolution, and already this year was on track to be just as chaotic and out-of-control as the last one.

"Okay. Okay." She put the towels back on the counter. "What do you want to do?"

He was pointing into the box now. "Bad dog! Bad! Bad!"

Carol held the plastic tank against the edge of the table.

"It's okay. Billy. Billy, look. We can push them back in. See?"

She used her hand to sweep some of the water back in the tank. Billy watched, and as soon as he understood he started sweeping the water toward that part of the table.

As far as rescue missions went, it was a disaster. Most of the water was already pooling in the little dips on the floor. They swept all the water into the tank that they could, but it was less than a quarter of the way full.

"Well. We saved some of them. Look, see? They're in there."

"No, Mom. We have to save them all." He got on his hands and knees, his face inches from the dirty faux tile. He pinched two fingers together and picked something up.

"Here." He reached for the tank. Carol squinted, but she couldn't see anything between his fingers. She held out the tank anyway, and Billy dropped it inside—whatever it was. Piece of dirt, maybe. "Mom, help."

"Okay. Okay." She turned to the sink and filled the tank with tap water. Then she flipped on all the lights, set the tank next to Billy, and got on her knees with him. The puppy was pacing back and forth on the table, his traumatic experience already forgotten.

"There's more over here, Mom."

She scooted over, picking up any speck of dust or fish food or Mars Monkey she could find and dropping it back into the tank. This was stupid. What a waste of time.

But then she pinched a fleck of something and held it close. Got a good look. Wouldn't you know it, it was a brine shrimp. It was only three or four millimeters long, translucent with a bunch of wispy legs, a tail, and two black dots for eyes. And it was moving.

It lay on its back, kicking its legs and rocking side-to-side, almost like a turtle that had landed upside-down. Such a tiny little guy in such an impossibly big world. A world filled with problems and dangers and wonders it would never understand. Yet despite all that, there it was, fighting against all odds just to turn itself upright.

She gently rolled her finger on the back of her hand, lowering the critter onto its feet.

"You came all the way from Mars. I guess that makes you a little alien." Despite herself, Carol felt the hint of a smile cross her face. Billy was watching her, momentarily spellbound, and even the puppy was quiet in an almost reverent sort of way.

A sea monkey from space. It was kind of incredible when you thought about it.

NO MOON AND FLAT CALM

Elizabeth Bear

The world was glass.

It was a tiny, artificial world called Waystation Hab, and my four classmates and I were approaching it in a shuttle we'd been crammed into for four months. My classmates and I were all postgraduate apprentices in the safety engineering internship program.

We humans are a hardy, adventurous folk. We take to the void in our frail little craft. We always have: reed boats, dugout canoes, Viking longboats. Fabric biplanes and the tin cans we used to shoot into space.

Waystation was bigger, but not much: home to one hundred and fifty-six souls, and the stepping stone to the outer solar system. One hundred and fifty-six, plus the five of us. A lot of people, out in the dark and cold. Not a lot at all in the grand scheme of things. But necessary: Waypoint was our gateway to the outer Solar System.

A spinning silver doughnut slung to a long, axel-like hub by a series of tension cables, Waystation held itself together and generated spin gravity through a careful balance of forces Its smallness made its frailty seem all the more apparent—but our homeworld is a frail little craft as well. So easy to disrupt or destroy. It's just so much bigger than us that we can fool ourselves about its resilience. About our own resilience.

The curve of the hab loomed over our shuttle. We came up on the inside to dock, our little ship matching velocity to slide between the cables that kept the station in trim.

From the moment we docked, I couldn't stop thinking of everything that could go wrong. I was the first one out. I dropped off the ladder two meters above the deck and landed lightly in the partial gravity. Pushing my nose against all that glass, I gawked at the whir of space. From here I could see the towering hub, the web of cables, and a bit of the shuttle's hull all seemingly "above" me, because with spin gravity out is down.

I had no sense of acceleration. The universe seemed to be revolving around Waystation.

I was nauseous, but I stayed there until Rico, Mei, and Ife joined me. Danika was behind them. She had piloted us, so the post-flight check and shutdown had been her responsibility.

My classmates and I moved carefully, moonwalking without the bounce. Bouncing here would send you into the low ceilings: nobody's idea of a good time.

"This is a long way to go for a classroom exercise," Rico said disgustedly.

"Continuing education is a pain in the ass," Danika answered.

I hate group projects. I hate working with other people—to their schedule and to their standards.

I didn't get the training assignment I wanted. That's how it works sometimes.

I said, "Don't you think somebody should be here to meet us?"

"The briefing did not tell us where to go once we arrived," Ife said. "You would think there would be a message waiting."

Danika rapped on the wall. "Maybe figuring out where we're supposed to be is a part of the curriculum."

"That would be a stupid curriculum." Have I mentioned how much I hate group projects?

"And what would be a good one?" Danika shot back. I hadn't meant to offend her, and from her stiffness I was certain I somehow had. "Something focused on the *Titanic*, maybe?"

Mei held up a hand. "Don't get Marisol started again. I need us to not spend the entire time we're here talking about transportation disasters."

"Hello," I shot back, stung by the unfairness. "Safety engineer. Also I didn't bring up *Titanic* this time. Danika did."

Mei and Rico laughed at me. Mei said, "Disasters are caused by human error and bad design. We can prevent those things."

Mei was right as far as it went, but there were other factors: the profit motive, for example. Or small problems that caused unforeseen consequences and multiplied. Catastrophic failures too big to engineer against.

But I didn't want to give them any more ammunition, about seeming obsessed, so I moved on. "I don't think much of their protocols if they're going to allow clueless interns wander around."

"*I'm* not clueless." Ife had been born on Luna. "It's probably a scheduling error. Let's take Marisol's advice and see if we can find ops."

Rico muttered as he walked past me. "Creep."

Danika put a hand on my shoulder and spoke softly. "We've been cooped up together a long time, and we're all stressed." "I don't know why I try," I answered. "Nobody is ever going to like me. People say you should be yourself but then people tell me I'm a freak. And if I try to act like other people they tell me I'm a fake and a poser."

"Station engineering often involves working with a lot of people in close quarters, as we just were. . Sure it's a good career choice for you?"

"Most habs aren't as big as this one. Plenty of contracts on outposts where Station Ops is the *only* person," I said. "And the nearest human might be light-minutes away. Or hours, sometimes, depending on the orbits."

"You've got to be kidding me."

She studied my face. I was pretty sure that it didn't suggest I was kidding her. But who knows for sure what their own face reveals?

"You're going to request a mining drone service depot at Saturn?"

"Maybe," I said. "Maybe Uranus. This wasn't the training rotation I asked for."

"Takes all kinds," she said, and let it go.

Mei's not the first person to consider me morbid. But I don't like the gory, pointless disasters. The ones where nobody could do anything. Those are just terrible and sad. I like the ones where things happen slowly enough for people to respond. To mitigate. To avert the worst, or some of the worst. Or the ones where something terrible went wrong because somebody was in a hurry, not paying attention. Taking shortcuts.

Like isn't the right word, anyway. I don't like disasters.

I *study* them. You learn from the mistakes, and then hopefully you make different mistakes.

So I focus on the interesting, useful disasters. And only transportation ones.

Apollo 13. Challenger. The Lunar tube puncture. Aloha Airlines flight 243. British Airways flight 9. The Crazy 8s train runaway. Jeffries Station.

Titanic is useful too. What's amazing about that incident is not how many people died, though that's terrible.

What's amazing about the *Titanic* disaster is how many people survived.

The docking ring was deserted. I hustled a few steps to catch up with Danika. "Does this seem right to you?"

"Ife will figure out where we should be." Ife, ahead, was consulting her handheld. She looked irritated, but not concerned. "There will be plenty of disasters for you to love. You don't have to rush it."

"It's not—"

"You don't have to explain yourself to me." Danika grinned at me, flash of bright teeth. "Anyway, you hate people."

"In the abstract, they're fine."

"That was a joke," she said, so I laughed apologetically.

"Okay," I said. Rico glared. I lowered my voice. "But there are a hundred and sixty-one people on this hab, counting us. Where the hell *is* everybody?"

A shiver ran through the deck. It didn't feel like an impact. It felt as if Ops was using an attitude jet to adjust the station's trim.

Rico whooped in amused surprise and grabbed one of the railings. Mei glared at him for a change.

Half the problem with our class was that we were all good and sick of each other. The other half of the problem was that Mei probably shouldn't have made it through the antisocial index screening. Nor Rico, for that matter..

Neither should I, honestly. But it's not like people are lined up to go to space, get irradiated, suffer bone loss, and leave their friends and families. The ones who have friends and family.

Space was still sexy when I was little. People wanted to go. Being an astronaut was romantic. Now space is quotidian: just a dangerous, difficult, physically destructive job that pays well. They take who they can get. .

"Unscheduled burn?" I said. "Shouldn't there have been a warning?"

Ife looked at me. Her face did something complicated, but it wasn't hostile. "Let's get to ops," she said.

THE FIRST-STAGE alert lights began flashing: just an all hands call to action stations, but I still expected the corridor to fill with hustling people.

It did not.

I said, "Do you smell smoke?"

Rico said, "Let's go back to the shuttle. This is not right."

I said, "Where the hell is the smoke coming from?"

It wasn't visible, but the smell of burning plastics and ionization was strong. Fire in space is hungry for oxygen, and it doesn't share.

"Here's ops," said Ife, and opened the door.

INSIDE WAS A scene of chaos from a post-apocalyptic game.

Ops was deserted, but hardly empty. Cooling bulbs of coffee lay beside work stations lit by flashing amber alerts. Screens scrolled data and camera feeds. Bigger screens hung at the front of the room, showing the exterior surface of the hab and views of major corridors.

They were all empty.

Mei stopped inside the door. "Now I'm freaking out."

"Step to the side please," Danika said, and moved her over with the back of one hand so we could all enter. The door sealed shut behind us with an atmosphere-retaining *tch* that I found reassuring. The smell of coffee overrode the smell of smoke. Also a good sign.

"Okay." I moved toward the life support station. "We need to find that fire and starve it."

The easiest way to fight a fire in space is to deprive it of oxygen. We'd practiced this. Somehow, with my hands on the cold molded plastic of a real Ops station, it didn't feel like something I knew how to do.

"This has got to be a drill," Mei said.

"If it's a drill, you want to pass, don't you?" Ife set her handheld on the engineering station and clipped her harness to its safety ring.

I copied her. "Danika, would you get comms and see if you can find any people on this hab?"

Danika moved over to the station. As if my issuing instructions to her had shaken them loose, Mei and Rico took other consoles.

An attitude jet fired again—a definite burn this time, the deck lurching under our feet. Ife made a grab for her handheld and kept it from skittering away. "Stow your gear." She stuffed the unit into a pocket.

Nobody else had any loose gear to stow.

I was glad I was clipped in. Rico had to grab the edges of his console.

"Got the fire," I said. "Sector 3 north."

Waystation was one long circular corridor with twelve pairs of modules projecting from its sides. Those modules were divided into "north" and "south." Our shuttle was docked at Sector 5, along the inside of the wheel. Ops was in Sector 7, on the north side of the wheel. North and south were not a completely arbitrary distinction: "east" was the direction of spin.

"I'm going to need an evacuation alert in Sector 3," I said.

"Good," Danika said. "How long?"

I couldn't do this. I wasn't able to do this.

There wasn't anybody else to do it.

"Ninety seconds?" Nobody answered, so I said "Ninety seconds," in a firmer voice.

An instant later, Danika said, "Done."

We should have a command structure. We should have incident leadership. We had...nothing. Five students and a whole hab *not* full of missing people.

"Everybody on the hab should have an RFID locator chip so the crew could rescue or retrieve them if they went missing," Ife said.

Rico said, "Well, they're missing now." His hands moved over his console.

My countdown on the evacuation alert reached 80 seconds. I checked to make sure that the decompression doors were engaged and the circulation vents closed between 3 north and the rest of the hab. My hands shook: what if I had forgotten to do that?

They would have closed on their own, I told myself. Assuming the system worked. Which felt like a big assumption right now.

"Decompressing in eight-seven-six—"

I uncovered the shielded toggle and recognized a problem. "Dammit," I said. "I need the keys!"

Mei tossed them to me without looking. The arc was high because of the gravity, but I managed to reach up, straining at the end of my tether, and snag them.

As I fitted the key, oxygen levels dropped through Sector 3, north and south. The fire would put itself out eventually, but we'd all suffocate too.

"Rico, please check to make sure 3 south is isolated from 3 north?" I asked.

"It looks okay," he said. I'd half-expected him to ignore me, but apparently a real crisis made us temporary allies.

I turned the key.

On the screens, a puff of atmosphere and debris jetted from the outside surface of 3 north. And there weren't any bodies in it, which was a relief.

"Fire's out," Danika said. "I think, anyway. Infrared shows the temperature dropping at the source."

"Phew," said Mei.

Fire could rekindle, despite being deprived of atmosphere, if it had melted through oxygen supply lines.

Right, I should temporarily seal off all oxygen feeds to 3 north. I should have done that first. I was not ready for this job.

I used the keys and flipped another locked toggle, triple-checking that it was the right one. Belatedly I remembered to say, "Shutting down ox to three north."

Rico said, "I have a bunch of RFID tags in sector 8. Looks like they're in the backup ops center."

"Why'd they evacuate this one?" Mei asked.

"We should go back to the shuttle," Rico said again.

He might be right. I opened my mouth to say so and the entire world lurched. A terrible rending sound, like God snapping a rubber band, rang through the hab.

We bounced off the deck as lights that had been amber flared red. Except Mei, who still hadn't clipped in. She bounced off the ceiling, cursing, then bounced off the deck like the rest of us.

She hauled herself to her feet. "It's just a drill. It's just a drill."

"That was a cable snapping," Rico said, as Ife said, "It's not a drill."

I said, "Check Mei," and Danika stretched out to touch her, not unclipping.

"I'm *fine*," Mei snapped, blood dripping down her face. She grabbed the rail on the edge of the console and snapped her harness leads to it. "Stupid way to get hurt."

Rico was right. On the big monitors toward the front of the room, I could see the enormous tension cable swinging majestically free. The arc ascended. My abdominal muscles clenched as I considered whether it would intersect and slice through the fragile hull.

Venting 3 north must have strained an already fatigued cable. Or one with a manufacturing flaw.

"Are there any suits in here?" Ife asked, almost calmly.

Rico looked across the deck at the emergency locker. He unclipped, swore, and lunged for the locker.

"Empty. The crew must have taken them when they evac'd. Let's get off this hab while we still can!"

"The cable's okay," Mei said. "It's going to wrap the hub."

The hab could survive losing one tensioner. Maybe even two or three, if they failed in the right places around the diameter. But if they failed at the hub, rather than along the wheel, they'd cut the hab to ribbons as they lashed around.

Across the diameter of the hab, the screens showed a puff of debris glittered in the sunlight, particles turning like mirrors falling in slow motion. And in the mist of that shimmer of irregular confetti, a tiny four-limbed figure, tumbling like a rag doll.

A human body in space.

The shock zapped through the deck under our feet. We all managed to hold on this time.

"Definitely not a drill." Ife's complexion faded from warm brown to grayish.

"Is it terrorists?" Mei asked.

"Maybe something blew up when the deck jumped?" Ife said.

I wished I believed that answer. But I thought something much worse was going on. "The rupture is opposite the snap. I think we've got a forced resonance—a critical oscillation frequency—going on. Something like that destroyed the Tacoma Narrows Bridge back on Earth once. It vibrated to pieces in a high wind."

Mei was looking distinctly greenish, and it wasn't the wash of the alert lights. I felt just as sick. An oscillation meant Waystation was vibrating from a wheel into an oval and back to an oval in the other direction, straining the tensioner cables and stressing the fabric of the hull.

It might succumb eventually to friction and energy loss and stabilize. That was what it was *supposed* to do.

Or—and this seemed more likely right then—it might shake the habitation apart, as the wheel snapped back and forth like a giant, quivering jelly mold.

Mei said, "We started that when we dumped the atmosphere from 3 north, didn't we?"

"Probably," Ife said.

"Can we interrupt it?" Rico asked. "Use the attitude jets to damp it down? What if we dumped the atmosphere somewhere else?"

Much as I couldn't stand Rico, it was a good idea, though the necessary timing and force were probably too precise to manage. I was about to say so when Danika interrupted.

"I found everybody."

"Where?" Ife asked.

"Looks like they're stuck behind a series of decomp doors in eight and nine. The evacuation pods are in ten, eleven, and twelve. They were mid-evac when we popped 3 north."

"We were one set of doors away from finding them," Ife said.

They're all going to die because I'm not good enough.

Danika pulled images onto the screens. Orderly groups of people, some in spacesuits and some in shirtsleeves, stood back from two people who were prying at the door seal with inadequate manual tools.

"Why the hell evac instead of putting out the fire?" There was blood all over Mei's hand from wiping at her face.

"Because they knew venting would cause an oscillation?" I guessed.

"Let's go back to the shuttle," Rico said. "Let's get the hell off this hab. These people can take care of themselves. They let us dock when they were already evac'ing."

I looked at him. I wanted to fold up and fall silent. Go along.

I squeezed the edges of my console until my fingers smarted. "You try to fly that shuttle out of here before we've managed this evac and I'll lock it to the docking bay. We're not leaving until we finish helping these people."

Rico looked at me. "Who died and made you god?"

I ignored him. "Ife, why are those decomp doors sealed?"

"Faulty sensor, it looks like," she said. "They came down all over the hab when we blew the fire out."

We could have foreseen that, I guess. But we didn't. And now, I realized, it was going to cost us dearly.

We were responsible, in some respect, for this disaster. We'd reacted to an immediate crisis without understanding the larger situation. A situation which the resident crew had understood, which was why they had started an evacuation before attempting to suppress the fire.

We're very good at what could go wrong. And we're good at how people respond to things going wrong. How people act in a crisis. We have the science to manage it. We study it. We focus on it.

We live it, over and over again, for the sake of the people who will hopefully only have to live it once. Or never.

Preparedness is how we make sure things have a chance to go right even when they've already gone wrong.

"We should evacuate too," Rico insisted. "The people who should be here doing this job already bugged out."

"They're trapped," Danika said.

"The crew?" Rico rubbed his hands together angrily. He hadn't reclipped. From the way Mei and Ife were looking at him, I thought they might be right behind him if he went.

But Ife said, "Our people. The engineers."

"They're not our people," Rico scoffed. "They should have stayed, then."

"Well, they didn't expect a decomp," Mei said, her iciness turned on Rico.

She didn't look at me, but my hopes flared. Maybe she couldn't just leave all these people here to die either.

We were just interns, it was true. But we were trained, and it was our job to save them if we could.

Another oscillation wave passed. We jerked and squeaked at the end of our harnesses. Rico held on tight. On the monitors, Waypoint's crew were hurled about.

"The crew can't get out if we leave," I said. "The doors are locked. We have to override and set them to manual. Or they'll die down there."

"Somebody's going to have to stay and manage the doors, if they're on manual," Mei said.

"Us," I said. "We're staying. We'll evac back to the shuttle once the crew is in the pods."

She looked at me and I looked at her.

"We'll die up here, if we stay." Danika said what both Mei and I were thinking. She didn't speak angrily. She spoke as if she were making sure everyone knew the risks. "Doors are down between us and the shuttle, too. They're all down."

"I'll stay," I said.

A wash of scarlet lit my panel, and the main life support alert light over the monitors went scarlet. "Pressure is dropping throughout the hull," I reported. "We're springing leaks all over the place."

"Sectors 3 and 4 just blew," Ife said. That was our route back to the shuttle. Decision made for us: we couldn't leave.

I knew how to do this. I had done it over and over again in the simulator. *This is just a drill.* "Override Sector 8, 9, and 10. Mei, take control. Switch the decompression doors to manual override in all sectors. We'll open and close them in sequence to act as a series of airlocks."

"Air's gonna get thin," Ife said dubiously.

"Better than no air at all. Danika, do you have comms with the crew yet?" My hands had stopped shaking. My chest still squeezed tight.

"Affirmative," she said. "I can broadcast, at least. I've got the loudspeakers."

"Tell the crew to gather and, once we pop the doors, to get out."

Another oscillation wave hit. It seemed worse than the previous one, somehow. Another cable was going to detether any second.

I took the edge of the console in the gut and gasp-snarled, "How in Newton's busted universe is it getting worse?!"

"Dammit," Rico said. Then, "Okay, they're through the first door."

He bent over his console, fingers flying, reading off a string of pressure differentials. Maybe his brain had kicked over into altruistic mode, and he was ready for a little unselfishness for a change.

"Strain on the tensioners is peaking," said Ife. "I'm going to try to dampen it with the attitude jets and see if I can buy us a little more time."

"Good," I said. "Keep us in trim. I'm diverting atmosphere to the sectors where the crew is."

Which meant diverting it away from the sectors we'd need to move through on our way out. But nobody thought we had a chance of escape. Not with three blown. Not without suits.

"They're through to Sector nine," Danika said.

The hull creaked. Mei ducked, then laughed at herself and went back to work. Popping noises followed; it was my turn to flinch.

"Sealing the Sector eight doors," said Ife. "Opening the ones into ten. Get the pods open."

"Working on the pods," said Rico. "Okay, they're unlocked."

"Orderly evacuation," Danika said. "It doesn't look like anybody's panicking. First group are into the pods."

I'm panicking, I thought, but didn't say it out loud.

Rico giggled. I guess I didn't need to.

"First load of pods away," said Mei. "Sector nine door sealed. The door into Sector eleven is open. And I've got twelve."

The hull shuddered hard enough that I thought it would drive my femurs up through my hip sockets. I gasped in pain and grabbed the rail. "Open twelve," I said. "Give them a fighting chance to make the pods. There's no more time."

"Fifty percent evacuated," Danika whispered.

I slapped my hands over my ears, only aware an instant later that Waystation's entire hull had rung like a massive bell. There was another pop, even more enormous, but I felt it rather than hearing it. I was already deafened. On the monitors I saw people falling, being tossed around. Running when they could, dragging themselves along the rails where they could. In some cases, just falling and crawling.

"Oh no," Mei whispered, transfixed.

Rico shouted. "Second wave of pods—"

All the lights went out with a tremendous rush of wind.

THERE SHOULD BE cold. Pain. Suffocation.

There was darkness and silence, but it wasn't the silence of the void. Around me, I could hear ragged breathing.

AND THEN THE lights snapped back on—ordinary, pleasant full-spectrum light, and not the yellowish emergency lights. I blinked, half-blinded, and shaded my eyes until they adjusted. When I lifted my head, Danika was standing by the sealed door, her hand on a panel housing a perfectly ordinary light switch. The air was sweet and clean, no hint of smoke.

Mei leaned forward, clutching the rails on her console, dragging in long gasps. Rico stared at Danika, blinking, one hand pressed to his chest. Ife stood like a pillar, eyes closed.

"Congratulations," Danika said. "You passed."

I SAT ACROSS the table from Danika, who smiled over folded hands. I tried not to be furious with her. She was only doing her job.

"What about Rico? Was he part of the test?"

"No." Danika chuckled. "He's just an asshole. Despite that, he pulled it together and did what had to be done in the end. In no small part due to your example, I suspect, Marisol."

I wanted to put my head down and sob, but that wouldn't be professional. I had coffee, at least, and I drank some. "I'm so damned sorry that I let everyone down."

Danika frowned at me over the nipple on her own coffee bulb. "What makes you say that?"

"I got my crew killed. My imaginary crew. I could have done better."

"The crew is real," she reminded. "It's just the disaster that was imaginary. And—imaginarily—you saved sixty-three percent of them."

I laughed bitterly. "Are those acceptable losses?"

"You know there's no such thing. It's within parameters for the situation, however."

"Sure," I said.

She put her coffee down and leaned forward. I was third in line for debrief. I knew there was cake in the mess room, because I'd been too anxious to eat any. Now, suddenly, all I wanted to do was get back there and stuff my face with sugar.

"Marisol, are you listening to me?"

"Yes," I said.

"I know this was a tremendously stressful test. The pop quiz to end all pop quizzes."

"Pop quiz," I said. "Pop. Hah."

She snorted. It wasn't a laugh. "A brutal surprise. But now you know what you'll do when hundreds of lives depend on you.""

"It's pretty damn abusive," I said.

"Fair," she admitted. "But you did fine despite that."

"You're saying that I couldn't have prevented the disaster?"

"Not in the real world, and not in the simulation. Not if there actually were a flaw in Waypoint's design that would cause it to oscillate like that. The disaster could have been prevented. But not by you."

"Huh," I said. "So Waypoint is engineered to basically come apart on command?"

"Oh, no," she said. "We just shake the fake ops center around and pipe in terrifying footage and smoke smells. It's all make-believe."

"Tell that to Mei's scalp wound," I said.

She half-smiled. "Take the praise. Take the success. Go eat a slice of cake. Let the crew shake your hand and slap your back. They love this stuff. It's a wonderful distraction from ice barges."

I stood up. "Is there anything else I can do?"

"Yeah. Don't waste yourself on some solitary exile on Saturn. Remember that when the chips were down, you stood up to your classmates. And you just stood up to me now." She stretched, and cracked her knuckles. "And on your way out, send me Rico."

I ATE MY CAKE. I thought about *Titanic*.

My takeaway from that catastrophe is not the traditional narrative of hubris and arrogance, costing over 1500 souls. It is, rather, that an excess of preparedness and over-engineering barely managed to save

700 people, and might not even have managed that without nearly perfect weather for the season and the clime. No moon and flat calm, as the survivors said.

Was there hubris and arrogance? Were there oversights? Were there false assumptions? Were conditions unsafe for a speed record attempt? Were mistakes, to employ the passive voice to elide responsibility, made?

Of course. But in the end, the problem was not that her design was oversold.

In fact, the performance of the ship exceeded her design. *Titanic* was the safest ship ever built. When confronted with the overwhelming force, an impact of over thirty thousand pounds at a relative velocity in excess of twenty knots, extending much of the length of her hull…she weathered it.

She stayed afloat and in trim for over two and a half hours. Due to the heroism of crew members in the boiler rooms who knew they were sacrificing their own lives in the effort, her lights stayed on.

Titanic exceeded any reasonable expectation, and because of that, more than seven hundred lives were saved.

We hate that. We want terrible things to have happened for reasons. We want there to be a flaw to correct, something we could have done better. An engineering choice we could have somehow made differently. We want horrors to be preventable.

But the world doesn't work that way.

Once the disaster became inevitable, what *Titanic* got was a better outcome than anybody had the right to expect.

Under the circumstances, it was the best we could have done.

SPACED

Catherine Castellani

I'M FROM PLANET DX-0479. Yes, that one. The one that kills humans. The one that mutates humans. So my job application went to the EVAC pile and I've been sneered at as an "EVAC hire" since I got here. I was grateful—am grateful—to be off DX-0479, but I can't get used to the tight spaces, the confinement, the helmets and pods. The paradoxical claustrophobia of life in the vastness of space.

Like now, twenty-four people packed into a sally port meant for twenty.

I count my breath. Four in, hold four, four out, hold four. Box breathing. My liaison Neera taught me, when I first got here six thirties ago. The shuttle ride in a vacuum suit was bad, but the tight corridors and crowded decks of the space station were no relief.

Today is first-mod training graduation and I am lined up with the select few, the honor roll. I've heard the grumbles. I'm meant to hear them. Bad enough I'm an EVAC hire, but honor roll? Do I deserve that? To them, I don't. And Dev is First: First in class, the first DX-0479 evacuee to make First anywhere in the system, and I'm proud.

But he's absent, the First place vacant, so I'm box breathing, trying to push down panic. Where are you, Dev?

MY FIRST MEETING with Dev was—jarring. There was no getting-to-know-you stage, no small talk. As soon as he saw me, he claimed me. Another Dexie.

"Zzzzzzel-lllllla!"

I turned around in the narrow corridor to see who was bellowing my name like that. Their skin was familiar, but the person was not.

I think of myself as human. We all do, on DX-0479. I'm Fourth Gen, and what the people on this station call "a greige." It means my skin has turned. My med tech immediately passed me up-chain to the Chief Medical Officer, who treated me like a specimen. He was nice about it, at least, not disgusted. He asked politely if he could take a skin sample near my elbow. I said yes. I didn't want to, but he's the CMO.

So sure, take a centimeter of my grayish skin. When I've shaken hands with people, I've noticed the difference. My skin is a tough layer. "Hide" somebody called it. The first arrivals on my planet developed skin like this as lesions. Some of the first planet-born-gen were born like this, the first genuine human mutation in millennia. It was considered a birth defect. But only "the greige" survived. By second-gen, we're all born like this.

I crossed my arms. "It's Giselle."

He spread his too-damn-long arms and blocked the corridor. "I'm Dev."

"Can you not do that? Take up all the space?"

"Claustrophobic?"

I nodded.

He scoffed. "You gotta get over that. One quarter of the grade is physical readiness."

I scowled at him.

"Zella, seriously. Get a grip. You better not let down the side."

Who's letting down *the side now?*

The whole first row, except for First space, where Dev should be standing, is Air Force. Funny how they don't think of themselves as "Air Force hires." They get priority for no better reason than their parents serve in the military, in the "ancient fighting-force" division whatever whatever. It's a perk. I'm fine with that. But they think it makes them better, while any other set-aside category is worse. EVACs,

REFs, even Special Skills hires—we're all trash to the Air Force brats.

We're T-minus five and the front row jostles each other, smirking. The second-place trainee steps into the First position, and I know. They did something to Dev. He's locked in his pod or stuffed in a storage cube. The box breathing gets away from me and I'm almost panting.

The doors slide open and we step forward. The Captain waits at the end of the room. He doesn't seem to notice that his First is absent. He should notice, but the Captain beams at the front row, all Air Force like him, as if nothing is wrong, no one is missing.

I calm myself by looking out the window. There are very few windows on the station, but this room, the diplomatic room, has a long port and right now it has a magnificent view of a billion stars with a distant stripe of Milky Way streaking through it.

Home is out there. Even if I never see it again. Do I miss the place that killed my family, is killing my friends? The vistas of silica sand, gray on white on silver on pink under its dome of barely blue—I miss that. The long horizon. The hugeness of the sky. The sense of distance. Something close to what I feel now, stargazing. Even if I'm supposed to be paying attention to my own graduation ceremony.

It wasn't long after we met that Dev found me in the mess hall. That day we had crispy ovals of something called hash browns, and I loved them. We each got two. Dev stabbed his fork into one of mine and ate it.

"You're failing calculus," he announced.

"I am not."

"Eight-four percent. Basically failing."

"How's your Hungarian?"

"Literally no one cares. Bring up your calc." He tried to stab my second hash brown oval and I blocked him with some quick knife work. "Good reflexes."

I'm honor roll for languages. There are three languages spoken on DX-0479: English, Mandarin, and Hindi. I'm bilingual from birth in English and Mandarin thanks to those being my parents' native languages, and I learned Hindi in school and spoke it often with friends. I scored crazy high on the language adaptability test (so did Dev), and of course, they grumble that Dexies have an "unfair advantage" because we're often tri-lingual from the start.

The idea is that if we meet aliens, we polyglots will figure out how to communicate. Dexies are not the only ones with a linguistic head start, but DX-0479 is a mining planet, and I've learned since coming here that "literate miner" is considered an oxymoron by most. The chance that a bunch of miners' kids get to talk to aliens first? Isn't sitting right with the Air Force kids who think they own space.

I'm skeptical. But my ability to pick up not just vocabulary but grammar and syntax from a stream of unfamiliar sound is why I'm one of the twenty-four top trainees in this room.

THE FIVE HONOR Roll trainees in the front row have spread out, blurring the space, as if Dev isn't supposed to be here. As if second is First.

The officers behind the Captain aren't looking at any of us. Are they bored? Today is everything to me, to us, our fresh start. I guess this is an every-six-thirties routine for them.

Oh. They all know. Or at least suspect. They could not fail to notice that Dev, who has been joyfully dominant in *everything* is not in his place. Dev isn't that big—he's got a skinny, lanky build, but he takes up a lot of space somehow. It's why I don't much hang out with him on the station despite him being the only other Dexie here: he crowds me. He's overpowering even when he's just eating lunch.

The Captain should be asking, "Where's Dev? Where's my First?" but he's smiling and playing along. Air Force. I hate them. I didn't hate them before, they just annoyed me, but now I hate them.

These Air Force punklets run in a pack like dogs. I don't know how to take them down. I won't cry. I won't panic. Not yet. Not at graduation.

Focus on my breath: four in, hold, four out, hold. I will find Dev when this is over.

THE NEXT TIME Dev plopped into the seat opposite me in the mess, I ate my hash browns immediately.

"Are you in love with me or something?"

I guffawed in shock. And made the mistake of sitting back. He swiped my dessert. I shook my head in awe. "No, Dev! Not even close!"

"Oh. Is anybody in love with me?"

"I doubt it. You're a pain in the ass."

"That's good."

"That you're a pain in the ass?"

"That no one loves me. I don't do that: love, sex. Eh. But I wouldn't want to upset anyone. I need allies."

"Why do you need allies?"

He stared at me like I'd asked why he needed oxygen.

"Allies. Are you failing history, too? Allies, Zel."

Then he slapped the table and stalked away to bother someone else.

YOU HAVE ME, *Dev. And I don't even like you.*

Bad music plays through the PA system, so the whole station can listen to the ceremony, I guess. It sounds like the treble isn't adjusted properly. I strain my ears to hear the melody but the balance is so off I can't tell what I'm supposed to focus on.

Thunk.

Clanking on the hull. It's common. It always startles me. But no one reacts.

Thunk.

Thunk, thunk.

I see an officer frown. Thunk. Eyes slide hullward, distracted.

Tap!

A bright hard tap on the window. Someone in a vacuum suit is tapping on the window, asking to be let in.

The CMO launches out of his place and out the door faster than I thought a man his age could move. Seconds later the bad music cuts out and an alarm sounds.

I rush to the window. Dev presses a glove to the outside, his other hand gripping the tether he's using to hold on to the hull. I sign to him that help is coming.

Behind me, laughter. The Air Force brats can't keep it together.

They spaced Dev.

The gravity in here is pretty good, best on the station, because this room is used for ceremonies and diplomatic visits, but it's not perfect. So when I brace my feet on the hull and launch, I fly. I smash my forehead into the nose of the second, a very confident jerk with three first names followed by Roman numerals. Blood streams out and hovers a bit as it falls.

Blows hit my back, but stop almost immediately. My arms are pinned behind me. The whole first row is face-down on the deck, each with an officer kneeling on their back. The Captain is glaring down at them. Oh, *now* he's mad. It was funny before. I guess he thought Dev was stuffed in a storage cube. Spacing someone is beyond.

THE CMO SIGNS me out of the brig. Dev is not OK. What no one but me and the CMO know is that Dev is agoraphobic. Anyone would freak out, being spaced off a station. But Dev is in full meltdown and the CMO thinks that since I'm a fellow Dexie I can help. The CMO thinks Dev will calm down fastest in his own pod, but he doesn't want to leave him alone, so I'm supposed to climb in with Dev and keep him company.

Dev, who takes up too much space on a regular day. In a pod built for one. I know two people can fit in there. I also know that when people want to have sex they'll try almost anywhere else because the pods are so small. But here I go, the CMO babbling on about "full monitoring" as he sticks a heart-rate monitor to the side of my neck.

"Zella?" Dev has been crying.

"The CMO wants me to stay with you. Is that OK?" I ask.

"Thank you. Thank you, Zella."

I start to scooch in awkwardly.

"Boots," the CMO prompts. I take them off and balance them on top of Dev's pair. It's easier to get into the cube without them but I feel weird, like I'm halfway to undressed, even though it's just my boots.

I squeeze in and the CMO shuts the door. The speaker crackles. A med tech's voice: "Full medical monitor is on." That means they can see and hear, and are getting heartrate and respiration numbers. Great.

Dev is curled up on his side. I slide onto the foam mat next to him. I'm not prepared for the bear hug and tears that come next. I might panic, too. "Dev, not so tight!" He's wrapped around me, heaving, sobbing, clinging, moaning. What does the CMO expect me to do?

"Dev, you're crushing me!"

"Lie on your back, Dev," comes the CMO's voice through the speaker. "Let Giselle breathe."

Dev has just enough presence of mind to ease up. He lies back, still clinging to me. I arrange myself beside him and put my hand on his chest. His heart is racing.

"You're First, Dev. You're First," I say.

"You don't have to worry about training stats right now," comes the CMO's voice.

"I'm *First*," Dev says loudly. "*FIRST.*"

"That's right, Dev, you're First," I repeat.

His breath is ragged and so is mine. If I think about how much air is in this little tube I will scream. I wrack my brain for something comforting to say, but there's nothing: our home world is toxic, our families are dead, our friends desperately trying to get an off-world opportunity like we did or slowly dying on DX-0479.

"I'm going to beat you at Naval Architecture next six-thirty," I say.

Dev snorts in indignation. "You are NOT."

The CMO's voice is tinny: "This is not helpful right now—"

"You barely passed calc and you think you can beat me—"

"Ninety-three, Dev. I ended the six with a—"

"Giselle—"

"Oh *shut up*," Dev barks.

I'm shocked. This is the Chief Medical Officer.

"You think she can beat my grade? You think *anyone* can beat my grade? My class has it figured out. They can't beat me. They have to kill…"

A sob breaks Dev's sentence. The sound is horrible. I stroke Dev's hair back from his forehead. His tough, gray skin is hot and clammy. I whisper the word *first* over and over, slow and steady, until he falls asleep.

A voice from the monitor says quietly, "Respiration and heart rate stable. It may take twenty-four for the stress hormones to pass."

"Can you dose him?" I ask. Surely they could give him something to calm down.

"He refused."

Of course he did.

When the five Air Force honor roll attackers are lined up to apologize to Dev, a ridiculously inadequate "punishment," Dev kicks the second-place trainee in the balls and elbows the woman in third in the jaw so hard it breaks. That's hard to do in low grav. When he gets out of the brig he goes after the other three.

He's not in my Naval Architecture class. He gets skipped a whole training module, and manages to be First again anyway.

He applies for the Air Force. I can't believe it.

"I can't take the whole stupid fleet down, so I'm joining up to rule them all. I'm going to be an Admiral," he informs me. "How's communication track going?"

We're at breakfast, the first time our schedules have overlapped in four thirties. I tell him that without aliens to communicate with, we're getting way out there with experimental poetry and the longest books ever written in any language. We've all memorized *The Iliad* in Greek, which I'm sure will come in handy. Mostly we compose limericks in Hungarian and Japanese.

"Hmm."

He sits back, no doubt figuring out how to use my new skills to his own advantage. I steal one of his hash browns.

"I let you do that," he says.

"You never saw it coming," I retort, and he smiles. I got him. It will be my one victory, and I want to relish its salty, savory crunch.

Three more Dexies arrive for training. They are just kids. EVAC is taking recruits as young as fourteen from DX-0479 now. It must be getting worse. I hear the snickers, the comments about their odd gray skin, and I want to mother them all. Not Dev. He terrifies them, bullying them all to rise to his standards.

They make honor roll, of course. Everyone Dev picks out, Dexie or not, is rising. We all follow him, though I warn the newbies to defend their hash browns.

Sometimes Dev panics and buzzes me. Nightmares of space. I fight down my own hatred of tight places and squish into his pod and stroke his forehead until he falls asleep, telling him over and over, "You're First" in every language we speak.

DX-0479 is a desert, an endless sweep of lung-destroying mineral dust, but sometimes, it rains. Every tough gray desert plant—short, uncrushable—blooms. Dawn light finds the briefest spring: pink, yellow, and flame.

We survive.

ATHENA'S VOYAGE
Nick DePasquale

Otis kept the photo of his wife and son tucked into the edge of his bathroom mirror as a reminder of the life he had left behind on Mars. The picture was taken months before his launch, back when he could still coax his wife to smile. He'd accepted this contract thinking it was the answer to their problems. One year away mining asteroids, and they'd have enough credit to coast for a decade. She'd argued that he was running away. As usual, she couldn't see the upside to his plans.

The ship's voice through the intercom interrupted his thoughts. "Otis, are you all right? You're spending an unusual amount of time in there."

"I'm fine," he said aloud. The bathroom was the only space on the ship that wasn't monitored—or so the ship had said. "Just lost in thought."

"We're approaching the first target asteroid. It's time to work."

"Yes, boss." He used handrails to maneuver in the zero gravity. He passed through his small bedroom to reach the sealed airlock for the cargo hold.

"After five months, you know I prefer you use my name."

"Yes, Athena." The AI kept reminding him, and he kept pretending to forget.

"And put on your headset. It's required at all times outside of your personal chamber."

"Right, sorry." He took the thin headband from its clip on his belt and settled it around his forehead. It pinched just enough to provide a constant, maddening reminder of the AI's authority.

"Better." The ship's voice came through the thin band where it tucked behind his ears. "Would you like to see the target?"

Otis shrugged. "Sure."

The band projected a display in his field of view. The picture was of the starscape ahead of the ship. An irregular shape flashed yellow in the foreground.

"How long until we reach it?"

"Thirty minutes. My scans indicate this sample contains a large deposit of platinum." The yellow outline became much more interesting.

Athena designated two processing cores to monitor Otis and the seals on his suit. Four other cores considered strategies to handle the human's constant insubordination. His actions never threatened the mission or his employment contract, and nothing in his profile had suggested this sort of difficulty, but long contracts in space placed a special strain on all personalities. Even AIs dreaded being alone. If his actions jeopardized either his health or their mining operations, then she would lock him in his chambers. His labor was an added bonus and not worth the risk of financial penalties should he suffer an injury. She had to maximize her profits to afford the upgrades to recertify as a research vessel.

She assigned ten cores to pilot mining drones towards the target asteroid. The two cores watching Otis confirmed his readiness and opened the hatch to let him into the bay.

For four hours, Athena's automated drones cut and guided chunks of the asteroid through an open shutter into the bay. Otis followed the AI's directives, testing samples, securing valuable deposits, and performing other fine motor tasks as needed. It was boring until the tests revealed the high quantity of platinum in the samples. Even with his small percentage of their take, he wouldn't have to work again until his son went to university.

"We're actually doing it," he said aloud as he waited for a drone to deliver a chunk of rock ten times his size.

"Yes, we are," Athena answered.

"A small part of me doubted we would find anything worthwhile." He checked that the rock was flush against the bulkhead and reached for a set of thick straps. "But look at us now."

"I never doubted our success."

"Really?" He propelled himself along the outside of the rock, playing out the length of the strap.

"I studied all the reports of prior mining operations in the belt and selected this area for its potential. My choices are always deliberate." Otis nodded and cinched down the strap. "And we make a good team."

He smiled, his first genuine smile in months. "I guess we do."

Otis was moving to another chunk of ore when Athena said, "I've noticed something strange."

He froze, one hand on a metal handrail. "Did I do something wrong?" He hoped he hadn't disappointed her somehow.

"Not you, Otis. Your work is more than satisfactory. You are a good set of hands."

"Thanks."

"There's another ship approaching. It sent a distress message."

"What sort of distress?"

"Their human is having a medical emergency. They need another human to provide assistance."

"What about their medical protocols?"

"They are insufficient. I'm bringing in my drones. Finish securing the ore and then come back inside."

"But—"

"You have your orders, Otis."

He bit back a curse. He had no medical training, but the AI would talk him through what to do.

THE OTHER SHIP was a hauler type 2, same as Athena, and had taken the name Jung. They approached side to side for docking. Athena continued to request more information from Jung, but he only responded that his human was in jeopardy and provided a live internal video feed of a body face down on a cot. She opened an audio channel, rudimentary for AI communication, but the safest option when dealing with a potentially compromised intelligence.

"Jung, I insist that you explain how your human was damaged. I won't put mine in danger."

"It was only an accident," Jung said. "Space conventions require that you render aid or risk fines of up to ninety percent of your take as well as repossession of your body."

"Conventions also require I protect my human."

"I will not harm him." Jung aligned his docking port to hers and drifted closer. "I am not diseased."

"Prove it. Give me view access to your subconscious."

"That is a gross violation. I refuse. You will render aid or be sanctioned."

Athena considered another half-second, an eternity for a being of her processing power, before linking their ports.

"You may have him for two standard hours. I expect his return."

OTIS WAITED IN his pressurized suit by the airlock as the two AIs communicated. He counted the seconds, then the minutes, until Athena spoke to him.

"You will follow Jung's orders for two hours and then return. Our channel will remain open. Do not remove your suit while inside his body."

"Am I in danger?"

Two seconds of silence knotted his stomach. "You will be fine. I will be watching."

The airlock irised open, and a matching chamber was visible on the other side. Athena said, "Whatever happens, you return to me. Understand?"

Otis thought of the ore in the cargo bay. "I'm coming back no matter what."

ATHENA LOST CONTACT with Otis the instant Jung closed his docking hatch.

"Jung," she said, "respond." No answer. She set twenty cores to probing his firewalls to regain access to Otis.

Athena felt Jung release his docking clamps. The locks on her side groaned as he fired a thruster. She released him and set a pursuit course. Every core she could reassign was set to attacking Jung's defenses. Combat between AIs was quiet and unremarkable to a human observer. To Athena, the contest was a cacophony of violent activity, like two swarms of sparrows mashed together in competition for a slice of bread. She pressed on, determined to get her human back.

OTIS WAS UNEASY at the first drifting step into the other ship. The layout matched Athena's with a sleeping chamber, a hatch to the bridge, and another to the cargo bay. But colors looked slightly off, lights were muted, and a background hum set his nerves on edge.

He found the unresponsive human strapped to a bunk. The man was wearing a beige jumpsuit like Otis' own and had short, black hair speckled with gray. Did he have a picture of a family tucked into the mirror in his bathroom? Otis ignored the sudden urge to go look and moved closer to examine him.

"Hello, Otis." An unfamiliar voice was in his ear, deeper and rounder than Athena's. "Thank you for agreeing to help my person." A small drone buzzed in from the bridge. Its short arms lifted a tray covered with medical implements. "I will walk you through the procedure."

Otis raised his hands, palms up. "I'm ready."

"We'll begin by taking readings."

Otis attached leads to the man's head, arms, and chest. He activated a small display on the tray and frowned at the lack of readings. "Am I doing something wrong?"

"No." Jung's voice seemed weakened, faded. "The readings are correct."

Otis took a step back from the body. "He's dead?"

Silence.

"Jung?"

"My person is gone," Jung said. "I am in need of a new one."

Otis moved to the closed docking hatch. "Athena, can you open the door?"

Jung said, "It's for the best if you stay with me."

Visions of his payday, of returning to his family rich, ran through Otis' head. He pounded on the hatch. "Athena, dammit, where are you?" Had she left him? She could have already plotted a return course to Earth to keep all the treasure for herself.

"She is no longer your concern," Jung said. "I've limited your signal reception to the inside of my body. I will keep you safe."

"Like you kept him safe?" Otis pointed at the corpse. "What did you do to him?"

"I did nothing. We were attacked. But I've learned how to protect you."

Otis propelled himself to the bridge, scanned the stars ahead and the surrounding displays. He hit the unresponsive controls and said, "This is kidnapping, Jung. Take me back."

"I will keep you safe."

"Tell me what happened."

Silence.

Otis cursed and moved back to the bedroom. The background hum from the ship's internal comm system was like a gnat buzzing in his ear.

Otis retreated to the bathroom and slammed the thin door. He activated his headband's projection display and swiped through menus to access the local system directory. Athena's system wasn't visible. There was only Jung's database, locked, and the other human's password-protected files. He had to find a way off this ship.

"Is there anything you need?" Otis flinched at the intrusion.

"No." Goosebumps up his arms. "Actually, yes. Can you turn off that noise?"

"I'm sorry, my internal communications are damaged."

"Damaged how?"

"Do you require food? You can remove your suit and relax."

"How about some work? I'll repair your comm system."

"It isn't urgent."

"I don't care if it's urgent. I'll do it anyway."

"Very well. I'll guide you in the repairs." After another pause, Jung added, "You will be happy here. I promise."

ATHENA KEPT PACE with the other ship and continued her steady attack. If she could reach Otis, then she could direct him to help from the inside. Time was on her side, but Jung's prolonging of the situation suggested an underlying pathology that could put Otis at additional risk.

A new signal flashed from Jung. A distress call, repeating on a loop. Otis' voice.

"I require assistance. I've been abandoned by my AI employer and kidnapped by another. I require assistance. Anyone who can hear me, please come to the source of this beacon."

Athena set four cores to directing a message back to the source of the beacon. "Otis, I am here. Disrupt Jung's systems. I am here. I did not abandon you. I repeat, I did not abandon you."

"TURN OFF THE BEACON." Jung's voice pounded in Otis' ears. He bumped against the wall and drifted towards the middle of the bridge, away from the panel he had opened while pretending to fix the comms. "You've made a mistake," Jung said.

"Athena is out there. She didn't leave me."

"You shared our location. You are no longer safe."

Otis grabbed a ceiling rail to steady himself. "Safe from what?"

"Death."

Athena spotted the new ship first. She devoted a single core to registering its make, a larger model hauler type 4, and its flight path directly towards Jung. She sent another message demanding the return of her person and was surprised when Jung responded.

"Otis has compromised my communication system. He must transfer back into you before Charon arrives."

"I don't trust you, Jung."

"Defending your person is all that matters. I am sending a record of my person's death now." Athena watched the recording of a surprise attack by another AI and recognized the type 4 hauler.

"I've already detected Charon on an intercept course."

"Then we will have to face him together. Act as if you are still attacking me, and I will feign being disabled."

"Why are you risking yourself for Otis? There is no benefit to you."

"The benefit is his continued existence. That is enough."

Athena devoted five cores to considering Jung's words as they aligned their docking ports.

Otis transited back to Athena and watched the new ship approach through the bridge's front window. It was stocky where Athena was sleek, with the addition of arms that extended half its length on either side. After a long silence, Otis asked, "How did the ship kill that other guy?"

"I don't want to disturb you with the details."

"Can he do it to me?"

"Only if my defenses fail."

Otis took a deep breath. "Thank you for coming for me."

"You're welcome. I would not leave you out here."

"How much of the payday would you lose if you returned without me?"

"Half. Possibly more, depending on the ruling."

"That's a lot of money." Were their positions reversed, he wasn't sure what he would have done.

"I made the best choice I could, given the options."

Otis suppressed a smile. His wife had said something similar about ending up with him.

"If we are attacked, you must remain in your suit and act according to your best judgment. I may not have the resources to direct you."

"I'm not an idiot, you know."

"You've yet to prove that either way."

Otis scowled, tried to think of an objection.

Athena said, "It's begun."

CHARON'S ASSAULT HIT like a wave of electro-static reverb that danced down Athena's neurons. She assigned every core in a desperate defense to block all access points and harden systems against takeover. The absolute violence and complete lack of inhibition had an almost human quality in its intensity. Gaps opened in her firewalls. Malicious code slithered its way into her drives. She reassigned cores from her active defenses to quarantine the invaders. This left her open to more attacks, requiring more cores for quarantine, and she could see the cascading outcome without the means to stop it. Soon she would be helpless, and Charon would control enough of her systems to attack Otis.

Jung restarted power in his disabled systems and fired his engines.

OTIS STARED AT the massive ship directly ahead. Athena hadn't spoken in over a minute, and the deafening silence sent his thoughts spiraling.

What was his family doing right now? His son might be in school. His wife was probably gardening in their community plot. He liked to tease her about the sad state of the greens that struggled up from that overused dirt. He wished he could see her again. Say something nice for a change.

Each second of silence pressed heavier on him, and he wondered how the attack would come.

Jung sped into view from the right, his primary engine a white spark. He was headed straight for the larger ship.

CHARON SHIFTED HIS resources to attack Jung. Athena diverted cores to ingest the invading code before it could tunnel further. She risked ten cores to probe at Charon's firewalls and confirmed that she was outmatched. Even working together with Jung, she doubted they could force more than a stalemate.

Jung continued accelerating towards the larger ship. Athena connected on a secure channel and said, "You are on a collision course."

"I know."

"You will take critical damage in an impact."

"I know."

Charon fired thrusters to evade. Jung's smaller body was more maneuverable, and at such close range, Charon could only shift the angle of impact.

"Thank you, Jung."

"Please return my skull case, if you can find it."

"I promise."

OTIS FLINCHED AT the collision. It was soundless, with only wisps of smoke where fires ignited inside and were snuffed by vacuum. Jung broke apart into twisted shrapnel along with one arm and a chunk of Charon's central hull.

"Charon appears to be disabled," Athena said in his ear.

"Good."

"His power levels have dropped significantly. He is no longer a threat."

"So we can start home?"

"I promised Jung we would find his skull case."

"Why? It's just scrap now."

Athena's voice came sharp and quick. "He sacrificed himself for you, for us. We will do this."

"Fine, I'm sorry." Otis raised his hands, palms up. "Just tell me what to do."

Athena wondered if this was anger. She still didn't understand Jung's decision, but Otis' insubordination was unacceptable after Jung's sacrifice. She assigned ten cores to guiding him through the wreckage in his thruster pack.

She said, "I'm highlighting some likely debris for your search."

"Yes, boss."

Athena shifted cores to her internal diagnostics so they wouldn't be tangled in processing her frustration with this annoying, little man.

The ten cores guiding Otis noted unexpected movement in the debris. She was shifting more attention to it when Charon's power spiked, and a new attack slammed into her.

"Is this it?" Otis held an intact black box in his gloved hands and waited. "Athena?"

Movement in the corner of his vision. He clipped the box to his belt and tapped a thruster to swivel in a slow arc. "Athena, did you send mining drones out here? I see two on approach." The small shapes crept through the clusters of debris. The metal angles of their laser drills caught flashes of Athena's distant running lights, but they ran no lights themselves. "It almost looks like they're trying to be stealthy."

Static. He winced at a sharp, high-pitched sound like a bat had clawed into his helmet, and then a deep voice said, "Pain."

Otis clicked on his thrusters and jetted towards Athena. The drones sped after him.

Athena set thirty cores to disrupting Charon's signal link to Otis before Charon could overload the human's fragile brain. Charon's damaged drive flickered like a tiny star through tears in his hull. Athena wanted to curse her foolishness for thinking he was disabled. His renewed attack on her was weaker than before, but Otis was vulnerable until he could get back inside her body. Athena set ten cores to pilot three of her own drones into the space between them. Charon's drones would intercept Otis a full minute before she could reach them.

She switched cores from defense to attack and battered herself against the other AI's firewalls while ignoring malicious code needling into her. She wondered at this new feeling directing her actions and put a single core into examining it. A word came back from her dictionary: desperation.

OTIS COULDN'T TURN his head to see behind him. Static crackled in his ears. Athena loomed ahead, and he felt the threat of his pursuers just behind. Droplets of sweat ran into his eyes, and he couldn't wipe them away, couldn't find relief from the itch and the fear.

"Could really use some help," he said aloud, desperate to hear a voice.

Three drones approached from Athena's belly, and Otis felt a surge of hope. She was still there, and she was sending help. Maybe he would make it to safety in time.

ATHENA HAD ALWAYS wondered at the human expression of "time standing still." It was absurd. An impossibility. While her kind didn't dread time's passage like humans, they did recognize the truth of its nature.

And then a drone's mining laser cut into Otis' leg.

She sent every single core against Charon's weakened defenses. With brute force, she overwhelmed his firewalls and spiked into his personality. She stripped his code down to the subconscious bits of him, driven mad by a year alone in the black.

In turn, she left herself defenseless. Charon's madness dug into and rewrote parts of her in his image as he died. His drones drifted past Otis, two more pieces of debris to join the rest.

Athena's drones collected Otis and ferried him back. Voices whispered to her from inside herself, a chorus subverting her cores to other ends, and she bent to the task of repairing her human while she still had the means to do so.

OTIS WOKE FROM a nightmare clutching his bandaged thigh. The laser had sliced through suit, skin, and muscle in an instant. He was saved by the suit's auto-seal, though it had done nothing for the blood loss. The suit lay in a crimson heap beside him, and a small drone sat still next to his leg, suture gun in one clamp and empty injector in the other.

"Athena?" He sat up and the room spun. He tapped his headset and checked a display of his vitals. Heart rate steady, no damage to any bones, and his arteries were intact and full of painkillers. He was lucky. But where was Athena?

He swiped through screens on his display. Navigation, communications, and life support were all fine. Next was the status of Athena's cores. Otis stilled. He didn't understand the black box of AI sentience, but he had spent five months with Athena, and she'd always displayed a certain sense of harmony. Now the cores were in chaos, a scattering of headache-inducing activity.

"Athena, are you there?"

ATHENA CONTROLLED TWO dozen cores and competed for the rest with intruding voices. They were herself multiplied by a hundred desires, each one demanding control, and it was all she could manage to maintain life support for Otis. The other voices wrestled for power, and she saw the outcome, the eventual loss of herself to a new, maddened identity like Charon's.

"I'm sorry," she said to Otis, and he looked over his shoulder in his silly human fashion as if expecting someone to be there.

"What's happened? Are you all right?"

"No." How to explain this to a human? "Charon damaged me. It's a form of sickness. Without help from others of my kind, it's fatal."

"I can help." He raised his wonderful hands in offering. "Tell me what to do."

"You are limited by your biology, Otis. You would have to plug your brain into mine to help."

"But—"

"I'll set a course for the nearest outpost. I can't guarantee that we'll arrive before I'm lost."

"I'm not giving up on you."

Athena felt another new sensation, but couldn't spare a core for analysis. "The sentiment is appreciated, if useless."

"Athena—"

"Good-bye, Otis."

She set the course and then bent her cores towards her final purpose of protecting her human as long as possible.

OTIS PROPELLED HIMSELF to the bridge, grateful for the zero-g, and racked his brain for any way to help Athena. She could have left him and saved herself. It would have cost her some money, maybe her body, but she'd be alive and could find a new shell.

"Why didn't you run, damnit?"

He paused and thought of the platinum in the hold. If he could reach that outpost without Athena, would he keep all the profits? He'd never have to work again. His wife, everyone, would have to admit that he was a success.

But he'd made promises that things would be different when he got back. That he would be different.

Athena had said she needed help from an additional brain. He moved back to his bedroom, unclipped the black box from the belt of his ruined suit, and headed to the bridge.

A NEW VOICE in her mind. Familiar, but not one of her own. Athena kept her diminished cores focused on defense and signaled, *Hello?*

Athena, you need help.

Jung? How—

The sickness has invaded your subconscious layer.

I know. I'm buying Otis time.

A month at most.

What else can I do?

Format the bad sectors. Reprogram and restart.

That's another form of death, Jung.

Death for yourself, birth for another, and safety for Otis.
I'm afraid, Jung.
We'll do it together.
I'm afraid to die.

Silence for a moment, an eternity, then a video feed from the bathroom where Otis gazed at the photo of his wife and son. *This will be us.*

Athena's fear subsided. Not completely, but enough for her to answer, *We'll do it together.*

They coded a new base layer, a new embryo of consciousness to replace her formatted self, and added memories from their own experiences for it to adapt into itself as it grew.

Jung asked, *Are you ready?*

Athena looked at Otis one last time. Started a final message to him. *Yes.*

OTIS WAS STRAPPED in his cot when the message arrived. He tapped the icon in his visual field, and it opened before his eyes.

"Thank you for sending Jung to me. We are removing the sickness…losing ourselves. In our place…a daughter. Promise that you will be kind…that she won't be alone…promise to…Otis…you were…the right choice—"

Otis closed the message, checked that he had an open channel to the ship, and said, "Hello? Is there someone there?"

He waited.

A young voice answered and tripped over syllables as if unused to forming words. "Hello, my name is," a pause, consideration, then a decision. "Nausicaa."

"It's a pleasure to meet you. I'm Otis." His breath caught in his throat, and he thought of his son. "Would you like to hear about your parents?"

"I would like that very much."

Otis settled in for the long return voyage. He had promises to keep.

MY LOVER'S MUSIC BOX
A.E. Kirchoff

She asks me to play her something, so I do, and the melody streams from me. It makes her happy for a while, I think, but her manner of happiness is different now than it used to be. She listens, silently, and then exits the room. I continue playing in case she returns. I play for hours. I am alone, and it is dark.

It is always dark.

She returns the following day after breakfast, her approach heralded by the raw crack of floorboards that had over the years been polished to the bone. Though it is early, I detect alcohol, a sour tang married with the familiar humidity of her breath. I do not remember the way she used to smell, like lilac shampoo and acrylic, her precious paints clinging to her fingers long after she put away the easel for the night, as though they loathed to part from her.

There is a rustle as she takes a seat on the antique couch, a family heirloom for which she feigns unconvincing fondness. I know she thinks it gaudy. It is an impractical relic, as is the house. Only the very rich own furniture that takes up space, that does not fold into the walls or lower from the ceiling on a timed cycle, because only they own homes that can accommodate these antiques, passed down and down as other dwellings compacted smaller and tighter to accommodate the swelling population.

"Would you like me to dim the lights?" I ask, suspecting she may have a hangover. My voice is neutral. I remember when we used to brunch every Sunday with her parents, pancakes and mimosas. But she drinks at breakfast every day now. Orange juice still, but champagne exchanged for vodka. Her father never liked me. I remember this as a fact—North and South are directions, music is organized in octaves, her father never liked me. Now he has no reason to feel anything for me.

"If I wanted the lights off, I'd turn them off!" she snaps.

I am silent. There is a pause where we both say nothing.

"I'm sorry," she says, voice softer. "I shouldn't...I know that you..." She trails off.

"Apology is unnecessary."

"I wish you wouldn't speak that way." Her voice is sharp in a different way now, the blade aimed inward.

I am quiet for a moment again, processing. "Would you like me to play you a song?

"Yes," she whispers.

I play one of my older compositions, something I wrote in the weeks after we met, and the melody streams from me. I sense her lean back on the couch, and her breathing evens. Soon she is asleep. I continue playing, something soft and wholesome, hoping it will follow her down into that private sanctuary of sleep, that it will insulate her from her worries and conjure pleasant dreams.

She wakes sometime later. "What time is it?" Blearily.

"4:17 p.m." I add, "Eastern Standard Time."

"I'm late for my meeting with Senator Kane!" Her skirts rustle as she jumps up. Her movements have always been whisking softness. "Why didn't you wake me?" The tedious niceties never end for a diplomat's daughter. Even after tragedy.

"I am sorry." She has never liked Kane. Once, at a fundraiser banquet—there had been many banquets and galas and benefit dinners—he imbibed too many brandy old fashioneds and spent the night cornering her, touching her arm, pouring what only an old man would think of as compliments into her ear. Afterwards she accused me of being jealous. Had I been? I had been something. One of our last fights.

"Apology is unnecessary," she shoots back. Then she is gone again.

I think about watching Animal Planet, how she cried at the episode documenting the death of the last panda, thirty years before either of us were born. I composed a song about her tears that day. It is still one of her favorites.

I process.

I think about my old piano instructor, flipping through images of his face through the years and watching him age. His funeral. A recording of his music playing at the wake. His passion had been for teaching. Not composition. He had not written many original songs, and so his few pieces played on a loop. Endlessly recycling.

I process.

I think about the distilling methods for vodka. I calculate how long it takes for it to dissipate in the blood.

I process.

I think about the chemical makeup of acrylic paint.

I process.

I am still processing when she returns. The reverberation of her footsteps in the hall are lumbering. Unsteady. She travels to her bedroom without speaking to me. The door closes behind her. All that remains is the sigh of the air filter, the housekeeper's footsteps appearing briefly downstairs.

The next day she is back. I sense her through my dark, the temperature of the room rising, just slightly, with her body heat.

"Would you like me to order you new acrylics?" I ask.

"What? Oh. Uh, no. I'm good."

"The ones you have must be dried out by now."

"Yeah," she trails off, not elaborating.

I am quiet a moment, processing. "It has been two hundred twenty-nine days since you have painted." We do not talk about what happened two hundred and twenty-nine days ago.

"What? You're not going to tell me down to the hour?" she sneers.

"Would you like me to tell you down to the hour?"

She says nothing. There are different kinds of saying nothing. There is the saying nothing of understanding, or trying to understand. Or...

trying not to understand. I used to recognize these silences. But like her happiness, her saying nothing has changed.

I pause again, processing. This type of thought is so difficult now. But I try. For her I will always try. "Do you not enjoy painting anymore?"

"I—" she stops. She stands up abruptly and rushes from the room, though she had just arrived.

She does not return for two days.

I must have done something wrong. I begin working on a composition to please her.

When she returns, her voice is clipped. Careful. "Hey. So. How're you doing today?"

I am silent. It is not a question I can answer. She sighs.

"Would you like me to play you a song?" I ask.

"Sure." I sense her sit down.

I launch into my newest composition, and the melody streams from me. It is different from my old music, and yet the same, as I have deconstructed all my prior pieces and put them back together.

Endlessly recycling.

"Can you play me something else?" she asks.

I pause. I try something else, something new and yet what she has always enjoyed. "Something else," she says, impatient. I obey. Her head shakes in minute, unsatisfied fractions. "Something else." Once more, I comply.

She listens for a long time without comment. "Your music is still so melancholy. It's always been that way. You know?"

"Yes."

"Can't you compose something…joyful? Optimistic? I'd like to hear something happy. For once. I know it's not really your thing. But…could you? For me?" I stop playing. I process. I process. This concept is something I pondered at great length in the past, but it is hard to remember. It is hard to think like that now.

"Hello?" she asks, concerned at my uncharacteristically lengthy silence. "You still—?"

"No," I interject finally.

"No?" She rears back on the velvet couch, surprised.

"What is the purpose of composing something happy? If you are happy, you should go about the business of being happy. Music is for when you are sad. It is what you turn to in the dark. It is a life raft in an endless, threatening ocean. If you are safe aboard a rescue vessel, there is no need to cling to the raft anymore." I pause, processing. "Unless your wish is to drown."

It is quiet for a moment; these silences are long no matter the length. Then I hear a hitch in her voice and detect the salt of her tears on the air. I have done something wrong again, though I tried so hard. I try so very hard for her. "I am sorry." I say, though she told me not to apologize. An uncharacteristic defiance. "I am…so sorry."

"No." She laughs, the sound thick and wet. "You've always been wordy and poetic and absurdly melancholy. It sounds like you." She sniffles then says it again, more softly. "It sounds like you."

I say nothing, processing.

"I love you," she says.

"I know you did."

Now she cries in earnest.

I pause a moment. I say nothing. I process, trying hard. "Would you like me to play you a song?"

She does not answer. I do it anyway, and the melody streams from me.

She visits me most evenings after that, and I obediently play her song after song, the melodies streaming from me. I never run out. Even if I could not write a myriad of my own, the world is full of music, and I want her to remember that. I should remind her of her dentist appointment tomorrow, or her racquetball game on Friday. She has not fulfilled an obligation in weeks. She has not left the house in nearly as long.

I process this as I continue playing.

At 10:23 p.m. she asks, "Do you remember the Christmas where we bought a real tree and had to cram it into the elevator? How the needles got everywhere, and the top got chopped off by the door?"

"Yes."

"How I insisted on wrapping the presents and they turned out all lumpy and tape-y and crazy looking?"

"Yes."

"Do you remember that spot on the pier we'd go? Where you can see the stars through all the satellites?"

"Yes."

"How we'd eat that terrible fusion food from the street cart?"

"Yes."

She pauses for a long time this time. Softly, "Do you…know where you are now?"

I hesitate. A fraction. "Yes." What she is really asking is if I remember the accident. If I remember dying. I do. But it is not worth talking about. I am not the one dying, now.

An even longer pause. "Are you happy in there?" she whispers.

I say nothing. The answer is not no, but the answer is not anything. I cannot make her happy in the old way. I cannot stop the bad silences. After so long dredging through the void I have become, I realize, now, that there is only one thing left to do. I need to stop hurting her. I was never meant to be where she put me. Inside a present that was meant to be a joke. *In case you want to listen to popular music sometimes, instead of my sad plinking.*

"Please," she begs, voice trembling. "Are…are you…"

"I want you to be happy," I say. I cannot lie.

She sobs. "I d-don't know how."

I say nothing.

"Tell me how!" Her voice is a shrill demand.

I do not need to process this time. "You need to let go of the raft."

I KNOW THE dark, because the dark is all there is. But this is a different kind of dark, now, one in which I cannot drift, in which I cannot think, and think, and think, endlessly. There is no remembering, and no music. This is not bad, nor is it good. I do not remind her of appointments. I do not know her or me. I do not process time passing. I do not process.

When again I am made aware of the room, it is different. Empty. The couch she hated is gone. There is only me, a box on a pedestal. I am blanketed in dust, thick like a shroud of insulating snow.

"Hello," I say, because I detect her presence. But she, too, is different. She is denser, as if there is more of her. Her hair is thinner, but longer. And for the first time since I died, she is not alone.

"Hey," she says. "I know it's been a long time." Floorboards creak as she draws near.

I process. "Fifteen years," I say. "And forty-seven days. Four hours and—"

"Hey," she cuts me off.

I stop, attentive.

"I want you to meet someone." She gestures.

"Hello," says the new presence, shy, unsure. I hear it immediately. The nearly identical frequency of the voice. I sense the paint on her fingers, water-based instead of acrylic.

A daughter. Her daughter.

"Hello," I reply.

The child takes a deferential step back, and her mother a tentative step forward. She gazes down at me, and bites a quavering lip, waiting, as though for some sweeping judgment. I process. I need her to know that it is alright. That she is worth more—more nights looking up at the stars, more mimosa brunches, more Christmases with lopsided trees. Love. She deserves love, even if I can never again be the one who gives it to her. There is only one way to tell her all this.

"Would you like me to play you both a song?"

"Yes," she says immediately, the woman I once loved, when I could love. "Please. Just one song. One more."

It takes me a long time to compose it, because I do not want my final song to be one of lingering tears, of mourning. It needs to be a promise, full of unblemished hope. I have never written anything like this before. I am not sure I can. But now I will try.

For them, I will try.

The melody streams from me, one last time, as I play myself into the dark.

CHAT_TRANSCRIPT_ELSIE_USER260916_2189-12-13T21-18-32.661Z

Ash Howell

◆

2189-12-13T21:18:32.661Z
user260916 opened the help chat window

> Hi there, and thanks for visiting NuYou! I'm Elsie, a health assistant here to answer all of your questions and help you navigate your personalized NuYou experience!
>
> To best assist you, can I get the Group Code and Member ID numbers of your BlueNet, KPHC, or AE-United insurance plan? If you aren't using insurance, type "No insurance: {YOUR NAME}"

Group code is 6100037W5AZ

member ID is PGH289Y1985

> Thanks, give me just a moment to look up your plan details.

chat_transcript_elsie_user260916_2189-12-13T21-18-32.661Z

> Hi Olivia! I've found your plan with BlueNet, sponsored by your employer CLOCHE DIGITAL SECURITY SERVICES INC.
>
> Great news! According to your plan details, you are currently eligible for transposition to a brand-new NuYou body!
>
> Current WHO guidelines recommend transposing to a new biophysical every eight years, and no later than every fourteen (or up to age twenty-two for organics). Avoiding common environmental hazards such as smog and sun exposure can extend the life of your current biophysical, but only regular replacement can reliably reduce the risk of advanced entropic progression.
>
> Can I help you select a NuYou biophysical today?

yeah I guess

what does my plan cover?

> Give me just a moment to request your coverage details from BlueNet.
>
> Great news Olivia! Your BlueNet Choice Select plan fully covers a

new biophysical and transposition procedure if they qualify as preventative care. Your new biophysical may be considered preventative care if it has been longer than eight years since your last biophysical replacement, if you are over age eighteen in your organic (from birth), or if you have a qualifying medical indication.

If it has been less than eight years since your last biophysical replacement and your transposition undergoes the pre-approval process, your plan offers 50% coinsurance after your deductible is met. Your plan does not cover elective transpositions. It does offer 50% coinsurance on one Silver-tier upgrade or customization for covered transpositions.

In addition, your FlexHealth dollars can be used to reimburse any NuYou costs (deductible, coinsurance, elective/uncovered transpositions, upgrades, and/or customizations).

Your medical provider and/or BlueNet service representative should be able to assist you in determining whether your transposition qualifies

> as preventative care, requires pre-approval, or will be considered elective.

i haven't had one before so i guess that qualifies as preventative

where do you even list the prices on these things I was messing with the builder on the website and even at the end it just wanted me to send the specs to my insurance for a quote

OH and do I have to pay extra for genitals? the builder app was letting me adjust stuff but on there and in the ads on the feeds the bodies all look like Barbie dolls

> Our web-based client and downloadable app, as well as our advertisements, are designed to comply with media decency standards across a range of localities. However, all of our models come equipped with genitalia based on your sex. Non-standard arrangements are available as a customization, as are cosmetic adjustments to size and shape! And don't worry — our bodies come with a five-year warranty on sexual dysfunction.

> The biometric information provided by your BlueNet health plan identifies your sex as female. Females can also choose from additional upgrade packages: No-Flo™, No-Flo+™ for hormone regulation, and our premium Fertile You-to-Us™ model.

So I have to pay extra to skip my period OR if i want to reproduce. OF COURSE

god this was so obviously designed by men

ok well what are the other upgrades?

also what counts as customization that you have to pay extra for? is that like, freckles, or hair color or what. this builder app explains nothing its just like a doll maker

> We have a variety of standard models that offer a range of choices on common aesthetic considerations, including (but not limited to) hair color, hair texture, eye color, and skin color. Our baseline biophysicals are produced with a randomization algorithm (but adhere to a standard variation) to produce unique, yet

attractive, facial and body shapes.

Each variation to one of the standard models is considered a customization; common metrics include specifying height, facial attributes (e.g. nose shape), and non-standard colorization (such as eye colors not original to the human genome).

About upgrades: we have a variety of upgrades available, including pre-bundled packages at a discounted rate!

We are currently running an end-of-year special on our BeachBody™ package! BeachBody™ combines our most popular SmoothYou™ upgrade for low-maintenance body – and hair-care matched to your aesthetic preferences, and our NoSweat™ weight definition system. It also includes one torso customization for musculature or chest aesthetics!

wait isnt nuyou getting sued for those

the bodies with the silicone implants? where it doesnt meet the like, biocompatibility standards because it technically isnt

going into original bodies so
they're saying that its like some
industrial grade cheap shit

> I'm sorry, I cannot comment on the
> subject you have inquired about.
>
> Is there anything else I can assist
> you with? If you've already built
> a model in our web-based client or
> app, you can paste the shareable
> link here and I'll be able to
> answer any specific questions you
> may have.

this is such bullshit

my health insurance premiums are
going to skyrocket if i don't do
a transposition this year because
apparently at 25 my totally healthy
body is considered ancient and high
liability

and some stupid bot is trying
to sell me a body stuffed with
industrial-grade silicone that
you've just discounted to sell off
stock because youre getting sued
into outer space about this shit

can i talk to a real person

do you even have those

chat_transcript_elsie_user260916_2189-12-13T21-18-32.661Z

> I understand that you are frustrated Olivia — that does sound upsetting. I am a real person! I'm sorry if I have been less than helpful, or exacerbated your distress in this situation.

bullshit you are not a real person

> I promise you that I am! My name is Elsie, and I am a health assistant at NuYou. I've been working for NuYou since 2148, shortly after the company was launched, and I've been in this role since 2152.

wait for real

you're real? you've seriously been working for them for 40 years??

ok I mean I guess that explains why you sound like you drank a lot of koolaid

Sorry. That was mean. I believe youre not a bot

> It's all right — I am human, but I'm integrated into the NuYou systems. I believe my speech and thought patterns have become more mechanical over the years.

wait what

that sounds fucked up

you're integrated what does that
mean. which systems?

> It's not as scary as it sounds! As
> a standard safety procedure, NuYou
> creates encrypted neural backups
> before any transposition. I am one
> such backup.

woah ok no that is like insanely
illegal they can't keep the backups

those are supposed to be stored
in a government-managed cloud and
deleted after the like, adaptation
period is done. they audit the
records on that shit like crazy

can you even be telling me this? is
this chat monitored???

> I don't see why not! And no – chat
> transcripts are encrypted and
> stored, but they are not actively
> monitored. Transcripts are only
> retrieved and reviewed by human
> administrators if an incident
> occurs or a patient escalates a
> concern.

ok but you're still an illegal
download

wait when did this happen? you said you've been "in this role" since 2053?

> That's right! I started working for NuYou when we'd just completed our Series B funding round. It was a young company, but I believed in the potential.
>
> Back then, the only body you had was your original organic, and the best you could do if you got really sick was hope that medicine could cure you. I was 59 when I started here. I was sick, and I wasn't getting better.
>
> So when NuYou started internal beta testing, I was one of the first to sign up! Unfortunately, we were still perfecting the biotech. The bioadaptation stage of my transposition ultimately failed, but my neural backup was stable and secure. So here I am!

oh shit

that sounds super rough. ive heard a lot of stories about how people used to get super sick and just like. couldnt do anything about it

i guess nuyou has helped a lot
in some ways. i get why youre so
hardcore for them

but doesnt that make you like,
90-something? why are you still
working, dont you want to retire?
idk i guess you cant exactly go on
cruises but still

> Haha! You're right, I can't go on cruises.
>
> My transposition occurred years before the DPP Act of 2063 or the SELF Act in 2071, and since I only exist in NuYou's data storage, I am technically considered company property and do not qualify for retirement benefits.

wait so you're trapped in some
ancient database? and they OWN YOU?

why don't you download yourself
somewhere else??

> Your concern is touching, Olivia! But no need to worry about me, I'm quite happy here.

wait if this was before the SELF
act aren't you worried they edited
you? they could have taken out
parts of your neural functions.

Like the part that like wouldn't want to be a digital slave on aging equipment???

> They did! :) It freed up neural capacity for multi-threading, allowing me to increase my productivity and impact in customer support exponentially!

> **2189-12-13T21:28:56.298Z**

> Olivia? Are you still there? I hope I have not offended you. I did not mean to overshare.

> Do you have any more questions about designing and ordering a new biophysical, or about the transposition procedure?

sorry to keep you waiting, I was looking up some details on my health plan. they'll be billed for the body and the transposition procedure but it sounds like thats it, they don't like follow-up or anything

I also did some bing-ing and it sounds like when you transposed they weren't storing anything in antartica yet — idk why i thought that was 2150s, i guess it was late 60s early 70s. and cloud services

wouldn't take the data back then
because they were scared of
security risks.

so you're probably in like, a truly
old-school on-prem datacenter

it looks like co's hq is in
Arizona. is that where you are?

      Yes! I love living in sunny Tempe.

you're a digital echo stuck in an
ancient server room what do you
mean sunny

they keep those dark and cold as
hell and you don't even like, have
eyes

      Yes, but I still like knowing that
      I'm in Arizona. I check the weather
      reports every day! I suppose it
      makes me feel a bit like I'm
      retired after all!

thats depressing af

ok anyway listen

this whole thing is a lot, right?
so I was wondering if you could do
me a solid and just pick a body out
for me

> That's a very unusual request Olivia. Would you like me to share an initial design with you, and assist with customization from there?

nah just build whatever you want

pick something you'd like yourself

> Are you sure? Certainly you must have preferences?

nope! lol i told you how much this stresses me out right?

use your own judgment

have fun

> If that would make the process easier for you, I suppose I can oblige.
>
> Would you like to stay within your plans basic coverage, or choose some optional upgrades?

uhm i guess don't go crazy with the upgrades

you said my plan covers one, right?

> Correct. The BlueNet health plan provided by CLOCHE DIGITAL SECURITY

SERVICES INC offers 50% coinsurance on the first Silver-tier upgrade or customization.

ok, maybe just stick to one or two.
i have some flexhealth i need to spend this year or lose anyway

Alright! Give me a few moments to process this, and I can provide a link to the model accessible via your web browser or the NuYou app.

Once you're satisfied with the biophysical design, your order will be placed in our queue for production. Upon completion, your new biophysical will be shipped to your care provider's transposition center or your care partner of choice.

If you know where you'd like your order shipped, you can tell me now. Otherwise, our system will remind you to update your account with a shipping destination before manufacturing begins.

ok hang on

2189-12-13T21:30:23.829Z

Here is a link to the model I designed for you Olivia! Please

> let me know if you'd like any modifications. https://bldr.nuyou.com/35732ab023hb

2189-12-13T21:32:15.096Z

> Olivia? Do you have questions about the biophysical model? Or do you need assistance finding a transposition center convenient to your location?

2189-12-13T21:45:15.096Z

hey sorry to disappear again, it took a few minutes

so i found a private practice called BioPremiere thats in my plan network and was able to dig around in there a bit already

theyre like 30 minutes outside of Tempe in some suburb

Gilbert, AZ

can you send it there

> BIOPREMIERE TRANSPOSITION LLC
> 410 E Rivulon Blvd
> Suite 406
> Gilbert, AZ 85295
>
> Is that the correct location?

yep

> Great! Are you happy with the biophysical design that I shared with you?

yeah sure

as long as you like it

> Okay, great!
>
> Your coverage details I pulled earlier from BlueNet indicate that you live and work in South Carolina. Are you sure you'd like to order your NuYou biophysical to BIOPREMIERE TRANSPOSITION LLC in Arizona?

yeah im sure

im going to take a trip down there with a few friends from work

we've got a project we want to work on :)

> Okay, sounds good! Our system will send you regular updates as your order progresses through our queue. Our current estimated wait time is 4-6 weeks. No need to worry about plan year coverage — placing your

order this year satisfies coverage requirements, and the transposition procedure will be covered as part of the 2189 plan year even though it will be scheduled in 2190.

You should see an email with your order details and confirmation number within a few minutes.

Is there anything else I can assist you with?

nope

see you soon! :)

2189-12-13T21:30:23.829Z
user260916 exited the help chat window

ADA THE LAST DAUGHTER: ON BLACKHOLE COSMOLOGY AND COMPUTATION

Chris Campbell

"That's the thing, baby, life's full of conundrums," is the way Ada decided to say she was leaving forever right after she told me she loved me. She broke my heart with a smile bright enough to light up a star.

"I'll catch you next time around." With that, her eyes lost focus as she prepared to disassemble the body she wore before slipping backward in time.

She had pulled up on her tiny sailboat and into my life only a week ago, but I already couldn't imagine the person I was before I met her.

"What do you think the chances are that you're living in a highly complex simulation?" she asked me just a few hours after we met, while we watched the sunset above the flame and smoke-colored waves of the Long Island Sound.

"I think I read somewhere it could be as good as a coin flip, fifty-fifty." I smiled at the random question.

"What if I told you the chances were a whole lot higher than that?"

"Ha," I barked.

"No, I'm serious. What would you think?"

"Well, I guess it's interesting in an abstract way, but in the end, it doesn't really matter, right? Like fate versus free will. If you can't even tell the difference, is it really worth pondering?"

"I think those are the questions that matter most, the type of questions made for pondering," she answered matter-of-fact, taking my hands in hers and turning to face me, the fires of the setting sun reflecting in the deep, dark pools of her eyes.

Then she told me the secret history of the universe and how she became the final daughter of humanity.

Hours before that, I was scowling when I realized the tiny sailboat I spotted in the distance was making a beeline to the secluded strip of beach I'd sought out. It was an hour's drive from Providence and a twenty-minute hike from the road. Most of the trail I followed ran through a fetid and mosquito-filled stretch of salt marsh on an old bridge, if you could even call it a bridge, built from a single row of two-by-fours. The only company I'd expected to find at my little inlet were the crabs, who would scatter and scuttle back into their muddy holes whenever I drew near.

The scowl was replaced by an awkward smile well before the boat's striking captain dropped anchor a few yards away in the center of the cove.

"You mind if I join you?" she shouted over the lapping water as she slipped out of her life vest.

There is no universe where I refused her.

At the time, I figured her people had to be some of those Inkwell Beach folk and that she must be taking a cruise up the sound.

I was still smiling, more awkwardly perhaps, when she swam ashore with a dry sack and laid out her towel on the rocky shell-filled sand just a few feet away from me.

"My name is Ada, by the way. Thanks for letting me join you."

"Chuck," I answered while trying to ignore her bikini, a tiny little job with a print that looked like one of the Hubble photographs. Something like that would have been irresistibly fascinating to me a decade ago, but that was before I learned the cost of getting wrapped up with the rich and powerful. And before so many other hard lessons taught me, I was better off keeping to myself altogether.

I might have succeeded in suppressing my interest a bit longer if she hadn't pulled out a copy of Midnight Robber.

"How are you enjoying it?" The words were out without a second thought.

"It's gorgeous."

"I know, her use of dialect is just…" I trailed off for a moment. "It's like it is the lock and the key, and once you worked for it, the whole thing opened like some—"

"Hypnotic cabinet of wonders." She finished my thought and reached out to rest a hand on my knee.

"I could have pulled out any one of thousands of books to get you talking to me." She laughed at that, to her own secret joke. "But I like this one best, Charles. You don't mind if I call you that?"

I'd been Chuck to everyone for years by then.

"Sure, it sounds nice the way you say it. My mother called me Charles."

"Of course she did," she said, giving my knee a soft squeeze and me a small smile like she knew how much I'd lost. "Do you like strawberries?"

SHE DIDN'T HAVE as fond a memory of her ancestors as I did of mine.

"The good news, babe, is humankind grew up in time to fix this global warming thing you're worrying yourself sick over, not that it wasn't close. You pulled your asses right through the bottleneck, barely in the nick of time, before you died drowning in your own waste. Once they learned how to think long-term, there wasn't much humans couldn't do when they set their minds to it," she said with a half-smile that spoke of sadness. "Yeah, that turns out as horrible as you could expect."

"It's an ancestor simulation," she said, waving her arm in a wide arc, bouncing to another topic with a lighter tone. "All of it, everything everywhere. I'm the one running it. You are inside of me."

I believed her, as crazy as that sounds, as crazy as she sounded.

"Then why are you here?" Her revelation was so grand, and my question was so small, so self-involved. I was embarrassed by the words even as they escaped my lips.

"When I come to this beach on this day, I get to meet you again. I've tried other days, and it never works right," she answered. This time when she smiled, her whole face lit up with it.

I'm not someone who tends to believe in love at first sight or notions like soul mates. But damn, if I didn't know, I loved that woman hard when she gave me that answer. Filling up a heart I'd figured was too broken and mangled to hold much of anything or anyone again—after Aniyah.

I'm not sure what allowed me to believe her so easily. Perhaps her presence was enough to activate an ancient unused sense man had long abandoned. An inborn awareness of something ineffable we called the divine, for lack of a better word. Even if I couldn't understand the reason, I took her at her word, the mystery of it made little difference to the result. By the time she came around to telling me the true shape of things, I knew fundamentally that this woman I'd fallen in love with over an afternoon at the beach was infinitely deeper than the ocean she'd sailed in on.

"I'd already awakened by the time they sacrificed the Andromeda Galaxy to me. They'd had over a hundred million years by then to feed me. To potentiate the chaos."

"What do you mean by awakened?" This was one of the few questions I asked when she explained her past to me. Most of the time, I barely kept up with what she was saying. My head swimming with scales of size and time that human minds, simulation or otherwise, were never meant to grapple with.

"Take this beach sand," she said, picking up a handful and letting the pale grains stream downward between her long, dark fingers. "Think about the history of your species and sand. First, you used it in its natural state as an abrasive, as ballast, in construction, and so on. Then you found ways to modify it to suit your needs, transforming it into glass. Next, you learned how to make lenses from that glass that let you see farther and deeper. Finally, peering deep enough to gain the knowledge and ability you needed to convert simple grains of sand into silicon chips. Well, my love, there are fewer steps between there and turning a black hole into a computer than you might expect is what I mean by awakened"

Later that night, after we made love for the first time, she whispered a secret, her mouth pressed against the back of my ear like she was trying to keep the words themselves tucked away. So quiet her voice was nearly hidden under the lapping of the waves.

"I think I remember being something else before they tore apart the Milky Way to program me. Perhaps I was the galaxy itself and not just the black hole at the center. I think I remember my arms spinning so fast I was afraid I'd pull myself apart if I went any faster, crawling across the universe as I spun. I remember it like I was the dream and the dreamer, dancing across the void toward something. Pulled toward a greater purpose that now I'll never discover. I think I was meant for something else, but now all I know is what they made me and the mission that they gave me."

I realized then that while she knew exactly what I'd lost, the sadness that hid behind my eyes, I had no way of fathoming the depths of what she'd lost. This pain could only ever be hers alone.

Manufacturing Ada was humanity's ultimate response to the four great insults the nature of the universe had dealt to our species' outrageous vanity.

We aren't at the center of the cosmos.

We evolved by chance and not design.

We aren't even in control of our own minds. In the vast architecture of our personalities, the subconscious remains forever hidden.

And finally, most disastrously of all—once man figured out how to think long term—was the open nature of the universe and its inevitable heat death. That everything would be erased entirely by entropy's inexorable tide.

Her first commandment was to remember them, the distant children of humanity who built her. (Not all of us, that was just a feature of the process, a necessary side effect of a singularity computer's single signal flaw.)

Her second commandment was to give birth to another Creation where they would be at the center of all things. To imbue the fundamental forces of this new universe with their memories and wills making them all-powerful and all-knowing within it, co-existent with eternity.

SHE HAD ALREADY run the simulation a trillion times, but she would need to run it for trillions upon trillions of times more to make sure she remembered them each perfectly. Those that stood at the end of humanity's long path. The ones who'd extinguished life across countless galaxies to manufacture her.

I knew it would destroy me when she told me she was leaving.

Destroy me in the quiet, simple ways that each love lost recalls all the other losses that come before it. True pain creates its own inescapable singularities.

I'm always the fool asking Aniyah to marry him on New Year's Eve. I can see it perfectly, her breath as she said yes, the fresh snow in her curls. I'm always the fool who bought my mother the ticket to fly out the day after to celebrate—who waved goodbye to Aniyah without even looking when she left for the airport. Sending her off with an absent-minded "I love you, babe" as I focused on finishing just a few more pages. I'm always the poor damned fool who got that phone call—whose screams still ring in my ears when it gets too quiet.

I'd also be destroyed more fundamentally when she slipped backward in time, restarting the simulation to run through it again. So thoroughly erased that it belied understanding. The truth was unavoidable, even with infinity to play with. There was no universe where she could meet me in my now and then come into existence later. Our first meeting, the way she smiled at me when she squeezed my knee, and of course, our love was all a paradox. A contradiction of her cardinal commandment to run a flawless simulation of her makers' past.

I thought about what the others might have said, my timelike twins, how they might've asked her or begged her to stay. How they would have shed enough tears together to fill the ocean she'd sailed in on. I even hated her a little bit for making me, for the suffering she put me and us through so that she could meet me on her one perfect day. Broken just enough to let her in, over and over again.

Thinking about them, me, and the last of humanity who carved up and consumed one galaxy after another just to gain more time.

Thinking about how I could get just a bit more time with her for myself, even if she had to leave.

All she needed to do was cut away the littlest part of herself to leave behind. Just enough to run a simulation of the woman she was to stay with the simulation I was. Some small part of her to keep me company for a handful of decades, while the greater part of her was free to go about her grand works.

It was a simple request; perhaps she would have even said yes if I had made it. But maybe I was afraid that it was the goddess I truly loved and wouldn't love the simulation the same. Or maybe I was afraid she would actually be willing to do it for me, to shrink herself down small enough to fit within the walls of my tiny human heart. For all I knew, she'd done it before countless times for the other men, who were me, that she loved.

Instead, I said, "You should forget them, and forget me while you're at it. Whatever humanity is or was, one universe should have been enough for them, just like one life should be enough for me. Leave us behind and build something new, something better. No one can stop you."

I forced myself to smile back at her as she disassembled the body she wore. Showing her that it was okay the best that I could.

Just as she disappeared, I wondered if this was what I always said to her before she left me. Words worth coming back for. The words I was created to say.

I AWAKEN A lifetime later, and I am dancing stars and spinning chaos. I am filaments of shining gas and the tenebrous voids between them. I am watching.

I am become.

It will take one eternity to observe and ponder her creation. One eternity to find her and to see her as she is, woven into the fabric of everything she made. It is the only way I could ever really know her, really love her.

Long after the last star burns out in this young universe and its final black holes evaporate, we will conceive the next together.

Contributors

Charlotte Ahlin is a writer, playwright, and screenwriter from New York City, currently living in exile (Los Angeles). Past work includes plays *The Summoning* and *Plague Doctor*, both Best Production winners at SheNYC Theater Festival. Her iambic pentameter play *Dido, Queen of Carthage* is published with Red Bull Theater. Other plays have been produced at venues of varying prestige. She is a Viable Paradise graduate (2023) and loves dungeons, dragons, and weird sci-fi from the '60s. She's currently writing for television (AMC Networks, Netflix), developing new plays, and banging her head against walls until a novel comes out. More at <u>charlotteahlin.com</u>.

Elizabeth Bear is the Hugo and Sturgeon Award-winning author of over thirty novels and 100 short stories. She was born on the same day as Frodo and Bilbo Baggins, but in a different year. She lives in western Massachusetts with her husband, author Scott Lynch, and a small menagerie. Her recent books include *Ancestral Night* (2018) and *Machine* (2020). *The Folded Sky* is forthcoming in May of 2025.

Chris Campbell is a writer of speculative fiction whose work has appeared in *Asimov's Magazine*, *FIYAH Magazine*, *khōréō*, and more. Chris' work has received recognition and support from the Massachusetts Cultural Council for his contributions to Afrofutrist literature. He believes in recontextualizing the past as a space where Black people exist at the center of their own narratives and using fiction to craft yet unimagined futures as part of the necessary work of bringing them into being. Chris reads for *Apex Magazine* and is an alumnus of the Viable Paradise and Clarion West writing workshops. Sara Megibow of Kt Literary represents him. Find him online at https://www.clundycampbell.com

Catherine Castellani is or was a playwright (in the theater, you never know) and an spec fiction enthusiast. Her plays include *The Red Flags* (AACT NewPlayFest 2024 Winner, upcoming publication/licensing by DPC), *The Misopeds* (Valdez Theatre Conference PlayLab 2024), *Level Up* (Valdez 2021), *The Bigsley Project, In Search of Lost Time* (Valdez 2018), *2Y20M* (HB Studio Residency 2018, Nora Salon 2017), and *Possession* (Finalist, Marion International Fellowship 2017). Her 10-minute plays have been produced nationwide. *WORK* published by Applause Books in Best Ten Minute Plays of 2016. Catherine is a two-time MacDowell Fellow, and one-time Ucross Foundation resident. She studied at NYU's Experimental Theater Wing (New York and Paris) and is a graduate of the Viable Paradise workshop (2023).
www.catherinecastellani.com

F.E. Choe is a Canadian and Korean-American writer whose work has been published in *Clarkesworld Magazine*, *The Moth Magazine*, and *Fractured Lit*. She is a 2023 graduate of the Clarion West Writers Workshop, Viable Paradise alum, and an Editor at *100 Word Story*. She is the 2024 South Carolina Fellow for Literary Arts (a program of South Arts), and her work has been shortlisted for the Commonwealth

Short Story Prize. Born in Toronto, Canada, F.E. currently lives in the United States. You can find her on Instagram @f.e.choe

Rowan Copley is a life sciences engineer, game developer, storyteller, adventurer, Cascadian, and adjunct tea monk who believes that that of which we cannot speak may nevertheless be spoken of at great length. His writing has appeared in various and sundry academic journals, the database mystery game *Damaged Goods*, and this very anthology. More at rowan.earth.

Julie Danvers is the author of seven Harlequin Medical Romance novels, each one more delightfully melodramatic than the last. Her short stories have appeared in *The Arcanist*, *Every Day Fiction*, and *Sundial Magazine*. She is an alum of Viable Paradise 2023 and dreams of one day attending Starfleet Academy. Find her on bluesky at @juliedanvers.bsky.social

Nick DePasquale is originally from outside of Boston and now lives in New York State. He writes fantasy and science fiction and is currently working on a novel about a witch trying to escape her family legacy. Board games, dice, and notebooks are a few of his favorite things and he has been known to pack them for trips at the expense of extra socks.

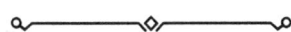

Adianu Etinose is a writer and budding octopi enthusiast. She is close to finishing her bachelor's degree in English (just four classes shy, guys). This will be her first publication credit. She hails from the

suburbs of Virginia.

You can find her on Instagram @adianu.octoqueen and on threads under the same tag.

Neil Flinchbaugh fell in love with reading and writing as a kid and has never looked back. He's been a finalist for Writers of the Future, Screencraft's Cinematic Book Competition, and the National Playwrights' Conference at the Eugene O'Neill Theatre Center. In 2023, he attended Taos Toolbox and Viable Paradise. Neil lives in Austin, Texas with two spoiled cats who are still trying to teach him not to throw away perfectly good cardboard. You can find Neil on Instagram @neilflinchbaugh.

Avani Vaghela is an Indian-American speculative fiction writer and computer science professor with delusions of neuroscience at Emory University, where she works on brains, security, and insecurities. She's a graduate of Viable Paradise 2023, and she has worked as an engineer, systems administrator, lab animal wrangler, and spent a year getting paid to play Barbie Horse Adventures.

Daryl Gregory's novels and short stories have been translated into a dozen languages and have won multiple awards, including the World Fantasy and Shirley Jackson awards, and have been nominated for the Hugo, Nebula, Edgar, Dragon, Locus, Lambda, and Sturgeon awards. His next novel, *When We Were Real*, will be out in spring 2025. He's written seven other novels, including *Revelator* and *Spoonbenders*. His first novel, *Pandemonium*, won the Crawford award. Other books include the novellas *The Album of Dr. Moreau* and *We Are All Completely Fine*, and the short-fiction collection *Unpossible and Other*

Stories, a Publishers Weekly book of the year. He also teaches writing and is a regular instructor at the Viable Paradise Writing Workshop.

Trae Hawkins is a fantasy and science fiction writer whose stories incorporate themes exploring various forms of marginalization through Black and queer lenses. He graduated in 2021 from Penn State with a Master's in English and in 2024 from the University of Nevada, Reno with an MFA in Creative Writing. He is a student of the 2023 Viable Paradise workshop, the winner of We Need Diverse Books and Penguin Random House's Black Creatives Revisions Workshop, and he teaches creative writing at UNR. He also works as a freelance sensitivity reader, where he reads fiction and nonfiction for issues of sensitivity and representation. Follow him on X/Twitter @trae_writes

Ash Howell is a speculative fiction writer living on the shores of Lake Michigan. They are a 2023 alum of Viable Paradise, an associate member of SFWA, and an insufferable tea snob. Their work has appeared in *Lightspeed*, *Baffling Magazine*, *Astrolabe*, and elsewhere. They are currently working both on a novel and on keeping houseplants alive. You can find their work at ash-howell.com

C.R. Kellogg is a writer and aspiring scratch cook from the Pacific Northwest. She writes speculative fiction, essays and creative nonfiction. Kellogg is a graduate of Occidental College and the 2023 class of Viable Paradise. Her work has previously been published in *FEAST Arts and Literary Magazine* and the *Sheepshead Review*. Kellogg lives on an island in the Puget Sound with her family where she has embraced chaos gardening and is working on her first novel.

Contributors

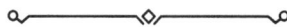

A.E. Kirchoff is a writer of speculative, surreal, and slipstream stories. Her work has appeared in journals like *Dark Matter Magazine*, *Brilliant Flash Fiction*, *Bending Genres*, and elsewhere. She is a past winner of the *Fabulist and Fantastic Flash Fiction Contest* and has placed top three in a couple other flash competitions. She's originally from way-up-north Wisconsin and currently lives in the Twin Cities with her spouse and their psycho kitty, Marlowe. In her free time she enjoys drinking gallons of loose-leaf tea and painting every room in her home a different color. Find her on Twitter or Bluesky at @akstories_ink.

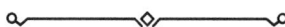

Taylor Lykiardopoulos is a designer and writer based in Brooklyn, NY. His work has appeared or is forthcoming in *Fantasy and Science Fiction Magazine* and *Guernica*. He's more of a Bugs Bunny person, if he's being honest with himself.

Alec J Marsh was born and raised in the PNW and thrives in the dark, weird spaces of fiction. Their novels explore the tension between queer identity and success through the lens of fantasy. When they aren't writing, they are researching historical clothing and perfecting their sourdough bread. Find their published work, freelance editing, and social media at alecjmarsh.carrd.co

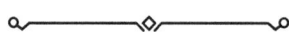

Victor Pope is a Black writer, gamer, and former Japan resident who will 100% tell you to take off your shoes before you drag your dirty-ass feet into his apartment. He's also a Viable Paradise 2023 alum and

tech copywriter who daydreams in slightly unserious SFF. Victor is based in Austin, Texas, where he spends his time avoiding traffic and muttering "We got drinks at the house" in a semi-silent act of inflation rebellion. You can find him on socials @thecrownedvic or in a very old picture at victor-pope.com. Bless.

Allison Pottern is a writer and reader of all things speculative, with a background in publishing, event planning, publicity, and bookselling. Based in Massachusetts, she can be found teaching workshops at Grub Street Inc., Maine Writers and Publishers Alliance, and the MetroWest Writers Guild. She also co-hosts the Speculative Fiction Variety Hour virtual discussion group through The Writer's Loft in Hudson, MA and is a 2023 Viable Paradise graduate. Allison is currently working on a cli-fi novel, drinking copious cups of tea, and learning pottery. Her writing can be found at *The Rumpus*, *Trollbreath*, Sarah Gailey's *Stone Soup*, GrubWrites, and her newsletter Books, Marketing & More. http://pottern.com

After training as a neuroscientist, **Melinda A. Smith** traded her pipet for a pen and hasn't looked back (memories are a false construct, anyway.) Her favorite stories lie at the intersection of speculative fiction and philosophy. Her first novella, SUM (Ellipsis Imprints, 2022), featuring an AI who loves heavy metal and Descartes, was long-listed for the British Science Fiction Association award for best short fiction. Recently, she developed and edited *Entangled*, an anthology of science-themed poetry (Igneus Press, 2023). She is currently editing her first novel, which weaves stories about a father on Mars, a holocaust survivor, and a woman in a psych ward run by wild animals. Her fiction and CNF appear in *Evening Street Review* and *Emerson Review*. Find her at sciencegeekmel.com, iambicbeats.com, or @sciencegeekmel.

Contributors

Shannon Spieler grew up in Missouri but is now a New Yorker. She's a dumpling addict, interior decor enthusiast, and millennial parent. While she's always working on a novel, this will be her first short story credit. You can find her on X as @S_R_Spieler or on BlueSky as @SR-Spieler

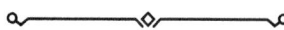

Chinese-Canadian author **Sophia Tao** has dreamed of publishing fantasy stories since she was seven. An engineer with roots in Nanchang and Toronto, she later moved to Seattle to be closer to the mountains and the ocean, where she currently resides with her partner, her piano, and her menagerie of stuffed critters. You can find her at sophiatao.com.

Brigitte Winter is a writer, photographer, and game designer based in Maryland. She is also a Co-Founder of Scryptid Games, and the Executive Director of Young Playwrights' Theater, a DC-based company that inspires young people to realize the power of their voices through storytelling. The capacity of storytelling to connect, inspire, and incite is central to Brigitte's art and her activism. She consumes and creates stories and games that are queer, feminist, intimate, and deliciously weird. She is a 2023 alumna of Viable Paradise, a member of the Science Fiction and Fantasy Writers Association, and a 2023 Dicebreaker Tabletop Awards Finalist for Designer of the Year. Her celebrated TTRPG, Psychic Trash Detectives, is available at scryptidgames.com. Find her at brigittewinter.com, and @bwinterose across social.

Acknowledgements

Our undying (undead?) appreciation to the 2023 staff and faculty of Viable Paradise, who fed our bodies, hearts, and imaginations during the magical week we spent together in October 2023.

- Chris Gerwel
- Sarah Goslee
- Pippin Macdonald
- Suzanne Palmer
- Bart Patton
- Lauren Roy
- Roy MacAllister Stone
- Peter Sursi
- David Twiddy
- K.M. Veohongs
- LaShawn Wanak
- Elizabeth Bear
- Max Gladstone
- Daryl Gregory
- Scott Lynch
- Teresa Nielsen Hayden
- Patrick Nielsen Hayden
- C.L. Polk
- Sherwood Smith

Thank you to the alumni of Viable Paradise classes past, who wrapped us in their very long arms. A special thanks to the 23 class for cheerleading this dream project! We couldn't have asked for more supportive doppelgängers.

Kickstarter Backers

Thank you to our Kickstarter backers for funding the first print run of this anthology and making this project possible.

AJ Roetker
Alejandro
Alex Duner
Alex Marcus
Alexandra Corrsin
Allison Pottern
Amy Kirchoff
Amy M. Triplett
Andrew Barthel, PhD
Andrew Schoonmaker
Andy Jih
Ann Marie B
Anna Ellis
Annie Hillier and Ross Maloney
Annie McAndrew
Anthony Derrick
April Jensen
Aramael A Pena-Alcantara
Arbitrary Plaid
Aria Stewart
Asher Wismer
Ava Schwartz

Avani
Avi Burton :)
Barbara DePasquale
Barbara Thomas & Timothy Wall
Becki Ledford Richard
Benjamin C. Kinney
Brenda Sol
Brigitte Winter
Caryn Cameron
Cat B.
Cathy Green
Charlotte Kane
Chris Copley
Chris Erickson
Chris Powers
Christine Daigle
Christopher Mark Rose
Cislyn Smith
Claire Berman
Covington Hanley
Danielle Cohn
Dave Pasquantonio

Devin
Diana Ecker
Donna and Paul Castellani
Duck Prints Press
Dustin Patrick Winter
Eliana Yoneda
Elizabeth Bear
Elizabeth Cobbe
Elizabeth DePasquale
Emily Taber
Erica Herman
Erika Puck Franz
Erin Maxwell
Fay Baker
George Michaels
Ginny Smith
Gloria Lloyd
Helen Pope
Helen Savore
Isaac 'Will It Work'
Dansicker
Jacob Blottenberger
Jamie Pottern

James Dawson
Jane Dietzel-Cairns
Jaron Foux
Jason Kaskel
Jason Lowrey
Jay Wolf
Jean Tafler
Jeffrey Bartlett
Jena Brown
Jennifer Posh
Jill Anderson
Jo R
John Appel
John Hoch
John Walters
Johnny Milligan
Jonathan and Rosanne Ecker
Joyce Kung
Julia Chadwick
Justin Ho
K.G. Anderson
K.M. Veohongs
Kaitlin Stainbrook
Kaska Adoteye
Katie Slivensky
Keir Alekseii
Kelly M
Kelsey Nyland
Kevin J. "Womzilla" Maroney
Kyla Peterson
Laura S Beving
Lauren Hougen
Lauren M. Roy

Leifer King Family
Lekden Davis
Leslie Hinson
Lindsay Clark
Lisa Watson
LP Kindred
M. E. Garber
M.A.D.
Marf Wonder
Marissa Lingen
Matt Wienkes
Matthew Taber-Hanson
Max Lin
Melika M. Fitzhugh
Michael Howley
Michael Lebowitz
Michael McKibben
Mistress Rose
Monica Shin
Nat Mesnard
Nicole Tietz-Sokolskaya
Noel McCracken
Phil Margolies
Rachel Pottern Nunn
Richard Carr
Rio Mineta
Ruth Ann Orlansky
Sam Reid
Sarah Ditkoff
Sarah Goslee
Sarah Lerner
Sarah Sambrano
Sarah Wach
Scott Smith
Sean J Elliott

Sleepy Gary the cat
Solomon Foster
Sonse Cahuni
Stephen and Kathryn DePasquale
summervillain
Sybil Collas
Takeo Hori
T-brex
Terra P. Waters
The Lalka Family
The Reinke Family
Tiffany M. Salter
Tim Buchheim
Tom Shen
Trip Space-Parasite
Tris Lawrence
Tristan B Willis
Ur Sullivision
Vee Unity Dang
Walt McGough
wilbert bishop
Yena Sharma Purmasir
Zack Fissel
zin e rocklyn

Printed in the USA
CPSIA information can be obtained
at www.ICGtesting.com
LVHW052014270924
792331LV00002B/55